DEATHBLADE

A TALE OF MALUS DARKBLADE

Tightening his grip on the Warpsword of Khaine, Malus leapt out from the darkness. Some slight sound, perhaps the shift of his harness as he lunged, betrayed his presence to the armoured tyrant. Malekith started to turn, fiery eyes blazing from the black depths of his helm.

Then the warpsword was chopping downwards, catching the king's shoulder, ripping through the ancient mail. The enchanted edge of Malus's blade tore through the Witch King's body, shearing through flesh and bone, cleaving ribs and breastbone before exploding from his chest.

Malus panted, gasping for breath, his entire body shivering from the magnitude of what he had done. He had killed Malekith! He had killed the Witch King! By his own hand he had made himself master of all Naggaroth!

WARHAMMER®
THE END TIMES

WITHDRAWN

WARHAMMER®
THE END TIMES

DEATHBLADE
A TALE OF MALUS DARKBLADE

C L WERNER

BLACK LIBRARY

For Dan and Mike, who blazed the trail.

A BLACK LIBRARY PUBLICATION

First published in Great Britain in 2014 by
Black Library,
Games Workshop Ltd.,
Willow Road,
Nottingham, NG7 2WS, UK.

10 9 8 7 6 5 4 3 2 1

Cover and internal artwork by Clint Langley.
Map by Nuala Kinrade.

A CIP record for this book is available from the British Library.

ISBN13: 978 1 84970 799 2

Product code: 60040281022

See Black Library on the internet at

blacklibrary.com

Find out more about Games Workshop
and the world of Warhammer at

games-workshop.com

Printed and bound by CPI Group (UK) Ltd, Croydon, CR0 4YY

The world is dying, but it has been so since
the coming of the Chaos Gods.

For years beyond reckoning, the Ruinous Powers have coveted the
mortal realm. They have made many attempts to seize it, their anointed
champions leading vast hordes into the lands of men, elves and dwarfs.
Each time, they have been defeated.

Until now.

In the frozen north, Archaon, a former templar of the warrior-god
Sigmar, has been crowned the Everchosen of Chaos. He stands poised
to march south and bring ruin to the lands he once fought to protect.
Behind him amass all the forces of the Dark Gods, mortal and daemonic. When they come, they will bring with them a storm such as has
never been seen.

Already, the first moves have been made. Valkia the Bloody led the hosts
of Khorne into Naggaroth, homeland of the dark elves, laying waste to
the north of realm and bringing war to the great cities of Naggarond and
Har Ganeth. Ominously, the tower of Ghrond, home of the sorceress-
queen Morathi, gave no warning of this attack. Only the return of
Malekith the Witch King saw Valkia cast down and Naggarond saved.

And in the fastness of Hag Graef, Malus Darkblade, undisputed master
of that city of slaves, plots and schemes, determined to increase his
power. His armies are the equal of any in Naggaroth, and his ambitions
are lofty – he would topple Malekith from his iron throne and take his
place as lord of all the druchii. But the Witch King has his own plans
for Darkblade, plans that will put Malus at the forefront of an invading
army as the final battle for the fate of the elves begins.

These are the End Times.

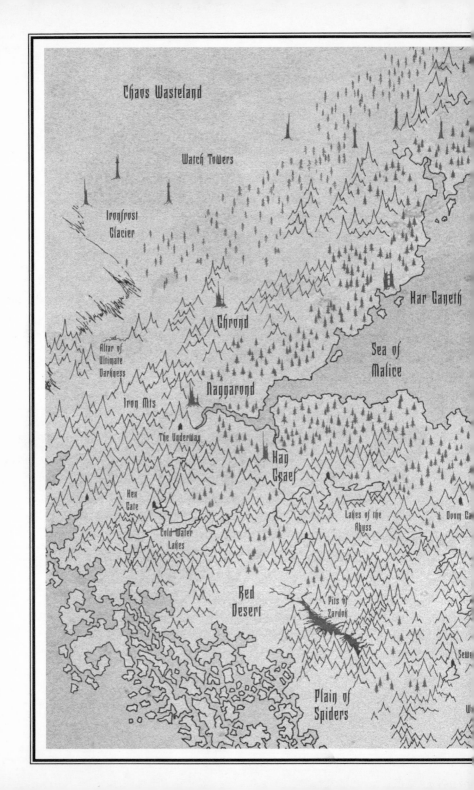

PART ONE
NAGGAROTH

Winter 2523–2524

ONE

The enemy of your enemy is your friend.

The words reverberated through the drachau's brain like rolling thunder. Sharp. Persistent. Insinuating. They spoke to him with an intensity beyond that of simple speech. No sound could convey the depths of meaning and suggestion entwined within them.

The drachau stiffened in his throne of polished malachite and hydra-hide, feeling the dried scales of the seat creak beneath his weight. From the corner of his eye, he gazed longingly at the tiny whalebone table and the bottle of dark wine resting atop it. The promise of release was almost too great to resist. A few glasses and he could silence the slithering inside his skull.

Malus crushed down the urge, strangled it before the merest flicker of his desire could betray itself in his features. The wine would indeed ease the turmoil inside him, but the price for such peace was too high. More than the dark presence boiling inside him would be stifled by the brew. His own wits would be dulled, his own senses retarded by the liquor. He couldn't afford that, not now when he needed every last dreg of cunning his mind could conceive.

Look at it, Malus. Look at that simpering bag of vice and corruption. Listen to it scheme and plot. Is this petty intrigue the best you can aspire to? You who have walked in the realms of the gods themselves!

The drachau's eyes narrowed as he studied the elf who knelt before his throne. He watched the ripple that passed through the thin spider-silk cape draped across the druchii's shoulder each time the elf drew a breath. He scrutinised the subtle play of hue and texture in each scale of the elf's hauberk. He inspected the quality of the swords thrust through the elf's dragon-skin belt, the craftsmanship of the engraving on hilt and pommel. His nose drank in the smell of exotic spices and perfumes exuding from the elf's pale skin and long dark hair. His ears deciphered the practised tonalities and courtly inflections laced into each word.

Yes, everything was there. The druchii crouched before him looked, smelled and sounded the part. If there was deception here, it had been very carefully prepared. Not so long ago, Malus would have still entertained his doubts. A clever enemy would take such pains and invest such care into a plot against him. Now, however, he doubted there was anyone within Naggaroth who had the patience for such delicacy of deception. There simply wasn't the time for such games any more.

Naggaroth was a land besieged, tearing itself apart in the wake of an unprecedented invasion from the north. A tide of human barbarians, beastmen and daemons had exploded from the Wastes and smashed their way through the ring of watchtowers that guarded the borders of the druchii. There had been no warning, the sorcery of Ghrond and Morathi had failed to alert Naggaroth to its peril. The hosts of Chaos had descended, slaughtering all they confronted, despoiling and destroying everything in their path.

The time for games was over. All the craft and subtlety, the scheming and politicking, all of it was over. A new age was come upon the elves of Naggaroth, an age of crisis and cataclysm, an age that demanded actions, not words.

It was a call to action that had been brought to Malus. As drachau of Hag Graef, he was the most powerful of all the dreadlords, his armies second only to those of Naggarond itself. No, Malus corrected himself, the armies that bent their knee to his banner were mightier now than those who served the black flag of Naggarond. To the soldiery of Hag Graef had been added the warriors of vanquished Naggor and the refugees from Clar Karond, to say nothing of entire tribes of shades who had abandoned the wilds to seek sanctuary within the spires of the drachau's city. As Malus expanded his forces, those of the Witch King had lessened, bled away by constant conflict against the barbarians and monsters seeking to conquer his kingdom. How many thousands had been killed to break the horde of the daemon-thing Valkia? How many more had been lost on that long march to Ghrond to seek a reckoning with the treacherous Morathi?

Your star rises, Malus, but beware. The star that burns brightest is the first to be extinguished.

Malus gripped the arms of his throne, feeling the cold of the malachite beneath his fingers. He nodded to the messenger, the highborn emissary who had brought him the most tantalising proposition. In every line of the messenger's face he could read the smug arrogance of breeding and privilege, the surety of one who has had his every whim obeyed without question. By using such a messenger, the one who had sent him was displaying before Malus the magnitude and severity of what he was being offered.

'You may tell her ladyship that I will meet with her and her confederates,' Malus decided.

The messenger raised his eyes, just that little spark of

condescension betraying itself at the corners of his gaze. 'The tzatina was certain her offer would appeal to your lordship.' He bowed his head again. 'Is there any message you wish me to convey to her?'

'I will send my own message to Khyra,' Malus said. In a single, impossibly swift motion, the drachau sprang from his throne and lunged at the messenger. The highborn was quick, fast enough to raise one hand in a warding motion while he reached with the other for a dagger cunningly sewn into the lining of his cape. Malus drove the black edge of his sword down through the messenger's hand, the enchanted metal ripping through the elf's mail as though it were butter. Fingers danced across the floor as Malus brought the Warpsword of Khaine shearing through the messenger's arm and into the druchii's breast. As blood bubbled over the dying highborn's lips, the dagger he'd been trying to free from his cape clattered against the ground.

Malus stared down at the bloodied carrion. Breeding and position counted for nothing now. The time for such frivolities was over. All that mattered was ability and ruthlessness, the vision to see and the power to take.

'Silar!' Malus called out as he wiped the edge of his sword clean with his victim's cape. From the shadows of the audience chamber a tall, powerfully built elf marched into the fitful witchlight cast by the overhanging lamps. Like the recently slain messenger, he wore an elaborate cuirass of steel scales and there was upon his face the similar qualities of breeding and nobility. There, however, the resemblance ended. Silar Thornblood was of Hag Graef and none of the sons of the Hag sneered at Malus Darkblade; even in their innermost thoughts they held their drachau in a place of fear. They were too familiar with the dreadlord's deeds and the fates of his enemies to harbour any delusions about defying him. The nobles of the Hag might hate Malus, but they would never underestimate him.

'You wish that to be removed?' Silar asked, pointing to the butchered messenger.

'Place him somewhere that the tzatina's agents will be sure to find him,' Malus said.

Silar bowed his head, not quite daring to match his lord's gaze as he spoke. 'The tzatina will know it was you who killed him.' It was true. No weapon in Naggaroth left a wound such as the warpsword dealt.

'She will,' Malus agreed. 'That is as it should be.' With a wave of his hand, he dismissed Silar, leaving the warrior to his grisly task. Soon, Silar was trudging off, the messenger's body wrapped in the silk cape and slung across his shoulder like a sack of meal.

They offer you the scraps of power. I offer you a feast. Why be content with a mortal's appetite when you can aspire to so much more?

Malus turned and made his way to the table and the bottle resting upon it. He could feel the wine calling out to him, sense the shudder of longing that coursed through his flesh. Freedom lay within that bottle, if only he was weak enough to take it.

You are weak, are you not, Darkblade?

The mockery crawled through his skull, stilling Malus's hand even as he reached for the bottle. His hand closed into a fist. With an animalistic snarl, he brought his hand smashing across the table. The bottle shattered against the floor, splashing the precious wine everywhere. Malus stared down at the spilled liquid. In his head, the voice suggested he might still drop to all fours and lap it up like a thirsty dog.

'Was that wise?' a disapproving voice called out to Malus.

Malus looked away from the wine. Advancing towards him across the audience chamber with a stately, unhurried step, was an elegant figure bedecked in flowing black robes, her carriage framed in a lacy meshwork of tiny pearls and crushed sapphires, her dark tresses bound in a coiffure of gold and jade. Her skin had an alabaster paleness beyond even that of most druchii, telling of an existence spent without the attentions of even Naggaroth's sickly sun. Across the harsh beauty of her features was stamped the fiercest determination, the sparks of her terrible will blazing in her eyes. In aspect, the elf presented a vision of both desire and dread.

'Hello, mother,' Malus greeted the elf as he stepped away from the shattered bottle. 'Your health looks as inviolate as ever.'

Lady Eldire didn't allow her son's remark to bait her. It was only through her intrigue and her assistance that Malus had survived to become drachau of Hag Graef. It was only by her sorcery that he was able to conceal the terrible affliction that gripped him and which, if exposed, would see him torn limb from limb by his own slaves. Her hold over her son was great, but so too was his over her. Lady Eldire was that rarest of creatures, a sorceress who owed no loyalty to Morathi or her convent. She had been a Naggorite, taken from the Frozen Ark by Malus's father. Only the protection of Hag Graef had kept her from being returned to Naggor or surrendered to Morathi. In placing her son upon the throne of Hag Graef, she had helped to ensure the continued protection of Naggaroth's second city.

Of late, however, Lady Eldire had been compelled to demand further indulgence from her son. She had discovered her vitality beginning to ebb, the old spells to ensure her youthfulness beginning to slip. The solution had been restorative magic that hearkened back to the forbidden pleasure cults that had corrupted the cities of Ulthuan long ago. Baths drawn from the heart's blood of elf youths and maidens, the blood of innocence to wash away the stain of age and corruption. Only through the connivance of

Malus had Eldire been assured of a steady supply of sacrifices to maintain her vigour.

'I wish I could say the same for the steadfastness of your mind,' Eldire reproved him. She smiled at the flicker of disquiet that appeared on his face. 'You needn't worry. There are no spies here. I would know if there were.' She ran her fingers across the curve of her cheek, feeling the silky newness of her revivified skin. 'As you observe, my vivacity is as keen as ever it was.'

Malus scowled. 'The Hag pays a high price for your sorcery, mother. I should feel cheated if your powers were not quite as profound as you claim them to be.' He shook his head and stalked back to his throne. 'Just the same, I don't want my... affliction... mentioned in Naggarond. Not even between ourselves.'

Eldire stepped around the shattered glass and spilled wine. 'I didn't know you were so afraid of the Witch King. Certainly not after your entanglements with Lady Khyra. A usurper who fears his sovereign has lost before he begins.'

'Anyone who doesn't fear Malekith is either mad or a fool,' Malus returned. 'No, to have any chance at all, I cannot deny my fear of him.'

The sorceress circled the malachite throne, her boots clicking against the tiled floor. 'Then you will expose the tzatina's plot? Forget the chance that providence has given you?' She leaned close to the throne, her hand closing on Malus's arm. 'They are offering you his crown, the Circlet of Iron itself. You would be lord of all the druchii, master of Naggaroth!'

Malus glanced past his mother, staring regretfully at the spoiled wine. 'I will expose no one. Not yet, at least. I will hear Khyra's offer, learn how much support I can expect. The killing of her messenger was a warning to the tzatina and the other dreadlords. They must know it is I, not they, who hold the reins of power. They think to make a present to me of something only my strength and the might of the Hag can secure. When they find their highborn messenger lying in the gutter like so much garbage, they will understand that. When the Black Guard fails to arrest Khyra, they will know I haven't exposed them, that I will listen to what they would pledge to their new king.'

Eldire brought her hand up to Malus's head, running her fingers through his dark locks. 'The land is in turmoil. There is talk of treachery everywhere. The noble houses snap at one another's throats even as the daemons come crawling across their walls. It will take a strong arm to bind them once more to the service of their kingdom. It will take ruthlessness beyond that of the Witch King, savagery unmatched even by daemons, to break their pride and bind them in the shackles of terror.'

Taking hold of his mother's hand, Malus pressed it to his lips. 'I have been schooled in the cruelties of Hag Graef, I have endured the horrors of the Wastes themselves. The blood of my own father is on my hands. There is no brutality I would not indulge for the sake of power. You know that.' The drachau's grip suddenly grew tight and with a sharp pull, he brought Eldire to her knees beside him, her face level with his own. 'From the first, I think you foresaw this moment with your magic. Every torture and torment I survived, you saw before it happened. All that I have suffered was known to you, wasn't it?'

'And if it was?' Eldire demanded. 'If your entire life stood revealed to me while you were still growing inside me, how should that change this moment? Will you curse me for what you have endured or thank me for preparing the way?'

Malus shook his head. 'Neither,' he said. 'The past is done. It is the future I seek. You have brought me to this moment. Tell me what waits beyond.'

The sorceress turned her face, unable to hold the suspicious glare in Malus's gaze. 'I have seen this far, but no further. There are rules to magic, boundaries that cannot be defied. This land draws but faintly upon the lighter vibrations within the aethyr and only so much can be achieved with the lower harmonies. Your doom is obscured, but this much I can tell you – the fate of Naggaroth is bound to your own.'

Malus released his mother, sinking back against the rest of his throne. 'Mine is the doom of Naggaroth,' he mused. He kept his eyes on his mother as Eldire withdrew from the chamber. He was cautious about trusting her too far with her portents and prophecies. After all, she had benefited the most by placing him on the throne of Hag Graef. Conquest of Naggor had eliminated most of Eldire's enemies. Malus had to wonder what foes she hoped to involve in this 'doom' she now foretold.

It will be a terrible doom. An end to all things, Malus. You will lose all you possess. Nothing will be left.

The drachau pressed his fist against his forehead, trying to blot out the foul whisperings inside his skull. He'd thought himself so strong to deny the succour of the bottle, but now he wondered if he'd been clever. Hadn't he simply responded to that goading mockery? Done exactly what it wanted him to do.

A different path can be yours. A path of unending glory and horror.

'Shut up, daemon!' Malus growled at the voice creeping through his mind.

The caustic laughter of Tz'arkan was the only response to Malus's fury. The daemon could wait. What was time, after all, to something truly immortal?

'I expected more of you,' Malus said as he marched out from a concealed doorway and into the dank crypt.

The crypt was buried beneath the tower that had once been the stronghold of Oereith Kincutter. Oereith and his house had been abolished years ago, exposed as devotees of the profane god Slaanesh. The Witch King had flayed every member of the house, from Oereith himself to the lowest slave, and impaled the wet, raw bodies upon the walls of Naggarond. It had taken weeks for some of the cultists to finally die, the slobbering moans from their tongueless mouths serving as a morbid warning to all druchii that some obscenities were too much even for Naggaroth. Since the abolishment of Oereith's title, no new dreadlord had been bold enough to claim the shunned tower for his own. There were too many whispers that some of the things Oereith had called from *beyond* continued to linger in the deserted passageways and chambers. With survivors streaming into the city, with the Black Council and their entourages flocking to answer Malekith's call, the cursed tower was perhaps the only place in the city that offered the isolation the tzatina's gathering required.

Resplendent in a silver-lined gown of black, a wispy filigree adorned with bloodstones entwined with the cascade of her raven tresses, Lady Khyra looked incongruous with the macabre surroundings of the soot-blackened crypt, the smashed bones of Oereith's ancestors strewn about the floor. She looked as though she were attending a royal banquet, not orchestrating a secret plot to overthrow the Witch King. Always possessed of a flawless grace and poise, there was nevertheless something about Khyra that made the blood turn cold in Malus's veins. Looking past the beauty of her face, the enticing appeal of her body, there was a malignance ghastly even by the jaded standards of the druchii. Gazing on Khyra, for Malus, was like watching some great spider spinning its web, always wondering if the trap was being spun for him.

Malus had been fortunate to escape Khyra's web when it had

been fashioned for him once before. Then he had been foolish enough to underestimate the tzatina, to think that sharing her bed gave him some immunity in her intrigues. It was a mistake he'd been fortunate to survive. Only by a shrewd piece of treachery had he been able to shield himself and leave the Witch King's wrath to fall upon Khyra.

Khyra had been fortunate, too. Malus felt his eyes drawn to the slender curve of the tzatina's right arm. It was covered in a sleeve of black adorned with sparkling diamonds and the shimmer of crushed pearl. There wasn't a real arm beneath that sleeve; it covered a surrogate carved from ivory. Khyra's real arm was adorning a spike on the battlements of the Black Tower, the price of Malekith's merciful indulgence. Being one of the Witch King's consorts, Khyra had rated such beneficent consideration.

Khyra swept past the dozen nobles and highborns who were with her in the crypt. Even the least of her companions had an air about them that betokened outrageous wealth and power. They'd made some effort to conceal their rank by adopting simple cloaks and girding themselves in the plain armour of household knights, but they couldn't efface the stamp of their breeding from their bearing. Subtle variances in costume suggested to Malus the slave markets of Karond Kar and the mines of Storag Kor, even the now-desolate shipyards of Clar Karond. He even saw a bit of scrimshaw bone adorning the dagger of one elf that was certainly in the decadent style of Har Ganeth. Khyra had cast her web far to draw in such disparate conspirators.

'I expected you to come alone,' the tzatina said, her eyes sliding past Malus to glare disapprovingly at his companions.

'You forget, Lady Khyra, I know you,' Malus reminded her. 'I will be able to concentrate on our negotiations better if I know I have someone here to watch my back.' He made a point of using his right hand as he indicated his two companions. 'Lord Silar Thornblood of my household guard. Captain Vincirix Quickdeath, commander of the Knights of the Ebon Claw.'

Malus fought down a smile when he saw the slight flush that came into Khyra's face as he introduced Vincirix. It was probable that the tzatina knew she was his current companion. Was it possible Khyra was jealous? No, not true jealousy, just the bitterness of a spoiled child who sees someone playing with one of her toys. Malus would have to remind Khyra which of them enjoyed the dominant role in this conspiracy.

'You killed my messenger because you worried if he could be trusted,' Khyra said. 'Why should we believe your *lackeys* can keep a secret any better?'

'Because they know that to betray me is to betray themselves,' Malus said. 'They each have powerful enemies. It is my strength that keeps them at bay.' Malus marched towards Khyra, pausing before he reached her to run his mailed fist across a section of fire-blackened wall. When last he'd set foot in these crypts, those fires had been raging at full force, devouring the foul creatures Oereith had bound to his service. From the corner of his eye, he watched Khyra, studying her for any trace of unease. He could find none. After what she had endured in these crypts, the hideous fate Oereith had planned for her, she must have ice water in her veins to come back.

Perhaps that was exactly why she'd chosen this place. If anyone suspected her, they'd never think to look for her here.

'The drachau places great faith in his strength, in the might of the Hag. Maybe too much.' The speaker was one of the supposed knights. Hearing his words, Malus recognised the voice as belonging to one of the elder sons of Dreadlord Ghalir of Shroktak.

Malus turned a withering look on the noble. 'The might of Hag Graef is why I'm here, and you all know it. If you didn't need my armies, you would never have invited me into your confidences. Without the strength of Hag Graef, you have nothing.'

Angry hisses and grumbles rose from the conspirators, idle threats and empty curses that Malus brushed aside like buzzing insects. Before coming here, even before he had cut down Khyra's messenger, he'd carefully considered every angle. This conspiracy had been hatched without any intention of including him. Likely, it had started as an opportunistic play to take the crown when Malekith failed to return from Ghrond. The Witch King had spoiled those plans, however. He'd survived and come back, putting Khyra and her allies in the worst possible position: a revolt all ready to unfold but without the military might to keep what it seized.

'You are sure of yourself, drachau,' Khyra said.

'Only necessity would make you welcome me back into your *arm*,' Malus answered. The look of total hate Khyra darted at him was so black that Silar took a step towards the tzatina. Malus waved him back. He'd read the situation right. Khyra did need him and would put up with anything until that was no longer the case.

'The Witch King is weak,' one of the nobles declared. 'The tyrant's grip falters. He failed to destroy the daemon-consort Valkia. He lacked the courage to relieve Clar Karond. He couldn't even bring himself to execute Morathi for her treason. He can dominate us no longer.'

Malus paced across the crypt, digesting the noble's treasonous words. There was truth in them, even divorced from the greed and hate that made them so enticing. Never in Malus's lifetime had Malekith been pressed so closely by his enemies. Driving off Valkia's horde had taxed his strength, while confronting his mother in Ghrond had tested his will. He was weakening, even as the might of Naggarond was weakening. Jackals like Khyra's allies could smell it, slinking ever closer to seize whatever they could take.

'But if the Hag were to support Malekith. If my armies were to flock to his banner, who would dare oppose him?' Malus enjoyed the looks of horror that crept onto the faces of Khyra's allies.

'You would not side with the Black Tower?' one of the highborn gasped.

Malus stopped pacing, let his fingers scrape across the scorched lid of a sarcophagus. 'Not unless it was in my best interest.' He turned towards Khyra. 'You invited me here to make a proposal. What am I promised should my armies support your cause?'

Khyra's eyes were as cold as a glacier when she answered the drachau. 'I think you have already decided what you want.'

'What I demand,' Malus corrected her. 'What I demand is the Circlet of Iron. What I demand is rule of Naggaroth. In exchange, I will support your own claims against your enemies and rivals.'

'Agreed,' Khyra said. Her answer came much too hastily for Malus's liking. 'We will acknowledge you as our king. But if you would be king, you must remove the current one.'

'Malekith's armies cannot oppose my own,' Malus said.

'Your armies cannot fight Malekith and protect the land from the hordes now despoiling it,' Khyra told him. 'It will take all the strength of Naggaroth to drive them back this time. If we spend our blood fighting among ourselves, everything will be lost.

'No, Malus Darkblade, it is not your armies alone that we need. We need you. We need the one swordsman in all Naggaroth who can do what must be done.

'You must kill Malekith, the Witch King.'

TWO

You know they are just using you. Once you have done what they need you to do, they will betray you as quickly as they betray their king.

'You have things backwards, daemon,' Malus growled at the presence inside his head. 'I am using them. They serve my purpose, even if their pride refuses to make them understand it. When their usefulness is at an end, even the tzatina will find that she is disposable.'

All flesh is disposable. Ponder this, when the dark reaches out for you.

Malus fought down the impulse to argue with Tz'arkan. The daemon took a perverse delight in goading him into empty arguments. The extra distraction of its poisonous advice was something he couldn't afford right now. The odds were stacked too heavily against him already.

Lady Khyra's plan had worked flawlessly thus far. Her knowledge of the Black Tower and the routine of the Black Guard who defended it had proven invaluable. Malus had been able to eliminate the sentry patrolling the desolate stretch of wall abreast of the suspended bridge that connected the tzatina's own tower to the outer ring surrounding Malekith's fortress. Silar, bedecked in the armour of the Black Guard, had assumed the sentry's place, adopting the gold sash that denoted the present rotation of warriors. The sentries wouldn't be relieved until the first light of dawn. Silar would have to make good his escape before then. Once his vassal withdrew, the empty post would be quickly discovered and real Black Guard would converge on the tzatina's bridge. Malus was certain Khyra already had some subterfuge prepared to absolve herself from any blame, but that wouldn't help him. If dawn found him still inside the Black Tower there would be no way out.

He'd be abandoned to the wrath of the Witch King.

That thought was enough to give even Malus pause. The drachau of Hag Graef, stealing through the Black Tower like a prowling shade. It wouldn't need a mind as crafty and twisted as that of the Witch King to figure out his purpose. In the long centuries of Malekith's rule there had been many assassins who had tried to depose the tyrant. Their fates had been obscene enough to horrify even the druchii.

Now, Malus was courting just such a doom. His mother's prophecy did little to cheer him. If there was one being in all the world who had the strength of will to force even fate to obey him, that being was Malekith.

Cold perspiration beaded Malus's forehead, his breath came in hot little gasps. He could feel the blood quickening in his veins. How much of it was the cocktail of herbs and elixirs he had imbibed to enhance his reflexes and heighten his senses? How much of it was his own fear, the fear that he tried to deny even to himself? He'd braved the quest for Tz'arkan's five treasures and the long quest to reclaim his soul from the devious daemon. He'd journeyed alone through the wastelands of Chaos and stood within the insane realm of the Screaming God-Child. He had dared the cursed black ark of Naggor and escaped. He'd deposed the former drachau of Hag Graef and installed himself upon the throne. All these things he had faced and survived, yet it was the spectre of his sovereign that filled him with dread.

Here, in the forgotten lower halls of the Black Tower, Malus was surrounded by the essence of the Witch King. Room after room of richly appointed chambers, their walls covered in masterworks that would have driven many a druchii noble to sell his own children into slavery simply to gaze upon them. Rugs of intricate pattern and artistry, their threads so fine that they rippled like water at the softest touch of his foot. Statues rendered from obsidian and amber, jade and crystal, their subjects rendered with such detail that they seemed to breathe as the eye passed across them. Carved tables of the rarest wood, their every curve possessing a grace and dignity that defied estimation. Jewelled goblets, platters encrusted with diamond and ruby, bowls of gold and silver and ithilmar, all of these were arranged upon the tables, awaiting the attention of some passing guest, oblivious to the faint discolouration left behind by the long-decayed viands they had once held.

Wealth beyond measure, enough to overwhelm the greed of the most avaricious druchii, yet here it stood abandoned and forgotten, caked in layers of dust that bespoke centuries of neglect. By their cast and craftsmanship, Malus knew much of the art he stalked past were relics from Nagarythe, the shattered homeland of the druchii. To any of the great houses of Naggaroth, such relics would be priceless heirlooms. To the Witch King, they were naught but idle baubles.

Nothing could impress upon Malus the absolute power of Malekith so demonstrably as this forsaken opulence. It was before the years of any living druchii that the Witch King had last employed these halls. Any living druchii save the immortal Malekith and his witch mother.

Malus ran his fingers across a goblet mired in a patina of dust and decay. Time had worn away the cup to a hollowed-out shell of corruption. It crumbled beneath his touch, collapsing to the floor in a clump of corrosion. Jewels long cheated of their lustre stared forlornly at him from the pile of decay.

The drachau felt cold fingers rush along his spine. These chambers were a lost and haunted place. Each step through the silent halls reinforced the eerie impression. It did not need the daemon's words to feed the urge to turn back, to flee to the grim horrors of Naggarond's streets, to be quit of the uncanny malignance of the Black Tower.

Hunger stayed Malus from retreat, the insatiable hunger for power that had ever driven him onwards. He stood before the ultimate power now, the promise of the Circlet of Iron and the throne of Naggaroth.

The spectre of that promise lay etched across the floor – a line of footprints pressed into the scum of dust caked upon the tiles and rugs. Malus wasn't so versed in the skills of tracking and hunting as the shades who lurked in the wilds or the beast-breakers of ravaged Clar Karond. Even he, however, could read the signs in the dust. The tracks were made by a single elf, his boots long and broad at heel and toe. The steps overlapped several times, denoting repeated circuits of this trail. All of it feeding back to what Khyra had told him about the strange turn the Witch King's habits had taken.

Since his return from Ghrond, Malekith had become prone to leaving the confines of his royal apartments at the top of the Black Tower. Many nights he spent wandering among the residue of ancient glories, pondering the relics of Nagarythe. No retinue of Black Guard protected him in these solitary forays, no complement of sorceress-consorts to follow behind him and watch over him with their magic. Whatever strange mood had gripped Malekith's mind, it was a boon for his enemies.

If that enemy was but bold enough to exploit the opportunity.

A bitter smile pulled at Malus's face. For all her intrigues and the conspiracy of powerful nobles she had gathered to her, Khyra lacked that boldness. All of them did. Only Malus had the determination to strike and slay!

Through the neglect and decay of a thousand years, Malus crept, pursuing the trail written in the dust. Every nerve in his body felt as though it were afire, and his heart beat a rapid tattoo inside his breast. His senses clawed at the stagnant air, straining it for the slightest sound, the merest odour – anything that would betray to the hunter the nearness of his quarry. His hand tightened around the warpsword's hilt. He could feel the eager pulse of the hungry blade racing up his arm, the sword's essence impatient to claim a royal soul. Soon, Malus promised, soon he would glut the warpsword's appetite.

Past a gallery of statuary that might have graced a Nagarythe garden into a broad arcade lined with wooden screens upon which some past master had painted exotic landscapes and ancient legends. Malus licked his lips, tried to moisten a mouth that felt as dry as an autarii's wit. His eyes roved along the trail he followed, watching with calculated paranoia for evidence of a trap.

The world froze around the drachau as he stepped from one gallery into another. His gaze didn't linger upon the dust-obscured portraits that filled the hall. He didn't stare at the jewelled frames and gilded settings. His attention was riveted entirely upon the lone figure who stood amid the desolation.

Tall, armoured from head to toe, an aura of imperious disdain exuded from that apparition of rune-etched metal. It was impossible to mistake the plates of black meteoric iron, the tall helm that supported the horned Circlet of Iron itself, the sheathed evil of the Destroyer hanging from the figure's hip. Malekith, the Witch King of Naggaroth.

The monarch had his back to Malus, turned to face the portraits lining the wall. Malus didn't dare breathe, felt a flush of fear at the sound of his own heartbeat. To strike now, to cut down the immortal tyrant, could he really do it? Who was he, after all, to kill an elf who had survived the Flame of Asuryan?

Now, when it is too late, do you question your pride?

The daemon's mockery poured the required measure of rage into Malus's veins. His fear was smothered beneath a surge of malice. Pride had indeed led him this far, and it would carry him still farther.

Tightening his grip on the Warpsword of Khaine, Malus leapt out from the darkness. Some slight sound, perhaps the shift of his harness as he lunged, betrayed his presence to the armoured tyrant. Malekith started to turn, fiery eyes blazing from the black depths of his helm.

Then the warpsword was chopping downwards, catching the king's shoulder, ripping through the ancient mail. The enchanted edge of Malus's blade tore through the Witch King's body, shearing through flesh and bone, cleaving ribs and breastbone before exploding from his chest.

Malus panted, gasping for breath, his entire body shivering from the magnitude of what he had done. He had killed Malekith! He had killed the Witch King! By his own hand he had made himself master of all Naggaroth!

For only a heartbeat, the grand images swam through Malus's mind. It took that long for him to accept the wrongness of what was happening before his eyes. Cut nearly in half by the warpsword,

Malekith was reaching for the blade sheathed at his side. Segments of torn plate flopped obscenely about the wound, yet still the ghastly figure persisted. Malus noted that there was no blood pumping from that wound, nor was there blood upon the warpsword's hungry steel.

As the tyrant began to draw the Destroyer, Malus struck at him again. Pride had fuelled his first assault on Malekith, but the king's horrible vitality had brought all of the drachau's fear racing along his spine. Panic drove Malus back to the attack, the panic that only a condemned soul can feel. Having struck the Witch King, he knew there were only two choices now: succeed or die.

Malus struck just as the Destroyer cleared its scabbard. The warpsword came slashing down, a blur of ravenous steel that bit into the Witch King's hand, cleaving through the rune-etched gauntlet and shattering the hilt of the tyrant's weapon. The Destroyer's blade went spinning across the hall, clattering along the dusty tiles. The severed hand flopped to the floor, rolling towards Malus.

Again, Malus was stunned by the lack of blood, the absence of pain exhibited by his foe. Instead of reeling back in agony or clutching at his maimed arm, the Witch King surged forwards, reaching for his attacker with the talon-like claws of his remaining hand. Malus took a single step backwards, then, uttering a snarl of defiance, he brought the warpsword whipping back around. It licked across Malekith's shoulder, striking sparks from the armour, and tore across the tyrant's neck.

The helm and its horned crown were sent leaping into the air as Malus chopped through the Witch King's neck. He gawked in disbelief as the helm went spinning away in the darkness. The headless body remained upright, still reaching for him with its hand. Malus felt cold terror clench his heart as the beheaded tyrant lumbered towards him.

The iron talons of the outstretched hand nearly closed around Malus's throat. It was more reflex than conscious thought that made the elf dart aside at the last instant, to spin around and drive the warpsword into his attacker. This time he caught the thing in the waist. Fear infused his arms with a desperate strength and the biting edge of his weapon tore its way through the iron plate as though it were butter. When Malus ended his destructive spin, his adversary crashed to the floor in two disparate sections.

Shocked, Malus watched as the armoured legs flopped impotently against the floor. The torso, with its single hand, struggled to flip itself onto its belly. Despite the continued havoc he'd wrought against the body, still there was not a trace of blood – not even a whiff of sanguine scent in the musty air. Malus could see why, now. As the bisected body flailed on the ground, he could see inside it. He could see that the thing was empty, nothing more than a suit of armour invested with the simulacrum of vitality by some profane sorcery.

It would seem you're not going to add regicide to your accomplishments.

Malus was about to growl a response to the daemon when the sound of strident clapping brought him spinning around. His hands tightened about the warpsword as he saw shapes manifest from the darkness, illuminated by the crystal lanterns several of them bore. Like the supposed Witch King, these elves were armoured from head to toe, and in a style that was impossible to mistake. They were the Black Guard, Malekith's personal army. Leading them, his hands coming together in jeering applause, was Kouran Darkhand, the Witch King's loyal dog.

'The drachau of Hag Graef,' Kouran said, his voice laced with vicious amusement. 'How low have the mighty fallen to come slinking into their lord's tower bent upon murder. Surely you might have hired another to do it for you?'

Malus glared back at Kouran across the still-writhing bits of armour on the floor. He'd been lured into a trap, that he understood the moment he saw the armour was empty, but to have it sprung by a common-born cur like Kouran was too great an insult to bear. As he glared at Kouran, Malus's mind was already racing. The rest of the Black Guard had come armed, but Kouran had neglected to bring either sword or halberd. That was a mistake Malus was going to ensure the dog regretted for the few moments left to him.

'When you want something done right, you do it yourself,' Malus snarled at Kouran. In a blur of motion, he charged the other elf, leaping over the twitching armour to reach his foe. The warpsword came swinging downwards, gleaming in the luminance of the crystal lamps.

Malus heard the wailing shriek as the warpsword bit into its victim, wrenching the soul from the victim as it ripped through his armour. The problem was, his blow had struck the wrong victim. As he lunged for Kouran, the elf seized the arm of the Black Guard closest to him and pulled the warrior into the path of Malus's blade. Even as Malus was trying to pull free from the warrior he'd struck, Kouran was in motion, smashing the helmeted head of the dead warrior into the drachau's face.

Blood streaming from his broken nose, Malus staggered back. The weight of the dead Black Guard dragged down the warpsword and as he kicked at the body to free his weapon, Kouran came rushing at him. The captain's fist slammed into Malus's face, knocking him back in a spray of blood and curses. The momentum caused the warpsword to tear free from its victim, and as Malus stumbled back, he was able to bring his blade whipping up.

The edge of the warpsword raked across Kouran's belly, scraping along the black armour in a shriek of grinding metal. The blade failed to do more than scratch the ancient plates, but its effect was pronounced nonetheless. Malus cried out as he was struck by a piercing agony, as though a candle had been set against every nerve in his body.

'This is the Armour of Grief,' Kouran laughed, slapping his hand against the breastplate. 'The enchantment Lord Arnaethron invested into it is quite zealous about punishing those who dare strike its wearer.'

Stunned by the magical backlash of Kouran's armour, Malus's blade slipped from his weakened grasp. He staggered back, fighting to recover command of his tortured body. Kouran's cruel face split in a sadistic leer.

'Take him,' the captain ordered his warriors, waving them forwards. 'I want to bring him alive before the king.'

Kouran's smile became impossibly colder as the Black Guard swarmed around Malus and beat him down with the butts of their halberds. 'His highness could do with an amusing diversion. It might be weeks before he tires of torturing this traitor.'

Malus felt a sharp pain against his skull as one of the bludgeoning warriors brought his weapon cracking against his head. He was unconscious when his head slammed against the dusty floor.

Are you awake, Malus? I should think you'd like to see this. There might not be a chance later.

Tz'arkan's jeers echoed through Malus's throbbing head. His body felt like one big bruise. He could feel cold iron against his arms and legs, and knew he was shackled upright to some sort of frame. The chill crawling over his flesh told him his armour had been stripped away. He guessed it would prove inconvenient for his torturers. They'd prefer a clean canvas at the start of their performance.

Slowly, Malus opened his eyes, squinting through narrowed eyelids at his surroundings. He wasn't surprised that he was in a dungeon of some sort. Richly appointed with ghoulish tapestries depicting imaginative cruelties hanging on the walls, it was a room designed to enhance the terror of its occupants. Malus hoped the tapestries were decorative and not a reference guide for his tormentors. He could see them, seven pale-skinned elves wearing long smocks of serpent-hide, their arms branded with tally-marks to commemorate their many victims. Several of the torturers were so scarred that they looked like they were wearing sleeves of boiled leather.

All of the torturers were fiddling about with an assemblage of ghastly tools, arraying them along a marble table, an altar to terrible Ellinill. Tongs and probes, cruel pincers and knives, bone-scrapers and flesh-hooks, each implement the druchii removed from their ebony reliquaries was more grisly than the last. Malus tried not to imagine what sort of havoc would be inflicted upon him for his attempt at regicide. The thought of biting his own tongue and cheating his captors flashed through his mind, but the taste of a metal bit in his mouth told him the same idea had already occurred to the torturers.

Groaning in frustration, Malus tilted his head enough that he could see the black throne standing between the tapestries. In the fitful light cast by the flaming braziers scattered about the torture theatre, the throne's malachite surface glistened with an oily sheen. He had a sense of foreboding as he looked over at the throne. He knew who it was who would soon occupy that seat, and when he did, then the pain would begin.

'His highness has a great many duties, drachau.'

The words came from just behind Malus, a scratchy whisper that made his gorge rise. He tilted his head back, drawing his arms up on the chains that bound them, feeling the manacles binding his feet bite against his skin as he stretched. His reward was a view of the speaker. A spindly, almost skeletal elf adorned in robes of black and gold. Malus recognised his old adversary, one who had nearly brought him to ruin once before. It was plain that Ezresor hadn't forgotten Malus's earlier escape. It was equally plain that Malekith's spymaster was eager to make up for that lost opportunity. He reached over his captive's shoulder and rudely pulled the bit from Malus's mouth.

Malus spat the taste of metal from his mouth. 'I won't tell you anything,' he said.

Ezresor stepped around the iron framework that held Malus. He stared up at the prisoner, his gaunt face probing into the druchii's bloodied features. 'You'll tell me anything I want to hear,' he said. He pointed to the torturers. 'They will make it happen. An hour or a day, it won't make a difference. They will extract every secret buried in that brain of yours. They'll pull it out of you and pin it to a board. If you try to lie to them, they'll know and they'll make it hurt worse. Keep that in mind, Darkblade. Whatever agony they inflict on you, know they always hold a little back. When you think it can't get any worse, know that it can.'

'If I told you what you want to know, it wouldn't change anything,' Malus said.

Ezresor tapped a finger against his chin. 'No,' he admitted, 'it wouldn't. But won't you feel better knowing the ones who convinced you to betray our king will share your fate?'

Malus managed a derisive laugh. 'No, carrion-face, I won't. I'll feel better knowing they might try again and that if they succeed their first order of business will be feeding your carcass to the harpies.'

The ghoulish spymaster's hand flew towards Malus. A dagger was in Ezresor's fist, projected there by some mechanism hidden in the sleeve of his robe. He brought it against Malus's cheek.

'You'll spoil the king's show,' Malus warned Ezresor.

Ezresor scowled as he pulled back the dagger. With the sleeve of his robe he wiped away the single bead of blood he had drawn. 'I can wait, Darkblade. I've waited this long, I can wait a little longer.' A smile slithered onto his emaciated face. He cocked his head to one side, assuming an attitude of attentive listening. He turned his grin on Malus. 'I think the wait is over,' he said.

Malus followed Ezresor's gaze as the spymaster turned towards a particularly horrendous tapestry. The hanging, with its depiction of mutilation and brutality, fluttered outwards as a sudden breeze struck it. Some concealed panel had slid open, ushering in a blast of air even more frigid than that of the dungeon. No, Malus corrected himself, the intense cold was nothing felt by the body. It was a chill that scratched at the soul, even a soul shared by a daemon.

The tapestry was pushed aside and into the torture theatre there marched the same figure Malus had so recently cut to ribbons. This time it was no sorcerous puppet of iron, but the puppeteer himself. Malus could feel the awful power exuding from the Witch King like an aura of cruelty. The eyes that burned within the face of the helm were like twin embers of hate, insatiable and implacable.

'Your highness,' Ezresor greeted the tyrant as he fell to his knees. The torturers mirrored his gesture of submission and fealty. Instinctively, Malus felt his own head start to bow. It was an effort to resist the automatic obedience Malekith had compelled from every druchii since the Sundering, but resist he did. As he raised his eyes, he found himself staring into Malekith's merciless gaze. There seemed a note of sardonic humour in the tyrant's stare.

'The fleshtakers await your pleasure, highness,' Ezresor announced as he started to escort Malekith towards the marble table and the cruel implements arrayed there so that his king might inspect them. Instead, Malekith turned away and approached the frame to which Malus was shackled.

'Did you really think you could kill me?' the Witch King asked, his voice like the rumble of an angry mountain. Malus shuddered as the tyrant came towards him, reaching out with a rune-etched gauntlet to close his cold fingers about the prisoner's jaw. 'Was your daring so great? Was your arrogance so mighty? Who are you, Darkblade, to think you can kill me? You are druchii, the spawn of this miserable land! You are my creation, moulded and forged like my armour and my blade! I raised you from nothing to command my armies, to lead my warriors in battle.' With a snarl, Malekith released the captive's jaw, shoving him back on his chains.

Malus glared back at the tyrant, pride crushing down his instinctive terror of the Witch King. 'You did nothing,' he growled. 'Everything I have achieved I won for myself. I clawed my way from being the vaulkhar's bastard son to drachau of Hag Graef. I did that, not you! I crushed the black ark of Naggor's legions and vanquished their Witch Lords! It was I who...'

Ezresor came charging at Malus, the glowing length of a poker held before him. The spymaster shouted in outrage at the temerity of the traitor in daring to defy Malekith. As he ran past the tyrant, the poker was plucked from his hand and sent flying across the chamber. A backhanded swat of Malekith's gauntlet knocked Ezresor to the floor, blood trickling from his split lip.

'If my armour fails me, if my blade breaks, I discard it and forge a new one,' the Witch King declared, still glaring at the shackled elf. 'But you aren't broken, are you Malus? You still burn with enough pride to defy me even here.' Malus could feel the tyrant's tone grow colder still. 'I should take great delight in making an example of you, but there is not the time, so I must grant you a reprieve.' Malekith waved his hand at Ezresor and pointed to the iron framework.

'Highness?' the spymaster asked as he picked himself off the floor.

'Release him,' Malekith said. His eyes continued to glare into

Malus's. 'Long ago, the pretender Bel Shanaar sent me into the wilds to be his ambassador among the dwarfs. Crude but clever things, the dwarf-folk. Do you know how they would check for foul vapours in their mines? They would bear with them a tiny bird and hang it from a cage where they could watch it. If the bird expired, they would know the air in the mine was becoming foul and hurry to the surface.' Malekith pressed his iron finger against Malus's chest. 'You are going to be my little bird, Darkblade. I know even you would not dare to strike against me without support from the other dreadlords. If there were time, I would rip each name from your flesh and savour every scream as I did so. But I cannot indulge in such pleasures now. Instead, I will pretend none of this ever happened. I will present the illusion that there was no attempt against my life, that you did not cut down my surrogate. I will restore you to your command of Hag Graef and none will be the wiser.'

Malus rubbed his cramped limbs as Ezresor unlocked his bindings. His mind whirled with the impossible things he was hearing, the unbelievable mercy and forgiveness Malekith was showing. Such qualities were the ultimate sign of weakness in any druchii. The society the Witch King had created was one that had long ago purged itself of such moral degeneracy.

'How do you know I won't betray you?' Malus asked.

The Witch King laughed, a sound that was far from pleasant. 'You mistake me. You are still my little bird. When I free you, when you go back among the dreadlords without any reprisal from me, what will they think? They will say that Malus has betrayed them. The cowardly ones will flee and I will have no need to worry about them. The bolder ones will stay. They'll plot against me, to be sure, but before they act they will strike against the bastard who betrayed them. You are my little bird, Malus! When the assassins come for you, that is when I will know to be on my guard.'

Malekith turned and stalked back towards the door hidden behind the tapestry. 'Ezresor will return your armour and sword to you. The Black Council meets tomorrow. I expect the drachau of Hag Graef to be in attendance.

'It would pain me to hear he has suffered an accident.'

THREE

There was no greater a concentration of malignance and evil in all the world than a gathering of the Black Council. From every corner of Naggaroth, the dreadlords came, hurrying to answer the Witch King's summons. Butchers who slaughtered for the simple pleasure of carnage, despots who crushed untold thousands beneath their heels, fiends who indulged in every depravity a mortal mind could conceive – all left their strongholds behind when Malekith called. Half the kingdom might be overrun by hordes of daemons and savages, the roads reduced to a nightmarish gauntlet of battle and horror, yet still the fear of their monarch was too great for anyone to defy his command.

The great throne room was situated high in the Black Tower, far above the streets and spires of Naggarond. The hall was of vast dimensions, its vaulted ceiling vanishing into shadowy heights so impenetrable that even the keen eyes of corsairs from the Underworld Sea couldn't pierce their darkness. Massive buttresses, every inch of their surfaces adorned with intricate carvings, loomed from the walls. Stone gods glowered down from the pillars: Ellinill, the Lord of Destruction, and his wrathful progeny. The eyes of each god were crafted from enormous gemstones, their lustre enhanced by an enchantment that caused them to glow with a smouldering malevolence. Between the buttresses, the walls were lost behind macabre tapestries fashioned from scalps encrusted with gore, a silent reminder of the many who had defied the Witch King's authority, and of the ultimate sanction for such defiance.

At the centre of the chamber stood the ancient throne of Aenarion, the first Phoenix King. Crafted from obsidian and iron, the massive seat was a stern reminder of Malekith's royal heritage. Of the Witch King's right to claim the Phoenix Crown.

Down the length of the hall, a blood-red carpet ran, streaming towards the great throne like a river of gore. Ornate chairs of lacquered wood flanked each side of the carpet. In each chair, some infamous leader of the dark elves reposed. Terrible names of might, equally feared and envied throughout Naggaroth. Behind each chair, standing in steely silence only a short distance away, was a warrior of the Black Guard. The halberds they bore were far from ceremonial affectations as would be normal at a meeting of the Black Council – as they had gruesomely demonstrated after Malus had himself announced by a pair of heralds. In response to the arrogant flaunting of decorum, two of the Black Guard had cut down the servants, leaving their remains strewn about the doorway.

The drachau scowled down the length of the hall to one of the chairs situated at the foot of the throne. Kouran matched Malus's glare. It had been on his order that the Hag Graef heralds had been killed, a not-so-subtle reminder to Malus of who was in command here.

Malus cast his gaze across his fellow dreadlords. He could almost smell the uncertainty and fear oozing from their pores. Ebnir Soulflayer, the general of the Witch King's armies, had died in battle – choosing death over Malekith's wrath, so the story went – and his successor tried his best to exude an air of scornful confidence and pride, but Malus could see through the warrior's pretence. The failure of Naggarond's army to utterly destroy the mongrel daemon Valkia was a responsibility that many whispered could be laid upon his shoulders rather than those of the king. He had passed blame to half a dozen lesser commanders, sealing each one alive within one of the obsidian mausoleums lining the approach to the Black Tower, but it was always possible Malekith would need one more life for his army to atone for the sin of failing him.

Hellebron's body was a shrivelled husk. The bloodthirsty Hag Queen of Har Ganeth was in her decrepit phase, but Malus had seen for himself the grisly vitality that remained in her withered bones. Entering the hall, she had paused beside the carcasses of his slain heralds to paw about in the gory wreckage. Fresh blood yet stained her fingers, and Hellebron would lick at them from time to time with her blackened tongue. Malus wasn't certain if it was magic, madness or narcotic delusions that so unhinged the Hag Queen, but whatever the cause, she was the most dangerously unpredictable of the dreadlords.

Shifting in his chair, Malus reconsidered that opinion. Hellebron might have a rival for the title of 'most dangerously insane'. Sitting across the aisle from her was Tullaris Dreadbringer, the feared executioner who had assumed the title 'Chosen of Khaine', an epithet that Malus himself had once affected when exploiting the religious mania of his half-brother Urial. With Tullaris, however, it was no mere affectation. The executioner truly believed himself marked by the Lord of Murder, to such an extent that he claimed to hear Khaine's voice inside his head. He was even bold enough to quietly decry Malekith's claims of being an avatar of the Bloody-handed God.

Lady Khyra, her false arm festooned with ornaments of pearl and silver in an audacious display of the favour Malekith had shown her – the Witch King had settled for just an arm when he might have had her executed – was several chairs to the left of Ebnir's replacement, but the way she leaned ever so slightly away from the general's direction made Malus suspicious. Was he one of her confederates, one she hadn't seen fit to let the drachau know about? The few nobles seated between the two were of such minor significance as to make their usefulness to Khyra too paltry to provoke any uneasiness. Malus was almost disappointed in the tzatina. Surely she hadn't taken it in mind to pit a fool like the general against him? A single troop of doomfire warlocks would be enough to rout any force brought against the host of Hag Graef. Malus caught Khyra's eye as he looked across at her, feeling a touch of bitter amusement at the mix of suspicion and alarm that flickered in those lustrous depths. It was natural she should worry, about how Malus was still alive and what he had told Malekith.

Ezresor, the sinister spymaster of Naggarond, was sitting further down the line from Khyra. The cadaverous elf sneered when he caught Malus looking at him. There was such a stamp of superiority in that caustic smile that the drachau at once found himself questioning his own security. Had Malekith reconsidered the usefulness of his 'little bird' and decided to make an example of him during the meeting of the Black Council? Or had Ezresor concocted some scheme of his own? Or was he simply trying to get under the drachau's skin? Malus smiled back at the spymaster and ran a finger along his cheek, mirroring the fresh scar Ezresor had suffered in the recent fighting against the barbarians. The ugly light that crept into Ezresor's eyes told Malus that the insult had struck home.

There were other lords, great and small. Venil Chillblade, Lokhir Fellheart and Drane Blackblood. Representing the Shade clans was the savage figure of Saidekh Winterclaw, his fur-trimmed armour festooned with the tongues and ears of foes slain in the recent fighting.

Seated opposite Kouran Darkhand at the foot of the throne was a newcomer to the Black Council. Never before had Ghrond been represented by anyone other than the Witch King's mother, Morathi, herself. Now, that ancient tradition had been broken. Drusala, one of the queen's handmaidens, sat in place of the exiled sorceress.

Malus had encountered Drusala only a few times over the years, typically trying to avoid any intrigues that involved Ghrond for the sake of his own sorceress-mother. Lady Eldire was the most potent enchantress in all Naggaroth who hadn't fallen under the sway of Morathi and her convent. That made her a valuable weapon in the arsenal of Hag Graef and a threat to Morathi's dominance of magic.

Malus remembered Drusala as strikingly beautiful. He found, however, that his recollection of her was far from reality. Her face was like that of a goddess rendered in flawless alabaster, milky and pale, unmarked by the stresses of time and turmoil. Her hair was a river of midnight, lustrous dark streams that swept across her shoulders and down past her waist. Charms and talismans of gold and silver and precious ithilmar were looped within her locks, tiny jewels sparkling from their polished settings. A gown of vibrant crimson hugged her shapely figure, clinging to her with all the affection of a second skin, slit at the sides to afford the greatest exposure to her slender legs. A jewelled girdle straddled her waist, tiny filigree spites clawing at one another with equal degrees of amour and violence. In her hands she held a silver chain, from which hung a pendant of Hekarti. A wispy necklace that might have been the crystallised ghost of a spider's web encircled her neck and fell across the swell of her breasts, a silver brooch in the shape of a spider holding the ethereal jewellery against the silk of her gown. Across her forehead sat a circlet of diamonds, each gemstone shaped and carved by magical rites until it looked as though it had been spun from the first frost of winter. Like icicles, two diamonds dangled from the bottom of the circlet, drawing the enraptured gaze of an observer down to the sorceress's eyes. Malus couldn't name a colour to describe Drusala's eyes. They had the same shifting, phantom quality as the aethyric aurora a bold fool might behold deep within the Wastes.

What intrigues was Morathi's handmaiden engaged in? Was she here on behalf of the king's mother, trying to pacify Malekith's ire, or was she here on some purpose of her own, without the knowledge of her patroness? And what of the Witch King? Was he privy to her schemes, a partner in them? Or was he simply keeping Drusala close as a way of monitoring a potential threat? What, Malus wondered, was her status on the Black Council? Was she Morathi's surrogate, her replacement or her scapegoat?

While he watched the sorceress from the corner of his eye, Malus saw Drusala's bosom exhibit the most momentary of shudders. A flicker of disquiet, something that senses less keen than those of an elf who had hunted a daemon lord alone across the Wastes would certainly have missed.

Malus felt resentment grow within him. He knew the cause of Drusala's disquiet. Brazenly, he looked about the hall and called out to his fellow dreadlords. 'So now we must await the pleasure of our august majesty?' He could sense the Witch King's presence, he knew Malekith was nearby. He also knew that whatever would happen had already been decided. There was nothing more to risk by making a bold show. 'I wonder how long it will be before he graces us with his presence.'

The Witch King's essence seemed to pour into the hall. The throne was suddenly filled with his cruelty, his fiery eyes burning from the depths of his iron armour. 'Not long, my good friend Malus.' The iron-encased monarch rose to his full, imposing height. He took a step down from the throne, the touch of his boot causing the carpet to smoulder. 'Not long at all,' the despot said, sweeping his gaze along the seated dreadlords.

The Witch King had kept the Black Council waiting most of the day. It was a common tactic he employed to remind his dreadlords of their status, to impress upon them who was master and who was vassal. In calmer times the king's tardiness was a necessary annoyance that the nobles knew they must suffer, but now, with cities being razed by barbarians and daemonic beasts, Malekith's eccentricity was almost unendurable. With each heartbeat, the dreadlords had wondered how far the invaders had progressed, how much of their own holdings and how many of their slaves had fallen to the enemy. To placate the tyrannical humour of their king under such circumstances was intolerable.

Malus quelled his petulant thoughts as he felt the Witch King's gaze upon him once more. He fought the urge to cower before that malignant glare. He was still somewhat in disbelief that Malekith had extended to him such left-handed leniency. He was certain that there was more to it than his king's talk of drawing out Lady Khyra and the other conspirators. Maybe if the kingdom weren't suffering such a crisis as now faced it, he would have accepted Malekith's words. But the last few weeks had shown just how nebulous the tyrant's reign had become.

Many of the dreadlords had been able to get away with acts of independence and defiance that would have been met with the most violent of reprisals only months before. The swelling of Hag Graef's armies to a point where they rivalled – if not outright exceeded – that of Naggarond was, to Malus, proof that the Witch King couldn't afford to check the autonomy of his subjects.

Naggaroth had to fight the enemy without; the king didn't have the resource to also fight the enemy within.

Let him claim he had extended mercy to Malus; the truth was that the Witch King needed him, needed him to hold the great host of Hag Graef together. He couldn't afford the time that would be lost as the Dark Crag's nobles fought for Malus's title and power.

The Witch King turned away from Malus and again looked across the assembly. 'Lord Vyrath Sor shall not be joining us,' said Malekith, his voice echoing across the chamber, as cold as the iron that encased his charred body. 'He was slow to answer my summons and only arrived this morning. I reminded him of his obligations to the Circlet of Iron. The harpies should carry what's left of him back to his tower by sunset. It would pain me if the garrison of Nagrar were to think their master had fallen victim to some lesser fate.'

To emphasise his story, Malekith tossed an object out onto the carpet. The gold chain clattered as it came to rest. Though caked in blood and shreds of flesh, there was no mistaking the sigil that had represented Vyrath Sor etched onto the chain's clasp.

'Do not mourn Vyrath Sor,' the king advised with mock sympathy. 'He decreed his own doom when he placed the defence of his miserable outpost before his duty to his master. The same doom any one of you might have earned by defying me.'

'Shagrath is lost, then?' The question was uttered by Venil Chillblade, one of the admirals of the eastern corsair fleets. With much of his power and many of his holdings concentrated in Karond Kar, it was easy to understand why anxiety had overcome prudence and gained mastery of the elf's tongue. The watchtower of Shagrath was to the north of Slaver's Gate; if the fortress had fallen, Karond Kar itself would be in jeopardy. To see it suffer the fate of its rival Clar Karond was a terror that threatened Venil's every dream and ambition.

The Witch King made a deprecating wave of his hand. 'An inconsequence,' he declared. 'The garrison will fight to the last because they have no choice. They will die as druchii should, shedding their blood on behalf of their king. When the tower falls, the advance of the barbarians will falter. They will be some time plundering their conquest and slaughtering such captives as they take. It will take their warlords still more time to gather their animals back into a fighting horde.'

'But they will continue their advance, your highness?' The hesitant voice of Thar Draigoth, the great flesh-merchant, sounded more like a rodent's squeak than the words of Naggaroth's most infamous slaver. Like Venil, he had extensive holdings in Karond Kar. After seeing his interests in Clar Karond massacred by the triumphant invaders, he was doubly worried about protecting the rest of his property.

'Let them come,' Ebnir Soulflayer declared. 'With the consent of his highness, I will lead the host of Naggarond against these animals and scatter them to the winds. You may send your hunters to collect whatever strays my army leaves alive,' he told Draigoth in a tone of haughty contempt.

'Your eagerness for battle is commendable, Soulflayer,' the king said, 'but I will waste no more blood fighting these savages and daemons.'

If lightning had struck the council chamber, it wouldn't have upset the Black Council as thoroughly as Malekith's hissed words. Many of the nobles sprang to their feet, all colour draining from their faces at the madness of what they had heard. The king wasn't going to fight? He wasn't going to loose the hosts of Naggaroth, the strength of the druchii, against these marauders? Was he simply going to sit back and watch his kingdom burn?

Malus could feel the incredulity of his fellow dreadlords

blackening into outright hostility. The Witch King ruled by fear, it was true, but the greater part of that fear wasn't that he could take a life, however slowly and inventively, but that he could take away everything a noble had schemed so long to possess. To lose one's life was inevitable, but to lose wealth and power before that life was through – this was a fate no druchii would accept.

With his own words, Malekith had fertilised the fields of discontent. Battle with Valkia and the treachery of his own mother must have upset the balance of his mind. It was the only explanation for why the king would incite such unrest at a time when his own reign was at its most vulnerable.

Malekith glared at his horrified vassals. 'The blood of the druchii belongs to me,' he snarled. 'I and I alone have made you what you are. Mine is the will that has stripped all weakness from your hearts. Mine is the vision that has poured strength into your bodies. All you think, all you dream, all that you are is as I have made it. The druchii are mine, formed from my hate, moulded by my spite. From the pathetic tatters of a vanquished realm I have built a great and terrible people.' The Witch King set his hand against the arm of his throne. 'To what purpose, then, have I done all this? To sulk in these black halls like a child of Drakira, supping from the poison of bitterness?'

Malekith let the question linger in the air. He waited several heartbeats, biding his time before springing whatever surprise he had in store for the Black Council. Malus was certain it could be no more shocking than the decision to keep his armies from the field of battle. In this, Malus soon found himself to be wrong.

'The *Rhana Dandra* is coming,' the Witch King proclaimed, his voice booming through the hall. 'These are the End Times. In your heart, each of you knows this to be true. Each of you has felt it in your soul.' For just an instant, Malekith stared directly at Malus. The drachau winced under that scrutiny, wondering if his king knew something more about his soul than he would like.

'Daemons and northlanders howl at the gates of our cities. They infest the land as never before. But it is not Naggaroth alone that is besieged.' Malekith paused again, letting anticipation build among his dreadlords. 'Ulthuan too is beset. Usurpers and faint-hearts strive to defend our ancient home against a foe they cannot defeat. If our people – all of our people – are to survive, they must have strong leaders. Leaders forged on the anvil of Naggaroth.'

A babble of voices rose as the dreadlords offered their full support to their king's latest campaign against Ulthuan. The nobles of Clar Karond and Karond Kar offered their warriors once the invaders were repulsed and their cities restored. The captains of the watch-towers likewise promised to dispatch elements from their garrisons once the present crisis was under control.

A grisly chuckle rose from the depths of the Witch King's armour. 'You misunderstand my intent. The End Times are coming. Chaos rises to devour the world. The northlanders will pillage everything that has not yet been warped by the storm of magic descending upon us. They will squat in our fallen towers to be preyed upon in turn by the daemons loosed by the Dark Gods they think they serve.'

Malus watched the Witch King stalk away from his throne, foot-prints burning into the carpet as he strode past the assembled dreadlords. Malekith stopped when he stood upon the great sigil of Aenarion set into the floor in lines of gold and malachite. An auric glow began to rise from the sigil as it reacted to the heat of Malekith's tread. Bathed in its light, the despot closed his hand about the hilt of the Destroyer hanging from his belt.

'This blasted wilderness has never been our home. It was a refuge, nothing more. Petty ambitions have allowed this place to become an anchor to the destiny of the druchii. Would you spend the blood of your warriors to protect a land that you despise, a bleak desolation that has within it nothing but scorn and mockery? I tell you, I tell all of you, this will not be! We will not bleed our armies defending this abominable wilderness. If we are to fight, then we will fight a war that is worth fighting. We will fight to take the land that belongs to us. We will fight to claim the land that is our heritage and birthright. Naggaroth? Let it burn. Let it rot. Let it fall to daemons and beasts. It is Ulthuan we desire, it is Ulthuan that is the destiny of the druchii. Ulthuan and the crown of Aenarion. Ulthuan and the birthright of Malekith!'

Ezresor was the first to raise his voice, the spymaster's tone cautious. 'The defences of Ulthuan are considerable. Even with the asur embattled by daemons, we must consider lines of supply and retreat...'

Malus could almost feel sorry for the spymaster when Malekith rounded on him and fixed him with his fiery gaze. 'There will be no retreat,' he declared. 'Naggaroth will die along with all who remain behind.' He turned, letting his gaze linger on each of the dreadlords. 'Any who try to return will die too. Do not mistake necessity for hubris. We *must* retake Ulthuan or perish in the Rhana Dandra. Victory or death, these are the only choices left to the druchii.'

The dreadlords sat in shocked silence, their outrage and resentment cowed by the mad passion of their king. Malus could guess their thoughts, for he doubted they were much different to his own. He had struggled hard to become drachau of Hag Graef. His rise had been bought with blood, far too much of it his own. Now, at the pinnacle of power, when he was the second most powerful elf in Naggaroth, it was all being cast aside, thrown away because their king believed the End Times were upon them. He was reminded of a warning Lady Eldire had given him once about prophecy: those who thought to see the future often brought it into being. Malekith believed the Rhana Dandra was upon them and now he was doing his utmost to ensure just such an apocalypse. Doom to both Naggaroth and Ulthuan.

Ulthuan. Malekith knew his people well. In his heart of hearts, every druchii coveted the lands of his forefathers. Naggaroth was a harsh, unforgiving desolation, a land of exile, not a land of glory. Nothing could change that brutal fact, not even the Circlet of Iron.

Even if he wanted to, Malus knew it would be impossible to hold Hag Graef on his own. Looking about the other dreadlords, he knew they would have reached the same conclusion. Their lands were forfeit, by royal decree. They would follow the Witch King in one final assault against Ulthuan, spending the last strength of the druchii. Either they would win new lands or they would give their lives in a final act of vengeance. Whichever doom was to be theirs, it was an ending that found harmony in the spiteful soul of every druchii.

The host of Hag Graef would follow Malekith in this final war against the asur. Malus would strip his city of every warrior, leaving only the old and the sick behind. He would muster the greatest warhost among all the druchii and, when battle was joined, the glory of victory would be his. The Witch King was selfish enough to believe this would be his war, but in any war, fortune was a fickle mistress. If Malekith showed any weakness, Malus would be there to seize upon it.

'Conquest or extinction,' the Witch King decreed. 'Naggaroth will never recover. Will the druchii stay to slowly dwindle and die, cowering behind our walls? No! We are scions of Nagarythe, the people of Aenarion. We will reclaim what is our birthright or die!' Malekith strode back to his throne as the assembled nobles cheered and shouted, each more eager to show his loyalty and support for the king than the elf beside him. Much of it was political theatre, but Malus could see that there were a few who seemed genuinely enthusiastic about the campaign ahead.

The Witch King motioned his dreadlords to silence. 'Before you depart the Black Tower, before you return to your cities to gather your warriors... a demonstration. A reminder of what must befall all who betray their king.'

Carefully Malus reached for the dagger hidden in the lining of his cloak. He froze as he saw Kouran rise to his feet. The captain wasn't interested in the drachau, however, instead marching towards the iron throne to stand beside his master. Any relief Malus might have felt vanished in the next instant. Emerging from the shadowy recesses of the chamber were the torturers who had so lately entertained him in the Black Tower's dungeons. One of the elves bore before him an ebony reliquary, which held the grisly tools of their trade.

Malus kept his hand around the dagger, every nerve on edge as he waited for some hidden foe to fall upon him. Was this why Malekith had freed him, simply to make an example of him before the whole Black Council? Watching Kouran approach the king gave him another idea. Perhaps it wasn't Malus the tyrant wanted to make an example of. Maybe it was Drusala who was the focus of the king's wrath. Making an example of her might silence some of those who thought him weak for not executing Morathi.

Kouran stood before the iron throne, the torturers flanking him at either side. The captain turned towards Drusala, then in a sudden whirl he fell upon Ezresor. The spymaster was caught utterly by surprise, the blade he'd hidden in the sleeve of his robe pinned against his wrist as Kouran restrained him. Ezresor was forced to his feet as the captain bent his other arm behind his back and pulled.

Malekith took hold of the struggling elf. His iron hand gripped Ezresor's gaunt face, forcing his mouth open. 'You were the eyes and ears of the Black Tower,' the king snarled. 'But what good are eyes and ears when the tongue will not relate what has been seen and heard?' The Witch King's iron talons reached inside Ezresor's mouth. A gargled cry escaped the spymaster as the tyrant ripped the tongue free. Malekith held the bloodied strip of flesh for all the Black Council to see. 'One of you bought Ezresor's tongue. Look well upon what you purchased.'

Dropping the gory talisman on the floor, the king withdrew from the chamber. Kouran waved the torturers forwards, supervising them as they helped him lower the mutilated Ezresor back into his chair. The elf bearing the reliquary opened the wooden box, disclosing an assortment of clawed mallets and long iron nails. While half of the torturers held Ezresor in place, the others began nailing him into his seat. When Malekith's armada sailed from Naggaroth, it would do so without the spymaster. He'd been condemned to remain behind and watch over the abandoned riches of Naggarond.

Malus shook his head. He'd suspected something untoward with Ezresor when the druchii had removed the bit from his mouth down in the dungeon. The spymaster had given Malus the chance to cheat Malekith by killing himself before any torture began. There was only one reason for extending such a mercy – Ezresor had been afraid of what Malus might say. Pride had kept Darkblade from taking such a cowardly choice. Now he rather suspected Ezresor regretted the transparency of such a mistake. He'd aroused Malekith's suspicions. Whether Ezresor was a part of Khyra's conspiracy or simply seeking to exploit it towards his own ends, the Witch King had paid him in full for his intrigues.

As he watched the torturers nailing the elf to his chair, Malus glanced across at Lady Khyra. Perhaps he'd been wrong; maybe she hadn't been leaning away from Ebnir but towards Ezresor. If so, with such a graphic display, Malekith had made the idea that the drachau had betrayed the conspiracy doubly convincing.

Malus knew Khyra wouldn't dare to act until the host of Hag Graef was embarked and on its way to Ulthuan. There was too much resting on the invasion to risk any delay in mustering the armies and setting sail. But after that, after that Malus would have good cause to worry.

His army might see the shores of Ulthuan, but would he be there to lead it?

FOUR

Malus watched as the towering spires of Hag Graef receded into the distance. The great black ark *Eternal Malediction* was bearing the bulk of his forces out into the Gulf of Naggarond. There they would join the rest of Malekith's armada before voyaging out into the Sea of Malice.

Hag Graef. How long and hard had he struggled to seize her crown? He'd fought against monsters and daemons, endured exile in the barbarous lands of humans and the deadly wastes of Chaos itself. He'd defeated the dread armies of Naggor on the battlefield and enslaved the Naggorites. The blood of brother and sister alike stained his hands, the life of his father had dripped down his sword. He had forfeited his soul to Tz'arkan and dared the forbidden world of the Screaming God-Child. Nothing and no one had been beyond the reach of his lust for ultimate power. Hag Graef, the second city of Naggaroth, and he had been its despotic master!

Now he watched as his kingdom faded away into the distance. Malus felt no regret at abandoning the city. The Witch King was right when he said that no druchii loved the chill wastes of Naggaroth. In their hearts burned the urge to reclaim the land to which they truly belonged, not the desolation of mocking exile. Hag Graef was a prison, a refuge, nothing more. It was in Ulthuan that true power and true glory lay, a realm worth ruling. The siren call of such a promise had fired the pride of Malus and every dreadlord in the land. Only the crazed inhabitants of Har Ganeth had refused Malekith's call, content to remain in their city, glutting their insatiable appetite for murder on the beasts and barbarians besieging their lands. Crone Hellebron and the Cult of Khaine had whipped up the people of Har Ganeth into a frenzy of blood-lust worthy of their ghastly city. It was as well for the druchii that Malekith had abandoned them to their madness.

The scenes Malus had left behind in Hag Graef were little better. Only the strong and useful had been taken aboard the *Eternal Malediction* and the other ships of the fleet. The rest of the city's population had been left to their fate, consigned to whatever horrible doom the creatures of the Wastes would bring to them once their hordes reached the Dark Crag. As his army withdrew from the city, the terror and turmoil boiling up around him had been thrilling to the drachau's black heart. He'd watched with amusement as corrupt old merchants and courtiers had tried in vain to bribe their way into the army, as though their wealth could make any warrior exchange the promise of glory in battle for the miserable end awaiting the city. He'd seen flesh traders auctioning off exotic slaves for almost nothing, seen those same slaves butchered on the spot by buyers interested only in indulging their jaded thirst for slaughter. He'd watched noble towers looted and burned, seen the mortuary vaults smashed open and the bones of ancient rivals ground into the streets under the vengeful boots of drunken wastrels. Some of the temples had been thrown open, their priests murdered by mobs of disillusioned elves, venting their feelings of divine betrayal against those who served the gods. Other temples, like that of Bloody-Handed Khaine himself, became centres of crazed worship and devotion, zealots dragging screaming sacrifices to the gore-soaked altars, as though in this last hour their religious frenzy might yet move their god to protect them.

As chaotic as the rioting and unrest in the streets was, Malus knew things were far worse in the mines below. In stripping Hag Graef of every able-bodied warrior, Malus had dispatched Kunor Kunoll's Son to gather the overseers and slavemasters in the pits below the city. He would need such experienced taskmasters to drive the captive Naggorites into battle. Leaving them behind to administer the vast numbers of human, dwarf and greenskin slaves under Hag Graef would simply be wasteful. There hadn't been time to massacre the slaves; Kunor simply withdrew the guards and locked the gates. Even as he was arranging the destruction of his own wine cellars so that no looter would profit off what he was forced to leave behind, word reached Malus that the mine slaves were in revolt. Panicked by their abandonment, the terrified throng was battering down the gates that confined them. It would only be a matter of hours before the horde won their way clear of the tunnels and spilled out into the streets.

Malus was irate he couldn't stay to watch that. It would have been amusing to behold the ragged host of starveling dogs tear their way through the decadent druchii he'd deemed unfit to fight against the asur. He was certain the carnage would be unprecedented in the history of the Hag, a final atrocity of epic scope before the foul city was blotted out.

'Do you mourn your kingdom, my lord?'

Malus turned as he felt the soft touch of Vincirix's hand against his forearm. He'd heard the knight's approach, of course. She was one of the few he trusted enough to get so near to him. It wasn't that she was beyond treachery – after all, she'd conspired with him to murder her own father – but the simple fact that she owed her position to him. Without his patronage, her own warriors would soon dispose of her. She was well aware of that. Malus wondered if that dependency added an extra note of urgency to her passion when they were alone. Certainly she'd proven to be the most delicious companion to share his bed in a long time.

The drachau rolled across the silk sheets and slid his hand down his lover's tender throat. The black arks were floating cities in their own right and the master of the *Eternal Malediction* had turned the tallest of its spires over to his fearsome passenger. The sprawling bed chamber Malus had taken for his own was very near the summit of that tower, with great windows set into three of its four walls. The resulting view was astonishing, making him feel almost as though he soared among the clouds rather than sailed upon the sea. It was easy to understand how the masters of the black arks could develop such a lordly opinion of themselves; feeling unbound by the very laws of nature, how could they respect the rules of kings and tyrants? Malus considered that it was a good thing his warriors outnumbered the black ark's corsairs by several orders of magnitude. It might remind them who exactly was in charge.

Lifting one finger, Malus stroked the knight's chin. There was just the hint of a scar there, the unhealed residue of a manticore's sting. She had far worse scars elsewhere. It had cost Vincirix much pain to impress her father, to rise through the ranks of her siblings. In some ways, her ruthless jockeying for position paralleled his own. Though, of course, his own ambitions had been much grander in scale and he, at least, had needed no help to kill his father.

He could feel Tz'arkan stirring deep inside him. Of all the things he had done, for some reason it was the vaulkhar's murder that actually seemed to disgust the daemon. Malus had never been able to figure out why. Perhaps it made the daemon question exactly how far its host would go to get what he wanted.

Vincirix tensed under his touch. She would never dare to say anything to him, but Malus knew she hated it when he ran his fingers along the lines of her scars. It reminded her that she had been weak, that she bore the marks of that weakness on her like the brand of a slave. Malus enjoyed reminding her of their respective positions. It reinforced how much she stood to lose if he tired of her.

'Do you still weep for Clar Karond?' Malus asked the knight, cupping her chin and drawing her head back so he could stare into the rich depths of her eyes. 'Do you miss the sights and smells of the slave markets, the roars from the beast-pits? Do you regret not walking the bridges between its great towers, passing between the great houses in the dead of night? How much of your heritage was lost there? How much of your blood is entombed within its tortured earth? How many companions did you leave behind, I wonder?'

The knight smiled at him, hugging him close against her in a tight embrace. 'I have no love but you, Lord Malus. What ardour could match yours? What passion could equal yours?'

Malus drew back, his hand twining Vincirix's dark locks. 'Then you are content? A pity. It is a mark of the petty that they become content. Those who aspire to greater things must never lose the flame of ambition.' Pulling her hair, he turned Vincirix back towards the diminishing image of Hag Graef. 'If I were petty, I should be content to keep the Hag. I would marshal my army and defy the Witch King's decree. I would strive to hold my realm against all foes. This I would do, if I were content to be master of a diseased dung-heap. No, Vincirix, the fire of ambition burns in me. I will have a kingdom worthy of me! Of what consequence then is the Hag or Clar Karond? Let them burn. Let them rot. They are the ghosts of the past, the symbols of our people's disgrace. The glory of the druchii doesn't lie with them. It is in Ulthuan, not Nagga-roth, where our people belong!'

'You speak like Malekith,' Vincirix observed. Malus laughed and kissed her neck.

'Does that mean I sound like a king?' he asked her. He leaned back and stared again into her eyes. 'How great is your own ambi-tion, I wonder? How far do you expect it to take you?'

Vincirix matched his stare. 'As far as it would carry my lord,' she said.

Malus laughed again and drew the knight to him.

In that moment, the great window staring out in the direction of Hag Graef burst inwards in a shower of glass and splintered wood. A lithe, nearly naked figure swept into the drachau's chamber, hip-high boots of chimera-hide and a gilded mask cast in the shape of a shrieking daemon the only raiment affected by the weird intruder. A small buckler ringed with razors was bound about the invader's right arm while in her left she gripped a hooked whip. The elf cast her masked gaze about the chamber and a hideous peal of gleeful laughter erupted from her as she spied Malus lying upon the bed.

Malus shoved Vincirix towards the masked intruder, at the same time throwing himself from bed to floor. The masked druchii swerved around Vincirix's diving form and lunged forwards at the bed. The invader's whip slashed down almost at the same moment, slicing into the bed and sending down billowing into the air. Before his attacker could fully recover, Malus kicked out with his foot, catching the elf in her shin. Instead of collapsing beneath the blow, she turned her fall into a violent spin, the razors lining her shield cutting across Malus's bare forearm. The bleeding drachau rolled away as his foe's spin brought the crooked sword sweeping towards him once again.

He knew this kind of enemy, Malus realised. He'd seen her like fight often enough in the arenas of Hag Graef. She belonged to the Sisters of Slaughter, foremost of Naggaroth's gladiator guilds – female warriors who devoted themselves to the ruthless god Eldrazor of the Blades. The gladiatrixes didn't master any technique or school of combat, instead honing their reflexes and plying their murderous trade on a savage, instinctual level. They were the most unpredictable of foes, constantly adapting and reacting to their enemy, existing only in the moment, devoid of the discipline and strategy of more refined warriors.

Whoever had sent this elf to kill him had known it was just this kind of enemy that would cause Malus the most worry. His cunning brain could outthink a normal foe, discern the pattern behind his opponent's training and plan his own strategy accordingly. Against a Sister of Slaughter, however, such ploys would be useless.

The gladiatrix was already whirling back to the attack, diving at him like a rabid wolf. Her spin brought both whip and shield slashing at him. The hooked whip gouged a furrow in the bedframe while the razored shield sent sparks flying from the stone floor. Still spinning, the elf kicked out, her boot cracking against Malus's cheek, spilling him onto his back.

More glass exploded inwards as two more of the pit fighters came crashing into the chamber, swinging into the room on ropes. Malus could afford them only the briefest glance before his first attacker was diving down on him again. His fist slammed into her chest, bruising the flesh and driving the breath out of her. As she gasped, the flash of her whip was diverted, sweeping through the drachau's hair instead of his skull. The gladiatrix's instincts recovered enough to smash the boss of her shield into Malus's face and dig the razors of its underside into his shoulder. Before she could work further harm, however, the invader was swept to the floor by Vincirix. The two she-elves rolled away, the knight's legs locked about the killer's torso, one hand trying to pry the hooked whip free while the other arm wrapped itself around the neck beneath the daemon-mask.

Malus sprang across the damaged bed, diving for the sheathed length of the Warpsword of Khaine lying upon its ebony stand. Before he could reach his sword, the other gladiatrixes were charging him, whirling at him in their eerie dance of death. The drachau recoiled before the storm of slashing whips and shields, throwing pillows and blankets at the savage she-elves in a desperate bid to hold them back. His gambit bore some slight success when one of the killers found her whip coiled around an upflung fur. Before she could disentangle herself, Malus caught her knee with a brutal kick. He heard a grisly pop as the warrior crashed to the floor.

Growling like a mother panther, the other gladiatrix lunged at him. Malus felt the murderous closeness of her whip as it snapped at his ribs. The elf's shield flashed upwards to swat away a pillow he threw at her, then her entire body described an impossible pirouette as the whip came into play once more. Malus could feel Tz'arkan's presence respond to the closeness of death to its host, the daemon's agitation threatening to intrude into his thoughts just when he needed them at their sharpest.

A shriek rose from his adversary as Malus drove his fingers into her mask. A wave of sadistic exultation swept through him as he felt the elf's eye beneath his finger. The gladiatrix tumbled away from him, pawing at her mask as she landed on the floor. With a wrench, she broke the leather straps and threw the bloodied mask at Malus. The exposed face was beauteous, or would have been but for the jellied wreckage dripping from one eye socket.

The bruising impact of the bronze mask against his bare flesh didn't stop Malus from making another dive for the warpsword. Instead, it was the brutal kick of a booted foot that drove him back. The other gladiatrix had freed herself from the blanket and was leaping to intercept the drachau. Raw pain flared through him as he was knocked back by the blow. He tried to roll as he landed back on the bed, but the pain only grew more intense. The killer's kick had fractured a rib, and blood streamed onto the sheets from the dozens of little wounds where the steel studs lining her boot had pricked his skin.

Before he could react, the mutilated gladiatrix was diving at him again. He grunted in agony as he was driven face-first into the bedding, his broken rib grinding against its fellows. The she-elf pinned him beneath her body, her legs pressing down into the small of his back. Cackling a laugh that was equal parts rage and murderous jubilation, she took hold of his hair and jerked his head back. He could see the sheen of her shield as she brought its razored edge spinning down. Desperate, Malus snatched hold of the soft flesh of the elf's thigh and gave her leg a vicious twist.

The gladiatrix was accustomed to worse pain, but the unexpectedness of Malus's assault caused her the briefest instant of surprise. Reflexively, she reared up and away from the drachau's tormenting clutch. The moment he felt her weight shift, Malus bucked up from the bedding, clenching his teeth against the surge of pain that roared through his body. His assailant was sent tumbling forwards, her uncanny knack for adaptation turning her fall into a roll. His intention had been to throw her full into the face of the other gladiatrix, but she displayed the same automatic reaction as her sister, darting aside and spinning around in a murderous counter-attack.

Malus reacted in the only way possible, doing the last thing his enemy would expect. Instead of diving back, he dived forwards. The gladiatrix adjusted the snap of her whip as he came at her; he felt the metal hook slice the skin along his shoulder. But he'd managed to slip beneath her guard, driving his head into her belly. The killer started to roll with the impact, twisting around so that she could drive her shield into Malus's neck. The drachau, however, drove a fist into her throat, crushing her windpipe. The warrior crumpled in a gasping, gagging heap.

From behind him, Malus heard a sharp cry. He turned around, putting his back to the wall and trying to keep both the choking gladiatrix and the one-eyed harridan in view. Across the room he could see Vincirix throw her enemy from her by bringing both legs up and under the killer's body. As the gladiatrix spun away, the knight kept a firm hold on her left arm. There was a sickening sound as the limb was dislocated. The crippled fighter managed to slash at Vincirix with her shield, but the knight slithered under the razored edge with an almost boneless undulation. The warrior kicked out with one of her boots, the toe cracking against Vincirix's jaw. It was a blow that would have stunned a less rugged combatant, but Vincirix had cut her teeth breaking the spirits of hydras and manticores. There was little punishment that could equal the pain of being splashed by the caustic venom of a kharibdyss. Grimly, Vincirix shrugged off the elf's kick and fell upon her foe. Wrenching the gladiatrix's knee about, she bent the killer's leg back upon itself. Even the intruder's mask couldn't muffle the resultant scream of agony.

Malus glared at the one-eyed gladiatrix, gesturing at the fighter Vincirix was dismantling piece by piece and the gagging wretch lying on the bed. 'You should have brought more help before you tried to murder me!' he snarled at her.

One-eye smiled back at him. Keeping her place near the warpsword, too cautious to risk touching the enchanted blade, the gladiatrix raised her fingers to her mouth and blew a sharp whistle.

Malus felt his insides turn sick when four more Sisters of Slaughter came rappelling down into the room through the shattered

windows. He could almost hear Tz'arkan laughing at him. The daemon was right. He had asked for it.

'I'm going to peel your eyes from your skull,' One-eye promised.
'Only when you forget how to scream will I let you die.' She dived
aside as Malus made a desperate lunge for his sword. The hand
that reached out for the blade was smashed flat by One-eye's shield.
The hook of the elf's whip cracked across his face, splitting his lip
and knocking teeth from his mouth. 'Slow, Darkblade,' the mur-
deress hissed. 'You die slow!'

The other invaders were rushing into the room now. Vincirix
was crouched over the naked wreck of her own foe, trying to break
the hold the killer stubbornly maintained on her whip. One of the
masked gladiatrixes danced towards the unarmed knight, lash and
shield describing a gleaming skein of death as she advanced.

At that moment, the door to the chamber burst inwards, blown
back by a force that snapped the bolt and the heavy beam that
had been set across it. A deafening roar raged through the room,
like the titanic bellow of an angry volcano. Malus felt his head ring
from the clamour, saw Vincirix and the gladiatrixes actually stag-
ger before the auditory assault.

Behind that monstrous din, warriors came rushing into the chamber, falling upon the stunned gladiatrixes before they could recover
their wits. Silar Thornblood led the rush, cutting down a gladiatrix with a double-handed slash of his sword. Charging past him
were Kunor and a pair of elves in the battered armour of Naggorite slave-soldiers. Their assault wasn't quite as unopposed as
Silar's, the gladiatrixes warding away the initial impetus with their
bladed bucklers.

A howl of fury that nearly matched the deafening roar of the
preceding moment struck Malus's ears. Close beside him, One-
eye twisted her body, snapping her whip at his throat. The arrival

of the drachau's warriors had cheated her of the opportunity to kill him slowly, but she was determined to kill him just the same.

Malus hooked his feet around One-eye's leg and threw his own body into a sidewise twist. The gladiatrix was forced to follow his motion, the whip falling lax as the two crashed against the wall. Before she could start to rise, Malus jammed the flat of his hand into her nose, crushing it into a pulpy mess. One-eye shrieked at him and raked the edge of her shield along his arm, ripping his flesh. The intense pain broke the hold Malus had gained on the killer's throat. Slamming her knee into his groin, the gladiatrix pulled back and tried to bring her whip into play once more.

Blinking through his own pain, Malus caught the butt of One-eye's whip. His tenuous clutch arrested the lash's motion, preventing the gladiatrix from drawing back for another murderous stroke. Spitting a mouthful of blood and the odd splinter of tooth into her last good eye, Malus surged upwards from the floor.

Before he could rip the whip free from the blinded gladiatrix, Malus felt his foe's entire body seized by a shivering convulsion. He could actually feel the warmth of life vanish beneath his touch. It was only the matter of a heartbeat, the pause between pulsations, and One-eye went from a living adversary to a mere carcass. He didn't need the uncanny clamminess in the air around him to recognise the taint of sorcery. He'd been around such dark arts all his life, between his mother and his treacherous sister Yasmir; he could recognise the residue of magic only too well.

Looking away from the dead gladiatrix, Malus was surprised to find Drusala standing in the doorway of his chamber. The explosive opening of the portal was now explained as well as the sudden demise of his own foe. Perhaps explained just a little too neatly.

'Silar! Kunor!' Malus shouted. 'I want one of them alive!' The drachau spared no more time for commands, but snatched up the warpsword. If Drusala didn't want any of the killers taken intact, the magic blade would make a good argument against her.

The conflict was winding down as Malus took up his sword. Two more of the gladiatrixes were dead, though they'd claimed one of Kunor's Naggorites before they went down. The last intruder was beset by the combination of Silar and Vincirix. Armed with the shield and whip of the gladiatrix she'd already killed, the knight from Clar Karond dived in upon the pit fighter as she spun away from Silar's blade. Vincirix's whip coiled around the wrist of her adversary, imprisoning both the weapon and the hand that held it. The tension of the tautened whip caused the hook at the end of the lash to tear through the gladiatrix's hand. Blood sprayed from a severed artery. Catching the masked warrior's shield with her own buckler, Vincirix pressed her assault. Closing with the gladiatrix, she drove both knees into the elf's midsection, driving the air from her body.

The crippled killer collapsed in Vincirix's arms. The knight shoved her foe away in disgust. 'Kunor,' she growled. 'Bind this thing's wound before she bleeds out.' Turning her back on the slave-driver, she smiled at Malus. 'You said alive, not whole.'

The smile Malus returned to her was as warm as a cold one's grin. 'You need to find a god and start praying that arena-meat lives long enough to tell me what I want to know.' His piece said, Malus turned away from his lover. He looked over at the gore-soaked bed. A final death rattle wheezed from the gladiatrix whose throat he'd crushed. He watched as the lithe body spasmed and fell still.

'It is fortunate that we arrived when we did, your lordship,' Drusala said, advancing into the room.

'Excuse me, I'm not really in a mood to receive visitors at the moment,' Malus told her. He directed a sharp look at Silar. The noble paused as he wiped blood off his blade.

'The sorceress saw an omen in the waves...' Silar started to explain. 'A shark in the coils of an octopus,' Drusala elaborated.

Malus didn't care for the amused twinkle in her eye as the sorceress strode towards him. Scowling, he reached for one of the sable-edged robes draped across a nearby divan. Irritated, he tried to shrug his way into the garment, his annoyance mounting when he found he'd grabbed Vincirix's robe by mistake.

'Which was I?' Malus grumbled as he threw the first robe at Vincirix and made a grab for the other. 'The shark or the octopus?'

Drusala waved her hand at the dead gladiatrixes. 'The shark ate the octopus, in the end, so you must have been the shark.'

'What does that make you?' Malus asked, not liking the superiority in Drusala's tone. 'One of the pilot fish?' He didn't give her a chance to reply. 'Silar, I want to know everything, but we can start with why you brought so few warriors to aid me.'

Silar couldn't hold his master's fierce gaze, staring instead at some imaginary fixture just over the drachau's shoulder. 'We... we weren't sure that... we'd be in time. If... if something happened...'

'You wanted only people who could keep their mouths shut,' Malus finished for him. He spun around, directing his glare at Kunor as the slavemaster finished binding the prisoner's wound. 'Can your Naggorite be trusted to hold a secret?'

Without hesitation, Kunor lunged and drove his dagger into the side of the surviving slave-soldier. The Naggorite cried out once, then wilted to the floor, his lifeblood spurting from the artery Kunor had severed.

'He can now, my lord,' Kunor said. The readiness of the slavemaster to indulge his blood-lust sometimes made Malus wonder if he wasn't the spawn of a witch elf rather than a son of Hag Graef.

'What of your captive?' Drusala asked. 'What secrets do you expect her to divulge?' The sorceress knelt beside One-eye's corpse, pulling down one of her boots and exposing a line of glyphs tattooed into her pale skin. At a glance, Malus could tell the glyphs represented various guilds, covens and noble houses. The uppermost, the most recently inked, was the glyph of Ezresor. 'Her employers are recorded here already.'

Malus smiled and shook his head. It was possible, of course, that Ezresor had made arrangements to murder Malus before his own doom claimed him in the Black Tower. It wouldn't be the first time that a schemer's designs for revenge outlived him. But such an answer would be too simple, too obvious. 'And what if she only records the mark when her job is done? No, I think it would be too reckless to trust so simple a solution.'

'Who else would want your death?' Drusala smiled. The question was much too obvious as well.

'Silar, take the prisoner to Lady Eldire,' Malus said. 'She can use her magic to wring what I want to know out of the wretch.'

Drusala snapped her fingers, calling Malus's attention back to her. 'I was handmaiden to Lady Morathi. I am a powerful sorceress in my own right. My spells can drag the truth out of that harpy-bait as easily as your mother's can.'

A twinge of amusement flashed across Malus's face as he noted the injured pride in Drusala's voice. 'Your spells are no doubt quite potent,' he told her. 'I have no doubt you could wrest the truth from this villainess. The only doubt I have is whether it would be the sort of truth I want to hear.'

Looking around the shambles of his bedchamber, Malus snapped orders to Kunor and Vincirix. 'Tell Fleetmaster Hadrith I will need a new apartment and get some of our people up here to clean this mess. Be discreet, we don't want the wrong people finding out about this.' He met Drusala's cool gaze.

'It might be dangerous if word got out before we knew who was responsible,' Malus declared. The sound of the wind whistling through the shattered windows seemed to echo his concern. An echo that rustled the bedclothes and the curtains, but somehow couldn't so much as ripple the thin silk gown that hugged Drusala's slender body.

FIVE

The empty wine bottle crashed against the stone floor, exploding in a nimbus of shimmering glass. Malus ignored the servant who hurried to clear away the debris and instead beckoned his mother's steward over to him. Korbus was a spindly, sour-faced druchii, with just a hint of yellow in his complexion that gave his skin a jaundiced look Malus typically associated with sickly human slaves. The expensive tunic and robe the steward wore always seemed to rest uneasily on him, like a snake not quite out of its old skin.

Korbus was an old retainer, long in his mother's service. She'd taken him on shortly after the vaulkhar's death. Malus had heard rumours that Eldire favoured him as a consort. That didn't trouble him particularly; he wasn't so insecure about his own position as to forbid his mother a toy now and then. No, what nagged at him were the stories that Korbus wasn't entirely without his own small talents in the black arts. It had been generations since Malekith, heeding some obscure prophecy about sorcerers and regicide, forbade any but she-elves to practise magic in Naggaroth. Certainly a number of sorcerers had remained, lurking in secret, but they existed under the pain of death not simply from Morathi and her convent, but from the tyranny of the Witch King himself. Why his mother, already an enemy of Morathi, should want to tempt Malekith as well by keeping a petty magician in her service was something Malus couldn't understand. One day, he felt, he would have to arrange an accident for Korbus and eliminate the potential for problems from that quarter.

For now, however, it was enough to have the dour little swine attending him like a serving wench. Korbus could do with a dose of humility and a reminder that whatever consideration Malus might accord his mother didn't extend to his mother's consort. As Malus beckoned to him, Korbus shambled over with another bottle of wine.

'Go any slower, Korbus, and I'll reconsider the wisdom of allowing you to remain on board,' Malus snapped as the steward proffered him the bottle.

'Forgive me, dread master,' Korbus said, bowing to the floor. 'I know your wounds pain you, but do you think it wise to imbibe so freely?'

Malus rolled the bottle along the side of his arm where Eldire's poultice covered the slash he'd received from one of the gladiatrixes. His mother's magic was mending his hurts well enough. It wasn't any physical pain Malus sought to deaden with the draught. It was Tz'arkan. The daemon was responding to the spells his mother had used, fattening on them like some phantom leech. The draught dulled its appetite, enticing it back into hibernation or whatever it was the daemon did when it wasn't nagging at his mind and trying to usurp his flesh.

At the moment, of course, the daemon was one of the less unsettling aspects of his life. Since sailing from Hag Graef and joining the rest of Malekith's fleet in the Gulf of Naggarond, Malus had come to appreciate the esteem with which his king regarded him.

The *Eternal Malediction* had been given the dubious honour of leading the rest of the fleet out into the Sea of Malice. The vanguard position offered more than the usual hazards. The threat of an asur ship might be minimal, but they'd already fended off the mindless violence offered by dozens of barbarian dragonships. There were strange blocks of luminous ice drifting through the sea, ice that exuded fingers of lightning and which seemed to chase after the black ark with an animalistic hunger. Reefs that had never existed before menaced the vessel as she sailed across waters that should have been as familiar to the corsairs as their own boots. Eerie storms of light and sound rumbled through the sky, flashing through the clouds like primordial leviathans, sometimes reaching down to draw up part of the sea in a shrieking water spout.

Naggaroth was slipping into the abyss. The invasion besetting the realm was far more than hordes of beasts and barbarians. The corruption flowing down from the Wastes was attacking the very fabric of reality, inundating the land itself with the corrosive energies of unrestrained and unfocused magic. The Witch King's decision to abandon his kingdom was more than a last thrust at the hated asur. It was the only way for the druchii to survive as a people.

Of course, it was his own survival that was of the utmost concern to Malus. When he'd seen Drusala and her entourage from Ghrond among the passengers aboard the *Eternal Malediction,* he'd thought her presence indicated that Malekith was trying to keep a close eye on him. Despite all the talk about the Witch King falling out with his mother and leaving Morathi to rot in her tower, Malus hadn't believed it. He'd been certain that the two were yet working in concert. Drusala had been sent to watch him because Malekith expected her to faithfully attend her duty.

The turmoil of their voyage into the Sea of Malice made him reconsider that idea. He knew how precarious his own position with his king was; now he wondered if Drusala weren't in the same boat. It would be like Malekith to put all of his enemies in one cage so they might be more easily disposed of. The sorceress from Ghrond and the drachau of Hag Graef might both be living on borrowed time.

Malus stared at the bottle of wine Korbus had brought him. A cold smile played across his face. 'Steward,' he laughed, knowing how the servile title upset Korbus, 'you are forgetting that the first glass always belongs to you.'

Korbus was usually much better at hiding his emotions than he was today, Malus reflected. There was almost a suggestion of anger in his posture as he retrieved a crystal glass and poured out a small measure of the dark wine. He'd have to talk with his mother about that. A suitably brutal corrective measure might remind the petty sorcerer of exactly where he stood in the grand scheme of things.

Betraying barely a breath of hesitation, Korbus drank the measure of wine from his glass. Malus leaned back in his chair, watching with the most intense interest as the steward replaced the glass on the table and folded his arms behind his back. Seconds stretched into minutes, master studying servant while the servant stared blankly at one of the tapestries hanging from the wall. At length, Malus gave an irritated wave of his hand.

'It seems you've succeeded in keeping poisoners away from my wine,' Malus said. 'That, or maybe you have enough magic that you can keep it from affecting you.' He gripped the neck of the bottle and sketched a mocking salute to Korbus. 'I wonder what my mother will do to you if that's the case. Letting your little spells protect you while failing to save her beloved son.' Laughing, Malus took a long pull from the bottle. He could feel the welcome rush of warm numbness spread through his body. Peering down the length of the upended bottle, he saw Korbus scowling back at him.

Losing patience with him, Malus gave an angry flick of his hand and dismissed his mother's consort. Considering these were the rooms Lady Eldire shared with the sorcerer, he was certain the added insult wouldn't be lost on Korbus.

As Korbus beat a graceless retreat from the room, Silar stepped away from the alcove from which he had been keeping guard. 'Is it prudent to bait him so, my lord?' he asked.

Malus shrugged his shoulders, feeling just the faintest echo of pain from the one the gladiatrix had slashed. 'No, probably not, but it is most satisfying. Someday Lady Eldire will tire of that arse-kissing conjurer and when she does, I'll get some real satisfaction out of him.'

'I shall eagerly anticipate the day, my lord,' Silar said.

A twinge of nostalgia tugged at Malus when he heard Silar speak. It was just the sort of thing Hauclir would have said, that insufferable mix of servility and sarcasm his old retainer had never been able to refrain from employing. Dear Hauclir. He'd been the closest thing to a friend Darkblade had ever had. Gone these many years, his memorial abandoned with the rest of Hag Graef...

Malus glared at the wine yet sloshing about the bottom of the bottle. It was making him maudlin, teasing out the weaker impulses and affections lying deep inside his mind. He'd almost prefer to give Tz'arkan free rein than evoke such puerile emotions. Angrily, he cast the bottle away, smiling as he heard it smack against one of the extravagant divans with which the apartment was furnished. The wine-stains would cost some corsair officer fair coin to remove once these rooms were restored to him. Allowing of course the sea-rat hadn't already been dumped over the side.

Yes, Malus reflected, there were a good many enemies who could have engaged the Sisters of Slaughter to take his life, among them the inhabitants of the black ark itself. When the drachau's enormous army had embarked, a great number of Fleetmaster Hadrith's people had been displaced, left to fend for themselves in the wilds around Hag Graef. The black ark was a floating city and, like any city, it had become bloated with the weak and wastrel. To make room for his soldiers, for their weapons and their beasts of war, Malus had ordered the removal of these worthless elves. At this stage of the game, there was no concealing from them that being left behind was a death sentence. There had been riots and rebellion, the corsairs forced to slaughter their own kin in order to maintain Hadrith's rule over the ship. The young, the old, the sick and the worthless – they had tried to resist, but it was a futile gesture against seasoned warriors. The eels and harpies had a grand feast when the black ark left Hag Graef.

Still, for all the necessity of his ruthless orders, Malus knew there would be many on the *Eternal Malediction* who bore him ill. Parents who'd seen their families cast over the side, sons and daughters who'd watched their progenitors abandoned as the black ark sailed away, any number of more torrid and unsavoury attachments that had been erased by the drachau's decree. Few druchii were so simple-minded as to let tender regards seep into their hearts, but there were even fewer who accepted their possessions being taken from them with good grace. In forcibly severing these ties of blood and intrigue, Malus had earned the hate of the corsairs.

'Someone among Hadrith's crew helped those she-daemons reach me,' Malus mused aloud. 'They must have had help getting into the rigging and knowing the right spot to rappel into my chambers.'

'Did the prisoner say as much before...' Silar shuddered, unable to finish the thought. He'd been present during most of Eldire's interrogation of the gladiatrix. The things he'd seen done were enough to shock even his sensibilities.

Malus frowned and shook his head. 'No, she didn't. But it stands to reason that they had inside help.' He tapped his chin as he considered just how obvious that connection was. Such bluntness was crude. No druchii would take any satisfaction from so direct a course of reprisal. It was the cunning behind a murder, the craft employed to conceal motive and perpetrator alike, that gave an elf pride in his sins. The very directness of the connection back to Hadrith's people made him doubt they were ultimately behind the attack. Certainly, someone had been involved at some level, but things weren't so desperate for the crew that they'd act in such a reckless fashion on their own. No, there was some other hand involved, some manipulator working from the shadows.

The question remained – who was that murderous plotter? The more Malus thought about it, the less he considered it possible Ezresor was striking at him from the beyond. The tattooed glyph on the leg of each gladiatrix was too obvious; besides there was the problem of the spymaster anticipating that Malekith would command the *Eternal Malediction* to carry the drachau and his army, a decision that the Witch King hadn't made until well after that final gathering of the Black Council. That, of course, still left entirely too many possibilities, starting with the Witch King himself. Lady Khyra and her fellow conspirators were likely candidates too, eager to obscure their own involvement in the attempt against Malekith.

Whoever was behind it, they'd had their own share of sorcery to draw upon. Despite the most heinous tortures her magic could inflict, Eldire had been unable to penetrate the barrier that had been raised inside the prisoner's mind. Some spell had partitioned the memory of whoever had engaged the troupe of gladiatrixes to kill Malus. Eldire was certain the memory was there – her own magic was powerful enough to uncover that much – but it stubbornly resisted every effort to pry it free. Before the end, after what she'd endured, Malus was certain the gladitarix would have gladly confessed if it had been in her power to do so. Instead, she'd taken her secret with her into Ereth Khial's underworld. Even Eldire's efforts to command the elf's departed spirit had been fruitless. It was rare when his mother encountered magic stronger than her own, and when she did it tended to put her into a dangerous mood.

Thinking of dangerous sorceresses made Malus turn his thoughts to Drusala. How far was he prepared to trust that her timely intervention had been caused by an omen and not arranged beforehand? What sort of game was she trying to play? If she was out of favour with Malekith, was she trying to inveigle herself into the good graces of Malus? If that were the case, anything that smacked of collusion between them would provoke the Witch King into some sort of response. Probably something involving a regiment of Black Guard. The prudent thing would be to keep the witch as far away as possible.

Malus hadn't risen to the rank of drachau by doing what was prudent.

'Where is Drusala?' Malus asked Silar as he rose from his chair.

Silar bit back whatever wise words of caution leapt to his tongue. Instead he took a moment to collect himself and tell his master what he wanted to hear. 'Lady Eldire and the witch from Ghrond have been in consultation all morning.'

That bit of information was intriguing. All his life, Malus's mother had lived in dread of Morathi's sorceresses, fearing falling into their clutches even more than she had being returned to the Witch Lords of Naggor. Why the sudden change? What had brought about such a dramatic adjustment in Eldire's sensibilities? Had the disgrace and exile of Morathi made his mother overbold? Or had her witch-sight told her she would need magic beyond what her own abilities could provide on the journey ahead? Eldire had a pronounced talent for prophecy, a quality that had made her valuable to Naggor and dangerous to Ghrond. What had she foreseen that made her entertain Drusala?

Malus scowled at Silar as he realised his retainer hadn't answered his question. 'I did not ask what she's been doing,' he warned the noble. 'I asked you where she is.'

There were only a few elves Malus considered dependable and even fewer he felt comfortable allowing close to him. Silar Thornblood, with all his quaint concepts of duty and obligation, was the nearest of them all. He could be depended upon to faithfully serve the drachau because he honestly saw his own prestige as being dependent upon the drachau's power. As close as he was, however, even Silar felt a twinge of fear when his master employed that cold, flat tone of voice against him.

'Lady Eldire is meeting with Drusala in the Star Spire,' he reported. 'Several of Fleetmaster Hadrith's diviners and astrologers are with them.'

'Some great effort on mother's part to see a bit further into the future,' Malus said. He nodded as he reached a decision. 'We'll just go and see the results of her divination.'

'Shall I call your knights?' Silar asked.

Malus uttered a sneering laugh. 'Let's wait and hear what sort of prophecies these witches have conjured before I have them massacred.'

Spanning the reaches between the great spires of the black ark, vast platforms and bridges had been erected. Supported by the most powerful of old Nagarythe's ancient sorceries, the black ark was a floating city unto itself. Incapable of expanding outwards, the city had built itself upwards. Gantries and walkways coiled around the stone towers, like fungus growing on a tree. Mazes of chain and rigging spooled downwards to anchor platforms of brass, bronze, bone and timber into place. Unlike a natural ship or even the strange bastions fitted to the scaly backs of helldrakes, there was little sense of motion when standing on the platforms. The turmoil of wind and sea were largely baffled by the magics that saturated the black ark. Fierce winter storms, even the deranged tempests of shimmering light streaming down from the Wastes, were incapable of battering the seafaring citadel.

As he prowled along the bridges, making his way to the Star Spire, Malus took a sardonic pleasure from the hastily downcast eyes of the elves he passed. How many of them resented him for abandoning the Hag? They were fools, and worse, they were hypocrites. Not one of them had forsaken his place on the *Eternal Malediction*. They had all accepted the choice between sacrificing the city or remaining behind to die with it.

He could have had much better followers if he'd only cast aside the title of drachau and ridden into the north. Malus would have become master of things no earthly lord could ever aspire towards! He would have stretched forth his hand and seen eternity itself coiling about his fingers. He would know the secret names of all things and understand the fragile skein that bound the essence of worlds. His heart would have despaired from the singing of the aethyr and the great truth beyond.

Malus stopped and leaned against the iron rail lining the platform he was crossing. He could feel the darkness of Tz'arkan boiling up inside him. So far, the wine had numbed the daemon too much for it to make itself coherent and understandable. Instead he could feel it as a shadow crawling through his flesh. 'Relent,' he hissed at the abomination inside him, smashing his fist against the rail in his frustration.

'Are you ill, my lord?' The question came from a young druchii in the studded armour of a beast-keeper. Malus directed a scowl at the elf so fierce that he stumbled back towards the pack of cold ones he'd been helping to keep under control.

Silar came up beside Malus, his face imperturbable but his tone carrying a note of worry. 'Is... your trouble... becoming a problem?'

Malus grimaced. 'My guest should be impotent for hours after all I've poured into my body,' he said. 'Instead I can feel the thing's dreams slithering into my thoughts.' He uttered a bitter laugh. 'Do you remember, Silar, when I would drink for the pleasure of wine, not to quiet a monster inside my head?' The drachau looked away from his retainer, staring across the platform, at the beast-keepers and their reptilian charges.

The beast-keepers looked absolutely puny beside the twenty-foot-long reptiles. Lizard-like, with great clawed hind legs and smaller forelegs, the cold ones were the natural inhabitants of the dank caverns beneath Naggaroth. Ages ago, the huge lizards had been adopted by the druchii as beasts of war. The powerful jaws of a cold one, its rending claws and tough scaly flesh made for a much more formidable steed than a mere horse. Through special scents and perfumes, an elf knight could deceive the reptile into believing him to be a member of its pack; through the cruellest training and privation, a beast-breaker could force the cold one to adopt the knight as a superior member of its pack. When a troop of cold one knights charged across the field of battle, only the most resolute of foes had the stomach to stand against them.

The cold ones, among their other nasty qualities, exuded a poisonous slime from their skin. Over time, this poison would deaden a rider's own sense of touch. The slime also contributed to the pungent, musky smell of the reptiles. In their own caverns, the cold ones would never gather in packs so large as to smother themselves with their own toxic reek, but in the confines of the black ark, the creatures had to be removed from their pens and allowed up into the open air periodically so that their cages could be fumigated. It also allowed the beast-keepers to exercise the reptiles so that they didn't become either lethargic or too aggressive. It was often a delicate thing to remind the savage brutes of who was master and who was beast.

Malus needed the creatures to be in prime condition when his army reached Ulthuan. Despite the Witch King's assurances that the hated asur were beset by other foes, invading the island continent would not be an easy accomplishment. It would take the steel of sword and spear and the strength of claw and fang. The cold ones would need to be at their most vicious when they were unleashed against Ulthuan.

Towards that purpose, Malus had squandered precious space in the black ark's holds to embark a supply of living captives. Elves too weak to fight, as well as many human and dwarf slaves. Fresh meat was the staple of a cold one's diet. When the reptiles had to catch their dinners it helped to keep their instincts sharp and their dull wits focused. The beast-keepers were even now preparing to feed the brutes. A cluster of ragged human wretches were being herded out onto the platform. The laggards were jabbed mercilessly by the prongs of the tridents their captors stabbed into their flanks. The coppery smell of blood excited the cold ones. The lizards swung their heads around, their tongues licking the air as they sensed the injured humans marching towards them.

It had been a long time since the cold ones had been fed. Two of the brutes started to lumber forwards. The beast-keepers lashed out with their whips, driving the creatures back. It was a necessary display of discipline.

Among the clutch of reptiles there was a smaller, more sparely built creature. Great horns jutted out from the sides of its head, stabbing back over its neck. The reptile belonged to a rarer breed called 'horned ones': beasts of slighter size but much sharper intelligence. This one was actually exploiting the punishment being dispatched against the over-anxious cold ones to start its own advance upon the slaves. In its display of craft, however, the horned one missed an unengaged beast-keeper off to its left. As the beast started forwards, the beast-keeper slashed at it with his whip. The steel barbs on the end of the lash raked across the reptile's muzzle, scarring the scales and drawing blood from the flesh beneath.

In a matter of heartbeats, Malus was upon the beast-keeper, snatching the whip from the elf's hand as he made to strike the horned one again. The druchii swung around, but the expression of outrage collapsed into one of mortal terror when he saw who had taken the lash away.

'You're beating my steed, pig,' Malus growled at the beast-keeper. The elf fell to his knees, started to whine some fawning plea for forgiveness. Malus looked over at the other beast-keepers and the slave-drivers. There were many times when a necessary display of discipline was in order.

'Feed, Spite,' Malus snarled as he kicked the pleading beast-keeper. The druchii fell flat on his back. The elf didn't even have a chance to scream before the horned one pounced on him. Spite's immense weight crushed the beast-keeper's ribcage, driving a fountain of blood from his mouth. The ravenous reptile chomped down on its former tormentor's shoulder, tearing away a ragged chunk of meat and bone.

Malus glared across at the other beast-keepers, savouring the fear he saw on their faces. 'This animal belongs to me. You will treat him accordingly,' he warned. Leaving Spite to continue its gory repast, the drachau resumed his march across the platform. Silar hurried after his master.

'After they take Spite and the others back below, I want every beast-keeper in that company stripped of rank,' Malus told Silar. 'They lose name, position and liberty. Give them over to Kunor.'

'Those are druchii of Hag Graef,' Silar cautioned. 'If they're put in with the Naggorites, they'll be killed.'

'If they are, we'll be able to feed the harpies a bit extra,' Malus said. 'They're not so particular about how lively their meals are.'

SIX

The Star Spire was a narrow spindle of stone and iron stabbing far above the black ark's foundations. It seemed impossible that such a delicate structure could soar to such a height, easily a hundred feet higher than Fleetmaster Hadrith's own tower. Unlike the other towers that rose from the foundation, there were few platforms and bridges connecting to the Star Spire. The mystics of the *Eternal Malediction* were fiercely protective of their privacy and the corsairs of the black ark were happy to allow them to keep their sinister secrets to themselves. Among the upper reaches of the spire, only a single bridge connected to it – a narrow ladder of steel rising from the parapets of the fleetmaster's tower. Malus eyed the high bridge with more than a little envy, but to trespass upon Hadrith's inner circle would be to expose his fears to the corsair king. He wasn't about to make a gift of his own weakness to Hadrith. It might give the fleetmaster ideas.

Instead, Malus and Silar were hurrying to one of the lower landings, the causeways that snaked up from the slave pits to the Star Spire's base. The bloody auguries and divinations of the black ark's seers required a constant stream of sacrifices. The more potent the ritual, the more blood and souls it needed to fuel its magics. Now, with the tide of slaves being herded into the tower, it seemed as though the Star Spire were trying to call up Khaine himself.

Malus was thankful for the slaves and guards trooping into the Star Spire. It would obscure his own entrance into the tower, at least from casual observers. He couldn't be too subtle; he'd need his position and authority to get inside. All he could hope was that the period of grace won by the confusion at the gate would be enough to put distance between himself and any opportunistic enemies.

The enemy is already here.

The daemon's voice was like thunder roaring inside Malus. It nearly sent him pitching from the bridge he was on, precipitating him down into the mass of slaves below. He reeled, snatching hold of a support pillar as his insides boiled from the force of Tz'arkan's intrusion. Silar started to reach for him, but quickly withdrew in alarm when he saw the distortion on his master's face. Despite the wine, despite the fierce will of Malus, the daemon was beginning to bleed through. Silar knew enough to be horrified at that prospect.

His retainer didn't know nearly enough, though. He didn't understand how Tz'arkan had mustered such strength. He didn't know the emotion in the daemon's cry. The monster was afraid. It was panic that had driven it to such a desperate exertion of power, risking the destruction of its mortal host in a bid to assert control.

'You'll kill us both,' Malus growled through teeth clenched in pain.

Death is already here.

The daemon's voice was weaker, only a whisper now. Tz'arkan had expended too much of itself in that first burst of panic. Malus could already feel it slinking back into the dark corners of himself, like a spider crawling along the threads of its web. For the first time, the drachau took no pleasure in Tz'arkan's retreat. The daemon wouldn't have panicked over nothing.

Malus was sent reeling once more, clinging to the support pillar as his legs whipped out from under him and dangled over the side of the bridge. He saw elves and cold ones hurtling past, thrown from platforms and bridges high above, their bodies smashing down into the herd of slaves below. Screams, cries of disbelief and confusion rang out from every quarter. Not simple fear, but the shrieks of beings confronted by the impossible.

The black ark, built upon the mightiest of ancient sorceries, floating inviolate upon its foundations of magic, was rolling and pitching, floundering in the sea like any mundane ship of wood and sail. The corsairs, in all the millennia since the city had ripped itself from the drowned shores of Nagarythe, had never been beset by such elemental violence.

The turmoil increased. The black ark began to list to port, throwing still more bodies from the higher ramparts and bridges. Blocks of stone, spans of iron and wood came crashing down as causeways buckled and stairways crumbled, the *Eternal Malediction's* yaw twisting them in ways and patterns never imagined by their architects.

Screams rang out all around, rising into a deafening bedlam. But that despairing din was preferable to the ghastly silence that followed, a silence so terrible that it struck Malus like a physical blow. A silence born from blackest terror.

It was *felt* before it could be seen or smelt or heard. The druchii felt the atrocity's presence like a foulness, a spiritual contagion that spread a skein of slime across their souls. It was the phantom touch of raw evil – not the petty evil as mortal beings imagined it, but the cosmic malignance that profaned the very essence of reality. It was the hate of things impossible and unborn, the bitterness of what could not be, the profaneness of the unknown.

From the depths, it slobbered upwards, a heaving undulation of carrion-meat, flesh bloated and necrotic. It had some semblance of form about it. The things that grappled the sides of the black ark were as much like arms as they were branches; the things that oozed from the ends of those arms were not unlike titanic hands. From each hand, ropy coils that rudely simulated fingers snaked around the towers, corroding stone and iron with their touch, engulfing flesh and bone until their victims were absorbed into the necrotic essence of the tendril that gripped him.

There was a head, of sorts, and it squatted upon bony, cadaverous shoulders. It was something like a skull that had been wrapped in a veil of slime and decay, each line of bone clearly defined yet still obscured by the encrustations it had accumulated. Hagworms writhed from the thing's sunken cheeks, while anemones and polyps squirmed between its teeth. Four cavernous hollows flanked a gash-like nasal opening. In the depths of those hollows, flickering at the ends of fleshy ribbons, were hundreds of blazing red orbs. As the behemoth surged upwards and wrapped its arms about the black ark, the eye-stalks extruded themselves outwards, whipping about the skull-like face to peer and probe the world the abomination had invaded.

'By the Gates of Nethu, what is that thing?' Silar screamed. The noble had lost his footing, sprawling across the bridge like an armoured crab. A jagged piece of masonry torn from one of the towers had ripped open his arm, but he was oblivious to the injury. Like every elf on the black ark, his mind was frozen with terror, his attention focused solely upon the oceanic horror that had crawled up from the nameless depths to seize the ship.

It is doom. Tz'arkan's voice was a mere whisper, but it was enough to stir Malus from his paralysis of terrified fascination. *It is obscenity made flesh. Such a thing as this might have been your slave, Darkblade, had you but the vision to embrace me. Now we are both doomed.*

Malus stared up at the daemonic giant's face. He thought he'd seen some of those eye-stalks shift and turn when Tz'arkan whispered to him. A horrible thought came to him. 'It's looking for something, isn't it?'

I vanquished it once. Tricked and betrayed it, bound it in chains just as I was later bound until you freed me. The chains that held it were stronger, but they relied too much upon mortal substance and mortal concepts. The mortal world is dying, Darkblade. The old barriers are breaking down. The old horrors are free once more.

'It is looking for you,' Malus snarled. Even as he said it, dozens of the eye-stalks unfurled from the depths of the atrocity's face, peering down through the nest of bridges and platforms. A crawling, crippling sense of insignificance smashed down upon Malus as he felt those hideous eyes trying to find him. It was like having a mountain suddenly aware of his presence, aware with all the limitless belligerence of eternity.

It is looking for us. You are my vessel, Malus. Do you think that power will pause to make a distinction between us? Do you believe it is even capable of bothering to do so?

'You'll destroy everything,' Malus gasped. The giant was reaching around with one of its arms, stretching into the heart of the ark, trying to bring its tendrils closer. He could see now that there were chains dripping from the daemon's flesh, corroded and rusted, caked in coral and salt. From each chain, swollen and decayed like the titan itself, was shackled a body. Bodies of men and elves mostly, but there were other things too – orcs and goblins and beings even the druchii had no name for. As each of the drowned corpses fell across a bridge or platform, they jerked into a twisted semblance of life. Like horrible puppets, the things stalked and slaughtered, falling upon the shocked druchii with cutlasses and tridents.

Now you see the deceit of mortal ambition. We must both of us suffer for your short-sighted pride. We will become another of that power's toys, doomed to languish upon one of its chains until...

Again, the bloated titan reacted to Tz'arkan's whisper. Its flabby arm came crashing downwards, smashing through bridges as it reached between the towers, groping its way towards the Star Spire. Towards Malus.

'Shut up, daemon!' Malus growled. Tz'arkan couldn't have failed to notice that its persistent mutterings were drawing the thing's attention. If it was truly afraid of the titan, why would it try to draw it out? Had fear usurped the daemon's reason, or was it playing its own game? Maybe the giant wasn't here to destroy or enslave Tz'arkan, but to free it. Maybe it wasn't the daemon's ancient enemy, but rather an old friend.

Would you gamble flesh and soul on your paranoia?

Malus almost allowed Tz'arkan to distract him. Very nearly he missed the long chain dangling from the bloated wrist that was yet far overhead. The corpse at the end of the chain slapped against the surface of the bridge, then jerked into grisly animation. It still had the beard and vestments of a human barbarian and its hands gripped the crude lethality of a double-bladed axe. The drowned carcass lurched towards him as it gained its feet, two tiny eye-stalks wriggling from the sockets of its skull.

The warpsword flashed in Malus's hand, raking across the drowned man, ripping through his tattered hauberk and the blue-tinged flesh beneath. Worms and crabs spilled from the grievous wound, but the ghastly creature continued to press its attack. Malus tried to defend himself, but found his strength ebbing. Tz'arkan was draining it from him, drawing it off. He could feel the monster trying to wrest control of his body away from him. Whether the daemon fought to save them from the giant's slave or deliver them to it, Malus neither knew nor cared. He wouldn't relinquish control. He'd die before submitting to that.

Then we die.

The double-axe came chopping down, its edge crunching into Malus's pauldron. The corroded state of the blade caused it to crumble from the impact, but it didn't need to penetrate the drachau's armour to send him sprawling. As he slammed down onto his back, Malus watched the drowned barbarian raise his ancient weapon for a downward slash at his face. The warpsword felt as though it weighed as much as the entire black ark when he tried to lift it and fend off the murderous blow. Even now, however, he wasn't going to submit to Tz'arkan. He might save his life, but he'd lose everything else.

Before the chained corpse could strike, Silar was rushing the creature, bowling him over and smashing him to the ground. The barbarian struggled beneath Silar, trying to throw off the armoured elf. The noble kept his foe pinned and began stabbing him again and again with a crooked dagger. 'It won't die,' Silar snarled.

The paralysis Tz'arkan had inflicted upon Malus diminished enough that he was able to stumble over towards his retainer. He glared at the hideous barbarian and the ghoulish eye-stalks. 'It will die,' Malus swore. Driven by some instinct imparted to him by the enchanted blade, or some fragment of knowledge Tz'arkan had inadvertently left behind in his subconscious, the drachau brought his sword slashing down into the rusty chain binding the zombie to the bloated giant.

Silar rose from his abruptly lifeless foe. The severed chain flopped and flailed, flecks of rusty ichor dripping from its broken links. For all that it looked like iron, the chain was actually an extension of the behemoth, an umbilical attaching its slave to its grotesque bulk. Once that connection was broken, the power animating the drowned thrall was extinguished. Even as Silar scrambled away from the corpse, it was rapidly dissolving into a mire of putrescence.

Any jubilation at their victory over the corpse-puppet was quickly stifled. From the arm of the giant, a dozen other chains were dropping and with them a dozen more of the hideously animated carcasses. Behind the creatures came the monstrous hand of the giant itself. Malus tightened his grip on the warpsword, fearful that any moment Tz'arkan would again exert its debilitating malignance.

'Maybe Hadrith's pirates will kill it,' Silar said, pointing with his blade at the towers overhead. The giant was indeed beset by the black ark's defenders now. Repeater bolt throwers peppered the thing's ghastly flesh with yard-long spikes of steel. Bold corsairs swung out upon lines to hack at the titan with halberds and axes. Flocks of harpies darted about its skull, trying to claw eye-stalks from its face. The flash and fire of magic crackled and flamed about its body, charring small patches of the monster's skin.

An army was doing its best to fight off the giant, but Malus didn't think it would be enough. Tz'arkan might have lied to him about many things, but he was certain the daemon was right when it claimed the mortal barriers were breaking down. With the gates of reality ripped asunder, the ability of mortal weapons to visit harm against a daemonic behemoth such as this was doubtful. Such magic as was being employed against it was too little to cause any real hurt. Malus looked up towards the heights of the Star Spire. Lady Eldire and Drusala were up there, along with many of Fleetmaster Hadrith's own seers and sorceresses, yet there had been not even the slightest suggestion of attack from that quarter.

While the rest of the black ark fought for their lives, the Star Spire remained inactive. Malus would have an answer for such treachery.

'We have to get to Eldire,' Malus told Silar.

The retainer scowled as the first of the zombies reached the bridge and stirred into hideous animation. He managed to cut the chain binding one of them before it became fully active, but then was forced to retreat as the rest slashed at him with their weapons. 'I fear that won't be easy, my lord.'

Snarling, Malus sent the head of a drowned pirate hurtling from the bridge. 'Then we make it easy,' he vowed, pressing home his attack and breaking the umbilical feeding energy into the head-less body.

A great shadow fell across Malus as he engaged another of the corpse-puppets. The drachau had only a second to dive aside before the gigantic paw of the giant came smashing down. The corpse he'd been fighting was obliterated by that huge hand. The whole bridge shook from the impact, chips of stone cascading down into the street below. The tendril-like fingers of the hand snaked about, squirming and oozing in every direction. Malus felt his gorge rise at the boneless, sinuous way the digits moved. Each was tipped not with a nail or claw, but a rounded leech-like mouth. He could see shreds of meat and armour caught in some of those mouths.

'You'll not feast on me!' Malus roared as one of the tendrils slith-ered towards him. The warpsword slashed across the finger, all but severing it. Wide as a man's body, the thing squirmed back, writhing and undulating. Other fingers came slithering around the bridge, some crawling up from beneath the span, to investigate the injury. Six gigantic tendrils turned upon Malus, their mouths utter-ing obscene ululations as they whipped out at him.

The warpsword severed one of the fingers, sending its wriggling hideousness into the crowd of terrified slaves below. Then the drachau was forced to retreat before the nest of abominable ten-tacles. It was all he could do to fend off the slobbering mouths and with each breath, the terror that Tz'arkan would immobilise him again grew.

Tremendous roars rang out from the end of the bridge. Malus was able to look past the nest of tentacles threatening him to see two enormous reptiles lumbering out onto the bridge. A company of beastmasters were goading them forwards with long spears and torches. Bigger than small whales, the reptiles stomped forwards on great clawed legs, their long bladed tails lashing angrily behind them. Bodies armoured in thick layers of scale, they ploughed through the corpse-puppets, snapping at them with their fanged maws. Each of the beasts boasted half a dozen heads, each one resting on a long, serpentine neck. There was no fear in their dull yellow eyes as they charged towards the titan's hand, only the limitless savagery of the most fearsome creatures ever bred by the beastmasters of Clar Karond: the war hydras.

Malus knew these beasts. He'd purchased them himself to augment the armies of Hag Graef, paying a small fortune to secure the biggest, most ferocious hydras ever to emerge from Clar Karond. He was still bitter over such squandered wealth. Only a few months after Griselfang and Snarclaw had been delivered to Hag Graef, the barbarian invasions and daemonic incursions had started. Clar Karond became a city under siege, desperate to sell anything and everything at any price just to bring more warriors to her defence.

Now, however, the colossal war hydras were showing their value. As they lumbered towards the titan's hand, Snarclaw reared its six heads. When it thrust them forwards once more, gouts of flame exploded from each maw, searing across the putrid meat before them. Griselfang roared, pushing past the other reptile in order to worry at the steaming flesh of the huge hand.

The tendrils that had a moment before been menacing Malus whipped back around, striking instead at Griselfang. The hydra bit back at the ropy fingers. Malus saw the hydra pull one of the wormy tentacles loose, as though uprooting a tree. The tendrils responded by wrapping around one of the reptile's necks and squeezing it mercilessly. Eventually the crushing pressure choked all life from the head. The tendrils withdrew, letting it flop lifelessly at the hydra's side. But even as life ebbed from the head, hideous new life coursed through Griselfang's frame. The dead neck and head burst, splashing gore across the bridge. Where the mangled flesh had been, two smaller heads now writhed, each snapping at the charred hand with vengeful ferocity.

Before the combined might of the two war hydras, the gigantic hand withdrew, retreating upwards. Bolts from repeater crossbows stabbed into the grotesque extremity, loosed by hundreds of Hag Graef's soldiers and the black ark's warriors. Nearer at hand, Malus saw a long spear hurled up at the hand to embed itself in the thing's palm. He locked eyes with the caster of that spear. The timely arrival of his war hydras was explained: Vincirix Quickdeath, making certain nothing dire could befall her lover and benefactor. The drachau started to walk towards her...

...Vincirix, Silar, the war hydras, the bridge itself vanished before Malus's eyes. One instant they were there, the next they were gone. Replacing them was a cold, dark room. Celestial shapes shone overhead, picked out in diamond and pearl with lines of platinum running between them to form the signs of the Cytharai and the Cadai. A great pattern glowed upon the floor beneath his feet, crushed rubies forming the lines of the Pantheonic Mandala. Upon the symbol designating each god and goddess, a disembodied heart lay in a pool of blood, the organs pulsing with impossible life. Only at the centre of the mandala, where the emblem of Khaine was depicted in bloodstone, was there no heart. Instead, a young elf boy stood, his body swaying in the grip of some hypnotic cadence.

Malus looked away from the esoteric scene, gazing instead at the people gathered around the edge of the mandala: Lady Eldire and the cabal of sorceresses she had gathered together. Somehow, he had been transported inside the Star Spire!

Eldire and the others stood in a wide circle, their hands linked. Crackling ribbons of aethyric energy played between them, provoking frost to form against their skin. Several of the sorceresses shuddered and shivered from something far more intense than the cold; two of them looked as though they had been shrivelled into mere husks, kept standing only by the hands of the druchii at either side of them.

There was only one gap in the circle. As Malus took stock of his surroundings, he saw Drusala waiting for him. Her expression was grave as she confronted the drachau. 'Your army will never reach Ulthuan if you do not protect this circle,' she warned him. 'The sea daemon will drown the *Eternal Malediction*. Our only hope for survival is to give it other prey.'

Malus looked over at his mother, but if Eldire was even aware of his presence, she gave no sign. 'How?' he demanded, returning his attention to Drusala. 'How will you save my army?'

Drusala indicated the young elf standing at the core of the mandala. 'A final offering to fuel the invocation,' she said. 'That is all you need to know. You must protect us until the ritual is finished.'

'Protect you from who? That giant?' Malus scoffed.

At a gesture from the sorceress, a door swung open at the end of the room, letting in a thin sliver of daylight. 'Stop the ones coming up the stair. If they reach this place, we are all finished.' She smiled, but it was a bitter, joyless look. 'My own precautions are not enough. Lady Eldire saw that much in her divinations.'

Drusala did not linger to explain more, but quickly returned to the circle, seizing the hands of the witches at either side of the gap.

Malus wasn't sure if it was his imagination, but a shadowy knife seemed to appear beside the hypnotised youth.

Sorcery! He didn't understand how such things worked and even less did he understand the strange price demanded by magic. It was enough that such forces could be harnessed and put to use. If whatever Eldire and Drusala were conjuring could save them from the titan, he would play his part to bring such magic about.

Grimly, Malus stalked through the door. Somehow he wasn't surprised when it slid shut behind him. He was standing on a landing high upon the Star Spire. Below him, he could see the whole of the black ark. From this vantage, he could appreciate the gargantuan size of the giant and the havoc it was inflicting upon the *Eternal Malediction*. An entire tower had been ripped free, thrown into the sea by the raging behemoth. The same sorcery that supported the black ark kept the tower afloat, broken as it was. Strange sea scavengers darted about the shattered tower, picking bodies from the rubble.

Closer at hand, Malus could see the giant's head. Several clusters of eye-stalks stared back at him. There was no mistaking the abomination's hungry interest as it redoubled its efforts to batter a path through bridges now swarming with bowmen and war machines. He could feel Tz'arkan stir deep inside him, but the daemon at least had sense enough not to speak and goad the giant to greater effort.

Malus forced himself to tear his eyes from the behemoth to the stair leading down into Fleetmaster Hadrith's tower. At the edge of the stair, he saw a lone warrior standing guard. The elf had a sinister, eerie air about him, his black armour looking as though it had been hacked from a slab of malachite. His helm was tall, moulded to look like a mass of writhing serpents. He reminded Malus of a medusa, though even those terrible creatures would have had more vibrancy about them than this stony sentinel.

Beyond the guard, Malus saw a troop of corsairs rushing up the stair. At their head was Fleetmaster Hadrith, his sea-dragon cloak and cephalopod-styled armour distinct among that of his retinue. As they saw him, a cry of utter hate welled up from the corsairs. From their tone, Malus could guess that all of them had lost family to make room for Hag Graef's army.

'The fleetmaster looks upset,' Malus told the guard. He expected some kind of response, but all he got was the same stony silence. He hoped that the elf was better at fighting than he was at conversation.

The corsairs halted as they neared the top of the stair. Hadrith stepped forwards, pointing angrily at Malus. 'Stand aside, Dark-blade. My business is with that scheming witch Drusala and your mother.'

'If you haven't noticed, there's a giant daemon ripping apart your black ark,' Malus said. 'I think you have bigger problems.'

Hadrith waved his sword at the drachau. 'They took my son, Dark-blade. What does the black ark mean if I lose my legacy to keep it? Stand aside, and I will spare you.'

Malus shook his head. 'You seem to forget who is in command here.'

An animalistic snarl rasped through the vent in Hadrith's helm. 'Kill them!' The corsairs charged forwards at the fleetmaster's command.

What followed was a whirl of blades and bloodshed. Malus caught his first foe just as the warrior was thrusting his halberd at the drachau. The warpsword slashed through the haft of the weapon and the elbow of the arm behind it. The crippled elf shrieked as blood jetted from the stump of his arm. Malus shouted his own war-cry and kicked the mangled corsair down the stair, tripping up the pirate behind him and leaving the elf easy prey for a butchering sweep of the warpsword.

Beside him, the silent guard played his own deadly swords-manship. Elves crippled by his blade fell screaming from the stair, hurtling to their destruction hundreds of feet below. The guard never uttered a sound, plying his gruesome art with the merci-less precision of a machine. Even when a corsair's axe managed to slash his thigh, the guard didn't cry out but simply returned the hurt with a backhanded slash that opened his attacker's throat.

Fighting from the high ground, Malus and the guard held the cor-sairs at disadvantage. Hadrith's concern for his legacy had provoked the fleetmaster to act rashly, to ignore the development of a more cunning strategy. He'd depended too much on numbers and force of arms, perhaps upon charms and talismans to ward away sorcery. He hadn't planned on warriors of such quality defending the spire.

Suddenly, the entire ark shook, a great tremor rolling through it, the quaking sending more corsairs hurtling from the stair. A bright flash in the sky blinded Malus, causing him to stumble back. Almost at once, Hadrith was flying at him, the fleetmaster's sword upraised. Malus caught Hadrith on the warpsword's point, the enchanted blade ripping through his breastplate and the ribcage behind it.

Spitting blood, Hadrith thrust himself along the impaling blade, trying to bring his own sword slashing across Malus's neck. 'They... killed...'

Malus didn't let the fleetmaster finish. With a twist of his sword, he cut the noble in two, the severed halves rolling obscenely down the gore-slick stair. The few corsairs left standing turned and fled as they saw their leader cut down.

'I'll set Vincirix and her knights to finding them,' Malus said as he watched the corsairs flee. 'They won't be able to hide for long.' Again, his words brought no reaction from the silent guard. The sinister warrior simply turned and marched back to his place at the head of the stairs. Malus felt a chill crawl across his flesh.

Even the corpse-puppets had been more lively than his late comrade-in-arms.

Thinking of the giant sea daemon, Malus cast his eyes downwards. He was shocked to find no trace of the abomination. The destruction it had wrought was all too visible, but the thing itself was gone. Vanished as completely as if the sky had swallowed it up. He could see equally shocked elves in the windows of the towers and on the bridges. He followed the pointing hands of several druchii. Far across the waves, another black ark floated upon the sea. That vessel was now listing to port, caught in the vicious embrace of the sea daemon.

Icy fingers played down Malus's spine as he considered the wrongness of what he was seeing, the uncanny magnitude of the magic his mother and the others had invoked. The shudder and the flash, that had been the mark of Lady Eldire's great spell. Hadrith had known that, recognised it as the sign that his son had been rendered up as the final sacrifice.

'The daemon has been given new prey.' Malus looked up to see Drusala standing at the head of the stairs, one arm draped teasingly across the blood-soaked shoulder of the silent guard. She smiled coyly. 'That is the *Relentless Retribution*. The ritual we cast allowed us to switch places with her in much the same way that I was able to transport you from the foot of the spire to the top. Only on a much grander scale. Six of the circle were drained completely by the spell.'

'My mother?' Malus asked.

Drusala drew back one of her raven locks, tucking it behind her ear. 'She was not one of the six. The experience has wearied her, but she will recover.' As though irritated by the question, she pointed again to the black ark. The giant was starting to pull it under, dragging it down into the depths. 'I believe Lady Khyra was on that vessel. We determined that she was behind the attempt on your life. I thought you would be happy to know she won't be able to do it again.'

'Then I will be able to focus on other threats,' Malus said, just the most subtle edge of menace underlying his words.

'Just be certain who is enemy and who is ally,' Drusala advised him. Stroking the shoulder of the guard, she beckoned the warrior to follow her back inside the spire. 'Come, Absaloth. The danger is past.'

Malus watched them disappear into the Star Spire, then turned to watch as the sea daemon finished sinking the *Relentless Retribution*. The deaths of thousands didn't move him; he'd seen massacres on a such scale before. It was the thought that such a fate could so easily have been his that made Malus sombre.

Be careful of that witch.

'I intend to,' Malus growled at the daemon inside his head, annoyed by Tz'arkan's renewed intrusion. Especially to state something he already knew.

She is more dangerous than you think, Darkblade. She can see me. She knows I'm inside you.

PART TWO
EAGLE GATE

Late winter 2523–Summer 2524

SEVEN

The ragged coastline of Ulthuan stretched away along the eastern horizon, shores so abrupt they might have been hewn by one of Addaioth's crooked swords. Here and there a crag of crumbling rock thrust itself up from the pounding waves, rotten fingers of stone that might once have been hills or mountains. At the height of the Great Sundering, when the treacherous followers of the false king Caledor sought to vanquish the faithful subjects of Malekith, the most powerful magic known to elves wrought destruction upon the realms of Nagarythe and Tiranoc.

Tidal waves a thousand feet high swept over the lands, drowning thousands, fouling the once lush countryside, obliterating the gleaming cities and soaring towers. Much of Tiranoc was sheared from the rest of Ulthuan, sent sliding into the sea. Beneath the waves, the streets of drowned cities could yet be seen, fish swimming through the weed-wrapped columns of palaces and temples.

Greatest of these sunken ruins was Tor Anroc, a place yet haunted by the ghosts of those who perished in the cataclysm. Even druchii invasion fleets gave Tor Anroc a wide berth, many of the corsairs claiming that sailing over any part of the drowned city would cause the sea god Mathlann to forsake their fleets.

As he studied the coast, Malus felt only contempt for the religious superstition of the corsairs. Mathlann had done nothing to help them against the great sea daemon that had tried to sink the *Eternal Malediction*. For the Lord of the Deeps, Mathlann had been noticeably reluctant to draw the creature back into the depths. If not for the sorcery of Eldire and Drusala, their voyage would have ended in disaster long before they came within spitting distance of Tor Anroc and the curse of its ghosts.

The real threat posed by Tor Anroc lay in that part of the city which the asur had rebuilt, a naval fortress that guarded the approaches to the western shore and whose artillery loosed pots of alchemical fire so fierce even the sea couldn't extinguish the flames. Flotillas of small, sleek galleys were anchored in the fortified harbour, ready to set sail at a moment's notice to harry any invader. The mages of Tiranoc were even known to conjure mighty merwyrms from the waters that had swallowed their old lands, and the great sea serpents were easily capable of crushing a ship in their coils, a menace to any raider not embarked on a helldrake or black ark.

And, of course, the biggest hazard offered by Tor Anroc was the simple fact that the city would spread the alarm to the rest of Ulthuan. The asur would be alerted to the return of their betrayed kin. They would muster their armies and march to repulse the druchii, to drive the invaders back into the sea. This time, with even their exile kingdom lost to them, the druchii couldn't allow their landings to be repulsed. They had to succeed, or perish in the attempt. Avoiding Tor Anroc would gain them precious hours, perhaps even a full day, to seize their beachheads. While the fleet of Drane Blackblood harried the asur naval patrols and Lokhir Fellheart led his fleet to the south and the harbours of Tor Dranil and Merokai,

Malus would have a prime opportunity to wage his own war and claim his own measure of glory.

Malus crushed the scroll he held in his hand, feeling the flayed strip of skin crinkle under his grip. Dictates from the Witch King were inked in the blood of traitors on the hides of their offspring, the seals affixed to them crafted from the fat of the selfsame traitors. Such gruesome missives were a reminder that Malekith was watching, and of what the recipients' fates would be should they fail their king.

The army of Hag Graef had been given a singular honour. They would lead the attack on Ulthuan. They would be the first to land in Tiranoc, the first to confront the wrathful warriors of the shattered kingdom. The *Eternal Malediction* was to beach itself, hurl itself far out upon the shore. The ancient enchantments that kept the black ark buoyant would be dispelled, severed by the Witch King's own cabal of sorceresses. The vessel would remain as a bastion, a citadel from whence Malus would stage his attack. The ships of the fleet would be broken up, their timber used to craft siege engines and cartage for the army, their iron fastenings reforged into shields and spears, their sails cut into tents and blankets for the long march to the Annulii Mountains and the Inner Kingdoms beyond.

This was what Malekith had spared him for! A suicidal probe against the most heavily defended of Ulthuan's Outer Kingdoms! A feint to draw the attention of the asur while the rest of the invasion massed in the south. Once the asur were committed, the Witch King would order the rest of the black arks to loose their warriors on the shores of Nagarythe, reclaim the old homeland. Malus knew he was being sacrificed; he had known it the moment the black dragon had descended from the stormy sky and its rider handed him the royal command.

Yet what else was there but to obey? Naggaroth was lost; there was nowhere to sail back to. The choice of retreat had been taken away the moment he'd abandoned Hag Graef.

Still, perhaps there was a way. The army of Hag Graef was larger even than that of Naggarond, bolstered by the enslaved Naggorites and the refugees from Clar Karond. He even had the expeditionary force from Ghrond that had accompanied Drusala. If he struck swiftly, if he was ruthless enough and spared nothing to move his army at speed, there was just a chance he could outwit the Witch King. If Malus's landing was intended as a sacrificial feint, then he would turn it into a victorious conquest! Even Malekith would have a hard time arguing with victory.

Malus turned from the balcony high upon the fleetmaster's tower. After the death of Hadrith, the drachau had assumed virtual command of the black ark, installing an opportunistic corsair named Aeich as the new fleetmaster. His sycophantic minion had rendered up the royal chambers for Malus's own use. He wondered if Aeich was still so eager to please now that the order to beach the black ark had been given. He rather supposed it put a kink in Aeich's ideas about the power he thought he'd inherited.

'You have conceived a plan, my lord?' Vincirix had cast aside the brief, loose robes that she'd adopted in her role as the drachau's consort. With the shores of Tiranoc just beyond the black ark, she again wore the steel plate and chain befitting a Knight of the Ebon Claw. Malus smiled at the cold lines of her armour, the slumbering lethality of the sword and clawed mace hanging from her belt. If anything, he found her more enticing this way. Nothing soft and weak, only the merciless strength of a true daughter of Naggaroth.

He waved the ghoulish proclamation at her. 'I have an idea,' he said. 'But it will take craft to implement it properly.' Malus tapped the rolled sheet of flayed skin against his thigh. 'It is a great gamble. The wager must be everything or nothing.'

'One wins nothing without risk,' Vincirix said. 'The bigger the gamble, the greater the prize.'

Malus laid his hand against his lover's cheek, giving it an ungentle pat. 'This isn't helping a nubile wench in her patricidal fantasies,' he said, draining some of the self-assurance from her eyes. After helping save his life by leading the war hydras to the attack, she'd become a bit too certain of her place. Malus needed her insecure. The hunger to prove herself, to maintain everything she'd managed to acquire would be a valuable asset on the battlefield. If she was worried about displeasing him, she'd push her knights to the limit of endurance and beyond.

The drachau turned and paced through the opulently appointed parlour of the late Hadrith. At each step, he slapped the royal command against his leg, reminding himself of the magnitude of the responsibility resting on him now. There could be no half measures if he was going to prevail. At the same time, failure would mean complete destruction. If his name was remembered at all, it would be as that of a reckless fool.

But to dare! To trick that conniving tyrant. If he won through, his name would be heaped with glory and envy. He'd be greater than all the dreadlords. Greater, perhaps, than the Witch King himself, for he would have done what Malekith had never been able to do. The Witch King expected to spend the lives of Malus's army and eliminate the enemy within by setting him against the asur. The last thing Malekith would be ready for would be a victorious Malus.

'It is a kingdom I gamble for now,' Malus told Vincirix. 'That is why the wager must be so costly.' His hand tightened around the decree, causing the traitor-fat seal to crack. 'But maybe there is a way that I can hedge my bet.' He spun around and pointed at the knight. 'Find that buzzard Korbus. Tell him that I want my mother to disembark with the first wave. I want her ready to perform one of her auguries as soon as she is set ashore.'

Vincirix looked uneasy as she heard her lover's command. 'Your mother will listen to no one but you, my lord. If you would have her obey, you should speak to her personally.'

Malus shook his head. 'No,' he said. He removed one of the rings from his fingers and set it in the knight's hand. 'Give Korbus this and he will know the command comes from me. I will not see my mother until she is ready to relate to me what the future holds.' A scowl briefly worked itself onto his face. 'If I saw her before, she might cause me to falter in my purpose.' With a wave of his hand, Malus dismissed Vincirix to hurry away on her errand.

Left alone, the drachau stepped back to the balcony, casting his gaze once more upon the broken shore of Tiranoc. How much blood had the druchii shed here over the ages, trying to seize the land from their hated kin? How much more would it cost before they were victorious? How much was he willing to sacrifice for that triumph?

He almost expected the sneering voice of Tz'arkan to slither through his brain, mocking him for his timidity and his ruthlessness. The daemon was capricious and saw no vice in hypocrisy. A lie wrapped in a truth disguised in a falsehood, that was the parasite's favourite manner.

The daemon, however, had been curiously silent since the sea titan had taken Lady Khyra to a watery grave. Malus hadn't even felt the need to drink his draught much, just enough to keep his senses at the proper degree of wariness. What Tz'arkan was about, he couldn't begin to guess. It had claimed Drusala had seen it when they were in the Star Spire. If so, the sorceress had made no move to denounce him. Daemonic possession was the sort of affliction that no dreadlord, not even the most powerful, could survive if it was exposed to his peers. His own subjects would rise up and tear him limb from limb, even more so now that Naggaroth had been abandoned to the bestial creatures of Chaos.

The prudent thing for Malus to do would be to have Drusala murdered. That would ensure the safety of his secret. Wisdom demanded such a course. It was for that very reason he was indecisive. He still harboured suspicions that Tz'arkan had deliberately drawn the sea daemon to attack the black ark. He couldn't trust anything the parasite told him. It might share his skin, but it didn't share his life. It had its own ambitions and desires. It would do anything to break free of him. Goading him into killing someone who could help him was just the sort of ploy that would appeal to Tz'arkan's perverse humour.

No, despite the danger, Malus couldn't act until he was sure. His mother had been incapable of freeing him from the daemon, but Drusala had been handmaiden to Morathi herself. She doubtless knew things even Eldire didn't, things that might be a threat to Tz'arkan.

Such concerns were for the future, however. At the moment, the success of his invasion was the only thing that mattered. Securing a victory that even the Witch King would be unable to take away from him. Without that, even if Drusala exposed him it wouldn't matter.

He could only die once.

Columns of spearmen and swordsmen marched from the black ark's belly, trooping down iron bridges and timber platforms. As each druchii set foot upon the shore, he turned his head and spit on the sands of Tiranoc, an ancient gesture of contempt for the hated asur who had driven their ancestors from Ulthuan. Even in this, the final battle with their treacherous kin, the druchii clung to the traditions of hate.

From a small hillock, seated in Spite's saddle, Malus watched as his army disembarked from the *Eternal Malediction*. Aeich had run the black ark aground, the huge vessel gouging a deep furrow in the rock and sand as its magic failed and it entrenched itself in the shore of Tiranoc. Corsairs were already scavenging timber from their ships to erect a palisade around the beached city, a wall to hold back any asur raiders. As yet, there had been no sign of Tiranoc's people, but the druchii knew it was only a matter of time before the vengeful natives came down from their cities to repulse the invaders. By that time, the fleetmaster intended to have defences in place to protect the black ark.

Malus had encouraged Aeich in his plans. He'd sent troops of doomfire warlocks and dark riders galloping off into the country-side to ostensibly spy out the land and determine the position of a gathering enemy. On their swift horses, the squadrons of cavalry could cover a vast area in a short amount of time. He'd impressed on them the urgency of their mission; the threat of failing the drachau was enough to make even the murderous warlocks set aside their need for slaughter. They'd soon bring back the intelligence the invaders needed.

Of course, if Eldire's prophecies were auspicious, that information might not be put to the purpose Aeich expected.

Across the beach, Malus could see the baggage train of his war-host slowly taking shape. Such slaves as hadn't been butchered during the long voyage from Naggaroth were now pressed into service, toiling away under the lashes of their cruel masters. He could see Kunor mounted upon a black charger galloping up and down the beachhead, plying his whip across the backs of his Nag-gorites, forcing the enslaved druchii to unload the ships the corsairs had driven up onto the rocky shelf. Kunor didn't need an excuse to indulge his sadism. When purpose was linked to his penchant for brutality, the slavemaster was utterly without pity or restraint.

A tumult around the black ark marked the unloading of Griselfang and Snarclaw. The gigantic war hydras struggled against the chains with which they were bound, their jaws straining against the steel muzzles that bound their snouts closed. More chains restrained their tails, keeping the reptiles from smashing their keepers with a slap of the long, scaly columns of flesh. As the straining, vicious beasts were led down one of the bridges by a small army of beast-breakers, Vincirix Quickdeath and her Knights of the Ebon Claw waited in a solemn formation along the shore, lances at the ready and their cold ones sniffing and snarling at the air. The gigantic war hydras were a powerful weapon in the arsenal of Hag Graef. Too powerful. If they broke free and raged among Malus's forces, the toll they would take would be hideous. Better to kill the brutes than have his own warriors massacred.

A low growl rumbled from the depths of Spite's throat. Malus could feel the reptile's body become tense beneath him. He slapped the side of the horned one's snout, warning it to be still. He knew what had agitated his steed; he didn't even need to turn around to know that a rider was approaching. Spite was an excellent judge of character, but the poor brute simply didn't have the wit to understand that people of low quality and verminous morality had their uses.

A lone cold one loped towards Malus's position. When it was still a dozen yards away, the reptile's pace slackened, and it dipped its head in an attitude of submission, trying to make its huge body seem smaller than it was. Deep scars marked the creature's scales, the reminder of the claws and fangs that had likewise left their imprint on the beast's tiny brain. The cold one had made the mistake of challenging Spite once before. It wouldn't make that mistake again.

The reptile's rider dismounted and removed his helm. Unlike his steed, the knight knew better than to ever challenge Malus. He'd seen for himself what happened to those who did. Indeed, he'd helped make it happen many times.

'Dolthaic, old comrade,' Malus greeted the knight as he bowed to the drachau. Dolthaic was the deposed heir of a noble house in Naggarond. His birthright usurped, he'd taken up the mercenary trail, gathering to him a vicious cadre of warriors he'd formed into the Knights of the Burning Dark. The sell-swords had long been in the service of Hag Graef, long enough that they'd earned too many enemies elsewhere to ever leave Malus's service. Calling Dolthaic comrade was like calling a loyal dog 'brother', and the hesitation the knight exhibited as he approached told Malus that neither the irony nor the insult was lost on him.

'Dreadlord, the offerings have been rendered up to Khaine,' Dolthaic reported.

Malus sneered at the knight's piety. He seemed to believe Khaine would smile down on them because they'd spilled a few bottles of wine and opened the bellies of a dozen slaves in his name. They asked their god to deliver to them victory over the asur and offered so little for such beneficence. It would be hilarious if it wasn't so pathetic.

'Khaine respects those who do not beg his favours,' Malus said, 'those who take for themselves what they desire! The only offering worthy of Khaine is victory, Dolthaic. Remember that.'

The chastened knight bowed his head once more. 'Yes, dreadlord.'

'Lord Silar has deployed the first cohort?'

Dolthaic nodded. 'They have assembled at the edge of the plain. The bolt throwers are in position just below the shelf. The crews have been given their orders. My knights are poised to support them, should the need arise.'

Malus smiled at the report. Silar was a capable lieutenant, but sometimes insufficiently ruthless. If the asur attacked while the core of their army was disembarking, the invasion would be over before it could properly begin. Against that possibility, Malus had dispatched a small force out beyond the beach, bait the vengeful elves of Tiranoc would be certain to seize upon. The small vanguard would be routed; they'd flee back to the beaches and draw the pursuing asur straight into the waiting bolt throwers. It would, of necessity, be costly for the vanguard, but if the natives fell into the trap, it would blunt their initial assault against the landings.

'Good, Dolthaic. If we can keep the asur off the beaches until the rest of the army disembarks, this enterprise may yet prove itself.' Malus eyed the mercenary, his expression growing thoughtful. 'There should be good pickings for your knights once we penetrate into the Inner Kingdoms.'

The mercenary's face betrayed no change in expression, but Malus could read the elf's avarice in his body language. The Knights of the Burning Dark were reckoned the most dependable troops in his army not because they owed any unusual loyalty to Malus or Hag Graef, but because they didn't. Their motive was simple greed – they took the drachau's coin and he paid them better than they could expect from any other dreadlord. Among the maze of hatreds and jealousies that ruled the hearts of most druchii, greed was pure and predictable. A warrior motivated by greed could be depended upon without the undue worry about what ulterior agenda might be lurking in the shadows of his soul. That was why Malus had set Vincirix and the Knights of the Ebon Claw the task of watching his war hydras. He could afford to lose the refugees from Clar Karond far more easily than Dolthaic's mercenaries.

'When do we march?' Dolthaic asked.

'Patience, old comrade,' Malus said. 'First I must know *where* before I can know *when.*' He looked back towards the beach, chuckling as he watched an elf hurrying across the rocks towards him. From the awkwardness of his movements, it seemed that he was unaccustomed to the heavy mail he now wore. 'Unless I am mistaken, I should be getting an answer to that question very soon.' Malus dismissed Dolthaic with a wave of his hand. He didn't want the mercenary around when the messenger arrived. Saluting his master, Dolthaic hurried back to his waiting steed and rode off to where his knights were lurking.

Malus let his eyes rove across the confusion of activity along the shore, the corsairs breaking their ships with mauls and sledges, the beast-keepers herding their ghastly creatures of war through the shallows, the infantry marching stoically towards the enemy shore. Tents and pavilions had already been erected, the banners of nobles and warrior companies fluttering in the salty breeze. A plume of smoke wafted into the sky from a hastily assembled shrine to Khaine. Harpies wheeled overhead as they emerged from the cramped cages that had borne them from Naggaroth.

The thing he was looking for defied his vision. Nowhere did he see the pavilion of Lady Eldire. He knew his mother had obeyed his command and joined the first wave of invaders. Somewhere down there, her shelter had been pitched. Perhaps she'd spared some small measure of her magic to disguise the place. After the sacrifice of Hadrith's son and the deaths of so many of the black ark's seers, there were many among the fleet who bore the sorceress malice. Enemies who had their own magic to call upon. It was only prudent that she would take steps to protect herself.

The armoured messenger finally reached the rise. Malus grinned coldly at Korbus as his mother's servant bowed before him. The petty sorcerer looked absurd in the old armour he was wearing. 'You look like a rat playing wolf,' Malus scolded the servant. 'What did you do, strip a drowned Naggorite on your way here?'

Korbus kept his eyes averted and emotion from his voice when he answered. 'Lady Eldire felt I would be more inconspicuous if I looked like a warrior.'

Malus laughed at the declaration. '*If* you looked like a warrior. My mother should have disguised you as a slave, Korbus. You would wear rags better than mail.' A kick of his heels brought Spite lurching towards the servant. The horned one's forked tongue flickered out as it tasted the conjurer's smell. Korbus recoiled from the reptilian brute.

'What word do you bring me from Eldire?' Malus demanded. A rumbling hiss from Spite added still more menace to the drachau's question.

'All is in readiness, dreadlord,' Korbus said. 'She is prepared to work her auguries. She but awaits your presence.' He hesitated, licking his lips nervously. 'She says that to ensure the accuracy of her divinations, she will need some of your blood.'

'So long as mother doesn't take too much, eh, loyal Korbus?' Malus joked. He glanced back across the beachhead, still unable to find anything that resembled his mother's pavilion. 'You lead the way,' he ordered Eldire's consort. A prod of his boot against Spite's ribs brought a growl from the beast. 'Not that I doubt your loyalty, or mother's, but you should understand that if anything happens, you die first. Remember that, Korbus.'

'Of course, dreadlord,' Korbus said. The conjurer's voice was firm and properly deferential, but he couldn't quite hide the anxious tremble in his step as he led Malus down from the rise.

Malus was careful to keep a few yards between himself and Korbus as they climbed down from the rise. Just enough space so he could keep his eye on his guide, but not so much distance that Spite couldn't leap upon the elf at the first hint of treachery.

Even when it came to his own mother, Malus felt it judicious to be cautious.

EIGHT

The smell of death struck Malus the instant he flung aside the curtain covering the entrance to his mother's pavilion. The stench lent a still more sinister air to the place, as though its sorcerous camouflage wasn't uncanny enough. Even with Korbus guiding him, Malus had been unable to see the pavilion until he was only a few feet away from it. It wasn't invisible; the magic in play was more subtle than that. It was as if his eyes had refused to focus on the tent, sliding away from its image, straying from it to gaze elsewhere. When he came within a dozen yards of it, a clamminess wrapped itself around him, an oily sensation that repulsed him and made him want to draw away. Spite had felt it too, refusing Malus's efforts to drive the reptile onwards. He'd been forced to dismount and leave the beast behind as he followed Korbus that last leg of their journey.

Now he stood within his mother's sanctum. Malus watched as Korbus walked over and ignited a brazier of coals with a wave of his hand. The drachau shook his head at the display. Whether the conjurer had evoked some petty spell or had simply dropped some caustic powder on the smouldering coals, Malus wasn't impressed.

He glanced at the rich tapestries draped about the walls of the pavilion, arcane glyphs woven into each one in threads of silver and gold. Dried heads and hands, desiccated herbs and bundles of roots and weeds dangled from the poles that gave the grand tent its shape. On the floor, a rug cast into the patterns of the Pantheonic Mandala stretched across the floor, the symbol of Khaine at the heart of the mandala glowing with an eerie crimson light. He could feel icy fingers of magic pawing at him, blindly groping at his flesh. A phantasmal music tugged just at the edge of his hearing, indefinable melodies that both enticed and horrified. In the depths of his soul, Malus could feel Tz'arkan stir, responding to some aethyric vibration only spirits could sense.

'Lady Eldire is beyond the veil,' Korbus announced, beckoning Malus towards a dark curtain. Malus recognised that curtain. It had been woven from the tresses of Hag Graef's fallen sorceresses, shorn from their corpses before the last warmth deserted their cold flesh. The Naggorites had called such a veil a 'soul hanging', believing that the spirits of those whose hair was bound into it were enslaved and compelled to ward away inimical magics directed against those who sheltered behind them.

'Leave us,' Malus ordered Korbus. There was only the briefest flicker of hesitation on Korbus's part, then his mother's servant bowed and withdrew from the pavilion. Malus waited until the conjurer was gone, then brushed aside the soul hanging and stepped into the gloom behind the partition. The stench of death intensified and closed around him, drawing him into itself in a cadaverous embrace. His hand tightened about the warpsword's hilt.

A strange blue light slowly grew from the darkness, illuminating a space that appeared impossibly vast for it to exist within the confines of his mother's pavilion. The curtains and tapestries lining the walls were familiar to him, recalling Eldire's sanctum inside the Scion's Tower in Hag Graef. Somehow, Malus felt that if he reached out and pulled aside those hangings he would find not the canvas of the pavilion but the stone of his abandoned palace behind them. It was an impossible prospect that made his heart clench inside his chest.

Seated on the floor, her legs crossed beneath her, was Lady Eldire. She wore the black silks of a sorceress, her hair bound within the claws of a filigree basilisk, its eyes shining with a strange luminescence in the weird blue witchlight. Around her was a circle drawn in powdered bone and around it a second ring rendered from the intestines of a harpy. Between the two grisly circles were drawn the astrological symbols of each of the Cytharai.

Eldire's eyes were closed, her face drawn and pale. She held one hand against her heart, while the other was stretched before her in an arresting gesture, as though pushing against some unseen barrier. She didn't look at her son when she spoke. 'I ask you, Malus, to reconsider what you would have of me. The aethyr is in turmoil. The old magic runs wild and is slow to heed the command of even Eldire.'

Malus stepped towards his mother, careful to keep beyond the arcane circles she had crafted about herself. 'I must know,' he told her. 'You are the only one I can trust to gaze ahead and tell me what waits there. Glory or death, I must know!'

A despairing sigh shook the sorceress. For the first time, Malus noticed wrinkles marring his mother's beauty, saw hints of silver polluting her black tresses. Until this moment, he hadn't considered the toll her divinations might exact from her. There could be no going back, however. If he relented now, he would lose everything. He would be nothing more than Malekith's pawn, cast aside while the Witch King's armies fought the real battle far away. His name would be reduced to a jest – the hapless dreadlord who'd been massacred while the host of Naggaroth made war against the asur.

'The future, mother,' Malus hissed. 'I must know what it holds. I must know the path to take.'

Eldire's outstretched hand trembled, her splayed fingers twisting into patterns that threatened to dislocate every bone. 'The pattern of what is yet to come is ever in flux. Every decision we make, every choice we abandon, every action we bring into being sends ripples through that pattern. To steal secrets from the future is to catch smoke in one's hand. Only the most powerful sorceries can lend solidity to the smoke, can pour reality into what is only possibility.'

'You have such power, mother,' Malus said. 'Among all of Malekith's fleet, there is no sorceress as mighty as you.'

Eldire shook her head slowly. 'I am alone, Malus. A manticore is mighty, but it is alone. The dogs are weak, but they are many. Their numbers make a strength that can overcome the might of that which is alone.'

Malus stood and glared down at his mother. 'You delay!' he accused. 'Who would dare raise their hand against you while I am still drachau. You aren't alone. You have the might of Hag Graef to protect you. What enemy do you fear? The witches of the black ark? I'll have Aeich slaughter them for you and bring you their hearts. Drusala? What can that enchantress do to threaten someone who defied Morathi herself?'

Eldire sighed once more. 'The answers you seek are already here,' she said. 'In my auguries, I saw you would not be dissuaded from your purpose, yet I refused to abandon hope.'

Malus felt a tremor of fear pass through him. 'The omens are ill, then? You have foreseen disaster?'

'To look into the future is to give it shape,' Eldire answered. 'To give it shape is to wrap chains around the present. Prophecy binds the present to itself, compels the purpose of now to fulfil the dictates of what is yet to be.'

For the first time, she opened her eyes. Malus recoiled when he saw that Eldire's eyes had become black pits, like chips of obsidian set into her face. Little fingers of pulsating darkness wriggled from her pupils, as though beckoning to him. 'The abyss of eternity holds all that is possible. To pluck from it what might have been and transform it into what will be is a magic even the gods fear to contemplate.' Eldire's voice trailed away, losing volume and vibrancy. It seemed the most colossal effort when she pointed a finger towards something lying sprawled on the floor.

His flesh cold from the dreadful emanations of such potent magic, Malus slowly approached the prostrate form. The stink of death clung heavy to it. The mutilations visited upon it made it impossible to tell if the corpse had recently been either man or elf. What he could tell was that the victim had been alive when the worst of the atrocities were inflicted upon it. The forbidden names of Hekarti, the Mistress of Magic, entwined with the obscene glyphs of Atharti, Lady of Desires. Even an outsider like himself understood the danger of invoking both of the Cytharai sisters in the same ritual, for they were the most dire of enemies. He could only wonder at what kind of ritual demanded such power that such evocation was unavoidable.

'Reach inside the offering and remove the heart,' Eldire told her son, her voice now not much more than a whisper. 'Crush it in your hand. Squeeze the blood from the dead flesh and you will find the future you seek.'

Through one of the ghastly cuts inflicted on the corpse, Malus worked his hand between shattered ribs and torn flesh. His fingers froze when he felt the heart beneath them. The organ was moist and warm to his touch, and as his fingers lingered, he felt a hideous pulsation pass through them. The heart yet beat! By some unspeakable magic, there was life still pulsating through this abominably tortured body.

Where another elf might have quailed in horror at so obscene a spectacle, Malus firmed his grip and yanked at the beating heart. Inch by inch, he worked it free from its fleshy moorings, drawing it back through the broken chest that had once housed it. As he removed it, he saw that the thing had turned black, cancerous with the same aethyric taint he'd seen in his mother's eyes. Black worms, no more solid than a shadow, slithered and writhed from the organ as he tightened his grip and began to squeeze.

Drop by drop, the blood began to seep from the heart onto the floor – far more blood than it could possibly have held. Soon there was a puddle at Malus's feet, and within that puddle he saw things, images that flickered and changed with each drop that fell from the heart.

He saw the great army of Hag Graef marching away from the shore of Tiranoc. He saw his warriors ranging across the land, seeking battle with the asur. He saw skirmishes with the bastard kin of Nagarythe and raids mounted by the chariots of Tiranoc – far too little to threaten the mighty host he had unleashed against Ulthuan. Onwards his army pressed, the asur refusing to give them the mighty battle they sought. Then the Annulii Mountains loomed before them, towering above the landscape. Between the snow-capped peaks, there was the pass connecting the Shadowlands of old Nagarythe and Ellyrion, joining the Outer Kingdoms to the Inner Kingdoms. Blocking that pass, its battlements soaring hundreds of feet between the mountains flanking it, was the Eagle Gate.

For an instant, Malus felt his ambition turn sour. This was the fortress Malekith had commanded him to take. This was the place where the despot expected him to die. He gazed upon the massive stronghold with its megalithic gates, at the glittering spears and helms of the army garrisoning it, at the fiery wings and cold claws of the giant phoenixes that soared above it. He heard the names of great heroes whispered to him – Yvarin and Shrinastor – and he felt despair begin to bind his hopes.

Then, in the pool of blood, Malus saw a sight no druchii had ever seen. He saw the titanic doors of the Eagle Gate torn asunder. He saw the towering battlements crack and crumble. He saw the gleaming army vanquished, their dead impaled upon their own spears, a grisly forest to honour Khaine and the ancient hate of the druchii.

Malus grinned. His mother had peered into the world beyond worlds, and brought back omens of glory and victory. Victory such as would shame even the Witch King's pride!

'You may rest now, mother,' Malus said as he cast aside the shrivelled heart. He saw her hand slip away from her own heart, watched as the blackness faded from her eyes and she slumped forwards. He rushed to her side, wondering if he should have heeded her warning, if maybe he hadn't demanded too much of her sorcery.

'You have seen?' Eldire asked. With the spell broken, there was already a bit more vibrancy in her voice.

'I saw,' Malus told her. 'Your magic has told me what I must do.'

Lady Eldire looked at him, her gaze penetrating deep into his soul. 'Prophecy is a lie we tell ourselves. Be certain of what you have seen. Beware that it is not what you merely wanted to see.'

Malus laughed. 'This vision is both. It is victory.'

Eldire pulled away from him. 'Then I am pleased,' she said. 'All I have done has been for you, Malus. Always remember that. You are my legacy. Your glory is my triumph.'

With his mother's words still ringing in his ears, Malus was stunned to find himself no longer standing in the blue light. He was back among the tents, right beside the place he had hobbled Spite. Ahead of him, he could feel the clammy wrongness attached to his mother's pavilion, but he could no longer see the place.

Malus shrugged aside the disorienting wrongness of his magical ejection from Eldire's presence. She had shown him what he wanted to know. There wasn't anything else he needed of her. At least for now.

'Come along, old comrade,' Malus said to Spite as he climbed into the horned one's saddle. 'I have new orders to give my army.

'Now I can tell them where they're going.'

Lady Eldire could feel the shadows of unborn potentialities clinging to her, trying to draw existence from the magic that coursed through her body. Removing the clinging embers of possibility from her was like burning leeches from flesh. It was a revolting, painful necessity. Each dream she burned away, each parasitic hope that thought to fatten itself upon her sorcery, each reflection of what could have been but would never be, all of them took their toll upon her stamina.

She should have refused Malus's command. In more stable times, when the aethyr hadn't been transformed into a raging cataract of magic and the tides of Chaos weren't spilling into the mortal realm in a deluge of arcane malignance, she would have been able to render her divinations more easily. They wouldn't have left her feeling like a dried-out husk.

No, Eldire corrected herself, even then, even with the full resources of Hag Graef at her beck and call, what she had done for Malus would have been no easy thing. She had indeed seen his future. She had seen what would be. With her magic, she had changed what was to come. Her vision had penetrated beyond the cascade of time, into the morass of possibility, into the streams of not merely what *would* be but of what *could* be. Merely gazing upon such things was a mark of the mightiest sorcery, but to reach into that pool of impossibilities, to draw it out and graft it to the stem of eventuality, to take the unreal and compel it to become real – that was a magic only the cold-blooded toad-mages of the jungle dared to harness. One misstep, the tiniest falter of heart or mind, and such magic would do more than destroy. It would obliterate. It would erase. What it consumed wouldn't simply die, it would never have been.

She had reached into the pool of never and brought forth victory for her son. She had bound a dream of conquest to the fact of Malus's army marching from their beachhead. She had seen that impossible vision, of Malus making war upon the shores of Chrace, and she had chained it to the flow of the present.

She hoped it was enough. She begged Hekarti that it was enough. Through Malus, she could carve a legacy. Without him, she could build nothing.

Had she done enough? Had she done enough to change that awful future she'd seen, the vision she dared not even whisper? To speak the future was to give it shape – that was the true threat of prophecy. How many divinations had brought themselves into being over the long march of history? She could not risk even a single gesture, a single word, that might bring Malus to the end she had foreseen!

Eldire rose to her feet, aware that she was no longer alone in her sanctum. This refuge existed in the spaces between space, neither fixed to her pavilion on the shore of Ulthuan nor her chambers in Hag Graef. It was possible some daemon might intrude upon such a shadow place, but the presence she sensed was mortal, or at least near enough to mortality to clothe itself in flesh, to have a heart beating in its breast and a brain thinking inside its skull.

'Who is there?' Eldire called out, her hands already tightening about the protective talismans hanging about her waist.

A soft laugh answered her. 'Is your sorcery so feeble that you do not know?' a mocking voice called out from the darkness.

The note of mockery vanished as the sanctum suddenly blazed with cold blue light. The gruesome conjuring circles, the sacrificial victim, the discarded heart and the pool of blood all stood revealed in the violent illumination. So too did a slender she-elf dressed in robes of purple and scarlet, a high collar of gold circling her delicate neck.

'Drusala,' Eldire hissed. 'You dare much. What errand has Morathi set you upon? Did your mistress think to settle one of her petty jealousies through you?'

Drusala paced slowly around the sanctum, careful to avoid the pool of blood Malus had squeezed from the heart. 'I came of my own accord,' she told Eldire.

'Then you are a fool,' Eldire said. 'Your mistress did not dare to strike against me. What makes you think you can do more than she?'

'Perhaps the opportunity never presented itself before,' Drusala said. 'Or maybe you were deemed unworthy of the effort.' She stared into Eldire's face and smiled. 'Until now.'

One instant, Drusala's hand was empty, in the next she held a long staff of iron and ivory inlaid with the carved teeth of vanquished elves. A grinning skull of crystal topped the staff and from its mouth there leapt forth an icy wind, a stream of polar energy that set its elemental fury upon Eldire.

The sorceress of Hag Graef was caught in the full force of that arctic blast. Hoarfrost formed around her body, engulfing her utterly in a shroud of ice. Soon, where she had stood there was only a snowy pillar cast in the rough shape of an elf.

Drusala didn't approach the pillar. Warily, she gestured with her free hand, swinging it back and forth as little orbs of molten fire formed on the tips of her fingers. After a time, she flung her hand forwards, hurling the fiery orbs across the sanctum. They struck the icy pillar, steam and slush exploding as they burned completely through the obstacle. Consternation gripped Drusala's features when she saw no evidence of a corpse beneath the ice.

'Your arrogance must be punished,' Eldire's voice snarled through the sanctum. Drusala spun around, trying to find where her enemy had translocated herself, but as soon as she started to move, she felt the floor beneath her feet lurch and sway. She tried to leap back, but it was already too late. What had been solid stone a moment before was now a viscous, gooey sludge that pulled at her feet and tried to suck her down into the floor.

A bestial roar exploded from the trapped druchii's lips, a cry that might have been bellowed by a mammoth. The icy blue light was transformed into a hellish crimson, scarlet shadows leaping from the walls and diving into the sucking floor. Grunting with the effort, Drusala pulled her feet free as the red pulsations compelled the floor back into a state of solidity.

Even as she regained her feet, she was beset by her adversary. Spectral blades struck at Drusala from every quarter, phantom swords conjured from boiling fumes of dark magic. She whipped her iron staff around her body, using it to intercept each blade as it came slashing at her, fending them off with her parries. Faster and faster the assault came, forcing Drusala to sharpen her reactions with her own magic. The whirlwind of attack and interception became a blinding blur, the purple robes slashed to ribbons by the spectral blades, the phantom swords blunted and shattered by the flying staff.

Finally, the assault faltered. The last of the ghostly swords evaporated back into the aethyr. Victoriously, Drusala drove the end of her staff against the floor. A pulsation of raw, unfocused magic swept through the sanctum. As it passed through the chamber, Lady Eldire's figure abruptly stood revealed, the cloak of darkness that had hidden her obliterated by the force of Drusala's power.

Eldire glared at the other sorceress. 'The hag of Ghrond taught you a few tricks,' she conceded. 'What I know, I learned for myself.'

Lady Eldire now held a staff of her own, a thing of crystal and bone. At her command, the exposed crystal began to darken, to exude crawling tendrils of night. The black fingers shot across the sanctum, reaching out to seize Drusala in their clutches, to rip the soul from her flesh.

Drusala took a step back and made an arcane gesture with her hand. From her palm, a ball of nebulous energy burst forth, striking across the black fingers that reached towards her, sending little slivers of magic flying in every direction. 'You should have learned more,' Drusala spat. 'Your divinations have weakened you too much for such a conjuration. Even a mere handmaiden would know this.'

A bolt of searing darkness leapt from Eldire's staff, shearing through the shielding orb Drusala had evoked. The bolt slammed into the handmaiden, flinging her back, ripping her own staff from her hands. She crashed against the wall, almost passing through its unstable substance into the shadows beyond. By some effort of will, the stricken elf collapsed back against the semi-reality of the sanctum wall.

Eldire was already evoking another spell to strike down her foe when her concentration faltered. She'd seen something in that instant when Drusala had pierced the sanctum's illusion. Something so unexpected that it caused her concentration to slip. For an instant, for the merest fraction of time, her enemy had a different appearance. Her adversary was cloaked in a sorcerous glamour!

'Who are you?' Eldire demanded. 'How did you penetrate the wards that guard this place?'

Drusala looked up from the floor, blood trickling from her lip. 'A traitor removed the soul hanging. That is how I found this place.' She slapped her hand against the floor, sending a magical tremor through the stones. 'And to you, I am the Pale Queen,' she declared with a snarl, evoking the Cytharai goddess of the dead.

From the pool of blood, sanguinary spears erupted, striking at Eldire. She raised her staff to ward away the gruesome assault, but her enemy had prepared the attack with vicious cunning. Too much of Eldire's own magic infused the oracular liquid, too much of her own essence was yet bound within it. Aethyric sympathies, harmonies of spirit tied the sorceress to what she had conjured. The spears of solidified blood stabbed through the counter-spell Eldire raised to defend herself. In a welter of gore, they impaled her, piercing her at throat, navel and heart. The crystal staff fell from lifeless fingers to shatter upon the floor.

Drusala studied her vanquished enemy, drawing a deep sigh of contentment as she watched Eldire's life bleed away. She didn't linger to savour her triumph. Already the sanctum was beginning to lose its substance, to collapse back into the nothingness from which it had been formed. Hurriedly, she dashed through the portal that linked the place to Eldire's pavilion.

As she rushed through the doorway, Drusala found Absaloth waiting for her. The silent guard bowed his head as he saw his mistress return. She gave the warrior scarcely a glance, but instead turned to the only other druchii in the tent.

'Is it done?' Korbus asked, the soul hanging folded across his arm.

Drusala smiled at the tremor in the traitor's voice. She slid her bloodied fingers down the elf's cheek, leaving a line of gore across his skin.

'It is only beginning,' Drusala told him.

NINE

A cry of agony sang out from the left flank of the column, rising above the clatter of armour and the tromp of marching feet. A druchii warrior, elegant and sinister in his armour of darkened steel and cloak of deep crimson, collapsed into the dust. An arrow trembled in the pit of his eye, expertly loosed so that the shaft merely grazed the metal nasal that guarded the elf's face. The warriors around the stricken druchii didn't scatter, but came forwards, locking their shields together to form a wall of steel. Crossbows were trained upon the rocky slopes the column marched past.

Malus Darkblade swung around in his saddle, glaring at the grey desolation of the hills, the crumbling toes of the Annulii themselves. Here and there, some pattern among the rocks suggested an ancient construction, the foundation of some tower cast down ages ago. There was nothing to betray the presence of enemies, not even to eyes as keen as those of an elf or the sharp senses of the cold ones. Yet they were there just the same, lurking in the dirt and dust, stalking the druchii army, harassing it every step of the way. The toll in lives the ambushers took wasn't even worth the drachau's attention. Of what consequence was a spearman here or a knight there? Even the odd noble wasn't a serious impediment; there were plenty of druchii only too eager to assume the command of a fallen highborn.

No, the toll the ambushers were taking wasn't measured in lives but in time. The incessant attacks were taxing the discipline and morale of his warriors. Their step wasn't as firm as it had been when they left the shores of Tiranoc and abandoned the beached black ark. They were constantly looking around, watching for the next ambush, waiting for the scream that would tell of another comrade brought down by the slinking asur. Several times, entire companies of soldiers had broken, their discipline shattered by the harassing attacks. They'd stormed up onto the rocks, vengefully seeking their tormentors. Many more had been lost to deadfalls and other traps in these futile retaliations than had been felled by the black-fletched arrows. Malus had ended these breaks in discipline by employing the most ruthless measures – ordering the execution of any officer whose troops broke ranks and commanding that any soldier injured by an asur trap be left behind. Most of these injured druchii would be seen again, their butchered remains strewn across the road before the marching army by their shadowy enemy. In this, however, the vindictive asur had helped rather than hindered the determination of Malus's troops. There were no more reckless forays into the hills.

Still, it sat ill with Malus to allow the asur to assault his host with impunity. Magic would have offered the best recourse, but Lady Eldire had yet to rejoin his column. She'd remained behind at the beachhead to recover her strength after the toll her prophecy had taken on her. Until she rejoined him, the only sorceress of note in Malus's army was Drusala and he was wary of depending too much on her arcane powers. The last thing he wanted to do was to appear weak to an enchantress who might yet prove an agent of Malekith.

To that end, he'd come up with his own method of retaliation. Among the vastness of his army were his war hydras. Not only Griselfang and Snarclaw, but all the other beasts the refugees from Clar Karond had brought with them. The maws of the grotesque reptiles were fountains of corrosive, viscous bile. It was hazardous to collect that venom, to milk the ravenous hydras. The beastmasters balked at the very prospect of such labour. Fortunately, the slave-soldiers of Naggor had no choice in the matter. Under the lash of Kunor and the other slavemasters, the Naggorites had set about collecting the venom, drawing it from the glands of the multi-headed monsters. Dozens of the slave-soldiers had been lost in the process when the jaws of a hydra would slip free of the chains holding them open. In the end, however, they were able to provide gallons of the corrosive venom, storing it in clay jars and glass bottles.

As the spearmen formed their shieldwall around their dead comrade, Malus looked over to Silar and nodded. His retainer made a broad sweep of his outstretched hand. In response, a clutch of elves came marching through the ranks – more of Kunor's slave-soldiers. The Naggorites each carried a jar or bottle of hydra venom. Reaching their positions behind the shieldwall, they lobbed their burdens onto the hillside. The slaves were most energetic in this exercise, knowing that those who threw their missiles the farthest would be excused from collecting the next batch of hydra venom.

Bottles and jars shattered against the rocks, splashing the vicious liquid in every direction. Small gaps appeared in the shieldwall now, as crossbowmen took aim. Once away from the poisonous jaws of a hydra for more than a few minutes, the venom lost most of its potency, but it was still able to inflict the most hideous burns. It would take a god-like discipline to ignore such pain.

Despite their ghostly attacks, the asur proved to be mortal things of flesh and pain. As the hydra venom spattered across the rocks, grey figures rose up. Some were in such agony that they tried to rip their burning cloaks from their bodies. Others retained a bitter sense of purpose, taking swift aim with their bows and loosing arrows into their hated enemy. Several more druchii fell as the arrows stabbed into their ranks, but the retaliation of Hag Graef's crossbowmen, with their repeating weapons, ripped through any asur before they could manage a second shot.

A vengeful cheer welled up from Malus's army as he watched a score of asur ashencloaks cut down. The camouflage afforded them by their garments was almost perfect; the fault lay not in the ability of the cloak to render the elves unseen but in the weakness of the asur themselves.

Malus looked over to Silar once more, giving his loyal retainer another unspoken command. Silar barked out a string of orders and a small company of Naggorites rushed out from the column. They scrambled up the hillside, several of them vanishing as a hidden pit opened up beneath their feet. The survivors pressed on, only one of them making the mistake of turning and trying to retreat back to the column. A bolt from one of the crossbows killed the wretch before he'd gone a dozen feet. The rest picked their way among the rocks, searching out the tokens that would be their only chance to rejoin the host.

A low grumble from Spite caused Malus to look away from the Naggorites on the hill. It was a general rule in any druchii force that cold ones and horses had to be kept away from one another. The reptiles relished nothing quite so much as horseflesh, a fact that made even the strongest warhorse skittish around the scaly brutes. Now a lone rider made her way through the mass of knights, and it was the cold ones that had become skittish, recoiling from the midnight-black courser as though it were a living flame. Even Spite was uneasy, flexing its claws so that the talons scrabbled at the ground.

Malus refused to share his steed's anxiety. He had endured too much to be frightened by a mere sorceress, whatever unsettling whispers Tz'arkan tried to fill his head with. He indulged in a patronising smile as Drusala rode towards him, injecting the nuances of annoyance and condescension that would remind her of her place in his army, emphasise who was in command.

'Dreadlord,' Drusala addressed him with just the slightest measure of deference. 'You have dispatched your soldiers to recover the cloaks of our enemies. I fear that will be of no avail. The enchantment that conceals them so well is keyed to the peculiar hermetic harmonies of the asur. The air, earth and water of Naggaroth have changed the druchii too much to appeal to that magic.'

Malus shook his head. 'I haven't risked soldiers to recover those rags. That is a task fit for dogs.' From the hillside, more screams sounded. Malus turned his head to watch as an ashencloak who had been feigning death suddenly sprang into action, striking with his sword in a blur of ferocity that saw three Naggorites maimed or dead before the other slave-soldiers were able to smash him into the dirt. The crooked druchii swords slashed across the prone asur, hacking away at him without mercy.

'Nevertheless, there are better uses even for dogs,' Drusala insisted. 'If you intend to take the Eagle Gate, you will need every warrior you have.'

Malus studied the sorceress from the corner of his eye, watching her face, scrutinising her gaze. Looking for any sign that she knew, that Tz'arkan was right and that she had seen the awful secret locked away inside his soul. She could destroy him with such knowledge. If she had it, why didn't she? He should have demanded the answer to that question when he'd consulted his mother. If her auguries could reveal to him the place for a great victory, then surely she could predict the motivations of a single elf.

'I *will* take the Eagle Gate,' Malus said. 'It is my destiny.'

Drusala's face curled into an enigmatic smile. 'Destiny is what the proud call fate and the foolish call doom.'

'Are you presuming to advise me now?' Malus asked.

'Never, dreadlord,' Drusala said. 'I am well aware that you already have an advisor in matters arcane.'

Try as he might, Malus couldn't read the subtleties of tone in Drusala's choice of words. He looked the sorceress in the eye. 'Beside the Witch King himself, I am the most powerful warlord among our people. Serve me loyally, and there will always be a place for you in my court.'

'I never doubted that,' Drusala said. 'You are many things, drachau, but you aren't wasteful.' She looked back to the hillside where another of the Naggorites had fallen victim to an ashencloak playing dead. 'At least not with anyone you think is still useful to you.'

'A sorceress always has her uses,' Malus declared. He could feel a flicker of fear pass through him as he spoke. Was Tz'arkan nervous? Maybe a closer alliance with Drusala was just what he needed. Eldire had been unable to free him of the daemon; perhaps it wasn't such a bad idea to see what Drusala could do. Assuming of course he could arrange things so that if his affliction were found out the sorceress would suffer the same fate as he did.

Drusala bowed her head. There was no misunderstanding the invitation in her smile. 'I will await your pleasure, dreadlord.' She started to turn her horse, but stopped and glanced past Malus. Her body became stiff and tense, reminding Malus of a panther scenting an intruder in its territory.

He had to stifle the urge to laugh when he looked in the direction Drusala was staring and saw Vincirix riding over to join them. So, the sorceress was trying to stake out new territory. If so, she was being presumptuous. She certainly had her useful aspects, but the captain of the Knights of the Ebon Claw possessed something much more important. She was dependent on Malus for her rank and power. That gave him control over her. He didn't have a similar hold over the witch. Not yet, at least.

'You have something to report?' Malus asked Vincirix as the knight dismounted and bowed before him. He noticed that her cold one was even less willing to be around Drusala's horse than Spite was, the reptile straining at the reins she held in her hand. 'Has my mother accompanied you back from the beachhead?'

Malus had dispatched Vincirix and her knights to return to the black ark and see if Eldire was rested enough to join the march. He was anxious about leaving her behind, worrying that when Tiranoc came to assault the *Eternal Malediction,* she would be cut off from his army. His mind didn't rest any easier with the dire predictions Tz'arkan kept feeding him, allusions that his mother was gone, that her sorcery had helped him for the last time.

'There was no trace of Lady Eldire,' Vincirix reported. The knight was aware of the magical barriers that obscured the pavilion of the sorceress and had concocted a clever way of finding the place just the same, spreading her cold one knights in a wide circle and seeing at what point the reptiles began to grow agitated. It would then be a simple matter of dismounting and heading for the centre of that circle. Malus had been impressed by the simplicity of such a ploy. Now the drachau wondered if his faith in his lover's cleverness had been misplaced.

Vincirix could see the anger and doubt in Malus's eyes. 'We found her pavilion,' she hurried to explain. 'But there was no sign of your mother there.' She rose to her feet and waved her arm at a small group of knights who had followed her. 'We did find this, however.'

The knights came loping forwards on their cold ones. Between them the two elves held a large leather bag of the sort corsairs used to stash plunder when out raiding. The way the bag squirmed and shuddered, Malus could tell it held something living. The size of the bag suggested whatever was inside would be about his own size. Gruffly, the knights tossed their burden to the ground. A muffled yelp of pain sounded from whatever was inside.

Vincirix stepped over to the bag. Removing the dagger from her belt, she slashed the rope binding the mouth. With a kick, she forced the contents of the bag to wriggle out through the opening. Malus found himself glaring down at his mother's consort, Korbus. The conjurer was bound and gagged, his body bruised from the rough treatment he'd endured at the hands of Vincirix and her knights.

'I found him among the corsairs,' Vincirix explained. 'He seemed reluctant to leave their company and rejoin the host of Hag Graef.'

Spite's saddle creaked as Malus leaned forwards and fixed his cold eyes on those of Korbus, fairly willing the captive to meet his gaze. 'Did this worm tell you where my mother is?'

Vincirix grabbed Korbus by the back of his neck and jerked the servant to his feet. 'He claimed that shadow warriors infiltrated into the beachhead and attacked the pavilion. He says your mother was killed in the fighting.'

Deep inside Malus, some forgotten piece of himself turned cold. When he spoke, his words were as sharp as knives. 'Did you see any evidence of this fighting? Did the Shadowland curs leave any mark after them?'

'There was nothing,' Vincirix said. 'The corsairs had fought off a band of infiltrators several nights before, but that attack had been at the other end of their perimeter.'

Malus saw the terror in Korbus's eyes. The conjurer was desperate to speak, to make the drachau believe his story. Malus started to give the order for Vincirix to remove the gag when he noticed the frightened look the prisoner directed at Drusala. He swung around and gave the sorceress a cold smile.

'He seems to recognise you,' Malus accused.

Drusala brushed aside the accusation. 'Naturally,' she said. 'I was Morathi's closest retainer. This maggot is a sorcerer, despite the Witch King's decrees against males practising the black arts. He has probably had nightmares about our meeting for decades.'

'Perhaps,' Malus mused. He waved Vincirix to cut away the gag. 'Let's hear what he has to say.'

Korbus at once began to speak, but an expression of utter horror gripped him, as though he was frightened by his own words. Malus could understand that. The worm had, after all, just invoked Malekith's name. He closed his mouth, licked his lips. When he started to speak again, it was the Witch King he spoke of. Once more, the conjurer clamped his mouth tight, sweat pouring down his face, his eyes wide with terror.

'I grow weary of this, pig,' Malus snarled. 'Tell me what happened to my mother!'

'He is too frightened to obey,' Drusala said. 'His horror of the Witch King is greater than his fear of you. If you like, I could use my magic to draw the truth out of him, despite his fear.'

Malus glared at the trembling conjurer. He already knew something of the truth even without Drusala's magic. Whatever had befallen Eldire, it had come about because of this maggot's treachery. He waved a warning finger at the sorceress. 'This scum has betrayed me. How do I know I can trust you any better?'

'Loyalty is sometimes displayed not in what one does,' Drusala replied, 'but in what one chooses not to do.'

Malus nodded, appreciating the unstated meaning behind her words. Even if he didn't trust her, he appreciated that in such a public arena he couldn't afford to call her loyalty into question.

Besides, if his mother was gone, he would need Drusala's magic. After that... after that it might be prudent to listen a little more closely to Tz'arkan's advice about her.

'So long as you do not kill him or strip away his senses,' Malus warned.

Drusala bowed in token of her understanding the restraint her powers were under. Looking back to Korbus, her eyes took on a fiery gleam, the pupils blazing until they assumed a golden hue. She reached out with her hand, the fingers splayed in a claw-like gesture. Strange words hissed across her lips. Spite and Vincirix's cold one growled, raking their claws against the ground and lashing their tails from side to side.

Korbus cried out, rearing forwards and almost slipping free of Vincirix's grip. There was absolute panic in his eyes, anguish on his face as he opened his mouth and tried to shout. The only sound that emerged was the name 'Malekith'. Hearing his own voice only increased the conjurer's despair.

'Speak, traitor!' Drusala snarled. A gibbous light began to shine from inside Korbus's mouth. Try as he might, the captive couldn't keep himself from opening his mouth. When he did, it could be seen that the light emanated from his tongue. 'Tell us what has befallen Lady Eldire,' Drusala commanded.

Korbus wept, his bound body thrashing violently in Vincirix's arms as the sordid tale of treachery and murder sprang from his tongue. He had conspired with the Witch King to kill Eldire and thereby weaken Malus. His part had been to remove and sabotage the protective spells Eldire had cast around her pavilion, opening the way for Malekith's assassins. His reward, he said, would be absolution, the Witch King's grace for Korbus's crime of practising sorcery despite the royal admonition.

Malus sat in brooding silence as the story was forced from the traitor. Drusala's magic wrenched every detail from his mother's betrayer. When the tale was told, the gibbous light faded away. All that was left in the conjurer's mouth was a burned and blackened nub of meat that had once been his tongue.

Vincirix let the traitor flop to the ground. Pulling the mace from her belt, she raised the weapon high.

'Halt! Do not touch the worm,' Malus called out before she could strike. His enraged gaze fastened itself on the shuddering figure of Korbus. 'He doesn't die so easily. This day or the next we will be at the Eagle Gate.' A cruel gleam shone in the drachau's eyes. 'I have a much better idea for how he can be paid back for the service he has rendered his king.'

The sound of rattling harnesses and marching boots echoed from the marble walls. The vibrations from two hundred warriors made the jewelled lamps sway on their golden chains, the wings of gilded eagles fluttering from where their silver talons clasped the rounded lip of each lamp. The deceptively delicate chains that held the enormous lamps high above the hall shivered in the bronze moorings that bound them to ceiling and wall. Servants in powder-blue livery hurried behind the two hundred, scrubbing and polishing the tile mosaic as they passed.

Upon a short dais, a great seat carved from the trunk of a white oak commanded the vast chamber. The back of the throne had been cunningly shaped into a lifelike semblance of a great eagle, outstretched pinions framing the sides of the throne, crooked talons making the seat itself. The brooding visage of the raptor's head loomed above the seat, the ferocity of its manner reminding all who met its gaze of the power and authority of the one who sat in the shadow of its sharp beak.

Prince Yvarin of Meletan had been commander of the Eagle Gate for only five years, a blink of the eye in the reckoning of elves. Many felt he was too raw, too untried to be given the prestigious duty of commanding the garrison, the responsibility of guarding the pass leading down from the blighted Shadowlands into the eternal summer of Ellyrion's sweeping plains. The beauty of Ellyrion, the tranquillity of that peaceful kingdom, depended upon the vigilance of the Eagle Gate. The threat of the exiled Naggarothi was perpetual, almost eternal it seemed. The pretender Malekith would never forsake his abominable claim upon the Phoenix Crown. So long as the foul Witch King of Naggaroth lived, he would never relent in his mad dream of conquest, to grind the lands of Ulthuan under his iron heel.

Amidst the turmoil besetting Ulthuan, the unprecedented numbers of strange beasts emerging from the Annulii Mountains to ravage the countryside, the burning of Chrace by mighty daemons, the horrific incidence of daemonic manifestations in the cities of Yvresse, Saphery and even Avelorn, somehow it was only to be expected that the Naggarothi would come again. Like jackals smelling a dying stag, they came from their forsaken land of chill to snap at the defences of Ulthuan. Yet another enemy at a time when the world seemed poised at the edge of the precipice. Was this, then, the final war?

Yvarin tried to banish such dire thoughts from his mind, but it was a difficult thing. It didn't need a mage to see the crimson slashes that stained the skies above the Shadowlands, a gruesome celestial corruption that grew and spread with each passing hour. The light of sun and moons had taken on a sickly quality – nothing that could be seen but something that could be felt down to an asur's very soul. The birds of summer had fled, spiralling skywards and streaming not to their winter haunts to the south but into the blighted north, the north of mutation and madness. The

wind that blew through the pass bore with it little flecks of irides-
cence, like shards of rainbows, vibrant motes of raw magic that
blighted whatever they touched.

Omens, as dire and fell as any Yvarin had ever read in the old-
est legends, had become commonplace. Foremost among the evil
portents had been the death of Finubar the Seafarer, last of the
Phoenix Kings. His death had left Ulthuan without a leader and
the turmoil besetting the land made it unlikely a new king would
be chosen soon.

Then there had come the great daemon host to assault the Eagle
Gate itself. That attack had been costly, both to the fortress and
the garrison. Replacements were slowly arriving to reinforce the
stronghold, but reconstruction of the walls the daemons had
breached was advancing at a sluggish pace. The gigantic plague
daemon that had struck the walls had done more than simply
knock down stone and mortar. The fiend's very touch had corrupted the rock, making the rubble brittle and unusable. Fresh
stone had to be brought into the pass to replace what had been
ruined, an ordeal that was made all the more laborious by the turmoil afflicting the land.

The prince ran his fingers across the wand of dragon-horn he had
been presented with by the last company of soldiers to arrive at the
Eagle Gate. It was a splendid, marvellous piece of artistry, inlaid
with rubies and fire sapphires so that whenever the light struck it,
Yvarin felt like he held a sliver of frozen flame in his hand. Shrinastor, the haughty loremaster from Saphery, would no doubt be
unimpressed by the token of esteem Yvarin had been given by the
contingent from Caledor. The secrets of its flawless beauty would
hold no surprises for the cynical mage. The prince felt it was just
as well Shrinastor had slighted the soldiers sent by Prince Imrik by
locking himself away in his chambers to consult his crystals and

his astrological charts. He could do without the added burden of Shrinastor's presence.

Yvarin looked at the wand, turning it over in his hands, then nodded in appreciation to Jariel, the captain of the Talons of Tor Caldea. 'We thank you for your gift, but more importantly, we thank you for your service. In this hour of crisis, when the old enemy comes upon us once more, it is more important than ever to remember the honour and tradition that unites the kingdoms of the asur.'

Jariel bent to her knee, setting her ruby-encrusted helm on the tile floor. Stolid and proud, her face seemed to be chiselled from the same marble as the chamber walls until she raised her eyes and stared at the seated prince. An expression of pained humiliation swept across her heroic features. 'I bring shame to you, highness,' she said. 'Please accept my apology for this inexcusable slight upon your noble house and do not hold my error against these valiant warriors who have come to serve you.'

Yvarin stared in confusion at Jariel, then, as his fingers continued to caress the wand she had presented him, he felt a roughness beneath his touch. Lowering his eyes just the smallest fraction, he saw the ruby he was touching and the deep flaw that ran through it, a blight upon the beauteous perfection of the wand.

'There is nothing to forgive,' Yvarin said. 'At a time of crisis, the fellowship of the asur is the only jewel that is without flaw. I know that the sons and daughters of Caledor will observe their duty to Ulthuan. I know that you will fight with courage and valour. I know that you will do honour to your ancestors.'

Yvarin watched as Jariel led the Talons of Tor Caldea from the grand reception hall. They were a magnificent sight in their coats of armoured scales and their tall, dragon-winged helms. The heads of their spears were broad and sported long tassels to sop up the blood of their enemies. Their shields were thick, reinforced with the cast-off scales of the great wyrms that slept in Caledor's mountains. Such a complement of warriors was a boon to his garrison.

Even so, Yvarin couldn't help but let his eyes fall once more to the wand he held and the flawed ruby.

Another ill omen for the lords of Ulthuan.

TEN

There was a chill in the air as Malus stared into the pass. The shadow of the Annulii Mountains cast the foothills at their feet into darkness, little wisps of snow wafting down from their peaks whenever the wind shifted. Malus covertly glanced at the druchii warriors who surrounded him. He smiled as he noted the briskness that crept into their step, the squaring of their shoulders, the almost imperceptible eagerness in their eyes. The dark, the cold, these might be hostile and unwelcome to the soft, pampered asur. But to the druchii, reared and raised in the bleak wastes of Naggaroth, darkness and cold were their element. The kiss of snow, the shroud of shadow, these were almost welcoming to them. It was as though the land itself were calling to them, reassuring them that they were indeed coming home.

Even the most jaded and cynical of his warriors took heart from the change. The more superstitious, those who bore charms of Khaine about their necks or wore rings devoted to the various Cytharai, took these things to be an omen of victory.

Malus wasn't prepared to go so far as that. Even with his mother's last prophecy burned into his brain, he wasn't going to place too much trust in the intrigues of fate. Destiny was something that was shaped by mortal hands and mortal acts. It was in a commander's power to squander a predestined victory through his own mistakes and his own hubris. Having seen the future, it was in his hands to bring it to fruition.

Horsemen came galloping out from the pass, their black cloaks whipping behind them, their steeds frothing at the mouth. White-feathered arrows protruded from several of the dark riders, the shafts stabbed deep into the flesh of elf and horse alike. As they stormed towards the army, one of the horses pitched and fell, crushing its injured rider beneath it as it rolled in agony on the ground. Malus swatted the top of Spite's head, warning the reptile to keep calm despite the smell of horseblood in the air. Along the line of his knights, he could hear the sharp crack of other druchii disciplining their cold ones.

The dark riders peeled away from the cold one knights. Now that they were beyond the arrows of their enemy, the threat posed by their own comrades was impressed upon them. Two of the riders drew rein some hundred yards from the cold ones. While one rider dropped down from his saddle, the other took his horse and led it away. Malus watched the returning cavalry gallop around the flank of his infantry, headed for the rear to rest and recover from their foray into the pass.

Silar Thornblood and a small group of heavily armoured spearmen intercepted the dismounted rider. The elf was wounded, an arrow pinning his left arm to his side, but Silar was careful to remove his sword and dagger just the same before leading him through the line of cold one knights to where the drachau waited.

'Dreadlord, the scouts have returned,' Silar reported as his guards helped the rider squirm between the scaly flanks of the reptiles.

'Really?' Malus grumbled. 'I thought it was some other band of horsemen wearing the colours of Hag Graef who just happened to be riding around in the pass.' He waved his retainer away and motioned the guards to step aside. The wounded scout struggled to keep his feet. Malus could see the jewelled badge fastened to the druchii's helm that marked him as a captain. A sense of duty, this one, to bring his report despite his wound. Or perhaps he just had enough ambition in him that he didn't dare allow one of his subordinates the distinction of meeting with the drachau.

'The Eagle Gate is intact, dreadlord,' the scout said. It had been a faint hope, but there had been whispers of earthquakes and elemental upheavals when Malekith commanded his kingdom into this final assault on Ulthuan. If such turmoil had broken the defences he might have pushed his army headlong through the rubble and into the Inner Kingdoms. What a feat that would have been. A wondrous glory for Hag Graef and her drachau!

Malus scowled at the news that the asur fortress was still as formidable as it had been during the druchii invasions of ages past. Those assaults had broken upon the Eagle Gate, floundered in a futile siege until relief could arrive. The proximity of Caledor worried Malus. Prince Imrik could unleash his dragons against the host of Hag Graef. The flying wyrms were a foe that Malus didn't have the resources to vanquish. Such dragons as remained to the druchii were with Malekith and the army of Naggarond – even the beastmasters of Karond Kar had been compelled to turn over their dragons to the Witch King. Without dragons of his own to call upon and drive off any force from Caledor, there were only two choices open to Malus. He could withdraw back into the Shadowlands and try to seek shelter among the rocky hills, or he could press forward and take the fortress. If his troops were in command of the Eagle Gate, even Imrik's dragons wouldn't be able to drive them out.

Sitting atop her cold one, Vincirix listened with mounting unease as the scout related the condition of the Eagle Gate. The dark riders had suffered five dead and twice as many wounded by the archers lining the battlements. He had marked the positions of at least half a dozen bolt throwers and suspected there might be a score more concealed on the walls. The scout had noted the banners of many asur nobles and even the colours of Caledor among the defenders.

'Caledor?' Vincirix said, running a nervous finger across the flanges of her mace.

Malus smiled at her alarm. When he spoke, it was in a voice loud enough to carry to the nearby troops. 'It is wrong to underestimate the cunning of the asur. Never let hate blind you to an enemy's ability. If the garrison is so bold as to display the colours of Caledor, it is because they want to frighten me with the idea that they've got a dragon or three hiding behind those walls.' He glared down at the scout. 'But if they did have dragons, is it not more likely they would do nothing to put that idea in my head? They'd want to lure me in and then unleash the wyrms on me.' In a single flourish, Malus drew the warpsword from its scabbard and drove the blade across the scout's neck. The stunned captain collapsed, pawing at the gushing wound in his throat. Whatever ambitions the elf had entertained were spurting into the dirt.

The drachau turned from the dying scout. 'They think to delay me here,' he mused. 'They are playing for time, trying to exploit my worries.'

'But, dreadlord, if the defences are as formidable as...' Vincirix fell silent when she saw the glare in Malus's eyes.

'I will test them,' Malus said. 'And when the asur have shown me their mettle, I will unleash my full fury against them. The Eagle Gate will fall. The glory of conquest will be mine.'

* * *

Bragath Blyte bit his lip as the lash cracked across his shoulder. The Naggorite's hands tightened about the spear he held. For the chance to drive that shaft into the belly of his tormentor... But to do so wouldn't lessen his misery or that of his people. Kunor Kunoll's Son had a vile imagination when it came to punishing rebellion. A clean death in battle might at least earn a reprieve for a slave's soul, see it carried into the Pale Queen's underworld rather than the infernal toils of Slaanesh. But broken by Kunor's tortures, his soul would be too foul to pass the Keeper of the Last Door.

No, there was nothing a war-leader of Naggor could do except swallow his pride and endure. Hope for a noble death in battle and to pass into the underworld of Mirai.

'Faster, you dogs! Close ranks!' The sharp voice of Kunor rang out above the cracking whips of his helpers. Under the bite of the lash, the slave-soldiers marched onwards.

It had been years since the Witch Lords of Naggor loosed their armies against Hag Graef. The Witch Lords had lost that battle, their sorcery and daemons unequal to the ruthlessness and cunning of Malus Darkblade. The bastard kinslayer had prevailed, seizing the crown of his own city even as he vanquished the legions of Naggor. The conquered had become slaves, chattel for the wars of the Hag. Once there had been several thousand Naggorites under Darkblade's banner. Now there were barely half that number. Privation, abuse and neglect had claimed many. Hundreds had died fighting hopeless battles when Malus rode to rescue the refugees of Clar Karond and bind what was left of their might to that of the Dark Crag.

How many more would perish today, Bragath wondered. Would his name be among those of the slain? Or would some perverse whim of providence sustain him yet again?

Staring out across the ranks of the slave-soldiers, the warrior inside Bragath cringed at the state of his comrades. Was his armour as sorry as that of his fellows, cracked and dented, crudely mended with bits of leather and scraps of cloth? Were his limbs as lean and wasted as those of the elves who marched beside him? Did his face have the same starveling thinness, the same sickly yellow colour?

Bragath turned his head and raised his eyes. Ahead, at the far side of the pass, there loomed the Eagle Gate. Hundreds of feet high, built from immense blocks of granite, the fortress blocked the pass utterly. Tier upon tier of battlements, each piled atop the last. At the centre, the gigantic sculpture of an eagle with outstretched wings. One wing merged into the side of the mountains that flanked the pass. The talons stabbed downwards, perched upon the lowest level of battlements. Between the legs, the great bronze doors rose, immense portals that were fifty feet high and nearly again as broad. The body of the eagle bulged out from the face of the fortress, each feather carved with lifelike fidelity. Bragath's keen eyes could see the little gaps between the feathers that marked the windows behind which asur archers were lurking. The enormous head of the eagle with its open mouth was more obvious in its menace, a pair of immense bolt throwers standing inside the beak.

A legion of Malekith's Black Guard couldn't take this fortress, yet Darkblade had commanded Kunor to drive the Naggorites to the attack. Bragath didn't need to turn his head to know that the rest of Malus's army was hundreds of yards behind them. They were following the advance of the slave-soldiers, but keeping well to the rear. It needed no tactical acumen to guess the purpose Darkblade had chosen for his captives. The Naggorites had been given the cheerful task of goading the asur into making the first attack.

Each step closer made the sweat drip into Bragath's eyes. It wasn't fear of death that caused his heart to pound and his back to shiver. He was resigned to death – all of the Naggorites were. It was the horror of anticipation, of knowing what must soon come but not knowing when it would strike.

At the head of the Naggorite formation, a tall standard rose into the sky. Bragath looked uneasily up at the frame of wood and iron atop the pole. Bound to that frame was the mangled body of a druchii. Korbus, the late consort-retainer of Lady Eldire. Darkblade had been especially vicious in dealing with the traitor. The conjurer's hands had been hacked off with an axe, his lips sewn shut with wire. A metal cage bound his head in place, so that Korbus couldn't hide his face. The elf's eyes had been pinned open with needles that transfixed his eyelids. Across his stripped body, glyphs representing the most abominable curses had been carved into his flesh. Over his heart, Malus himself had cut the most profane symbol of them all, the emblem of Slaanesh the Devourer. Even for a dreadlord, such a ghastly punishment as deliberately invoking the Prince of Chaos to claim his enemy's soul was obscene.

Stoutly, the slave-soldiers maintained their march while the slavemasters barked and snapped their whips. Then a new sound entered the battle. From the walls there came a noise of whistling. The tall standard writhed and jerked as arrows slammed into the living emblem of Darkblade's hate. Blood streamed down the pole as Korbus was pin-cushioned with arrows. Then the archers on the walls turned their bows against the warriors of Naggor. Driven by the powerful longbows, the arrows arched high above the pass before streaking downwards to skewer the druchii slaves. The rude, poorly maintained armour of the Naggorites was small protection against the broad-headed missiles. By the dozen, they fell, dead or maimed.

Bragath Blyte raised his shield, feeling an asur arrow slam into it a second later. He could see the dead steel head where it had punched clean through the laminated wood. He scowled at the missile that had come so close to finishing him. Was this the warrior's death for which he'd endured years of suffering as the captive of Hag Graef?

Hate caused him to crash the shaft of his spear against his shield, breaking the arrow embedded in it. Bragath howled his fury to the uncaring sky and the asur safe behind their walls.

It was a truth the druchii had long ago learned. Where hope is lost, hate alone can drive a warrior onwards. With enough hate in his heart, a druchii could accomplish anything.

Even revenge.

Malus studied the march of Naggor with the same intensity as a gem-cutter might inspect a diamond before deciding how best to cut it. He watched every step, observed each slave-soldier as an arrow brought them down. A hundred elves lay in the dirt, killed by enemy archers or trampled by the feet of their comrades, and still the Scion of Hag Graef sat and brooded. Sometimes his hand would move to pat Spite's head as the brute's senses became excited by the smell of blood, but otherwise he was as still as a statue.

Finally, with an abruptness that caused Vincirix and Dolthaic to jump in surprise, Malus turned to the captains of his knights. 'The shooting from the right is weaker than that of the centre and the left,' he declared. 'They've tried to hide it, but there's a break in the fortifications there. A swift strike by cavalry to secure the ground followed by a rush of infantry to assault the wall.' He clenched his fist, grinding his fingers against his palm as though he were crushing the enemy in his hand. 'They try to feign strength where they are weak and weakness where they are strong, but the asur panicked at the last. They didn't want Kunor's dogs to get close to that right flank so they loosed their arrows on him too soon. Their caution has exposed their weakness instead of protecting it.'

One of my brothers has paved the way for you, Malus. This place was beset by my kind not long ago. A great plague daemon smashed his way through six of the eight walls. It is that wound your enemy hopes to protect. Do you understand now the power that could be yours?

Malus clenched his teeth against the urge to snarl down Tz'arkan's voice. Always tempting, always trying to seduce him with the promise of power. The daemon knew the desires of his heart only too well after all the years the thing had been festering inside him. The urge to quiet the daemon with wine was even greater than the fiend's wheedling, but Malus could afford neither. He had to keep his head clear if he was going to command his troops. More, with Eldire gone, he didn't know how he was going to replenish the dwindling supply of the draught he added to his wine. Drusala could make more, he was certain, but that would make him dependent on her. He still wasn't certain how much of his affliction she understood. There was great risk in adding to such knowledge as she already possessed.

She knows too much, fool! Kill her and have done before it is too late.

Malus looked down the line of knights, to where a small squadron of horsemen were galloping out, weaving a path between the main body of the army and the embattled Naggorites. His doomfire warlocks, hurrying to the attack. Even at this distance, he could see the fiery runes blazing upon their exposed hands and faces. Little coils of smoke drifted away from them as the hellish curse Malekith had inflicted upon them slowly dragged their souls into the realm of Slaanesh. The warlocks could save themselves only by sacrificing others in their stead. The murderous souls of Naggorites had done little to appease the curse – they needed pure, courageous souls to sacrifice and earn themselves a few days of respite. They needed souls such as they would find among the defenders of the Eagle Gate.

The doomfire warlocks, on their dark chargers and with their black cloaks billowing about them, weren't the focus of Malus's attention, however. Among the warlocks rode Drusala. Just as he'd tasked Kunor with drawing out the asur's physical defences, so he had charged Drusala and the warlocks with engaging the gate's magical defences. Just as the only way to defend against a dragon was with another dragon, so the only way to defend against magic was with magic of your own.

She would wait, Malus decided as he watched the sorceress ride towards the fortress. Whichever way he decided, it would wait until after the battle. The daemon inside him would just have to be patient. For now, there was the breach in the wall to exploit.

'Wait until the riders are closer,' Malus told his captains. 'Then we use them as a screen while we rush the weak point.'

'That will be hard on the warlocks,' Vincirix observed.

Malus smiled at her. 'It's a hard life, being a warlock. They should have learned that by now.'

Drusala could feel the aethyric vibrations that pulsated around the Eagle Gate. She was surprised to find them in such a sorry condition, shocked to find the protective harmonies in such a state of discord. Extending her senses, closing her mind to the crude physical essences around her, she was able to fixate upon the ruinous energies that saturated the pass. It seemed that Malus wasn't the first enemy to try his luck against the Eagle Gate. The malefic discord of hundreds of vanquished daemons oozed all around the place. The asur had been thrown into such turmoil by the calamities besieging Ulthuan that they hadn't even been able to take the time for a proper cleansing ritual.

Such unpreparedness wasn't like the hidebound asur. This truly was the prime opportunity to attack. Malekith had been wise to abandon the wastes of Naggaroth and stake everything on this chance to seize the lands that were his birthright.

She let her witchsight canvass the walls of the fortress. She noted the great breach to the right of the gate, a gap in the defences that went beyond simply the physical. Whatever had wrought such havoc upon the Eagle Gate had done so on far more than a material level. The very atmosphere around the place was like an open wound. She could feel the dark energies bubbling and boiling there.

Turning in her saddle, Drusala wasn't surprised to find the cold one knights rushing for the breach. Both the 'household guard' of Malus Darkblade – the mercenary Knights of the Burning Dark – and the Clar Karond exiles of Vincirix Quickdeath – the Knights of the Ebon Claw – were charging down the pass. The Scion of Hag Graef was forsaking the idea of a prolonged siege and throwing his lot into a lightning assault. That he was using both the Naggorites and the doomfire warlocks to shield the initial rush of his advance was a bit of callousness that wasn't lost on her. Darkblade valued no life more than he valued his own ambition.

A flash of brilliant white light among the battlements drew Drusala's attention. Gazing upwards, she watched as a small flock of immense birds took wing. As they rose into the sky, the very plumage of the creatures burst into flame, scorching the air as they climbed. Phoenixes, great raptors whose very essence was saturated with the magical energies of the Flamespyres. Unlike most of the animals changed and twisted by the magic in the Annulii, there was a certain intelligence in the mind of a phoenix, a rationality that made the creatures respond with friendship towards the asur. The fiery birds were a powerful ally for the garrison and a terrible foe for the invaders. Attuned to aethyric harmonies, the phoenixes had been roused by the approach of the doomfire warlocks. Drusala had little doubt who the beasts had chosen for their prey.

As the birds came hurtling earthwards, Drusala urged her mount skywards. The glamour that had cloaked her steed fell away as great leathery wings unfurled from its sides. Snorting and stamping, the dark pegasus shed the illusion of being a common steed. It fanned its great wings, upsetting the ranks of the mounted warlocks. The riders cursed and raged as Drusala's steed climbed into the air. She had no need to fear reprisal. The warlocks would quickly have problems enough just surviving the assault of the phoenixes.

Soaring aloft, the pegasus gave the diving phoenixes a wide berth. Drusala could feel the heat from the creatures as they passed, could smell the acrid scent of their burning plumage. She wove her own sorcerous defences a bit more tightly around herself, hiding her presence from the hunting raptors. Soon, her flying steed had borne her high above the embattled warlocks and their bestial foes.

Drusala might have lent aid to the warlocks, but to do so would mean squandering some of her own arcane power. She needed her full strength right now, for it was her intention to go beyond the foes the warlocks had drawn out. From the aethyric harmonies of the Eagle Gate, she knew that someone, some powerful mage, had been making his own attempt at cleansing the daemonic taint. That he thought himself knowledgeable enough to attempt such a purification on his own was a testament to either his ability or his arrogance.

Drusala intended to discover which.

Warning trumpets blared from the battlements as eagle-clawed bolt throwers cast their missiles down into the pass. Drusala saw two Knights of the Burning Dark skewered by the immense shafts, their carcasses tumbling through the dust, crushed beneath the bodies of their cold ones. The rest of the knights charged onwards, however, goaded to the attack by the merciless fury of Darkblade himself.

The asur knew the objective Malus had in mind. The trumpets were calling troops down to defend the broken walls, to block the breach before the cold one knights could seize it. Archers scrambled along the battlements, but there were too few near the breach to render much help. A knight's armour wasn't so easily pierced as that of a Naggorite slave and a cold one's scaly hide was more resilient than that of a horse. The only hope the garrison had lay in the armoured spearmen who filed down into the gap.

The spearmen, and the mage whose presence Drusala now perceived. He must have worn some talisman or charm to conceal his aethyric aura, probably a ward prepared against the daemons raging across Ulthuan. Now, however, he was drawing too deeply from the stream of magic to conceal himself. Drusala could see him as a sun-like beacon of light, luminous with the power he was drawing into himself.

She could sense his purpose as well. The mage was conjuring a spell to strike down Malus, to cut the head from the force threatening the breach. There was enough power in his magic that Drusala considered the enemy had a very real chance of working harm upon Malus. There was no question that if the tyrant were incapacitated, the attack would falter.

Worse, if the mage managed to kill Malus, he might be freeing something Drusala wasn't certain she was ready to face. And that was something she wasn't willing to risk.

A bolt of rippling black energy leapt from Drusala's staff, cleaving through the crackling blaze of power the mage was loosing against Malus. The antithetical waves of magic, light and dark, collided with tempestual fury. A dull boom roared across the battlefield, a roar that had within it the violence of both spells.

The mage turned towards her. Drusala could see a lean elf in sapphire robes bedecked in gold and pearl, a tall helm rising above his thin visage. There was pride and vanity stamped across that face. In her mind she could hear the mage announcing himself. 'I am Shrinastor, Loremaster of Hoec, Hierophant of the Golden Way, Magus of the Emerald Light. This place is under my protection.'

Drusala could feel Shrinastor drawing power into himself. The loremaster intended to fight her, to pit his magic against her sorcery. Twisting the reins of her pegasus, she jerked the beast's head to one side and turned it back towards the druchii lines.

Let Shrinastor think he'd frightened her off with his magic. She'd achieved her immediate purpose. Malus had reached the breach. His knights were engaged with the asur soldiers. The loremasters were always squeamish about destroying their own troops with their magic. The drachau would be safe from Shrinastor for the moment.

More importantly, Drusala had the answer to her own question: whether her asur adversary was moved by ability or arrogance.

Their next encounter would end quite differently now that she knew who she was facing.

'Set spears! Hold your ground!' As the orders were shouted, hundreds of spears slammed into the earth, a knee set against each to help brace the weapon against the coming attack. Tall, iron-banded shields, each standing as high as the elf who carried it, were lowered across the body of each warrior. There was no expression of fright, no thought of retreat as the soldiers prepared to receive the charge of the most monstrous cavalry in the druchii horde.

Prince Yvarin, even in the midst of the battle, felt his heart pound with pride. Among his officers, he knew there had been questions about his decision to deploy these troops here, at the breach, when the position could be held by lesser troops. They had urged a sally against the druchii, to take the battle to the invader before a prolonged attack could be mounted. For such an assault, they had wanted the best warriors in the fortress. That meant these elves, the Eataine Guard.

The prince had endured the implications that he was unwise or inexperienced when he'd disagreed with the idea of an offensive attack. His officers were right – holding the Eagle Gate against a prolonged siege would be difficult with the breach in the walls. That was why he'd chosen to exploit the weakness. Turn it into a killing ground for the best their foe could send against them.

Doubt had ruled him as he saw the attack unfold, as he watched the Tyrant of Hag Graef himself leading a host of cold one knights towards the breach. Yvarin felt a sense of foreboding, the feeling that he gazed upon his own doom. It was hopeless to try and stand against such a foe. The Eagle Gate was lost, what good could come of selling their lives to no purpose? The temptation to call the retreat vexed him, nagged at him with songs of safety and peace.

The feel of the sword in his hand steadied his resolve. That blade had been handed down for fifty generations of his house. Many times, it had been borne home with the body of its owner laid upon a shield, entrusted to the living heir by a fallen hero. Never had that blade fled from battle. Ever had the elves who bore it done their duty to the Phoenix King and the people of Ulthuan. Yvarin knew what duty demanded of him this day.

He knew that to hold the gap in the outer walls was the key to maintaining the security of the Eagle Gate. Yvarin also knew that it was here the fighting would be at its hardest. The troops deployed here were effectively being given a death sentence. One and all had adopted cloaks of white before marching to the breach, a mark of purity and resolve before their final sacrifice for Ulthuan, the colour of mourning for when that sacrifice had been made. For that reason, if no other, Yvarin had decided to entrust this role to none but his personal retinue of warriors, the Eataine Guard. For that reason, he had determined to stand beside them in battle. If they prevailed, the fortress would hold. If they failed, no command he could issue would delay the catastrophe.

The stink of the Naggarothi steeds swept over the prince, bringing tears to his eyes and a cough to his throat. It was a mark of how far the druchii had degenerated since they'd followed the merciless Witch King into exile that they could abide such foul beasts.

'Ready arms,' Yvarin told his warriors. 'We fight for the Phoenix Crown! Let none of this scum past!'

The fierce cries of the druchii, the monstrous roars of their reptilian steeds rose in a deafening din. Many of the asur turned their faces behind their shields as the enemy charged their position. They could feel the ground shuddering beneath their feet as the weight of the attack came thundering towards them.

Lesser troops would have broken. The Eataine Guard held fast. Reptilian roars turned to shrieks of pain as many of the cold ones impaled themselves upon the waiting spears. Then there came the shrieks of elves as the druchii knights drove their cruel lances through the thick ironwood shields. Dozens of asur perished as the knights drove their attack home. The white cloaks of the first line were quickly stained red with the blood of friend and foe alike.

'Forward!' Yvarin cried. At his command, the second line of warriors advanced, thrusting their spears at the enemy. The druchii charge had decimated the front line, slaughtering four-fifths of the warriors, but the impetus of their assault had been blunted. Wounded cold ones flailed upon the ground, their claws slashing at anything that came near, forcing the knights behind to finish them before they could advance. Dead bodies tripped up those cold ones that tried to rush into the breach, leaving their riders exposed to the spears of the Eataine Guard. Black-armoured knights cast aside their lances, hurling them spitefully into the faces of their foes. The lance was the weapon of the charge, and the druchii charge had faltered. Now the knights drew sword and mace from their belts, the weapons best suited to close quarters.

Yvarin struck down one knight, his sword chopping through the killer's arm as he tried to negotiate his way past a thrashing cold one. The stricken knight's reptilian mount snapped at him, striving to bring him down. The axe of Yvarin's standard bearer smashed into the brute's skull, sinking almost to its jaw. The cold one collapsed in a heap, dragging the standard bearer down with it.

Before the standard bearer could regain his feet, another druchii knight was lunging at him. The reptilian mount's claws raked open his side while the knight's clawed mace dented his helm and shattered his skull. The knight snatched at the standard, catching it before it could fall to the ground. Viciously she raked her bloodied mace across it, tearing the ancient silk and fouling the emblem of the Eataine Guard.

Prince Yvarin felt fear roar through his veins. He'd watched this knight during the charge. She was one of Darkblade's war-leaders, a position she could have earned only through the most heinous atrocities. What was he beside such a fiend?

Surprisingly, Yvarin found the answer, felt it as a roar that deafened the fear inside him. Who was he? He was the commander of the Eagle Gate!

'For the Phoenix!' Yvarin screamed as he drove himself upon the war-leader. Her clawed mace crashed against his shield, but he ignored the stinging numbness the impact sent racing up his arm. Spun around by the brutal impact, he turned his rotation into a sidewise slash. It was a strategy he'd practised a thousand times in his father's palace. Now it served him well. Outstretched by the brutal blow she had struck, his enemy was exposed to the sweep of Yvarin's sword. The ancient blade rang out as it crashed against her armour, splitting the spiked pauldron and driving a sliver of the compromised mail back into the face of the knight's helm.

Blood gushed from the helm. A muffled scream rang from behind the metal mask. The clawed mace fell from a hand that now snatched at the chin-strap holding the mask in place. A moment later, it came free, or at least one side of it did. The rest simply hung in place, pinned to the war-leader's face by the sliver of steel that had impaled her eye.

Yvarin struck again, thrusting his blade at the knight. The thrust stabbed into her throat, drawing a hideous gargle from her as her body slumped sidewise in the saddle. The reptile, panicked by the dying elf slumped across it back, scrabbled away from Yvarin, snapping and barking at the other cold ones as it fled back into the pass.

The death of their war-leader appeared to embolden the knights who bore her symbol. Even as the Eataine Guard cheered Yvarin's triumph, the prince felt himself struck from behind. His shield shattered, the arm behind it cut almost to the bone. As he crashed to the ground, he saw a ghastly figure glaring down at him from the back of a horned reptile. The prince braced himself for death. He knew who this enemy was and he knew better than to expect mercy from Malus Darkblade.

The villain raised his sword, Yvarin's blood steaming on its blade; then the masked tyrant seemed to think better of it. Leaning forwards, he hissed into the earhole of his steed. 'Feed, Spite.'

Before the horned one could lunge at Yvarin, spears stabbed at Malus from almost every quarter. The tyrant lashed out, shearing through each weapon as it was thrust at him. Darkblade looked around and an animalistic cry of rage rose from behind his mask.

Painfully, Yvarin raised himself on one elbow and looked to see what had so enraged the infamous murderer. What he saw was beyond belief. The druchii attack had failed. The second group of knights, the ones following after the she-elf's company, had broken and fled. Sight of the dead captain's steed retreating through their ranks had panicked them and thrown them into headlong flight. The surviving knights of the first company, who had been holding the breach, were now falling back as well.

Seeing the fight was lost, Malus drove his spurs into his reptile's flanks. The horned beast spun around, smashing several asur with its tail, then leapt over the carcasses between itself and the breach. Archers chased Malus as he retreated back into the pass.

Attendants hurried to Yvarin's aid, but the wounded prince barely took notice of them. His wounds, his fatigue, even the terror he'd felt when he found himself facing Malus Darkblade, all of these were forgotten. His entire world now consisted of a sound. A sound that was like the roar of the ocean. A sound that rang from the walls and battlements.

The Eagle Gate had held against the druchii attack and now its defenders were cheering. A cheer that took the form of a name, a name that only days before they had still held in doubt.

'Yvarin! Yvarin! For the Phoenix and Yvarin!'

ELEVEN

Malus could feel the rage building up inside him. Gazing back into the pass, he could see the asur dragging the cold ones that had been killed in the assault out from behind the walls. They were building a rampart of dead flesh out ahead of their broken fortifications, an obstacle that was well within range of the archers on the battlements. There had been a chance to end the battle quickly, to establish a foothold within the fortress itself. Now that opportunity was lost.

The drachau stalked among the commanders of his knights. The Knights of the Burning Dark. His household guard. Mercenary trash that had broken at the first setback! If they'd kept their nerve, if they'd maintained the momentum of the assault... But, no, the slinking vermin had fled. They'd seen Vincirix's cold one come galloping back with her body hanging from the saddle and they'd fled.

The Warpsword of Khaine sang out as Malus removed the head from one of the disgraced commanders. Bound hand and foot, the scum awaited his rage. Silar marched behind his master, raising each gory head as Malus cut it free. Grimly, he lifted each one by its hair and cast it into the jeering mob of infantry and horsemen who'd been assembled to watch the executions. There was little sympathy for the arrogant, highborn knights. Not from the common soldiers, who were so often abused by their noble comrades.

'Have pity, dreadlord! When we saw Vincirix's body, we thought you had been slain as well.' The cries came from Dolthaic. The captain had been lashed to a skinning rack and positioned so that he could see every moment of punishment as it was meted out upon his officers.

Malus hesitated, as though considering Dolthaic's words. Then he stepped to the next bound officer. The warpsword came chopping down once again, shearing through the elf's neck. Deep inside his soul, he could feel Tz'arkan exult in the vindictive carnage. It annoyed Malus that the daemon found vengeance so satisfying when it had no vested interest in what was being avenged. For the daemon, it was all nothing more than an amusing game.

He thought again of the dwindling supply of the draught. Could he afford to indulge himself this way if it gave Tz'arkan strength? Malus dismissed the worry as unworthy. His attack had failed. If he didn't punish someone, discipline in his army would break down. His soldiers would think him weak, unfit to lead. They'd entertain ideas that someone more capable and ruthless should be their general.

The warpsword sang out again and another grovelling knight fell to the ground without his head. This last one had been a Knight of the Ebon Claw. They had their own responsibility for the failure to take the breach. If they'd fought harder, if they'd been more loyal to their captain, perhaps she wouldn't have been cut down by that damn asur prince!

When Malus struck next, it wasn't the neck of the knight he saw, but that of Prince Yvarin. The cursed asur! He'd killed Vincirix, taken away his lover and war-leader. Malus wasn't one to form deep attachments with his possessions, but he considered it an unforgivable slight when anyone took away something he owned. That the cretin had rallied the asur troops by killing Vincirix made the trespass still more insulting.

There would be retribution. Malus vowed that by Khaine he'd face Yvarin again. He'd make the prince answer for Vincirix's death. He'd make him watch as the druchii tore down his fortress stone by stone. He'd keep him alive long enough to see his family butchered like hogs. Only when the cup of vengeance had been drained to its dregs would Malus allow the scum to die.

Why stop there, Malus? It is in your power to make vengeance an eternal state of being. All you need do is stop fighting against me. Embrace the inevitable, and we can enjoy this sensation until Khorne's rage consumes all existence. You could take the soul of Yvarin and torture it until the moons crash into the sea and the sun collapses into a smouldering ember.

Quaking from the intensity of the daemon's presence, Malus hesitated as he raised the warpsword to strike down another victim. At the last instant, he kicked the wretch kneeling before him, knocking the knight into the dirt. In a loud voice, he cried out to the watching legions of druchii. 'Let this be a reminder to every captain and highborn. Let it be a lesson to every soldier and slave. The life of every one of you belongs to me. Spend it well, or by Khaine, I will claim your death for myself.' He raised the warpsword high once more, the blood of its last victim still sizzling upon the blade. The cheers and jeers of the infantry as they had watched the executions had faded now, the warriors cowed by the threat of the tyrant they served.

Malus glowered at his army, his eyes roving from elf to elf, fixing each with his merciless stare. He didn't need their loyalty, he didn't want their love. Those were the weak motivations of the contemptible asur. What he wanted was their obedience. What he needed was their fear. As he gazed upon them, Malus could see that he had claimed both. Sheathing the warpsword, the drachau dismissed his troops.

'Free the last of them,' Malus told Silar as he turned away. There were still a few officers of the Knights of the Burning Dark who had kept their heads.

Silar looked doubtful. 'Is that wise, my lord?'

An ugly chuckle rose from the drachau. He waved his hand at the officers he had spared. 'The knights will need leadership in the coming attack, and these will fight much harder than any others now that they know the fate which awaits failure.' Malus clapped his hand on Silar's shoulder. 'They are afraid of me now, too afraid to plot and scheme. By the time they gain the courage for revenge, I'll have already spent their lives taking the Eagle Gate.'

Leaving Silar to cut the bonds of the disgraced officers, Malus strode up to the skinning rack where Dolthaic's body was stretched. He stared coldly at the commander of his household guard, the mercenary renegade he'd taken into his service so long ago. 'You have wounded me, this day, old comrade.'

Dolthaic's eyes were like two pits of terror as he looked up at his master. 'Dreadlord, have I not always served you well? Have my knights not done everything you've asked of them?'

Malus scowled at Dolthaic. 'A drachau doesn't ask. A drachau commands,' he snarled. 'Your landless wastrels have accomplished the one thing that is unforgiveable. They've failed to bring me victory.'

Upon the rack, Dolthaic struggled in his bonds, his terror mounting with each word that left Malus's lips. 'Mercy! I will not fail you again!'

'Vincirix is dead,' Malus said, his hand closing about the jewelled dagger sheathed alongside the warpsword. 'You let that preening asur prince take her from me. The breach remains in the hands of the enemy. You allowed them to keep it from me. What punishment for a mere sell-sword who dares do such things to his master?'

Dolthaic cried out as Malus ripped the dagger from its sheath and slashed at him. His scream turned into a grunt of astonishment as he felt his left arm fall loose from the frame. When he dared to open his eyes, he saw Malus returning the blade to his belt. It took him a moment to fight through his own disbelief to understand that the drachau had cut him loose.

'Do not mistake a reprieve for forgiveness,' Malus cautioned. 'You've served me well over the years, Dolthaic. Because of that, I am giving you a chance to earn back your right to live. If the Knights of the Burning Dark redeem themselves, riches and glory await you. If they fail me again, it would be best for you to die on the battlefield.'

Turning his back on Dolthaic, a gesture of scornful disdain for one druchii to show another, Malus stalked off towards his tent. He could trust that Dolthaic would drive his knights mercilessly from now on. The dispossessed noble knew first-hand how vicious his master could be. There'd be no restraint any more; if Dolthaic were to fall in battle, he'd make sure his followers shared that fate.

What remained now was for Malus to decide exactly how he was going to spend their lives.

Execute them. Kill them all. Have a little fun, you miserable cretin.

'Shut up, daemon.'

The moment Malus stepped inside his tent, he could feel the icy touch of magic crawling across his skin. Deliberately he suppressed any reaction to the uncanny atmosphere. After his many audiences with his mother and the Witch Lords of Naggor, he'd become quite accomplished at denying the instinctual repugnance sorcery provoked. Calmly, he set his helmet on the ebony stand near the doorway. Without looking, he addressed the personage he knew was somewhere nearby.

'Make yourself at home,' he advised. 'Unless you already have.'

'I predicted your invitation,' Drusala's voice called to him as he started to unbuckle his sword belt.

The drachau turned his head, following the sound of her voice. To call the strip of black silk that Drusala had somehow squirmed into immodest would be like calling an orc irritable. Despite his distrust and, if he were honest, fear of the she-elf, Malus felt the blood in his veins quicken as he looked on her. She was lounging across one of the divans that had been brought all the way from Hag Graef. He'd kept it through the years, a memento of when he'd conspired with the old drachau's daughter, Malgause, to seize the Dark Crag's crown. How his ardour had burned for her and the power she had represented. He might even have kept her as his wife if she hadn't plotted to betray him with her brother.

Now, gazing upon Drusala, Malus couldn't even remember what Malgause looked like. He was sure the comparison wouldn't be favourable. It would take Atharti herself to equal that vision of seduction and desire.

Lose your head and lose your head.

Tz'arkan's voice was but the merest whisper, barely more than imagination, but it struck Malus like a peal of thunder. His nose wrinkled as he caught the subtle aroma, the soft hint of exotic perfume. He could imagine how exotic. He'd seen the degenerate slaves of Slaanesh, the barbarian marauders who devoted themselves wholly and unashamedly to the Prince of Chaos. Their shamans could obliterate the minds of those they offered up to their insidious god simply by holding a tiny flower under their nose. The scent would arouse such feelings of passion that the victim would tear out his own throat to escape the torment of longing and despair.

The key to defying any enchantment was being aware it was being cast. Malus didn't hang his sword belt on the stand with his helmet, but kept a loose grip about the sheathed length of the warpsword. Draped across the divan, Drusala's eyes exhibited just the tiniest flash of alarm. She knew Malus hadn't been caught in the web of her charms.

'Was I overbold in coming here?' Drusala asked, leaning back to better display the supple curve of her legs.

It was an effort of self-control for Malus to keep his gaze focused on her eyes. The witch didn't need perfumes or magics to enchant her prey. She was perfectly dangerous all on her own.

'I have not yet lit the pyre for Vincirix Quickdeath or entreated Nethu to allow her soul to pass the Last Door,' Malus said, trying to inject a steely firmness into his voice.

Drusala raised one eyebrow in surprise. 'Sentiment from the Scion of Hag Graef? I did not think you capable of such... indulgence. The little she-sword of Clar Karond is dead. Her usefulness to you is over.'

'And the usefulness of Drusala, lap-dog of Ghrond, is only beginning,' Malus replied venomously.

The sorceress smiled at his anger. 'Magic is always useful, drachau. Your mother should have taught you that.'

Mention of his mother only inflamed his anger. Malus stalked towards the divan. He started to reach for Drusala, but something even more primal than Tz'arkan warned him back. She was trying to goad him. He might not know why, but that didn't mean he had to walk blindly into her trap. Shaking his head, he lowered his arm and walked away.

'Your magic wasn't terribly impressive today,' Malus scolded her, 'for all your airs of arcane power and your claims of being Morathi's favourite disciple. My warlocks have been decimated by the phoenixes, but a few survived. They tell me you abandoned them when the birds came.'

Drusala matched his cold smile. 'I went to fight another, still greater enemy. He calls himself Shrinastor, one of the asur loremasters. Quite a formidable mage. Left unchecked he could have wrought great havoc on your forces.' A scolding note entered Drusala's tone as she wagged a finger at Malus. 'When you tried to kill the asur prince, did you not wonder that the warpsword failed to slay him outright? That was Shrinastor's doing. He worked a charm to dull the efficacy of your blow and allow the prince to live.'

Malus was silent a moment, thinking about Drusala's claim. It was true, the warpsword should have killed the asur prince with one blow. Instead the elf had only been wounded. If the frustration of his revenge was the doing of Shrinastor, then he owed the mage a debt of slow death.

'My warlocks have been reduced to a mere shell of their former strength,' Malus said. 'I am told they were unable to overcome the phoenixes. Lady Eldire cautioned that the birds are drawn to magic like a leech to blood. If that is true, how do you hope to prevail against both the birds and the mage?'

'Reinforcements are coming,' Drusala said. She glanced at her hand and a large ring fitted to one finger, a band of obsidian with a great sphere of crystal. 'I have seen it. By nightfall, Fleetmaster Aeich will reach your camp, bringing along a small army of corsairs and all of his surviving seers.'

'Aeich will bear me no friendship after leaving him to rot on the beach,' Malus observed.

'True, but after you left, the Tiranocii attacked. They managed enough damage to scare Aeich away from the black ark. You might have no friends among the corsairs, but they understand that their one hope for survival is to join your horde.' The sorceress tapped a finger against her chin. 'I doubt Aeich will try to have you assassinated until after the Eagle Gate is taken. A pirate knows it takes a general to capture a fortress.'

Malus clenched his fist in frustration. If it needed only a general to take the fortress, it would already be in his hands. No, after failing to seize the breach today, it would need something more. It would need luck. He had but the briefest window in which to take the gate. After that, the Eagle Gate itself would be reinforced. Worse, the dragon princes of Caledor might send a few of their wyrms to intercede. If that happened, Malus would have no chance of victory. He'd be disgraced, at best. Dead, at worst. Most likely, that had been Malekith's plan all along.

The drachau walked across the tent to the mahogany cabinet where he kept his special wine. For the first time in many months, he needed the drink not to quiet Tz'arkan but to stifle his own fears.

'You should be careful not to imbibe too freely,' Drusala called to him from the divan. 'A general must keep a clear head... and a clean spirit.'

Malus turned and scowled at her. 'Be careful how much you presume, witch. No one is indispensable.' Returning to the stand near the door, he snatched up his helmet and stormed from the tent.

Drusala watched the drachau depart. 'We shall see,' she whispered. By her estimate, a few more weeks and there would be no more of Eldire's draught left. If Malus lived that long, things would get quite interesting.

She would make a fine match for you. She wants to be lover and mother all at once. I wonder which you need more, Malus.

The most frustrating thing about the daemon was having nothing to lash out against when its taunts cut too deep. Malus growled at Tz'arkan to relent. Much more of its baiting and he'd go back to the tent and drain an entire bottle to smother the daemonic presence. That might play right into Drusala's plans for them – and he emphasised that concern. The triumph he felt when Tz'arkan receded back into the shadows of his subconscious wasn't as satisfying as he needed it to be. Something had to suffer for all the rage bottled up inside him.

Malus found that his lonely walk through the camp had brought him to the crevasse where the slave-soldiers of Naggor had been bivouacked. The grubby survivors of the day's fighting lay heaped on the ground, panting like dogs beneath ragged blankets and threadbare cloaks. A few of the vermin had been granted the privilege of starting small fires to warm themselves against the night. It was an indulgence that Kunor typically reserved for those Naggorites who informed on their fellows – or those Naggorites he wanted their fellows to believe were informants.

As he glowered at the slaves, Malus thought of the many battles he had fought against them. The war between Naggor and Hag Graef had been vicious and bloody, but in the end he had been the ultimate victor. He'd risen from being an outlaw and outcast to becoming the Dark Crag's greatest hero and drachau. In a way, he owed his position to the Naggorites. Perhaps that was why he despised them more now than even at the height of the war. That vindictiveness was why he'd brought them along, shackled in the holds of the black ark, when he'd left so many others behind.

To be strong, a druchii needed something to hate.

Malus saw the empty, beaten looks the slaves gave him – at least those brave enough to even look at their conqueror. Dogs! Vermin! To call these wretches druchii was to defile the name.

The despot turned as he heard armoured figures come rushing towards him. Silar Thornblood and a few of his guards. With them was Kunor Kunoll's Son, fresh blood smearing the leather smock the slavemaster wore. Malus knew it was Kunor's custom to personally attend the most sorely wounded of his slaves. Any Naggorite with half a brain in his head made sure to bite his own tongue rather than fall into the slavemaster's hands.

'Dreadlord!' Silar shouted, anxiety in his tone. 'You should not be alone.'

Malus waved his hand in contempt at the exhausted Naggorites. 'Your concern amuses me, old friend. What danger is there here? A whipped dog forgets how to bite.'

'And we have ways of making them forget if they remember,' Kunor grinned.

Silar stiffened at the slavemaster's mirth. He'd always pressed Malus to treat the Naggorites with some measure of consideration and restraint. They were, in his mind at least, fellow druchii. 'I was worried about asur infiltrators,' Silar said. 'The ashencloaks continue to strike down our pickets and spoil our supplies. If one of them should have the chance to strike at you...'

'Then he would end this battle with one arrow,' Malus said. The drachau's gaze became almost murderous. 'If such is my doom, the gods will answer for their jest.' He turned back around, staring across the huddled Naggorites. 'Kunor, how many troops do you still have?'

'Dreadlord, the asur struck down three score and six,' the slavemaster replied. 'Another score or so have expired from their wounds.'

Malus nodded. A grotesque strategy was occurring to him. If Drusala's prediction was right, and she would hardly have made the claim unless she was certain, he'd soon have Aeich and a host of corsairs for the next attack. Warriors accustomed to scaling the battlements of their black ark, they'd be the perfect shock troops to send against the walls of the Eagle Gate. But for him to do so, the asur would need a more immediate threat to keep them occupied.

'Your entertainment is over, Kunor,' Malus said. 'The injuries of the wounded are to be bound. You'll also pick out a hundred of the dogs in this camp. Once you've gathered them together, march them to where the beastmasters have penned the war hydras. Tell them to slather every one of the Naggorites you bring them with fellbrew.'

Silar's face went pale with shock. 'You can't mean to do such a thing?'

Malus laughed. 'Old friend, I need the war hydras at their most ferocious when we attack tomorrow. When they devour prey that has been coated in fellbrew, it will drive them berserk. Given their slow digestion, six hours should suffice to gain me the results I want.'

'But you could use horses or cold ones...' Silar protested.

'You are too timid to ever amount to anything,' Malus reproved the highborn. 'I need every horse and every cold one. I have extra Naggorites.'

Laughing at his cruel jest, the despot stalked away. Silar ordered the guards he had brought with him to follow Malus. The future of Hag Graef depended on the drachau. He wasn't going to risk that future because of their lord's hubris.

Kunor lingered long enough to give Silar a cold look of contempt before he rushed away to rouse his henchmen and carry out the drachau's command. Silar was left alone at the mouth of the crevasse. He stayed there while he heard the cries rising from the sick-tent where the injured Naggorites had been taken. It would be like Kunor to tell the wounded what was going to happen to them even as their hurts were being bandaged.

Disgusted, Silar started to walk away from the slave compound. He had only gone a short way, however, when he found his step restricted. He looked down just as the noose his foot had stepped into was jerked tight and he was sent crashing to the ground. Before he could roll onto his back, he felt the weight of a body slam on top of him, pushing his face into the dirt.

'Now, Darkblade, vengeance!' a venomous voice hissed.

Silar felt a blow against the back of his head. The thick steel of his helmet prevented the blade from striking his neck, but he knew his attacker would correct his aim for the next blow. Flailing about, Silar tried to rise, but there were other foes now, enemies who had hold of his arms. Growling in frustration, he struggled to break free before the killing blow could be struck.

'This isn't Darkblade!' a shocked voice rang out.

Silar's head was pulled back, his chinstrap snapping as his helmet was ripped free. He found himself looking into the scarred countenance of a wiry Naggorite. The slave returned his scowl with interest.

'Who is it, Lorfal?' one of the other ambushers asked.

'Silar Thornblood,' Lorfal grunted in contempt. 'One of the tyrant's lapdogs.'

The pressure on Silar's back vanished. To his surprise, the elves holding his arms released their grip. Slowly, the highborn rose to his feet. There were half a dozen slaves around him, each armed with some manner of blade. Silar was careful to keep his hands away from his own weapons. He was surprised to recognise the ambusher who'd been on top of him as Bragath Blyte, one of old General Ralkoth's captains. They'd crossed swords before, when Naggor had still been free.

Bragath saw the recognition in Silar's eyes. 'Yes, it is I. You see, I've survived all these years. When Darkblade conquered us and put all the captains of Naggor to the sword, you could have pointed me out to him.'

Silar nodded, his eyes watching the other Naggorites, wary for the first sign of treachery. 'You were a worthy foe. You deserved a death in battle, your chance to impress Khaine and Ereth Khial.'

The slave-soldier clenched his fist. 'Many years have passed and I've often wondered if I should thank you or curse you for that, Silar. I've watched you keenly when I've seen you and listened with sharp ears whenever one of our people spoke of you.' A cold smile formed on Bragath's face. 'You've always tried to deal fairly with us. You've risked Darkblade's wrath to temper the cruelties he'd heap upon us.'

'If you would kill me, give me the same chance to die with a sword in my hand I gave you,' Silar said.

'That is my intention,' Bragath said. He pointed his dagger at the scarred Lorfal. 'We thought you were Darkblade himself. That is why we attacked. It was an opportunity that could not be squandered.'

The chastened Lorfal hung his head in contrition. 'The tyrant was here. I heard him speak.'

Bragath motioned the elf to silence. 'We didn't intend to attack you, Silar, but we were looking for you. Alone among those close to Darkblade, you might give us a chance to get close to him. I know you have disagreed with his ruthless orders. A drachau must be merciless, but Darkblade goes beyond what his title demands of him.'

'You seek to draw me into a conspiracy against the dreadlord?' Silar asked, stunned by the outrageousness of such a thing.

'Indeed,' Bragath said. 'That is what we ask. What is your answer?'

Silar started to reach for his sword; then, in the distance, he heard another of the wounded Naggorites scream. Druchii fed to war hydras like so much carrion. It was a callous waste of life, an almost unthinkable atrocity.

Silar let his hand fall to his side. Looking Bragath straight in the eye, he answered the slave's question.

'Whatever you are planning, I don't think you could do it without me.'

TWELVE

Malus hefted the warpsword high overhead, shouting at the black legions of his horde. He evoked all the old indignities that had been heaped upon the druchii by their despised asur kin. He spoke to his warriors of the ancient hate that had divided a people. He smiled coldly as he recounted the theft of the Phoenix Crown from Malekith by a petty and ungrateful people. With his words, he conjured the vision of lost Nagarythe, now a wasteland haunted by ghosts and monsters and the deluded aesanar. He recited the promise made to the Black Council by the Witch King: that the lands of their birthright, the kingdoms of Ulthuan, would belong to them if they but had the strength to take it.

'Death and blood to the traitors!' Malus roared, his voice amplified beyond the merely mortal by the excited daemon boiling inside him. Tz'arkan was in its element now, poised upon the edge of slaughter and massacre. Briefly, Malus had considered dulling the daemon with wine, but had at last relented. He might need the accursed might of the daemon to draw upon. After all of these years sharing his flesh with the malignant fiend, he was confident that he knew how much he could tap into Tz'arkan without going too far.

Without losing control.

Without losing all that he was and all that he would ever be.

At his cry, the drachau's commanders issued the order to attack. The breach was blocked now by the piled carcasses of his own cold ones. No lightning strike by his cavalry would allow Malus to slip behind the walls and seize the Eagle Gate swiftly. No, now he would be forced into a longer fight. His army must outnumber Prince Yvarin's asur a hundredfold; there could be no question of the final outcome if he had only the garrison to worry about.

But Malus knew time was a greater enemy to him than the asur guarding the Eagle Gate. The host of Hag Graef had been bolstered during the night by Fleetmaster Aeich and those corsairs who had fled their doomed black ark. Adding thousands of battle-hardened corsairs and militia from the abandoned *Eternal Malediction* had swollen the ranks of his army, and the addition of Aeich's surviving seers and sorceresses had added a good deal more magic to his force, making Drusala not quite as essential as she so dearly wanted to be.

The problem with the arrival of the corsairs was the news they bore with them. They'd been harried by the asur along the entire line of march. Not just by the black-feathered arrows of ashencloaks, but charioteers from Tiranoc too, the advance elements of an entire Tiranocii army that had pursued them from the beachhead. Only a day or so behind Aeich, the Tiranocii force wasn't big enough to pose a threat to Malus's army. However, if they struck against the rear of his horde while they were trying to break through the Eagle Gate, the carnage they could wreak would be prodigious.

Malus didn't care so much for the loss of warriors, but he was worried about the loss of time. Every hour might bring a relief force from Ellyrion to support the Eagle Gate. Or worse, the skies might fill with dragons from Caledor. The drachau had campaigned against the asur often enough to know that whatever enmity might exist between the kingdoms, they set aside such resentments when faced by a mutual foe. If the dragons came, Malus would never take the Eagle Gate. His army would be smashed and scattered, his own disgrace absolute.

It is not too late, Malus. Set me loose and victory will yet be yours!

Spite hissed beneath its master as the horned one sensed the brief flare-up of the daemon's presence. It took an effort of will, but Malus forced Tz'arkan back into the hinterlands of his soul. Now wasn't the time to indulge the fiend's bloodthirsty ambitions. Malus had his own dreams of conquest and slaughter to achieve.

Blocks of infantry marched into the pass. Malus watched their banners snapping in the wind. He wondered how many of the asur inside recognised the bloodied flags of Hag Graef. He wondered how many hearts had filled with terror as the nature of the foe they faced became apparent. Those who didn't know the druchii would soon learn.

The warriors of Clar Karond, the enslaved Naggorites, the soldiers of the Dark Crag itself, all marched behind a screen of skirmishers drawn from the black ark's militia. Why squander his own slaves when he had those of Aeich to spend? The fleetmaster had been a good deal too vocal about blaming Malus for abandoning the beachhead. Well, now the fleetmaster would be thinking the slaughter of his slaves was his punishment. That mistake would make Aeich less appreciative of the role he and his corsairs were to play in the battle. The best illusions, after all, were those who believed in their own deceit.

Spite trotted alongside the armoured mass of spearmen, a regiment that had held the line during the final attack by Naggor against Hag Graef. For their unrivalled brutality on the field, Malus had awarded them the banner of the vanquished Witch Lords. As the spears slowly advanced on the Eagle Gate, that banner was held high before them. A sheet of leathery skin, flayed from the bodies of enemies the Witch Lords had offered in sacrifice to dark Hekarti, the banner had been endowed with powerful enchantments by the Naggorites. As arrows came whistling down from the battlements, they veered sharply away from the dreadspears and deflected into the regiment of swordsmen marching on their flank. A few of the bleakswords fell, their armour pierced by the diverted arrows, their bodies kicked and trampled by the warriors who hastened to fill the gaps in their ranks.

Orbs of blazing arcane fire came crashing down from the Eagle Gate, incinerating dozens of druchii with each impact. In response, the sorceresses Aeich had brought unleashed their own dark magics against the walls. Lances of writhing lightning, blacker than death and lethal as the kiss of a medusa, seared along the walls. The scorched bodies of asur soldiers hurtled from the battlements, cooked inside their own armour. After an initial assault, the barrage of magic broke into isolated duels as asur mages pitted their abilities against druchii sorcery. Malus could see the white fire and the black lightning crackle and explode as the antithetical conjurations collided. Here and there, the white fire would fade, but along the front nearest the breach, it was the darker sorcery that failed. Malus scowled as he looked in that direction. The loremaster Drusala had spoken of seemed to be taking a hand in defending the gap. The asur's power must be prodigious to overcome so many sorceresses. Malus wished he could have matched Drusala against him. Whichever way such a contest went, it would make things simpler for the drachau.

Drusala, however, had other duties at the moment. Her magic was the key to this second assault on the Eagle Gate. The sorcerous deception she had worked to make her dark pegasus seem an ordinary horse had inspired Malus. He'd tasked her with working a still mightier glamour, an illusion that would conceal the true strength of the attack until it came smashing down upon the asur.

Malus laughed grimly to himself as he watched the mass of slave-soldiers being herded towards the walls. The Naggorites were again acting as a screen for better, more valuable fighters. Every arrow that pierced one of the slaves, every bolt that skewered the marching spearmen, was directed, naturally, at those nearest the wall. The asur didn't target the ranks behind, that great solid mass of druchii who stormed onwards, the whips of their masters snapping at them and forcing them on. Perhaps, if Shrinastor and the other mages weren't already occupied, they might have noticed something, detected some hint of the glamour Drusala had worked. But the mages didn't have the luxury of such wariness, not with their arcane duels unfolding all along the wall.

Piercing, bestial cries announced that other foes had noticed the deception, or at least had become aware of the great magic being worked at the rear of the Naggorites. Rising from the walls, their plumage burning like molten bronze, the phoenixes circled above the Eagle Gate, a fiery flock that was now stirring itself to action.

Malus had anticipated this as well. He'd placed his most dependable vassal, Silar Thornblood, with the contingent from Clar Karond. Silar had strict orders. When the phoenixes took wing, the beast-masters were to throw open the cages they had wheeled all the way from the *Eternal Malediction*.

Looking towards the ground the warriors of Clar Karond held, Malus watched as a great swarm rose shrieking and howling into the sky. Harpies, cruel twisted beasts cast in the roughest semblance of she-elves, with great clawed talons for feet and leathery wings sprouting from their backs. They were vile, despicable creatures, eager to torment the weak and helpless, to glut themselves upon the dead. Great flocks of them had followed the black arks – indeed, many of them had been captured in the *Eternal Malediction*'s rigging – hungry for the victims the druchii slaughtered.

Sometimes exhibiting a vicious cunning, the harpies were still little more than beasts and it was the instinct of beasts that moved them now. It didn't matter to the winged fiends that there were scores of dead druchii lying before the Eagle Gate. It didn't enter their minds to question the battle unfolding around them. Neither hunger nor curiosity governed them now. It was simple brute aggression, the fury of an animal that senses a rival in its domain. Creatures of the sky, the harpies viewed the flock of phoenixes as trespassers, intruders to be destroyed or driven away.

Even as the largest of the phoenixes, a great bird whose plumage was the colour of sapphire and diamond, started to dive towards the shaded palanquin where Drusala worked her enchantment, the harpies hurled themselves upon the phoenixes. The aerial battle was primal, primordial in its savagery. The harpies were immolated by the fires of the phoenixes, their charred bodies sent plummeting down into the massed druchii below. Sheer numbers, however, overwhelmed several of the birds. As they were slashed by the talons of their foes, burning blood spattered across the battlefield, a sizzling rain that scorched the flesh of whatever it struck. One of the phoenixes, several harpies clinging to it with their talons and mauling it with their clawed hands, went smashing down into the battlements. The fiery bird exploded as it perished, immolating its killers and the hapless asur manning that part of the wall.

The immediate threat of the phoenixes removed, Malus gave the command for the second assault to begin. Nearby, a blood-red banner was unfurled. It was the sign the waiting reaper bolt throwers had been waiting for. The fiendish engines began to pepper the face of the great gates with enormous steel arrows, each as long and thick as an elf's leg. Dark enchantments had been invested into the bolts, and as the magazines of the repeating bolt throwers churned away, the face of the Eagle Gate was pitted and scarred. Cupolas disintegrated beneath the barrage, sending archers hurtling to their deaths far below. Turrets crumbled, raining rubble onto the walls and smashing the defenders into paste.

In time with the assault by the reapers, Aeich and his corsairs launched their own attack on the left flank. Grappling irons were hurled onto the battlements while crossbows strove to hold the asur back. From behind their screen of militia and slaves, the murderous corsairs raced to the walls, their sea-dragon cloaks glistening with an oily sheen as the sun shone upon them.

The attack by the corsairs threw the asur into a panic. Here, the defenders seemed certain, was the main thrust of Malus's attack. From his vantage, he could see them diverting troops from other parts of the wall, determined to keep the corsairs from gaining a foothold on the battlements. Dozens of corsairs fell screaming as their grapples and ladders were cast down; scores more died as they tried to climb the ropes, their bodies spitted by asur arrows.

Malus waited until the corsair assault showed the first, faint hint of being driven back. Again, he motioned to the highborn bearing his signal flags. This time the banner that was unfurled was green. Even Spite seemed to understand the meaning behind that signal, the horned one hissing lowly as the command was relayed. Malus laughed at his steed's temper. He wondered what horror the asur would feel when they saw the next attack.

The great block of troops behind the Naggorites burst through their ranks, charging through the slave-soldiers as though they weren't there. The Naggorites scattered in all directions, heedless of the arrows that continued to persecute them from the walls.

Some hundreds fell, smashed beneath the force that now surged through their ranks.

Drusala's glamour vanished, winking out like a snuffed candle. Where a body of slave-soldiers and their overseers had been, there now charged a dozen war hydras and their minders.

Absolute panic gripped the asur. Malus could see archers hurriedly reacting to the charging beasts, many of them leaning out from between the crenellations to loose upon the hydras. These fell victim to the bolts of druchii darkshards, plummeting from the walls. Some few sent arrows into the hydras, but the effort was far too feeble to arrest the reptilian assault.

Bolt throwers were hastily turned back to the gate, their powerful missiles smashing into the war hydras. The monsters simply snapped and gnawed at the spears embedded in their scaly flesh. Drugged by their meal of the night before, they felt no pain, the tiny brains in their many heads aware only of the burning hunger gnawing at their bellies.

More and more bowfire was unleashed against the war hydras. Now the crackle of magic struck at the beasts. Malus clenched his fist in triumph as he saw asur spearmen trying to dislodge rubble from the shattered turrets onto the heads of the monsters. Between the hydras and the corsairs, the asur were completely committed now. Two deadly foes snapped at their fortifications, enemies too dangerous to ignore.

The asur commander would doubtless be committing his reserves, any caution abandoned in the face of the double assault. Yvarin, like all of his weakling breed, valued the warriors who served under him. He'd project that same attitude onto his enemy. That was a bit of arrogance that was going to cost him. Malus didn't care how many lives he squandered. There were thousands more waiting to die so that he might have the glory of seizing the Eagle Gate!

Prince Yvarin would never guess that both of these perilous assaults were but feints. While the garrison was occupied with these distractions, Malus would be leading the real assault.

How many troops had the asur dared leave to guard the breach?

From behind the gruesome rampart of slaughtered cold ones, the Eataine Guard watched as the druchii assault intensified. Corsairs were mounting an assault on the walls, trying to secure even the smallest presence there so that they could open the way for the mass of black-armoured infantry below. The rampaging war hydras threw themselves against the silver and starwood doors of the gate itself. Two of the beasts had been felled by eagle claw bolt throwers, while three more of the monsters writhed in their death throes as magical fire was poured down on them from spouts and murder holes. Still, the surviving reptiles flung themselves at the gate, clawing it with their feet and spitting at it with their venom.

A grim silence held the Eataine Guard. They felt shame at watching their comrades fighting all across the wall while their own position was as quiet as the tomb. They longed to throw themselves at the enemy; in their minds rang the bloody song of Khaine, the call to war that stirred the heart of every elf. Unlike the foul druchii, the asur knew better than to give themselves wholly to the Bloody-handed God. Khaine had his place, he had his purpose, but the elf who harkened only to his war-song would soon become a monster. The example set by the druchii was proof of that.

A murmur swept through the white-clad warriors, astonishment as they found their commander, Prince Yvarin, returning to the breach. His arm was still swaddled in the arcane poultice Shrinastor had fashioned for him. It was crafted from feathers donated by the phoenixes and its glow shone out from beneath the prince's armour, exuding a warmth that brought beads of perspiration to the brows of those standing too near. Yvarin's shattered shield had been replaced by one gifted to him by the captain of the Silver Pelts, a mark of esteem and solidarity from the contingent from Chrace. Not to be outdone, the Talons of Tor Caldea had bestowed on him a breastplate of finely wrought ithilmar and obsidian, which, they claimed, had been forged in dragonfire by the mightiest dragon mages.

Prince Yvarin was uneasy about the heroic regard he was afforded by his troops. After the thwarting of Darkblade's first assault, Yvarin had been hailed as a champion of his people, his deeds at the wall magnified in the telling and the retelling until even the Caledorians were whispering his name in awed respect. He'd become the rallying point for his entire garrison. Elves who had gazed upon the size and evil of Darkblade's horde, who had felt the tremor of fear and doom in their hearts, now spoke of triumph and glory. Resignation to fate had been replaced with greater purpose: victory! To win the battle, not simply wear down the druchii host and break the impetus of their invasion. To finish it here and now, not lay the seeds from which would grow the triumph of another army. To be the victors themselves, not the martyred dead of future remembrance.

It was humbling to have such hope vested in him. But while Yvarin had dreamed of fame and glory, he now found it had a sour taste. Never before had he felt the weight of responsibility lie so heavily upon his shoulders. The entire garrison was united behind him; no longer disparate contingents from the ten kingdoms, they had embraced a new identity – the defenders of the Eagle Gate. He'd told them as much in the speech he'd given after Shrinastor administered to his hurts. He had been stunned by the cheers and salutes his sentiment had been met with. Not the cries of warriors resigned to their duty, but of true hope.

Darkblade's second assault was much grander than that first

bold dash to the breach. Yvarin had hoped to deceive his enemy away from where the fortress was weakest. As he'd commanded his troops from the ramparts, as he'd watched the druchii attack unfold, a terrible premonition had occurred to him. He'd shown guile in trying to draw Darkblade away from the breach. Why should he expect anything less from the infamous Tyrant of Hag Graef?

The corsairs on the walls, the war hydras at the gate, these were both terrible foes, but perhaps that was exactly why they'd been set loose. Thunder to distract from the lightning. From the beak of the eagle, Yvarin had studied the deployment of Darkblade's army. As the war hydras burst out from their glamour and trampled the druchii warriors screening them, the first alarm sounded in Yvarin's brain. The survivors of the treacherous assault by the hydras were being reformed, whipped and threatened back into positions away from the gates. The haste and brutality of the slavemasters indicated that whatever purpose the regrouping had, it was both important and urgent. As they reformed at the other side of the hydras and away from the corsairs, it appeared to Yvarin that there was only one possible reason for these actions. Darkblade intended another assault on the breach.

The commanders subordinate to Yvarin didn't agree with his conclusion. Jariel had demurred at his suggestion that the Talons of Tor Caldea withdraw from the fight on the walls and strike out to the slopes of the pass to support the Eataine Guard at the breach. She'd posited that the druchii were reforming in order to rush in once the hydras were through the gate. She didn't agree with Yvarin's observation that the enemy would have put fresh warriors at the ready to act as shock troops. The druchii were as merciless to their own as they were to their enemy – she'd seen as much fighting raiders along the coasts of Caledor. She wasn't about to pull her troops out of the fight to support an attack she didn't feel was coming. The other commanders held similar views, and impressed on Yvarin that to pull any warriors from where there was already an attack would be to weaken their positions just at the time when they needed them at their strongest.

Yvarin was certain, however, that the real attack would be here. So it was back to the breach, back to the Eataine Guard, where he felt his place must be. When Darkblade made his move, it would be too late. Yvarin felt he'd anticipated the enemy. If his commanders were right, the absence of one asur on the walls wouldn't count for much. If, as he was convinced, the druchii moved again against the breach, his presence there might make all the difference. He was, after all, a hero now.

The salutes of his soldiers warmed Yvarin even more than the poultice Shrinastor had provided him. He returned their salutes with the terse nod that was expected of an elven prince, but his shining eyes told them how deeply their esteem was valued. Of all his troops, there were none he felt closer to than these warriors. To have earned their respect was a richness beyond gold.

Oerleith, the captain of the regiment, his family heraldry picked out in crimson thread against the white cloak he wore over his silver-chased armour, bowed as the prince approached him. 'Your highness, you do us a supreme honour,' he said, his eyes downcast. 'Everything has been quiet in this quarter. Except for the odd harpy dropping down from the sky, the enemy has lost interest in us.'

A tinge of hurt crept into Yvarin's eyes. Even these, his proud Eataine Guard, felt he should be elsewhere, that he should be up on the walls or at the gates inspiring his troops where the fighting was at its worst. They too didn't see the threat that Yvarin saw.

'I haven't lost interest in you,' Yvarin said. 'The breach here is the key to the Eagle Gate. Darkblade knows that as keenly as I do. Why should we believe he won't attack here?'

The captain raised his head, turning a look of confusion and astonishment on his prince. 'The druchii are already assaulting the walls and the gate. Darkblade is losing hundreds of his soldiers. He'd gain nothing by such an expensive feint.'

'He'd gain something more precious to him than the lives of his warriors,' Yvarin said. 'He'd gain time.'

Even as he spoke, warning horns sounded from the battlements. Yvarin and Oerleith rushed to the piled carcasses of the cold ones. They watched as the reformed slave-soldiers came marching towards the breach. More significantly, however, beyond them marched thousands of druchii regulars, the banners of the Dark Crag itself flying above them. Too late, Yvarin's captains on the wall saw the accuracy of their prince's premonition. An orderly redeployment was impossible now. The dribs and drabs that could make their way down from the walls would be merely a gesture. If the breach were to hold, it would be thanks to the Eataine Guard.

Yvarin hoisted himself on top of one of the cold ones, his boot resting on the reptile's head. He drew his sword, the same blade that had killed the druchii captain. He turned and faced his warriors, the finest in his garrison, the comrades-in-arms who had held this position against the cold one knights. They'd braved the best Darkblade could throw at them. It was important that they knew this as the black tide of the tyrant's army came surging towards them.

'Sons of Ellyrion! Daughters of the Summer Kingdom! Gaze upon the desperation of your foe! You, who stood here and cut down the vanguard of his horde. You who shattered the point of his spear. Now he sends a flood of dogs to drown you in blood. He thinks to strike fear into your noble hearts by this show of force. I say to you that you spit on dogs! I say to you that your hearts know no fear! You are the Eataine Guard. Let Hag Graef send a hundred slaves against us. We will slay them all and ask the scum for another thousand. We will show them what the song of Khaine means when it is sung by those with valour in their hearts and courage in their souls!'

A great cheer rose from the Eataine Guard. With spears crashing against shields, the asur answered the fiery words of their hero. Almost eagerly, they ran to the grisly pile of dead reptiles, ready to repel the first waves of Darkblade's army. Their faith in their prince had blotted out the doubt that might have ruled them otherwise. They had longed for battle, and now that battle was coming to them. With Prince Yvarin fighting beside them, how could they fail to be victorious?

Malus's retainers stacked the corpses of the knights he had executed into a pile. Digging his spurs into Spite's flanks, he sent the horned one scrambling up onto the decaying mound. The reptile snarled, digging its claws into the dead flesh until it found the purchase it wanted. Malus waited until his steed was settled before he unsheathed the warpsword and raised it high. With a downward sweep, he thrust the blade in the direction of the breach. A single word left his lips, arctic in its tone.

'Advance!'

Obediently, the warriors of Hag Graef trooped towards the rampart of dead cold ones. Already the Naggorite slave-soldiers were engaging the asur, throwing themselves at the entrenched enemy with the fatalism of all sword-fodder. They were dying by the droves, but it was of little consequence. They weren't there to win; they were there to occupy the enemy long enough for Malus's real troops to bear down on the position. Indeed, if the Naggorites did manage to hold their ground they'd be slaughtered by the soldiers coming up from behind them for being in the way. Malus considered the promise of spilling Naggorite blood before laying into the asur to be something of a reward to the soldiers of Hag Graef. The heap of dead knights beneath Spite's claws was a reminder of the punishment they'd get if they proved unworthy of that reward.

The dreadspears stabbed their way through the few Naggorites holding against the asur. A blast from the serpent-tooth horn the first regiment carried announced that they were confronting the defenders. Malus watched for the signal flag to be raised, the signal that the spearmen were through. His patience wore thinner with each passing breath. After ten minutes had elapsed, he could see that the first regiment was beginning to fall back. The second regiment advanced, thwarting the withdrawal of the first. Malus smiled coldly as he saw the warriors of the reinforcing regiment cutting down any druchii trying to retreat from the front. The orders he had issued to his captains hadn't fallen on deaf ears. Every one of them understood what was expected.

Still, even the advance of the second regiment wasn't enough to break the defenders. Worse, they themselves were beset from the flank by Caledorian archers, who'd crept out onto the face of the cliffs flanking the pass. From their precarious perches, the bowmen harassed the second regiment. Darkshards were brought up to oppose the Caledorians, but the crafty asur had positioned themselves beyond the range of the druchii's crossbows.

The third and fourth regiments swarmed forwards now, rushing to bolster the flagging strength of the second and the remnants of the first. At last, Malus thought, the breach would be taken. His anger boiled inside him as the asur continued to hold. Minute after minute, with only the Caledorian bowmen to support them, the Eataine Guard held their ground. Outnumbered a hundredfold, they refused to yield!

Elsewhere, Malus could see that his feinting attackers were faltering. The corsairs were a ravaged shell of their original strength, their robust assaults reduced to cautious probes. The harpies had been burned from the sky by the phoenixes, leaving far too many of the magical birds free to menace the druchii sorceresses.

At the gate itself, the assault of the war hydras was likewise losing its impetus. Malus saw Griselfang scorched by a shower of arcane fire poured down on it from the spouts set into the fortifications above the gate. While the huge beast writhed in pain, bones popping through its charred hide, one of the phoenixes swooped down on it. A great bird of ice and crystal, larger and older than its fiery kin, the phoenix tore into Griselfang with talons that froze the hydra's mangled hide and caused its scales to crumble into shards of frost. As the phoenix beat at the hydra with its wings, each buffet seemed to drain more of the vitality and resistance from the reptile. Its heads drooped wearily as their long necks sagged to the earth. Its lashing tail became sluggish, incapable of swatting down its avian tormentor.

Too intent on Griselfang, the cold phoenix was taken by surprise when Snarclaw charged at it. Three of the hydra's heads sank their fangs into the bird, snowy ichor dripping from the grievous wounds it had inflicted. Even as frost began to form around the jaws that held the phoenix, Snarclaw was wrenching the creature free from the dying Griselfang. The bird slapped at the reptile with its great wings, freezing scales and sapping warmth with each touch of its icy pinions. Its other heads hissing at its prey, the hydra began to pull the phoenix apart with the jaws embedded in its body. Shrieking in agony, the phoenix was ripped to shreds, each portion of its mutilated frame freezing as it died, transforming into nothing more than slivers of ice.

Snarclaw had no time to savour its triumph. As it stood over the wreckage of the phoenix, the vengeful fire of the garrison stabbed down into it. Bolt throwers and bowmen all across the wall sought to avenge the cold phoenix. The hydra's scaly hide was pierced again and again by the missiles. In its agonies it threw itself towards the gates, there to have its flesh scorched by the same kind of molten fire that had burned Griselfang. Howling in agony, the reptile lumbered back, half of its heads lying dead and dragging behind it in the dust. Before it got more than a few yards, however, a great bolt of lightning hurtled down from the beak of the stone eagle, sent from the staff of the blue-robed elf who stood there. The arcane energies sapped the last of the hydra's monstrous vitality. With a final shudder, Snarclaw crashed to the ground and its remaining heads wilted into the dirt.

Malus cursed lividly as he saw his prize hydras cut down. The brutes had cost him a fortune. With them gone, he knew the runts Clar Karond had salvaged from their collapsing city wouldn't be able to batter their way through the gates. The asur would soon realise that, too. Then fresh forces would be diverted to the breach.

The breach! Seven regiments had now been thrown into the attack and still the Eataine Guard held their ground. What would it take to break those preening asur swine! Minutes of defiance stretched into hours. Fresh defenders could be seen scrambling down from the battlements to support the position, but the main opposition remained the Eataine Guard. Callously, Malus threw fresh troops into the assault. The ground around the breach became a mire of blood and bodies, yet he wouldn't relent. Any captain who dared think of withdrawal was butchered where he stood.

Finally, as night fell over the pass, even Malus had to accept the hideous truth. The attack had failed. He'd spent thousands of his soldiers, but the asur had held. With the darkness, the phoenixes diverted their attentions to the troops massed at the breach, swooping down on them in blazing dives that charred their victims and shattered the morale of those remaining. Assaulted from one flank by the Caledorian's arrows, the aerial attacks of the phoenixes were too much for the druchii. Their strength still in the thousands, the host of Hag Graef turned and retreated back down the pass.

Malus watched his soldiers run, cursing each and every one as a coward and worse. Threats of reprisal and revenge slashed across the fleeing warriors until the drachau's throat felt like a raw wound. Promises to torture their descendants to the fifth generation were not enough to turn his warriors back.

Turning away from the rout, Malus glared at the rampart of dead cold ones. He could see the Eataine Guard standing atop the bodies, jeering and mocking the fleeing druchii. One asur captain was even so bold as to hold out a captured banner, inviting the enemy to come back and take it.

These scenes were forgotten, however, when Malus trained his eyes on the solemn figure standing atop the rampart. There was a magical glow about the elf's shoulder and side, the place the warpsword had kissed. Malus recognised the helm and the sword in the asur's hand. Prince Yvarin, the foe who had cut down Vincirix!

Say the word, Malus. Set me loose and we can kill him. Now. We can avenge your little flesh-friend. Set me loose and we'll rip through the asur and make that princeling beg for death.

Angrily, Malus dug his heels into Spite, compelling the horned one to leap down from its perch. With a tug of the reins, he sent his steed loping back towards the druchii camp. He didn't trust himself to remain within sight of the enemy.

Not with the daemon's whispers in his ear.

THIRTEEN

There was no rest for the druchii warriors, no time for the drachau's slaves to lick their wounds. By dawn, the second assault against the Eagle Gate had been beaten back. An hour later, captains were forcing their regiments back into formation as slavemasters beat their charges back into the line. Through it all, the merciless gaze of Malus Darkblade swept across his soldiers. Every warrior could feel the hair at the back of his neck prickle and his skin crawl as he imagined the kiss of the warpsword against his flesh.

A stack of skulls rested before the drachau, heads cut from the latest victims of his ire. One soldier from every regiment, that had been the army's tithe to the dreadlord's wrath. Malus had personally cut down a hundred victims, playing the warpsword with such ferocity that his face was lost behind a patina of gore, his armour stained crimson with elven blood. Drusala and the sorceresses had been impressed into hasty service, atoning for their own failure in the battle by stripping the heads down to grinning skulls with their magic.

It was not enough. Not even the slightest gesture towards sating the fury burning inside Malus's black heart. He could feel Tz'arkan goading him on, growing stronger with each victim he claimed. He cared little. If these craven maggots lost the battle, he was dead anyway. It would be fitting punishment to turn the daemon loose upon them.

Malus crushed down that idea. That was the daemon talking, trying to make its desires sound like the drachau's own thoughts. There was still a chance for glory here, if he were bold and swift. But it had to be soon. Already, he knew his army was on borrowed time. Scouts ranging behind his army had reported the Tiranocii force drawing closer. Hours, perhaps, remained before they would reach the pass. Malus had the scouts executed before word of what they had seen could be disseminated. His warriors had only one purpose – to take the Eagle Gate. Anything else was but a distraction. If they seized the fortress, there was no need to fear the chariots of Tiranoc. If they floundered before the walls again, death beneath the wheels of the Tiranocii was a better fate than they deserved.

Despite the contempt he held them in, Malus appreciated that a reckless attack would get him nowhere. Once the regiments were reformed and the wounded dispatched, he restrained himself. Hard as it was, he sat on Spite's back and watched as the sun slowly climbed into the sky. He could see the gleam of armour on the battlements, the fiery glow as the light reflected off the phoenixes' burning plumage. The enemy was there, waiting. They too were biding their time, thinking it to be their ally.

Malus intended to teach them the error of their thinking.

When the sun reached its zenith, when its brilliant rays shone down upon the pass and straight into the eyes of the elves on the battlements, Malus drew the warpsword and again snarled out the order to attack.

Thousands of druchii advanced upon the fortress once more.

Great blocks of infantry moved towards the great gates of starwood and silver, their faces pitted and scarred by the war hydras the day before. Aeich and the corsairs were doubly eager to claim the glory of seizing the gates – from their regiments Malus had demanded two victims instead of one. At their sides marched Naggorite slave-soldiers and the dreadspears of Clar Karond, both forces employing their heavy shields to fend off the archery of the asur. Harpies, those that had survived the night and been recaptured, were set loose to harry the defenders. Minds maddened by torture and magic, the harpies ran amok as they reached the asur, dragging them from behind the crenellations and tearing into them with claw and fang.

Drusala and the other sorceresses acted in concert now. They didn't ply their magic in individual duels with Shrinastor and the asur mages. Instead, they concentrated it into a great protective shell, raising it above the druchii army. While the sun thwarted the accuracy of the archers, the witches thwarted the accuracy of the spells loosed by the dragon mages and astromancers. The dark magic caught and twisted the lightning and fire called down by the asur mages, pooling the arcane energies into a dark, writhing cloud. When the cloud was powerful enough, Drusala herself sent it hurtling into the battlements. Elven warriors were slaughtered by the roiling fog of aethyric malevolence, tendrils of darkness whipping out to corrode armour and devour flesh, leaving only glistening skeletons behind.

As the attack on the gate gathered momentum, a third assault on the breach was set into motion. This time Malus didn't trust the attack to anyone but himself. He didn't leave the first charge to a lover and her knights, he didn't delegate the first wave to vassals and their warriors. He didn't linger behind and wait to see how the attack fared. This time, he led the push personally, commanding the soul-bonded warriors of his own tower, the drachau's private guard. At their back rode Dolthaic and the Knights of the Burning Dark, eager to redeem themselves in the eyes of their despotic master, only too aware that no other dreadlord would give them sanctuary should Malus fall.

Spite loped along with the soul-bonded dreadspears, the horned one snapping at those warriors too clumsy to keep their distance. The reptile disliked the nearness of allies as much as it despised the closeness of enemies, traits ingrained into its tiny brain from the moment it had hatched and found itself the runt of the nest. Malus did little to curb his steed's hostility. It reminded the soldiers of their place and warned them that death needn't come from an asur arrow or spear.

The rampart of dead cold ones drew ever closer. Malus could see the asur spearmen defending the morbid barrier. One of them turned his head and shouted to someone behind him. A moment later, a volley of arrows came arching up from the ward beyond the broken wall. Dozens of the dreadspears were struck as the barrage came raining down upon them. Those who fell were trampled by those who followed behind them. It didn't need the threats of the drachau to keep the spearmen moving. They knew they were within range of the enemy bows now. The only remedy for that was to get stuck in, engage the Eataine Guard and force the archers to hold back lest they strike friend instead of foe.

The rank smell of decaying cold ones struck Malus's senses as his assault closed upon the ghoulish obstacle. Just as he came near the barrier, he gave Spite a vicious kick in its flanks. The horned one responded with a powerful leap that brought it pouncing onto the top of the barrier. The carcass of a cold one was dislodged, sliding free to drop onto the asur below. Malus laughed as the elves caught beneath the reptilian body tried to squirm free. With deliberate viciousness, he caused Spite to drop down onto the carcass,

adding his own and the horned one's weight to that already crushing the trapped asur. Screaming in pain, his white-clad enemies
flailed in abject misery.

The suddenness of Malus's assault caught the other Eataine Guard
by surprise. Prepared to stab their spears through gaps in the macabre wall at enemies trying to climb it, ready to repel foes who tried
to circle around it, they were unprepared for an adversary who
was already over the barrier. In a few heartbeats, the warpsword
wrought a grim harvest from the startled warriors. Spite's jaws
snapped shut upon the arm of an elf wearing the heraldry of an
Ellyrian noble. A turn of the reptile's head wrenched the limb from
its socket, sending the elf lurching back, feebly trying to staunch
the welter of blood spurting from his mangled body.

Before the Eataine Guard could concentrate their efforts against
Malus, soul-bonded druchii were scrambling up and over the reptilian wall. Spears stabbed down into the asur, spitting them like
pigs. It took only a few moments for the druchii to jump down and
secure the foothold they had gained, their iron-shod boots stamping out any life that clung to the elves they had impaled. Around
the flanks of the dreadspears came Dolthaic and the Knights of the
Burning Dark, who barrelled into the asur and hurled them back.

The orderly defence that had resisted the last assault was quickly
smashed aside by Malus's troops. The drachau exulted as he butchered every asur he could reach. Spite's jaws were foul with elven
blood and strips of elven flesh. Within, he could feel Tz'arkan
responding to the carnage, the daemon's presence swelling and
expanding.

'This is my glory!' Malus snarled at the thing inside him.

*Is this glory? Even for a mortal, you are delusional, Malus. Look
about you, fool.*

The daemon's mockery stabbed at Malus like an icy dagger. He pulled back on Spite's reins, forcing the bloodthirsty reptile to heel. He ignored the fray unfolding around him, seized the moment to appreciate the broader situation. His face contorted into a mask of inhuman rage.

The Eataine Guard weren't trying to hold the rampart, they were falling back. They were trying to draw his warriors deeper into the breach. They were trying to pull them into a trap! He could see Prince Yvarin, the glow of magic still burning beneath his armour, leading the slow withdrawal. Nothing that would alert the druchii and make them suspicious, but now Malus could see through the methodical retreat.

He could order his troops to withdraw, to avoid the jaws of whatever deceit Yvarin planned. To do so, however, would shatter the entire assault. He'd lose another day trying to orchestrate another thrust. Another day for reinforcements to arrive. The Tiranocii would be at his rear by then, certainly. The dragons of Caledor, too, might take wing and fly to the Eagle Gate's rescue. He couldn't risk that. There could be no more delays. This attack *would* succeed. It *must* succeed!

Victory is in your power, Malus. Do you have the courage to claim it?

The druchii continued to swarm the barrier and pursue the Eataine Guard past the broken walls beyond. Malus sneered. Yvarin had overplayed his hand. He was thinking like a soft, pampered prince of the Inner Kingdoms. What matter if his trap cost Malus a hundred soldiers? Two hundred? There were more. He could afford to drown the entire garrison in blood. The host of Hag Graef alone still outnumbered the garrison a hundredfold. He would mock Yvarin for his arrogance before he ripped out the maggot's heart.

Roaring, Malus goaded his troops onwards, funnelling them into the gap, driving them at the Eataine Guard with the fury of a tempest. 'One step back!' he raged. 'One step back and you shall feel the kiss of Khaine!' He brought the warpsword flashing down into the helm of the nearest dreadspear, splitting the reinforced steel and shearing through the skull inside. The murdered warrior collapsed where he stood. Those around him redoubled their efforts to gain the walls.

'What need have I of daemons?' Malus spat at the beast inside him.

What need, Malus. Shall I tell you?

Tz'arkan's slithering words stoked the furnace of Malus's wrath. He wouldn't let the daemon's mockery poison the moment of his triumph. Savagely, he kicked Spite and sent the horned one rushing through the ranks of dreadspears. The push into the ward beyond the wall had faltered. He would know why.

Through his soul-bonded soldiers, Malus forced his reptilian steed onwards. Those elves who failed to leap out of the way were crushed underfoot. At last he reached the open ground within the ward itself. He felt his heart turn cold when he saw the battle unfolding. His dreadspears were beset on three sides by Yvarin's troops. The Eataine Guard held the ground directly before the invaders, but from the sides it was regiments adorned in the colours and lion-skins of Chrace that fought the druchii, their heavy war-axes crunching through armour and snapping bones with each strike. Archers from Ellyrion stood upon the inner walls, loosing arrows into the rear ranks of Malus's troops, felling them before they could fight their way to the front ranks.

Magnificent, are they not?

Malus could feel the daemon snicker at him. It took but a glance to understand its meaning. The archers on the walls, the Chracian axemen – these weren't the beleaguered warriors from the last two days. Their armour and raiment wasn't grimy with the foulness of war. These were fresh troops, fighters new to the battle. In the early morning, while Malus waited on the sun, the Eagle Gate had been reinforced!

The blast of a warning horn far back in the pass carried to Malus's ears, magnified and made more distinct to him by the perfidy of Tz'arkan. Tiranoc! The chariots had reached the druchii camp. The rear of his army was now beset by yet another asur host.

What glory for a fool? But, then, your king didn't expect you to win here. He expected you to die.

Snarling, Malus drove Spite forwards. The horned one swatted the druchii in its way, lashing out with fang and claw. With a lunge, it brought its master into battle. The warpsword sang out as it cleaved through the breastplate of a warrior of the Eataine Guard. Spite's jaws clamped tight about the head of a Chracian hunter.

Victory, Malus. It can still be yours. You can still have the last laugh over your king. Free me. Release me. The wild magic of these mountains rages through this land, and I have supped deeply from the storm. The pain and anguish of these mortals invigorates me. If I wanted, I could free myself, but we have been companions for so very long. It would sadden me if you weren't able to enjoy the carnage with me.

'Lies,' Malus snapped. An asur spear glanced across his knee, the warrior behind it exploiting his distraction. The drachau brought his deadly blade sweeping around, reducing the elf's face to a bloodied pulp.

What need have I for lies? You know the truth as well as I. You can feel it in your very bones. Are there not enough enemies here already, Malus? Must we fight one another as well? Think of what defeat means, Malus. Think of the Witch King laughing at you. Think of the honour and glory Prince Yvarin will enjoy, slayer of Malus Darkblade... and his lover!

Malus felt himself turning sick inside. Defeat was bitter enough to accept, but to know that in defeat he would further the ambitions of his enemies was too much to bear. How long had he resisted Tz'arkan? How many sleepless nights and hideous days? Every hour feeling the daemon's thoughts nagging at him, urging him to relent, to allow it to go free.

He knew how mighty Tz'arkan was. He knew that it never made promises it wouldn't keep. If it claimed it could still snatch victory from the jaws of defeat, it could do so.

'Very well,' Malus whispered. 'I release you, Tz'arkan. Together we will kill them all.'

We will kill them all, the daemon repeated. In that moment, Malus felt the fiend's essence boiling inside him, rising up, flowing through every nerve and every vein. Spite bucked and flailed, the horned one's terror so great that the straps of its saddle snapped and Malus was flung to the ground. Dimly he saw his loyal steed fleeing back through the press of dreadspears. Around him, druchii and asur alike drew back, gazing in horror at the fallen drachau.

It was different this time. As the pain of possession wracked him, Malus knew something was wrong. Having his body usurped by Tz'arkan was never a pleasant experience, but this time the agony was unspeakable. Screams pierced his ears, and it took the greatest effort to appreciate that the screams he heard were his own.

Now, Malus, it is your turn to be the spectator. Your chance to be the parasite. After a few centuries, you may even enjoy the experience.

Malus's skin began to flow like water, dripping away from his body, exposing the raw meat and muscle beneath. His bones began to expand, popping and cracking as they assumed new dimensions and adopted new shapes. The drachau's screams rose to a piercing wail, a cry of agony that ripped at the souls of all who heard it, tugging at them, dragging at them, trying to pull them into the private hell of the damned. The druchii and asur around the stricken tyrant backed away, retreating heedlessly into the blades of comrades and foes yet unaware of the horror unfolding so near to them.

A cackle of daemonic mirth rasped from the elongated jaws that distorted the drachau's face. Armour cracked and split, sloughing away from the transforming body in patches of twisted steel. The torn rags of Malus's rich garments fluttered in the wind as his body continued to expand, doubling in size, then redoubling once more. Long, razor-like spines erupted from his back, great horns sprouted from his forehead. Facial features withered into a skull-like semblance, eyes burned away to become embers of aethyric malevolence. The elf's long black hair thickened into a mane of worms, writhing and squirming with obscene vitality. The bubbling mass of flesh reshaped itself into thick cords of muscle; legs lengthened and broadened into pillars of bone and sinew. Thick, ape-like arms ended in blade-like talons.

The warpsword alone remained unfazed by the transformation, seeming little more than a puny knife in the clawed fist of the unleashed monster. Then it too began to change, expanding, growing into a giant blade of darkness, the weapon of some primordial titan or maniacal god.

Tz'arkan threw back its skull-like head and roared in triumph. Free! It was free! The roar that erupted from its daemonic lungs deafened the elves nearest it, shattering their eardrums. Tz'arkan the daemon king walked the mortal world once more!

One of the Eataine Guard was Tz'arkan's first victim, cut in half by a single stroke of the warpsword, his torso flung far across the battlefield. The daemon could feel the elf's soul drawn into itself, feeding the insatiable furnace of its own malefic essence. The taste brought a howl of delight from the monster. Greed, the insatiable hunger for mortal energies, flared through the daemon's mind. It had intended to keep the spirit of its bargain with Malus, to kill only the asur and spare the druchii. Now, however, it was minded to obey only the letter of their compact.

'We will kill them all,' Tz'arkan hissed, enjoying the terror that flared up from that tiny parasitic awareness lurking at the edge of its consciousness, that impotent spectator that shared its eyes. The feeble ghost that had been Malus Darkblade.

The daemon king swung around, slashing the warpsword across the druchii spearmen in its shadow. A score of elves were cut down in the blink of an eye, torn asunder by the daemon's strength and the warpsword's bite. The released spirit of each victim was channelled into Tz'arkan, further stoking the dark energies within it.

Tz'arkan howled once more. It could feel the terror of its victims and its future victims wash over it. It could feel the envy of its brother daemons, watching it from beyond the veil, straining to pierce the barrier, to emerge from the Realm of Chaos and join it in the feast. A thought, a gesture on its part, and they would be through. The daemon king laughed. The feast was rich and it had no intention of sharing. It forced down the perverse temptation to tear wide the rift. Later, perhaps, when the screams of mortals ceased to amuse it, it would let its brothers indulge themselves.

Druchii and asur alike attacked the daemon now. Dreadspears fought alongside the Eataine Guard, Knights of the Burning Dark made common cause with Chracian hunters. Spears stabbed into the monster from every side. Lances pierced its back, fangs snapped at its legs, axes hacked at its belly, swords slashed at its flanks. Tz'arkan laughed at the pathetic assault. Ichor bubbled from its wounds, closing them as soon as the violating steel was withdrawn. It plied the warpsword to left and right, spilling its enemies in every direction, each slaughtered soul serving to speed its own regeneration and invest yet more strength in its limbs.

Then, for an instant, Tz'arkan hesitated. The Eataine Guard retreated before it, but a lone warrior came striding out from their ranks. The daemon chuckled. How bold and stalwart Prince Yvarin looked, how heroically he marched to his doom. What would his vassals think, what would they say, if they could taste the desperation and fear their leader tried to hide so carefully?

Look, Malus, he is here, Tz'arkan taunted the drachau's spirit. *Pay close attention, because you surrendered more than you know just to enjoy this moment.*

The daemon reached out for Yvarin, but its arrogance, its savouring of Malus's emotions, was a distraction. The prince dived under the monster's claw and struck. The runesword, the fabulous blade that had been handed down for thousands of years, burned brighter than the sun as it slashed across the daemon's hide. Ancient enchantments blazed up from the blade, searing through the ghastly essence of Tz'arkan. The ichor that bubbled from this wound didn't knit the flesh together, didn't undo the hurt visited upon the daemon. Steaming, blackening the ground it fell upon, the ichor slopped from the cut in a continuous flow, each drop sapping some of the fiend's hideous vitality.

Yvarin started to shout in triumph, to cry out to his warriors – even to the druchii – that the beast could be hurt, the daemon could be slain. The sound died on his lips as one clawed hand closed about his runesword as he drew it from the wound. Another seized him by the neck. Tz'arkan glared at the prince with a malignity far beyond anything even Malus could have shown him.

'That hurt,' Tz'arkan growled as it crushed Yvarin's neck like a rotten stick. A flick of the daemon's claw sent the dead hero's head spinning off into the battlements.

Tz'arkan looked across the horrified ranks of the Eataine Guard as the asur began to fall back.

'Which of you wants to keep your prince company?' it called out in challenge as it stalked after them.

Drusala sensed the moment when Tz'arkan was released. The daemon's essence blazed like a pillar of fire to her witchsight, an infernal flare almost blinding in its brilliance. Amid the tumult of battle, the aethyric reverberations struck with the impact of a thunderbolt. The lesser sorceresses around her were knocked off their feet, sent tumbling through the dust, blood trickling from their ears and eyes. It would be hours before they could recover from the arcane shock and once again unleash their sorcery. Only she had the skill and power to shield herself – left shaken but otherwise unharmed.

The one consolation was that the shock wave hadn't played favourites. The phoenixes had been sent shrieking away from the ramparts, spinning crazily up towards the mountains as they fled the daemon king's return. Drusala knew the asur mages would be suffering the same debilitation as the druchii sorceresses. They'd be out of the fight for some time.

Only one of the enemy wizards remained. Without any other mages practising their art, it was comparatively simple for Drusala to detect the workings of Shrinastor's magic. Like her own, the loremaster's willpower and knowledge had been strong enough to shield him from the aethyric blast. Now he was trying to conjure a spell that would curb the daemon's rampage.

That wouldn't play into Drusala's plans. She'd waited months for Malus to become weak enough to let loose the daemon. Now that Tz'arkan was free, she wasn't about to lose this opportunity to the loremaster's meddling. Snapping stern orders to Absaloth and the spearmen from Ghrond, Drusala dashed to her dark pegasus. A single word from her sent the winged steed soaring up into the sky. She laughed as archers loosed arrows at her, the missiles exploding into splinters as they crashed against the magical shell she'd woven about her steed.

High up in the beak of the stone eagle, Drusala could see Shrinastor siphoning magic down from the mountains into the head of his staff. It was a bold, even reckless conjuring for the mage to perform. She smiled maliciously. The loremaster was panicking, he was trying to draw too much too fast. He knew how powerful Tz'arkan was. He knew that no simple conjuration could restrain it. Pride, desperation, some foolish notion of duty – something made him unwilling to accept that reality. He was trying to hasten his spell by feeding more and more magic into it. The failing of the asur, the great weakness of their decadent breed, was that they couldn't accept when it was necessary to watch their own kind die.

The sorceress brought her pegasus soaring towards the eagle. A bolt of black lightning incinerated a clutch of archers who tried to drive her away. She stretched forth her hand and a cloud of dark, poisonous fog enveloped the bolt throwers as their crews tried to train the weapons on her. From the head of her staff, a finger of darkness struck out, ripping the souls from the armoured swordsmen who surrounded Shrinastor.

Laughing with murderous delight, Drusala leapt down from the back of her pegasus and danced over the bodies of her victims. She was alone upon the beak of the eagle. A blast of arcane fire melted the bronze door leading inside the fortress, transforming it into a wall of metal, ensuring that no rescuers would be able to rush up from below. Then she turned her attention to the loremaster.

Shrinastor had drawn a complex protective circle about himself, the asur rendition of the mandala employed by the druchii. Drusala scowled at the glowing glyphs, knowing the power they contained. It would be no easy thing, breaking such a ward.

The winds of aethyric energy Shrinastor was drawing down into the circle appeared to her magically attuned eyes as a translucent spiral of whirling colour and light. There was darkness there, too, but only the smallest traces. The mage was trying to strain the darker energies from his spell. That observation gave Drusala an idea.

Raising her staff high, Drusala whipped it through the air overhead. Faster and faster she spun the staff, and with each rotation, wisps of crawling darkness appeared in the air. The shadows coiled together, slithering into a thick morass of blackness, a patch of midnight thrust into the light of day. With a gesture, the sorceress sent the nexus of dark magic streaming into the aethyric spiral Shrinastor was calling down.

It wasn't malignant in its own right. All she had done was send more power into the energy Shrinastor was summoning. That lack of focus, that absence of immediate malevolence, allowed the dark magic to shower down into the circle. At once, it had an effect.

Shrinastor's eyes, previously unfocused and staring down towards the breach, now took on an expression of horror. His face became contorted, though his lips maintained the discipline to continue his conjuration. By degrees, the bright glyphs turned dark, their shine becoming more shadowy with each heartbeat. Threads of blackness began to ripple through the loremaster's body, squirming inside his veins.

Shrinastor's lips faltered, a syllable of his spell was lost. At once, the elf's mouth became distorted, twisting until the lower jaw tore away. Before it could strike the ground, flesh and bone had dissolved into soot. The dissolution spread as the rampant magic – far too much for the loremaster to control – ripped him apart. A hand detached itself, sprouted chitinous wings and flew away. An ear exploded into green flame, melting its way through the asur's tall helm. Lungs tore through the ribs that held them, expanding in an insane spasm of unrestrained growth.

Amidst the horrors assailing his body, Shrinastor was able to turn his gaze upon Drusala. In that last moment, a look of shocked recognition shone there. Then the eyes dissolved like wax, spilling down his face in a gelatinous tide.

Drusala sneered at the dying loremaster. Before she turned her own attention to the breach, she intensified the spells that guarded her. It might be that Tz'arkan's release had weakened some of them. It wouldn't do to take any chances.

Not until it was too late to stop her plans.

'Set spears!' Silar Thornblood shouted at the dreadspears around him. He could see the warriors hesitate. He could understand their alarm. The ground beneath their feet trembled with the fury of the Tiranoc chariots as they came rushing down the pass. Only the discipline of centuries as warriors of the Hag kept them in formation, that and the appreciation that if they tried to run now they would be slaughtered. If they held their ground, at least they had some slight chance.

Silar wasn't putting too much trust in those chances. As soon as his orders were given, he was falling back. He had other forces to command. Forces that had a real chance to blunt the asur attack.

The chariots came rushing from the distance, their silver-chased armour gleaming in the sun. Each of the chariots was drawn by two powerful horses, matched animals that had been paired for exactness of stamina, speed and strength. Two elves rode in each chariot, an armoured driver and a bowman. While the driver charged the lethal mass of the chariot towards the dreadspears, the archer loosed arrows into the massed ranks, felling warriors with each draw of the string.

Whether out of discipline or resignation, the dreadspears held their ground. Troops from the rear ranks stepped forward to replace those shot down by the archers. Horns blared, advising the soldiers how much distance yet lay between them and the enemy. When the chariots finally crashed into the ranks, a few were brought down by the wall of spears. Most, however, barrelled through, their pounding hooves and bladed wheels slashing through the packed druchii.

When the chariots won clear, however, they found Silar waiting for them. Two hundred darkshards arrayed in a double-rank opposed them now. At Silar's command, they fired their repeating crossbows into the asur. A thousand bolts punched into the chariots, slaughtering elves and horses alike. Of the Tiranocii who punched their way through the dreadspears, not a single chariot was able to retreat back into the pass and regroup with the rest of their army.

A shout, a cheer of murderous triumph, rose from Silar's troops. Even if for only a moment, the army of Hag Graef had driven off their attackers. The druchii gave small concern to the spearmen who had been sacrificed to bait the trap. Destruction of the asur was all that mattered at the moment.

With the cheers of his troops still ringing in his ears, Silar turned and gazed towards the Eagle Gate. If Malus could only seize the breach, they might yet claim the fortress.

Then his gaze rose to the skies above the Eagle Gate and Silar knew that the time for fantasies about victory was over. There was no victory for them here, only the ignominy of a useless death.

In the sky, Silar could see mighty shapes soaring towards the fortress, great winged figures of gold and crimson. What Malus had feared from the start had come to pass. The dragons of Caledor had been awakened.

The dragons were coming to save the Eagle Gate.

FOURTEEN

A resounding cheer rose from the battlements as the dragon princes of Caledor soared into the pass. Banners were unfurled, flags waved wildly, trumpets blared. The Eagle Gate was saved! There wasn't a chance the hated druchii could take the fortress now. In the hour of need, Caledor had come.

For the druchii in the pass, the immense reptiles flying towards the fortress were nothing less than heralds of utter doom. Many of these warriors had stood against the hordes of the Witchguard of Naggor and their doom-wings. The flying demi-reptiles had seemed terrible, then. Now the memory of the doom-wings was blotted out by the enormity of the dragons. The smallest was thirty feet from horned snout to spined tail. Many were far larger, two and even three times as great. Coated in thick scales of white and gold, each of their powerful legs tipped in mighty claws, their reptilian heads adorned with sharp horns and spiny crests, the dragons were a terrifying sight. Their great leathery wings fanned the air, sending a hot, mephitic wind into the pass, the musky odour feared across the world as 'wyrmreek.'

Silar Thornblood didn't bother to redeploy his troops. If they scattered into the hills, some of them might survive, for a time, until the shadow warriors of Nagarythe tracked them down. For Silar, the verminous existence of a hunted creature didn't appeal to him. Defiantly, he held his head high and watched as the dragons began to descend. Around him, most of the druchii followed his fatalistic example. They were resigned to die and dragonfire would present them with a speedy death.

The roars of the dragons were louder than any thunder as the ancient reptiles hurtled down from the sky. The druchii cried out, final prayers to Khaine, as they saw their doom rushing down upon them. Then, abruptly, the great dragons turned, swung away from the army of Hag Graef. Silar blinked in utter shock as he saw the wyrms dive upon the Eagle Gate. The dragonfire he had expected to feel melting the flesh from his own bones was now unleashed upon the asur behind the battlements. By the hundreds, the horrified garrison were transformed into living torches, their blazing bodies raining down from the walls.

Now, Silar noticed for the first time that among the red and gold wyrms of Caledor, there were creatures of a far different and darker cast. Black-scaled dragons from Naggaroth! He could see the Caledorian nobles on the backs of the other dragons, but astride each of the black beasts there was a druchii lordling.

Silar was slow to accept the evidence of his eyes. Caledor had betrayed the asur! They had sided with Malekith! Even when he saw a flight of dragons swoop away from the walls and glide down into the pass to assault the host from Tiranoc, the highborn had difficulty accepting the unbelievable turn of events. Even as he watched the dragons of Caledor burn the asur with their fire while the dragons of Naggaroth smothered them with noxious clouds of gas, he struggled to understand. It was only when four of the dragons launched themselves at the great gates themselves and tore them asunder with their mighty claws that the truth became undeniable.

The Eagle Gate was taken! Victory was theirs!

As the druchii swarmed towards the fortress they had fought so hard to claim, the greatest of the black dragons swooped down before them. Seated upon the giant reptile's back was a figure no elf could fail to recognise. The Witch King himself, Malekith.

From the back of his monstrous steed, in a voice that was magnified by magic and boomed across the battlefield, the despot addressed the battered warriors of Hag Graef.

'The Eagle Gate is mine,' Malekith thundered. 'Caledor has acknowledged my right as true heir of Aenarion.' He raised his sword and thrust it towards the broken fortress. 'Spare all who wear the dragon,' he commanded. 'Kill the others!'

A monstrous snarl rose from the druchii. The frustration and fear of the previous days of fighting burst forth in a mad rush towards the Eagle Gate. It wasn't the organised march of an army now, but the vengeful rage of a mob. The battle was over, the dragons sweeping the walls of all organised resistance. Even the phoenixes had fled, their magical fire no match for the power of dragons.

No, the battle was over, but as Silar joined the throng charging into the fortress, he knew the killing was far from finished.

Now was the hour of slaughter and massacre. The hour of murder. The hour of Khaine!

A veil of shadow cloaked Drusala as she hurried through the anarchy and confusion of the Eagle Gate. The betrayal of Caledor had shocked her every bit as much as the asur. Morathi had seen much in her divinations, but she hadn't foreseen the shift in alliance by the dragon princes. The entire purpose of her exodus from Ghrond seemed pointless now. Drusala had been scheming to thwart Malekith's invasion, to prevent the Witch King from gaining a hold on

Ulthuan. She'd decided her best pawn in this endeavour was Malus Darkblade. If the entire army of Hag Graef were lost to him, Malekith would have been forced to reconsider his plans.

Spells to excite and enrage the daemon inside Malus had worked on the mind of the drachau. Careful strategies had been discarded in favour of bloody, ruthless slaughter. Malus had hurled his army against the Eagle Gate like a stoker shovelling coal into a furnace. A few more days of siege, and the largest army in the entire druchii armada would have been bled white by its possessed general.

The treachery of Caledor had foiled that scheme. There was no keeping Malekith from taking the Eagle Gate, no preventing his forces from securing a presence in Ulthuan. Drusala would have to adjust her plans. To do so, she'd need to return to the one she had thought almost at the end of his usefulness.

Ghost-like, Drusala stole past the stunned asur defenders. Her dark pegasus had fled when the dragons came, even its twisted heart unable to withstand the terror of so many ancient wyrms. A simple gesture had burst the beast's heart and sent it plummeting from the sky. Drusala had no pity for those who betrayed her, be they elf or brute. Without her winged steed, however, she was forced to weave an enchantment over herself, a mystic obfuscation that redirected the gaze of those who looked at her. For the asur, the only hint of her presence was a flash of movement glimpsed out of the corner of the eye.

The sounds of fighting grew louder as Drusala neared the section of wall that had been breached by the plague daemon during the last battle for the Eagle Gate. From the battlements, she could see the hulking, monstrous shape of Tz'arkan unleashed. The daemon king had left a trail of mutilation and carnage behind it as the thing glutted its appetite for death and destruction. The horrendously maimed bodies of asur and druchii alike were strewn about it.

Most of the druchii, it seemed, had the sense to understand that this was a battle they couldn't win. They were retreating from Tz'arkan, fleeing back past the rampart of dead cold ones. She could see the commander of Malus's mercenaries, the renegade noble Dolthaic, trying to regroup his knights and drive them back to the attack. Drusala smiled at that absurdity. To think his knights had any chance against the daemon was idiotic. It was a testament to his fear of Malus that a cunning opportunist like Dolthaic would consider such a plan. She wondered what he would think if she were to tell him that his master was gone. The drachau was dead.

Well, to all intents and purposes, Drusala corrected herself. Unless she took certain steps and intervened.

While the druchii retreated, the asur remained stubbornly defiant. The ragged remains of the Eataine Guard continued to attack the ghastly daemon king, refusing to submit meekly to the monster's advance. Tz'arkan took vile delight in tearing its enemies limb from limb, sometimes deliberately presenting a weakness so that some elf would rush at it. It would endure the wound the warrior delivered, then snatch him up in its claws and take its time pulling its captive apart.

As amusing as the sight of asur being butchered was, Drusala had bigger things to think about. She looked out towards the breach. Fresh druchii troops were filing past the rampart now – her own spearmen from Ghrond. She could see the cold figure of Absaloth among them. The sinister warrior had been one of Morathi's lovers once, and for that pleasure she had burned away his will and his identity. He was somewhat like a puppet now, one of the merciless Voiceless Ones. With his mind and soul chained to Morathi by links of magic and blood, his larynx had been fused into a knot of useless meat so that his words might never betray his queen. But he still had a tongue, he still had a mouth. With a minor incantation, Drusala made use of both. She had some commands to amend.

'The mistress orders that the daemon be captured, unharmed,' Drusala said. Below, she could see the Ghrondian spears turn in surprise as Absaloth repeated her command in a dry, rasping hiss. 'Keep Tz'arkan from leaving. Your mistress will join you soon.'

Drusala didn't linger to watch her spearmen charge towards the hulking daemon. Already she was hurrying down steps littered with rubble and the corpses of fallen asur. Once or twice she encountered elves wearing the heraldry of Caledor locked in mortal combat with hunters from Chrace and swordsmen from Ellyrion. Such fratricide pleased her, despite what it boded for her plans. If only all of the asur could be so obliging.

She reached the ward at the base of the walls just as the last member of the Eataine Guard was torn in half by the warpsword in Tz'arkan's fist. The daemon bellowed mockingly at the asur archers and axemen who had been supporting the noble elves.

'Are there no wolves left?' Tz'arkan raged. 'Must I drink the souls of dogs now?'

In answer to the daemon's challenge, the purple-cloaked Ghrondian spearmen rushed at Tz'arkan. The daemon swung around in amusement. It wasn't surprised. With senses far more keen than those of sight and sound, it had detected the druchii warriors stalking towards it. Now the fiend exulted in the opportunity for new atrocities.

'Your countrymen, Malus,' Tz'arkan hissed. 'Tell me, flesh-worm, are any of these walking corpses your friends? I dearly hope so!'

Laughing, Tz'arkan pounced towards the Ghrondian troops. One was crushed flat beneath the daemon's hooved feet. Another fell clutching at the string of organs the monster ripped from his bowels. A third was cleft in twain by the warpsword, his body bisected so cleanly that for a single step, the elf continued his charge before his body slopped to the ground.

The daemon's laughter became a cry of pain as one of the Ghrondian spears stabbed into its side. Tz'arkan reached a claw to the wound, surprised at the fiery ichor dribbling from the cut. Like the runesword of Prince Yvarin, the spears of Drusala's warriors could hurt the daemon. It wasn't by accident that she had dispatched these soldiers to confront the fiend. They were trained and equipped to face such foes. The sorcery within Ghrond had acted as a beacon to the twisted entities of the Wastes, drawing them down across the frontier time after time like moths to a flame. The warriors of Ghrond had been that flame.

Tz'arkan staggered back, the daemon's arrogance and audacity faltering as it now saw dozens of spears exactly like the one that had pierced its side. With grim determination, the druchii warriors formed a ring around the monster, hemming it in with a fence of steel. The daemon howled and roared and raged; threats that would have chilled the hearts of vampires slithered off its tongue. The warriors remained unmoved, determined in their purpose: to hold the beast for their mistress.

'You cannot escape,' Absaloth's rasping voice declared.

Tz'arkan fixed the Voiceless One with a murderous stare. 'I smell your magic, witch,' it snarled. 'Show yourself! Let Tz'arkan treat with the master, not the plaything.'

Drusala stepped out from the broken corner of a wall. She knew it was a reckless thing to do, foolish and stupid. She could deal with Tz'arkan without exposing herself. But the fiend's words had crawled their way into her mind, nagging at her pride. She suspected some enchantment behind that vexation, the sort of wearisome magic the daemon had used so often to manipulate Malus.

The daemon snorted derisively when it saw Drusala. 'You played your game, little one, but there is no time for games now. Tz'arkan is made flesh once more. Tz'arkan is free!' Its blazing eyes smouldered with grotesque mockery, its forked tongue licked lasciviously at its withered lips. 'Perhaps I would allow you to be my slave. If you beg. And it amuses me.'

The sorceress could feel the daemon's mind wearing at her, trying to play out her pride, trying to make her forget her schemes and plans. Trying to make her give herself over to the impulses of emotions rather than the calculations of knowledge.

'You fear me,' Tz'arkan accused.

Drusala smiled coldly at the monster. 'I think it is you who are afraid.'

Tz'arkan started to laugh at that, but it grew quiet when it saw Drusala wave her hand. Some of the spearmen raised their weapons and stepped out of formation, opening a passage for her into the cage that held the daemon. As she walked through the line, there was nothing in her step that bespoke uncertainty, not the slightest flicker of hesitancy on her face. Even when her warriors closed the ring behind her, she didn't stray.

The daemon's eyes narrowed with suspicion. There was a trap here, but try as it might, it couldn't ferret the nature of that trap from Drusala's mind. Her magic was too powerful to penetrate; all it could do was try to exploit emotions that were already there, and even this had failed it. Exploitation and manipulation end with the target's awareness.

'Who are you?' Tz'arkan hissed, offended that any mortal sorceress should have such power to resist it.

'That is the wrong question,' Drusala told it.

Tz'arkan bared its fangs, streams of venom dripping to the ground. 'What, then, is the question I should be asking?'

'You should be asking me what I want,' Drusala said.

The daemon laughed. For all the arcane power she possessed, for all her mystic knowledge, this flesh-worm was no different from any other mortal. She wanted a pact, some petty agreement between them. What would it be? Wealth? Power? Love? Revenge?

The sorceress answered her own question in a voice that was like a razor. 'I want Malus.'

Tz'arkan glowered at her. 'Darkblade is gone. There is only Tz'arkan now.'

Drusala slowly circled the hulking daemon, like a lion stalking game. Tz'arkan had made a mistake trying to manipulate her through her pride. It had forgotten that the channel worked both ways. Without the daemon appreciating it, she was playing upon its pride, provoking it with every breath. The angrier it got, the less it was aware of what else she was doing to it.

'You shouldn't lie,' the sorceress chided Tz'arkan, stepping around the gory husk of a Chracian hunter. 'I know he's still there, inside you. You wouldn't destroy him so quickly. Not when you could make him suffer.'

The daemon took a lumbering step towards her. 'Would you like to join him?' it threatened. 'All eternity as Tz'arkan's captive audience.'

Drusala continued to circle the daemon, gingerly picking her way between its victims. 'Is this how you use your freedom? Petty massacre? The great daemon king Tz'arkan, nothing more than a maniac with pretensions of grandeur.'

The daemon lashed out at her, nearly striking her with the warpsword. 'Your mind of flesh can't conceive what I am. In your blackest nightmares, you couldn't imagine the tenth part of what Tz'arkan is!'

Drusala leapt away from the enraged daemon. As Tz'arkan rushed at her, the fiend stopped short, thrust back as though it had struck an invisible wall. The beast snarled as it made a gesture with its claw. At once a scarlet circle blazed into life all around it, the circle Drusala had been furtively drawing with her foot as she taunted the daemon.

'This won't hold me,' Tz'arkan mocked. 'The merest effort and I shall be through. Then I will peel your body like a piece of fruit and feed you your own skin. I wonder how long you'll have the strength to scream.'

Drusala set one hand on her hip and actually laughed at the beast. 'You think that circle is the only magic I have worked upon you? Would you like to hear your True Name? It is neither long nor complicated as such things go. A half-brute witch doktor could learn it.'

Tz'arkan roared, the daemon's fury of such malignance that stones crumbled from the battered walls, corpses shivered on the ground. 'I will–'

'You will do nothing!' Drusala sneered. 'Or I will say that name. I will send you back.' Her voice became even more threatening as she recalled an image she'd found while she rooted about in the daemon's putrid essence. 'How do you think your brothers will greet you when you return? How will they thank you for leaving them scratching at the door when but a gesture from you could have ripped the barrier open? That should be an amusing spectacle.'

The daemon quieted, its burning eyes fading into black pits. 'What do you want?' it demanded in a sullen voice.

Drusala was wary, making no mistake of trusting Tz'arkan's seeming acceptance of defeat. 'I want Malus,' she repeated.

'You can't have him,' Tz'arkan growled. 'I am free. Do you understand me, free!'

'Soon you will be free among your brothers in the aethyr,' Drusala said.

An inarticulate cry of impotent fury shook the daemon. It knew the battle was lost. But one battle didn't lose a war. 'You can have Malus back,' the beast hissed, 'but you can't have him without Tz'arkan. Our essences are too entwined to be separated. Where he goes, I must follow, otherwise it is death for us both.'

Drusala nodded. She had expected as much. Indeed, it was vital to the revision her plans had undergone that she have both Tz'arkan and Malus Darkblade.

'Bring back the drachau,' she commanded the daemon. 'Restore your prison of flesh.'

'Shall I tell him who it was that killed his mother?' Tz'arkan asked, expecting to horrify the sorceress with a secret only a daemon could learn.

Drusala glared back at the fiend. 'If you did that, I'd be obligated to kill Malus. Then you'd lose your anchor. You'd have to go back to your waiting brothers.'

Hissing profanities to disgust the most jaded ear, Tz'arkan cast the warpsword from its hand. The weapon landed blade-first beyond the circle. For a heartbeat, Drusala's eyes glanced over at it. In that brief span, Tz'arkan rushed the sorcerous circle holding it. Wisps of colour exploded in every direction as the daemon burst through the circle. It charged at Drusala, intent on ripping her head from her shoulders before she could invoke its name.

Before Tz'arkan could reach her, however, the daemon was forced back, its body pierced by the spears of the Ghrondians. The silent Absaloth stood before his mistress, sword in hand, directing the warriors to push the daemon back.

At once, Tz'arkan sank to its knees. Its final, desperate effort had failed. Before Drusala could retaliate, could use its True Name against it, the daemon hastened to appease her. It would give her back Malus... And it would wait.

As Tz'arkan shrieked and howled like a creature damned, its monstrous frame began to collapse in upon itself. Slabs of daemonic flesh oozed away, dropping to the earth in stinking heaps. Horns crumbled into powder, spines snapped off and evaporated into smoke. Inch by inch, the daemon was melting away, each transformation bringing it a little nearer to the size and shape that had constrained it for so very long. As Tz'arkan withered away, so too did the warpsword shrink, taking back its original proportions.

Agony nearly beyond endurance had heralded Malus's transformation into Tz'arkan; now the same waves of pain coursed through him. As the daemon receded, as it restored his flesh to him, he could feel every pop and grind of his shrinking bones, experience the ghastly reshaping of muscle and tendon, the emergence of organs from the black broth of Tz'arkan's substance.

When the change was complete, Malus lay strewn upon the ground, unable to move, steam rising from his naked body. It was torture to even breathe; he had to concentrate to make his heart beat inside his chest for the first few moments, until the rhythms of his body restored themselves. He could sense Drusala's magic flowing through him, the sorceress helping guide back his mind and soul, acting to maintain his shattered body until its restoration was complete.

Around Drusala, he could see Absaloth and the Ghrondians. The spearmen stared at him in shocked disbelief, unable even now to accept that their general, the Tyrant of Hag Graef, had been the hulking daemon they'd fought. Malus grimly wondered why Drusala had bothered to restore him. With so many witnesses, there wasn't a chance of keeping the secret now. When the Witch King learned of this, he'd have Malus executed on the spot.

'Dead tongues spread no rumours,' Drusala said, reading his thoughts. Throwing both hands wide, she sent a tide of dark energies sweeping through her soldiers. The druchii stumbled and staggered as the dark magic entered them. They dropped their spears and drew the short blades on their belts. Then, in pairs, they drove their daggers into one another. The suicidal massacre was as complete as it was swift. Before a minute was out, only Drusala, Absaloth and Malus remained to bear witness to the drachau's secret.

'You needn't worry about Absaloth,' the sorceress said, motioning for her bodyguard to lift Malus from the blood-soaked ground. 'The only thoughts in his head, the only words in his mouth, are those that I put there.' She raised her hand and stroked Malus's cheek. 'We are going to be firm allies, Malus.'

Deep inside him, Malus could feel the last flicker of Tz'arkan turn cold. In as much as it was able, the daemon had abandoned him to the sorceress.

PART THREE
REAVER'S MARK

Summer 2524–Autumn 2524

FIFTEEN

Malus moved through the carnage of the battlefield, pale and wraithlike in his nakedness. A bloodied cloak, ripped from the corpse of one of Tz'arkan's victims, was the only raiment he'd had time to adopt. Except for the Warpsword of Khaine and the icon of Hag Graef he wore about his neck, he was without accoutrements. The daemon's release had shattered his armour and destroyed his clothes. Drusala's spell to re-cage the monster had left Malus as bare as a babe. There hadn't been time to worry about propriety and modesty, however. He had to hurry if he wanted to save something more important than his dignity.

His own skin.

The Witch King himself had come to the Eagle Gate and Malus knew the dreaded tyrant would be expecting the drachau to present himself. Every moment of delay would only further provoke the despot's ire. Malus had to plead his case, make Malekith appreciate that he was still a valuable asset in the conquest of Ulthuan. Otherwise, he knew his head would be joining those of the asur lords decorating the battered walls.

Malus found his king just outside the broken fourth wall. Malekith was in conference with some of his lords and generals, poring over the maps pinned to the side of a dead cold one. As he tottered out from the shadow of a battered gatehouse, Malus was spotted by Kouran. The warrior favoured the drachau with an ugly smirk, and then hurried to draw his king's attention away from the improvised table and towards the nearly naked elf.

With an effort, Malus forced his head back and strode towards the king with such pride as his exhausted body could muster. The nobles gathered around Malekith whispered and pointed as he came shambling through the ruins, but it wasn't long before the whispers rose into open jeers and taunts. Even the harpies feasting on the corpses scattered amidst the rubble snarled and snapped at him. The columns of druchii soldiers marching into the captured fortress turned their faces towards him and laughed as they trooped past, delighted to see the high-handed Malus brought to such distress.

Each barb only served to enflame the boundless hate within the drachau. He drew upon that hate, using it to pour strength into his weary bones. He returned the taunts and jeers with a defiant arrogance that made many of his detractors choke on their laughter, suddenly appreciating just how injudicious their humour was.

Kouran stepped forwards as Malus approached the Witch King, the captain of the Black Guard closing his hand about the Crimson Blade. The drachau stopped his march when he was twenty feet away from the king, far enough away as to not provoke the uncertainty of either the despot or his hound. Malus could imagine the fearful sight he must present, his body riddled with scars and stained in blood, only the gore-soaked cloak to cover his nudity. If he were in Malekith's boots, he would be wary. It was the lone fanatic, crazed and determined, who was the greatest threat to any tyrant.

The Witch King stepped away from his maps and cast his gaze over the drachau. 'You are alive,' he said. 'Mostly.'

Malus dropped to his knee, bowing before his monarch. 'Mostly alive, your majesty,' he said. He could see the wariness on Kouran's face as he addressed Malekith. To ease some of the warrior's doubt, Malus thrust the warpsword into the ground beside him, the blade trembling ever so slightly as he withdrew his hand from its hilt. He dismissed the warrior from his mind and returned his attention to Malekith.

'Please forgive my tardiness, Lord Malekith. I was otherwise engaged during yesterday's triumph and could not share your victory.' Malus bowed his head as he made his apology, but he could hear the druchii nobles drawing closer, savouring this display of contrition and weakness, eager to see what would happen next. Jackals waiting to pick at a corpse, should the Witch King reject the drachau's apology.

It took all of Malus's willpower to fight down the fear that filled him as the Witch King walked towards him. Like a prowling lion, Malekith circled him. He could feel the despot's suspicious gaze burning against his skin as the king studied him, marking every scar and blemish on his body, trying to read on his flesh the record of his recent battle. If the Witch King guessed even a small part of the truth, Malus knew the last thing he would feel was the Destroyer stabbing into his body.

'Tell me, Malus,' the king's voice came in a low growl from behind the drachau, 'what could be so important as to delay you from my council?'

Malus tried to restrain the fear that swelled within him. He shifted his head, trying to catch some sight of the Witch King, the faintest suggestion of what the despot was doing. He strained his ears for the slightest sound that might warn him that the Destroyer was in Malekith's hand.

'Alas, majesty, I was so enthralled by the song of Khaine that I pursued the fleeing foe far down the pass. It is only this dawn that I returned.' Malus wished he could see the Witch King so he could know how favourably his lies were accepted.

'You were overcome by bloodlust?' Malekith asked, a trace of scorn in his tone.

'That is true, majesty,' Malus replied. The story had been concocted by Drusala and he'd been too exhausted by his ordeal to fabricate a better one. Now he wondered if trusting the sorceress hadn't simply guaranteed his own destruction at the hands of the Witch King.

'And you pursued the enemy so vigorously that it took you all night to return to us?'

Malus swallowed the knot that was growing in his throat. His bare back shivered, anticipating the Witch King's blade stabbing into his flesh. Malekith wasn't buying his lies. Even so, Malus knew there was nothing to be gained by abandoning the bluff.

'Which enemies did you pursue with such vigour, dear Malus?' the Witch King demanded.

Terror was racing down Malus's spine, raw despair pounding in his heart. Malekith was suspicious. A moment more and he would draw the Destroyer. Malus glanced over at the warpsword, wondering if he could reach it before either Kouran or his king could cut him down.

'I believe they were Ellyrians, your majesty.' Drusala emerged from the crowd of nobles who had gathered to watch Malus squirm under the Witch King's interrogation.

The drachau wondered if the highborn fools around her understood the power Drusala embodied. He could bear witness to the awesome might of the handmaiden. Only his mother, Lady Eldire, had ever been able to subdue Tz'arkan, and that had been with the daemon in a far less powerful state than Drusala had encountered it. How she had managed such a feat, how she had been able to not merely subdue the daemon but force it to restore his physical body, Malus couldn't begin to comprehend. He'd felt his own mind collapsing into a shrieking mire of horror and pain, but Drusala had called him back. She'd sewn his essence back together, made him once again who he had been.

Such power didn't make Malus grateful; it made him worried. He'd been forced into an alliance with Drusala. Why? What did she hope to gain from him? What was it only the Tyrant of Hag Graef could bring to her?

Malus quickly took up the thread the sorceress dangled before him, remembering more details of the story she had so hurriedly fed him before sending him to treat with his king. 'They fled towards Ellyrion, so that would make the most sense.'

'So ardent was your pursuit that you abandoned your horned one, Spite?' The Witch King's words slashed at Malus like knives. 'You abandoned your clothes? You cast aside your armour in the midst of battle?'

'Forgive me, majesty, for I made an imprudent decision when the fighting for the wall was at its fiercest.' Malus looked across the still-gloating faces of the nobles. He tried not to let his gaze linger on Drusala, but couldn't resist directing a sharp look her way. If Malekith didn't buy her story, if there was any opportunity at all Malus was going to make sure she shared his fate.

'To heighten my prowess in battle,' Malus explained, 'I drank some of the witch brew of Khaine. Just a mere mouthful to strengthen my sword-arm. I did not anticipate its effects. When an asur champion pulled me from Spite's saddle, my mind seemed to be engulfed by flames. I cut the traitorous cur in two almost as soon as I left the saddle, but that wasn't enough to satisfy the song of Khaine blazing through my veins. In my fervour, my Khaine-blessed fury to slaughter the Ellyrians, I stripped off my armour, which was weighing me down...'

Laughter rose from many of the nobles as they heard Malus explain his nudity. Before the drachau was fully aware of what he was doing, he seized the warpsword and turned on the jeering druchii lords. Belatedly he noted Kouran start towards him, but a gesture from Malekith called his hound back.

'You laugh?' Malus snarled at the nobles. 'You who allowed the king's enemies to escape? You would allow them respite? Allow the damned asur to rally and fight us again?' The drachau's eyes were nearly as fiery as those of the Witch King as he glared at the mocking crowd. Nothing so fanned the fires of his rage as the sneers of those who thought themselves his betters.

Malekith raised his hand and at once the laughter was silenced. He stared at Malus in silence for a moment. 'You cast aside your armour in order to pursue the enemy with greater speed?'

Falling to his knee once more, Malus bowed to his king. 'It is even as you say, majesty.'

The Witch King turned and pointed an iron finger at Drusala. 'You vouch for this story?'

The sorceress bowed her head. 'Even so, your majesty. Lord Malus may not remember, but he came to me last night in a battle-fever and confessed what happened.' Her voice took on the slightest note of amusement. 'He was seeking my advice, your majesty, on how to apologise for his excesses during the fight.' She produced a length of bloodied cloth and held it towards the Witch King. 'He came to me with this. He thought it to be of great importance.'

A flick of Drusala's hand and the cloth unfurled, displaying the device of silver wings upon a field of white and blue. A snarl came from Kouran as the warrior recognised the torn banner Drusala held. 'The banner of Eagle Gate,' the warrior said, reaching out to take it from the sorceress. 'The Ellyrians tried to escape with it?'

Malus looked at the banner, feigning astonishment, pressing his hand to his head as though to massage memories back into his mind. He turned to Malekith. 'Majesty, I have no reason to doubt the Lady of Ghrond's statements. My own recollections before this morning are, I fear, somewhat hazy.'

The Witch King gestured to Kouran. Malekith and his faithful dog conferred for a moment, only snatches of their conversation reaching Malus's ears. What he did hear made the drachau anxious. The king wasn't buying their lies. With that thought in mind, Malus was shocked when Malekith turned to address him.

'Your persistence in the fight is commendable, even if your tardiness to my council is less than exemplary. Your appearance is disrespectful, offensive to your king and the sensibilities of these refined highborn. It needs more than an asur shroud to be presentable at my court, whatever the custom might have been in Hag Graef.'

The king's mockery brought more jeers from the watching nobles. Malus started to raise the warpsword when Malekith again motioned for silence.

'I will overlook this discourtesy, friend Malus,' the king declared. 'The campaign ahead of us will need leaders as persistent and audacious as yourself. To you I will entrust the defeat of the Ellyrians. Your army has suffered keenly in the fighting. You will need fresh forces to bring battle to Ellyrion. To that end, I place at your disposal the warriors of Tullaris Dreadbringer. After your experience with the witch brew of Khaine, the two of you should have more in common than ever.'

Malus clenched his jaw tight as he heard the king's words. Tullaris Dreadbringer, commanding a force of executioners bigger than any left to the armies of the Witch King. With him were such warriors and soldiers as had left Har Ganeth before Hellebron declared her entire city one giant altar to Khaine. The lack of amity between Malus and the disciples of Khaine was renowned. His half-brother Urial had been a priest of the Bloody-handed God, determined to bring about an ancient prophecy surrounding the Chosen of Khaine and the Bride of Khaine. For a time, it had seemed Malus himself was the Chosen, but that had been the daemon Tz'arkan twisting fate so that his mortal slave might gain the Warpsword of Khaine and restore the daemon to corporeal form. Urial had been one of the casualties in that web of deception. So had a great many others who were involved in the cult of Khaine.

Tullaris had long been held as the Hand of Khaine, the Lord of Murder's favoured son. Now, he was universally accepted as the Chosen of Khaine by the entirety of the cult, not simply those in Har Ganeth. Violent, moved by dark dreams of carnage and slaughter, Tullaris had seized everything in his brutal life with his own hands. His accomplishments were littered with the corpses of his victims. To have the acknowledgement of his right as Chosen essentially passed over to him by Malus was a source of unending vexation to the executioner. Malus had often wondered how many of the assassins who'd tried to kill him had been dispatched on Tullaris's orders. He suspected very few – this was one enemy who would suffer no blade but his own to end the drachau's life.

One of his most dire enemies, yet Tullaris had one great mark in Malus's favour: he bore no love for Malekith. The Witch King had many times proclaimed himself as Khaine's mortal avatar. Tullaris made no secret of the divine dreams that moved and inspired him to his acts of atrocity and massacre. He presented himself as Khaine's herald, a mortal touched by the Lord of Murder. For Malekith, the executioner's claims were close to treachery. For Tullaris, the Witch King's posturing as a divine avatar was nothing less than blasphemy.

'In this war, the divine favour of Khaine is of more value than a thousand dragons,' Malus said, trying to make the statement sound sincere. 'I would deem it an unmatched distinction if I might be given command of the army brought here by Lord Tullaris. Unworthy of such command as I may be.'

'You will strike out with them across the interior of Ellyrion,' the Witch King commanded. 'It is a very simple task we set before you, Malus. We simply want you to put every settlement between here and Evershale to the sword. Do you think you can manage that?'

'If I didn't think I could achieve the task you set before me, majesty, I would be unfit for the command,' Malus said. He stood up and would have turned to walk away, but a last question from the Witch King stayed his retreat.

'What weapons will you use against the asur?' Malekith demanded.

Malus stared back at the Witch King. 'The greatest weapons of them all, majesty. The ones that have been burned into the souls of every druchii since we were cast from our homeland.

'Deceit and treachery.'

The flayed skin that formed the backing of the folding campaign chair creaked as Malus settled himself into his seat. He couldn't remember now who the skin had belonged to originally. He thought it had been one of his father's old retainers, one of the ones who had lacked the caution to treat him with proper respect while he was growing up. Emit? Razmat? He couldn't remember now. Whoever it had been, their skin surely hadn't been as comfortable to wear as it was to sit against.

Cold fury burned inside Malus every time his mind contemplated his surroundings. Despite the fawning obeisance he'd paid the Witch King, it *had* been his army that had beaten the garrison. It *had* been his leadership that broke the Eagle Gate and left it open to conquest. Malekith's contribution to the battle was little more than gutting a shark after it was already hooked and hauled into the boat. Yet the despotic monarch and his entourage were ensconced inside the fortress while Malus was left to the spare comforts of his army's camp. Instead of the prestige of sleeping in the chambers of a conquered foe, he was left to sleep in a tent like all the common sword-fodder of his army!

Despite, or rather because of, his rage, Malus was in a perversely good humour. It had been a very long time since he'd been able to indulge himself in a proper temper. Even under the influence of his mother's wine, he'd always had to be careful lest some excess of emotion allow Tz'arkan to exert too much control over him. Since Drusala's spell, however, there hadn't been a peep from the daemon. He could still feel it there, cowering in some corner of his soul, but the sorceress's magic had certainly curbed the spectral parasite.

That knowledge only further aroused Malus's temper. He hadn't risen to become drachau of Hag Graef by allowing anyone to have a hold over him. He'd refused the advances of Naggor's Belladon, refused to accept a throne on the witch's terms. It would have been easier, but to assume power at such a price would have been a shallow illusion. He would have been a slave dancing to the tune of a hidden master. He'd had enough of that sort of thing from Tz'arkan. He wouldn't simply swap the daemon for Drusala.

His eyes strayed towards the sorceress. Again, she lounged upon his divan, seemingly careless of her provocative appearance as Malus conferred with his closest advisors. She didn't fool anyone, of course, that she wasn't aware of either her beauty or the desire she provoked. But that didn't make it any easier for them to ignore her. Malus noted Dolthaic in particular attending a bit too much attention each time Drusala shifted her position and exposed a bit of her thigh. He'd have to remind the knight later about where his priorities should be. At least if he didn't want to end up as a chair.

By contrast, Tullaris Dreadbringer and his second, a noble warrior named Sarkol Narza, seemed to be sizing up a slab of meat any time their attention diverted to the sorceress. The two executioners were appropriately terrifying in their stylised armour, long-handled draichs slung over their backs, the withered heads of a few choice victims dangling from their belts. Tullaris was a tall, cheerless sort of killer, his face marked with the ghoulish imprint of the true fanatic. Sarkol Narza was more compactly built, almost stocky for an elf, but his face was no less villainous than that of his master. Matched monsters, two semi-rabid wolves in the service of Khaine. Malus had heard that Tullaris didn't even balk at offering up the hearts of those already devoted to his god when the mood struck him, once going so far as to kill a dozen witch elves during one of Khaine's holy festivals.

At present, fortunately, Tullaris gave the appearance of being far more controlled and rational. Indeed, after that exhibition of hate in the Witch King's court, the executioner had become strangely resigned to taking orders from his old enemy. What Malus couldn't decide was how much of the killer's attitude was genuine acceptance and how much was pretence. Either way, he wasn't about to let his guard down.

'If it pleases you, dreadlord,' Silar Thornblood addressed Malus, 'I think it would be best to integrate our forces gradually. Fleetmaster Aeich is dead and his corsairs almost exterminated on the walls, the Clar Karond contingent is a shell of its original strength, and the Knights of the Ebon Claw remain leaderless...'

Malus waved his hand as though swatting aside an annoying insect. 'Fold whatever is left of Vincirix's knights into Dolthaic's command. If any of them complain... the cold ones could probably use fresh meat after such a long battle. As for the rest, if they have any problems with our new allies, I suggest they get over them quickly.'

Silar turned and glowered at the imposing Tullaris, exhibiting more nerve than Malus would have given him credit for. 'I was more concerned about the discipline of our "allies", dreadlord. The denizens of Har Ganeth aren't renowned for their... professionalism... on the battlefield.'

An ophidian smile stretched across Tullaris's face. 'Is my lord Silar questioning the valour of my warriors?'

'Not their valour, only their restraint,' Silar said. It was clear he appreciated the menace in the executioner's tone. Even under the watching eyes of Malus there was no guarantee that Tullaris wouldn't kill him where he stood. It was a bold display on Silar's part. Maybe not wise, but certainly bold.

'Has it occurred to you that that is why Malekith threw this task to Tullaris?' Drusala asked. Her tone conveyed the disgust she felt, not just for the herald of Khaine but for Malus's decision to join his fate to that of the infamous marauder. 'The Witch King wants the countryside laid to waste. While we're running about butchering farms and hermitages, what do you think the Ellyrians will be doing? They'll be mustering their forces to march against us. Malekith expects us to bypass Tor Elyr and Whitefire Tor, to leave them unchallenged at our back while we strike towards Evershale and Avelorn. We will have two armies behind us and the forces of Avelorn before us.'

'Does the prospect frighten you?' Malus asked.

Drusala's eyes narrowed as she gazed over at the drachau. 'I am saying this force is nothing more than a sacrifice, Malekith's offering to Khaine so that his own victory may be assured. We draw out the hosts of Tor Elyr and Whitefire Tor, and once those armies are engaged with us, the Witch King can take the cities they've left weak and unguarded. We die while he claims all the glory.'

'Is that not the role of any dutiful subject?' Malus relished the flash of fire that came into Drusala's eyes.

'You've conveniently allowed the Witch King to put all of his worst rivals into a single force,' Drusala accused.

'And you've forgotten what I told Malekith,' Malus said. 'I warned him that my weapons would be deceit and treachery. I just didn't tell him who I'd use them against.' He rose from his chair and began to pace the floor. 'Tomorrow we march into Ellyrion, just as Malekith expects. We will begin carving a path of blood, as he has commanded. But we won't forget Tor Elyr, as he wants.' He pointed at Drusala. 'It will be your duty, witch, to observe the city. When their army sallies forth to put an end to our rampage, I need your magic to tell me.'

'And what will we do when the host of Tor Elyr comes seeking vengeance?' Dolthaic asked.

Malus grinned, his face becoming almost as bloodthirsty as those of Tullaris and Sarkol. 'We show the Witch King what a massacre really looks like.'

It was long into the night before Malus came stealing into the tent of Tullaris Dreadbringer. It was a gruesome spectacle, stitched together from the skins of sacrificial victims, the brand of Khaine still visible on each desiccated forehead. Scalps and dried fingers adorned the tent posts, fluttering in the fitful wind moaning down the pass. A mat fashioned from the facial bones of a hundred skulls grinned up at the drachau, taunting him, daring him to cross the threshold.

It would take more than that to give Malus pause, however. At his gesture, Dolthaic preceded him and drew back the curtain of witch elf hair that covered the door of the tent. A smell of blood and death wafted out from the darkened interior. Malus gave himself a moment to get accustomed to the stench. The bones in the mat cracked and creaked as his armoured boots strode across the flesh-less faces and into the executioner's domain.

Tullaris was waiting for him. The Chosen of Khaine knelt on the ground, clad only in a loincloth. A pair of thin, sickly looking slaves attended him, their scarred arms rubbing at him with blood-soaked sponges. A third slave lay crumpled in a wide, trough-like basin, her blood streaming from the dozens of cuts inflicted upon her body. Sarkol Narza stood over the bleeding slave, a strange instrument gripped in his hand. It was shaped like a branding iron, but what was fitted at its end was more like a set of razors, each blade cross-ing and recrossing the others to form a perfect representation of the Sign of Khaine. As Malus watched, Sarkol pressed the bladed instrument into the slave's side, leaving a crimson imprint for a brief moment before the streaming blood obscured it.

'Is this how you receive your master?' Malus growled, glaring at Tullaris and his minions.

Tullaris matched the heat in the drachau's gaze. 'I serve but one master, Darkblade, and you are not Him.'

Another elf, even a dreadlord, would have been intimidated by the cold passion in Tullaris's voice, the gleam of fanaticism in his eyes. Malus had seen too much, survived too much, suffered too much, to feel impressed. 'I wonder, Tullaris. Does Khaine truly speak to you, or are you simply mad?'

From the corner of his eye, Malus noticed Sarkol reach for the dagger on his belt. He could hear Dolthaic start to draw his sword and move to intercept the executioner. He kept his own gaze upon Tullaris. The slaves were retreating from their master, cow-ering away from him. Even now, they were more frightened of the unarmed executioner than the armoured drachau standing a few feet away.

'I should have killed you, Darkblade,' Tullaris said, every word dripping with hate and bitterness. 'Pretender. Imposter. Blasphemer. You used the title that belongs to me towards your own purpose. For your own gain you have profaned and defiled the holy name of Khaine.'

Sarkol had turned to face Dolthaic. If it came to a fight, Malus wasn't certain he'd put his wager on the knight, even with the longer reach of his sword. At close quarters, a fanatic was more dangerous than a professional soldier.

Tullaris turned his head towards his lieutenant and nodded. Reluctantly, Sarkol relented and slammed his dagger back into its sheath. Tullaris looked back at Malus, a bitter smile appearing on his face. 'I should have killed you, Darkblade, but I *do* hear the voice of Khaine. I have seen, in my dreams, that you are the key to destiny. It has been granted that you shall atone for your blasphemies by bearing me to my apotheosis. We will walk to the Throne of Khaine together, you and I. The Witch King's pretensions of divinity shall be cast down and the true glory of Khaine will be revealed.'

With each word the executioner spoke, Malus felt his anxiety increase. Better than anyone, he knew what it was to have another voice inside one's mind. He wasn't sure which possibility was more disturbing – that Tullaris was mad or that he really did have *something* speaking to him.

'Before the Witch King offered you the choice, I knew that our doom was joined,' Tullaris continued. He rose from the ground, his body dripping with the blood his slaves had anointed him with. His brawny chest was a confusion of scars, overlapping layers of cuts, each slash representing the Mark of Khaine. 'Before you knew what you would do, I knew we would march together.'

Malus scowled at the executioner. 'Prophecy is unerringly

accurate after the fact,' he sneered. 'It may interest you that my closest advisors urged me to join forces with Venil Chillblade.'

'But you didn't, Darkblade. You made the choice that Khaine demanded.' Tullaris's eyes narrowed, his tone dropping to one of warning. 'The sorceress. You must eliminate her.'

'She is... useful to me,' Malus said. He wondered if Tullaris had merely guessed or if the executioner really knew that Drusala was the 'advisor' who'd urged him against siding with the Har Ganeth exiles.

'She is a creature of the Witch King,' Tullaris said. 'She is the hand-maiden of Morathi, a product of her convents. All the sorceresses of Ghrond serve Morathi, however far they fare and whatever deceits they weave.'

That idea gave Malus pause. He was certain Drusala was play-ing her own game, trying to fulfil some scheme that would benefit herself. Was it possible that at the same time she was acting as an agent of Morathi or the Witch King? Could it be all the seem-ing disfavour in which Malekith held her was simply a pretence? He already considered the witch a threat, but one that could be attended to later when the opportunity arose. If she was an agent of Malekith, however, her elimination was crucial.

'It needs magic to fight magic,' Dolthaic said. Although Sarkol had relented, the knight remained on his guard, poised to protect his master's back and flank should treachery arise.

'Only those with little ability fall outside the power of Ghrond,' Malus said. 'It will need more than a petty enchantress to oppose Drusala.'

Tullaris stepped over to the basin and the bleeding slave. He ran his hand through the dazed she-elf's hair. 'Was the Lady Eldire a petty enchantress? She opposed Morathi herself and remained independent of her control.' The executioner locked eyes with Malus. 'Perhaps that is why she was murdered.'

It took the iron resolve of a drachau not to allow any sign of emotion to show on his face. The loss of his mother was a pain Malus had yet to face. Korbus had claimed he acted for the Witch King, but what if he wasn't alone? It would need powerful magic or careful treachery to overcome someone like Eldire. Or, perhaps, a mix of both. He was reminded of what he'd witnessed while locked inside Tz'arkan's twisted form. He'd felt rather than heard Drusala's voice rising from Absaloth's tongue. Had she employed similar magic when Korbus was exposed?

Malus looked over at Dolthaic. 'The problem remains. It needs magic to fight magic. As you say, my mother was the single most powerful sorceress to defy Morathi's control.'

Almost absently, Tullaris shoved the head of his slave forwards, pushing her face under the film of blood at the bottom of the basin. 'There is no single sorceress who can equal Lady Eldire,' he said. 'But there are three whose powers combined can suit our needs.' He smiled as the slave's body thrashed about. Drowning, she had snapped from her weary stupor. Her fingers clawed at the executioner's arms, scratching at him in her agonies.

Sarkol explained his master's words. 'Three sorceresses fled Ghrond long ago. They sought shelter in Har Ganeth and the protection of Hellebron. They have become the Blood Coven, their combined sorcery enough to oppose even the great daemons of the Wastes. Perhaps only Morathi herself is the equal of their united power.'

'This Blood Coven is among your entourage?' Malus asked.

Tullaris frowned. The resistance of the drowning slave was growing weaker. 'They are not with us, but they could be. Malekith mistrusts Morathi for failing to warn him of the daemonic invasion. That suspicion runs to all who serve the convents. He knows the value of having in his keeping a body of sorceresses with no love for his mother. He has kept the Blood Coven close in case he must use them against his mother's disciples.'

'The Blood Coven appreciates how precarious their position has become,' Sarkol continued. 'They know that should Malekith reconcile with Morathi as he has so often before, they would be lost. Given the chance, they should again like the protection of Har Ganeth and the favour of Khaine.'

'Say the word, Darkblade, and when we march, the Blood Coven will march with us,' Tullaris said. He released his grip on the now unresisting slave. There was just a flicker of life left in her. If she had the strength, she might yet save herself. If she was too weak, it was a sign Khaine had accepted this offering of murder. 'Sarkol Narza knows where they are being held. He will liberate them and bring them to you. By the time their escape has been discovered, we will already be deep in Ellyrion.'

Malus pondered the offer. Not for an instant did he doubt that Tullaris had motives of his own for rescuing the Blood Coven. But it might be that such motives echoed his own. Anything that might give him an edge over Drusala was a gamble he felt he had to take. Even more now that the seed of suspicion was there.

'Very well, Tullaris,' Malus decided. 'Bring your witches.'

Tullaris smiled as he watched the last bubbles of air rise in the basin and the first touch of death steal upon the drowned slave. 'Khaine blesses this compact, Darkblade,' he said, jabbing his thumb at the unmoving corpse. 'Together, He will lead us to our destiny.'

Silar could hear the cries of agony even before he reached the compound where the Naggorites had been interred after the battle. A ring of impaled bodies greeted him, the still-living husks of those slave-soldiers wounded in battle. There were scores of them, hands bound behind them, slivers of silverwood torn from the great doors of the Eagle Gate thrust through their vitals. It was a slow, hideous death, the kind of death usually reserved for traitors and cowards, not warriors whose only failing had been to fall victim to the caprice of battle.

Such was the viciousness of Kunor Kunoll's Son, however. An inveterate sadist, the brute never squandered an opportunity for cruelty. As Silar approached, he saw the slavemaster and two of his henchmen standing over a Naggorite who'd been staked on the ground. They were busy heaping the armoured bodies of fallen slaves on the wretch, gradually pressing the elf to death. Silar noted with a start that the druchii Kunor was torturing was Bragath Blyte. One word from the tormented slave and Silar could find himself branded a traitor.

There was nothing to do, however, except keep walking. Kunor had already noted the highborn and would think it curious to see him withdraw without some manner of explanation. Silar glanced down at Bragath. For just an instant there was a silent appeal in the Naggorite's eyes.

'Has the great Silar Thornblood decided to go slumming among the commoners?' Kunor laughed. 'I thought you didn't care for this kind of diversion. Too crude for your refined palette.' He laughed again as he hefted the corpse he was holding onto the one already on Bragath's chest. The weight of two fully armoured elves now pressed down on the captive.

'I find little to enjoy in savagery without purpose,' Silar said. 'There is an art to torture that I despair of you ever appreciating, Kunor. This,' he gestured to Bragath, 'is like comparing the murmur of an idiot to the song of a diva. They are alike only in that both are sounds.'

Kunor glared at the highborn. 'I'll teach the swine to sing,' he growled, motioning for his henchmen to lug another corpse onto the pile. The slavemaster's eyes narrowed with suspicion. 'What did bring you here?'

'Orders from the drachau,' Silar said, letting the weight of that statement sink in. 'He commands that you have your Naggorites ready to march in the morning.' He glanced around the compound, at the great dark stretches between the campfires of the slave-soldiers. Over half of the Naggorites had perished over the course of the campaign. 'Such as are left,' he added with a mocking smile. 'I wonder, Kunor, how long it will be before your command vanishes completely. What use will Malus have for a slavemaster without any slaves?'

Kunor raised his hand, arresting the action of his helpers as they prepared to dump the third corpse onto Bragath's chest. 'What do you mean?' he demanded.

Silar shook his head. 'Surely you don't expect Lord Malus to give you command of a company of dreadspears or a troop of dark riders? You aren't a leader, Kunor, you are a taskmaster. You don't lead, you drive. You bully and terrorise your warriors, but you don't lead them. The host of Hag Graef may need new leaders when this war is over, but it won't need a slave-driver. Not to command troops on the battlefield.' Silar glanced down at Bragath. 'I wonder what you'll do when they're all gone. Perhaps the drachau will reward you with a post in his kitchens.'

The slavemaster shook from an apoplexy of rage. He ripped the whip from his belt, but when he played his lash, it was across the faces of his henchmen. 'Put that carrion down! Go and check that the rest of these dogs are fit to march in the morning!'

Rubbing his slashed face, one of the henchmen pointed at Bragath. 'What about him?'

'Leave him,' Kunor growled. 'If he lives until morning, cut him loose and put him in line with the rest.' The slavemaster turned back towards Silar, but the highborn was already walking away. He glared hatefully at the noble, damning him for the doubt and fear he'd set in the slavemaster's mind.

Silar walked slowly through the darkness, away from the slave compound. He'd done what little he could for Bragath. He hoped the Naggorite understood that. He hoped it would be enough to keep the elf's silence.

'Unusual friends for a noble of Hag Graef,' a soft voice whispered to Silar from the darkness.

Surprised by the abruptness of the words, Silar spun around. He discovered Drusala staring at him, an enigmatic expression on her face.

'Beasts like Kunor are an unfortunate necessity in a time of war,' Silar said.

'War makes strange bedfellows indeed.' Drusala stepped closer and slowly turned to face back at the slave compound. 'You were a hero of the war that saw Hag Graef victorious against the black ark of Naggor. It is strange to see you with such sympathy for your old enemies.'

Silar tried to hide the flash of alarm that coursed through him. How much did the sorceress know and how much did she simply guess? Or was Drusala simply fishing for a reaction, trying to tease out from him with craft what she couldn't with magic?

'That war is over. The Naggorites fight alongside Hag Graef now,' Silar said. 'I simply do not like to see Lord Malus's resources squandered needlessly.'

'A most thoughtful vassal,' Drusala said. 'It is rare to find such loyalty among the highborn. Usually it makes them too weak to accomplish anything of merit.'

As abruptly as she had appeared, so too did the sorceress depart, vanishing into the darkness of the druchii camp. Even after she was gone, however, Silar could smell the tang of her perfume and feel the uncanny chill of her presence.

SIXTEEN

For five days the druchii raged across the Ellyrian countryside, slaughtering and burning everything in their path. No settlement was too small to escape their hate, no victim to insignificant to be spared their wrath. The crucified bodies of tortured asur marked the march of Malus Darkblade, every victim bearing the brand of Khaine upon their brow.

Dark riders ranged far and wide, scouting the terrain, studying the lay of the land. While Drusala and the other sorceresses kept their focus upon Tor Elyr, the Griffon Gate and Whitefire Tor, the scouts fed the army a complete survey of the land. On the sixth day of their rampage, Malus had cause to put that intelligence to use.

The ravages of the druchii were known to the asur. Day by day, the outrages inflicted by the invaders continued to build until at last an army stirred from each of the great Ellyrian cities. The hosts of Tor Elyr and Whitefire Tor marched to intercept that of Naggaroth, but Malus was careful to avoid being trapped between them. His army ranged deeper into the countryside, drawing the asur after them. Eventually, the two Ellyrian armies merged, forming a united front against the despoilers of their kingdom.

It was then that Malus ordered his army to retrace their march, fading back towards the Annulii Mountains. The asur were coming for his bait, now it was time to give battle. Battle under his terms and on ground of his choosing.

From a rocky outcropping on the foothills, Malus and his generals watched the asur army closing upon them. Around a stand of forest that had been partially burned by the druchii, the Ellyrians came, their banners fluttering in the breeze, their armour gleaming in the eternal summer of Ellyrion's sun. A war-chant, as old as Aenarion's reign, rose from the marching soldiers. As it reached them, some of Malus's warriors added their own voices to the song, a reminder to the asur that it was the druchii who were the true heirs of Aenarion.

'They outnumber us, dreadlord,' Silar cautioned Malus. 'Why give battle to them at all? We can fade into the hills and force them to divide their command to pursue us.'

Malus reached down and gave Spite an affectionate pat. He appreciated the horned one's unquestioning loyalty, especially at times like these. 'After all the hard work to bring my enemies together, dividing them again is the last thing I want.'

'If you were to draw them back towards the Eagle Gate, the dragons would be able...'

An icy glare silenced Silar. 'The last thing I want is to make a present of my victory to either Imrik or Malekith. This victory will be mine! It won't be stolen from me as the Eagle Gate was.' Raising his hand, Malus brought his mailed fist flashing down. At his signal, a horn sounded, its dolorous note echoing among the rocks. Below the rise upon which Malus and Silar conferred, a great body of troops rushed out towards the enemy. Mounted slavemasters cracked their whips against the soldiers, driving them like cattle.

Silar felt his insides go cold as he watched the Naggorites herded towards the asur. He knew the slave-soldiers were greatly outnumbered, that Malus didn't expect them to stop the Ellyrian push. Well was he aware of his lord's callous deployment of the Naggorites and the fiendish plan behind it. The knowledge didn't make him like the scheme any better. Vanquished, enslaved, the Naggorites were still druchii. That meant something to Silar, much more than it had before Naggaroth was abandoned. They were the last of a breed, the last sons of the Land of Chill. To spend their lives in such a ruthless manner made him sick.

'The passes will hide the numbers of Kunor's dogs,' Malus laughed. 'For all that the asur can tell, the whole of my host is descending upon them. Our magic will prevent them from piercing that deception. When the Naggorites break, the asur will smell victory and pursue.' Malus clenched his fist, his face contorting into a visage of complete hate. 'Then they are mine. Sacrifices to *my* glory. Not that of the Witch King!'

Silar looked down into the pass. The first line of the Naggorites was just emerging out onto the plain. Immediately, a rain of arrows and spears rose from the asur lines. Scores of druchii were brought down, falling in their droves as the missiles struck their formation. Kunor and the mounted slavemasters whipped fresh troops into the gaps, driving them on, allowing them no pause for thought or fear. Yard by yard, the Naggorites clawed their way across the field towards the asur front. Beneath their feet they trampled the bodies of their own dead and wounded, deaf to the cries of the maimed and dying.

Before the Naggorites could reach the Ellyrians, a block of swordsmen in suits of mail stepped forwards. They met the initial rush of the slave-soldiers with cleaving strokes of their double-handed blades. The asur swords scythed through the druchii, cleaving through armour as though it were paper and taking scant notice of the flesh and bone within.

Kunor and the slavemasters continued to beat and threaten their troops, forcing more and more of them into the fray. At last, however, even the fatalistic determination of the Naggorites reached its limit. The surge of black-armoured elves receded, turned back upon itself. Raw, primitive cries of despair and alarm rose from the druchii as they fled back into the passes, stampeding those before them into full retreat.

The asur, the song of Khaine already sounding in their souls, the smell of enemy blood in their hearts, pursued their reeling foes. Shouting triumphantly, the Ellyrians charged after the druchii, cutting down any unfortunate enough to fall into their hands.

Upon the rise, Malus smiled, an expression of such murderous glee that it might have provoked envy in Tullaris had the executioner been there to see it. Once again, the drachau raised his hand high. Carefully he watched the Naggorites pouring back into the pass below, studying the numbers and progress of the asur pursuing them.

'Can we not wait until our warriors are clear?' Silar asked.

Malus didn't bother to look aside at his retainer. 'The Naggorites die to serve the Hag. It is all they are good for.' Extending forefinger and thumb, he gave the signal the troops positioned on the rise had been watching for.

The sorcerous glamour that had cloaked the warriors on the rise evaporated as the druchii sprang into action. Their concealment had represented something of an abuse of Drusala's magic, taxing her to the utmost. Only by remaining completely still had the warriors been able to retain the illusion of rock and brush. In motion they were revealed to the elves below. Rank upon rank of darkshards, the hideous power of their repeating crossbows magnified by the half a dozen reaper bolt throwers ranged among their ranks. Naggorite and Ellyrian alike vented a cry of despair when they saw the druchii aiming down at them.

The ensuing slaughter was horrific by any standard. The crack of bowstring, the smash of bolt through armour, the scream of ruptured flesh, all rose into a deafening tumult. In the close press of panicked warriors, the dead were pinned to the living, the wounded skewered to the walls of the pass. Ellyrian knights were shot from their saddles to impale themselves on the swords and spears of the infantry around them. The floor of the pass became a churning sea of death and terror, frantic warriors struggling to escape the massacre unfolding all around them.

Malus had schooled his soldiers well, impressing on them the penalty for restraint or hesitation. Scores of Naggorites fell alongside hundreds of Ellyrians as the gruesome harvest continued. The ground became so soaked with blood that it was reduced to a muddy mash that sucked at the feet of those trying to escape it.

The butchery was more than the asur could endure. At last they broke, fleeing back through the pass and out onto the plain. Though they left hundreds of their dead behind them, the Ellyrian force still numbered in the thousands. The trap had bloodied them, but it hadn't destroyed them.

Malus paid little notice to the surviving Naggorites as they retreated back into the hills. He was watching the asur, staring with the keen interest of a gem-cutter tending a stone. The Ellyrians were out of the pass, fleeing onto the plain. Their numbers weren't greatly diminished. But Malus hadn't expected them to be. All his trap had been designed to do was inflict disorder in the enemy host, to break up the regimental formations, to confuse the discipline that brought them unity. If he had faced a single army, the commander might have restored order as soon as the asur were clear of the pass. That was why he had waited for both armies to merge before confronting them. Instead of bringing strength, the combination had brought weakness. Two command structures, two generals, two elves to which the panicked troops were looking for leadership, for orders.

The panic of the asur continued, the commanders unable to restore order in their mixed host. The retreat brought them close to the burned forest. The forest where the real jaws of Malus's trap waited.

It had been something of a gamble, entrusting the role to Sarkol Narza and the Bloodseekers. Malus had been worried about their discipline, fearing that their lust for carnage would cause them to act too soon and betray themselves. But Tullaris had impressed upon the executioners the importance of their role, the vital turn they would play in this battle. The individual slaughter they could work on their own would pale beside the wholesale havoc they could inflict by following the drachau's plan.

It had also proved a vital test of just how powerful the Blood Coven's powers truly were. He'd taxed Drusala's magic with her illusion and demanded the Blood Coven perform a similar feat. The red-robed witches had managed their spell with a good deal more bloodshed than Drusala, offering up a dozen sacrifices to Khaine over the course of their ritual, but in the end their sorcery had proven just as effective.

The seemingly capricious burning of the forest had been exactingly deliberate: to confuse the memories of any Ellyrian who knew this ground, and to make the asur oblivious that there were more trees in the forest than there had been before. As the fleeing army retreated past those trees, the glamour cast upon Sarkol and his executioners vanished. Howling like wolves, the murderous horde fell upon the asur. This time it was the Ellyrians' turn to be cut down like wheat.

The other set of jaws in the trap Malus had prepared came galloping out from the pass. Dolthaic, leading the Knights of the Burning Dark, and Tullaris Dreadbringer, leading the Ossian Guard, the elite of his murderous army. While the cold one knights carved a path through the rear of the confused asur, Tullaris led his killers into the gaps created by the mounted warriors. Left and right, the Ossian Guard played their heavy draichs, rending the Ellyrians at every step.

'A great victory,' Malus declared as he watched the slaughter unfolding on the plain. Pinned by Sarkol at the front, Dolthaic on the flank and Tullaris at the rear, the asur were being herded into a ring. It was still possible they might coordinate and break through, but that opportunity was quickly slipping away. The rest of Malus's army was now marching out from the pass. The survivors of Clar Karond, the veterans of Hag Graef, the Iceblades and Voiceless Ones brought by Drusala from Ghrond, the hordes of exile killers from Har Ganeth, the corsairs of the *Eternal Malediction.* The Ellyrians still outnumbered the druchii, but their numbers counted for little now. They'd lost cohesion and they'd lost the initiative. For too long, they had thought of themselves as the hunters. It wasn't an easy thing to understand that they were now the prey.

Silar listened to Malus's words. He stared down at the carnage in the pass below, at all the dead Naggorites. 'A great victory, dreadlord,' he agreed. 'But I wish it hadn't cost us so much blood.'

Malus shifted around in his saddle and favoured Silar with a withering stare. 'Be happy none of it was yours,' he told his vassal.

'I am ready to die for the Hag,' Silar answered, bowing his head.

'I will remember that, Silar,' Malus said. 'I trust you will not have cause to regret your choice of words.'

Shifting his attention back to the battle, Malus watched as the ring of asur was slowly cut to pieces. Undoubtedly some would still escape, but he actually preferred to leave some survivors. They would carry word of what had happened here back to their cities and when Malekith came to lay siege to them, the Witch King would know that it was Malus who was responsible for already decimating the asur armies.

Perhaps Drusala was already telling Malekith of what had happened here by means of her magic. Malus almost hoped she was. Anything that taxed her sorcery further was to be applauded.

'I will have need of your service this night,' Malus told Silar. 'Make yourself available. There is an urgent chore that needs attending to and I'd trust no one else to see it carried out.'

The wind carried upon it a strange warmth. By the starlight, Silar could see an eerie shimmer shining from the peaks of the Annulii. It was a fearsome thought, to understand that even someone without the uncanny gifts of a sorcerer could actually see the magic streaming down from the mountain tops. It was a manifestation of how rapidly the world was coming apart around him. Even if the druchii achieved their ancient dream of conquering Ulthuan, Silar wondered if it would be naught but a Pyrrhic victory. The might of Chaos had engulfed Naggaroth, obliterating the land that had sheltered and reshaped his exiled people for millennia. He had seen the seas tearing themselves apart on the exodus from the Land of Chill. Was it so strange, then, to question whether Ulthuan would be any more inviolable?

Silar pushed aside his doubts, focusing on the task ahead. The least distraction could prove his undoing. He regretted expressing his qualms about Malus's ruthless strategy now. Perhaps it was that discontent that had led Malus to question his loyalty, and made him decide to employ Silar on such a perilous duty. After all they had been through, he'd half hoped the drachau considered him as something more than just another replaceable lackey. But after all these years, he knew better than that. Whatever bonds they shared, Silar knew no one was indispensable if they stood between Malus and his ambition. Hauclir, Lhunara, even his own father, the vaulkhar Lurhan Fellblade, all had been removed when they became obstacles in Malus's way.

It was one such obstacle that it had become Silar's duty to remove. Malus had been unusually frank about his reasons for having the sorceress Drusala killed. In addition to his suspicions that she was an agent and spy of Malekith, he had come to suspect she was responsible for the murder of Lady Eldire. As one of the few who was aware of the condition that afflicted the drachau, Malus told Silar that the sorceress knew of Tz'arkan and had displayed her powers over the daemon. It could be only a matter of time before she determined to use that ability to exert control over him. To protect the legacy of the Hag, Malus had to break free of such a hold. For vengeance and freedom, Drusala had to die.

The battle against the Ellyrian host had weakened the sorceress. She had drawn heavily upon her powers to conceal the druchii forces from both the spells and the eyes of the pursuing asur. Even for one of her ability, Drusala had been drained by the demands placed upon her. After the battle, she had quietly left the encampment, stealing up into the hills with only her mute bodyguard, Absaloth.

Drusala had imagined her absence to be unremarked, but in that belief her magic had failed her. The witches of the Blood Coven were using their magic to observe her. They too had been impressed to use their spells during the battle, but because they were three, they'd been able to weather the storm better than Drusala. They had enough power left over to monitor her and to warn Malus when she left the camp.

As he quietly made his way over the rocks, Silar listened for even the slightest noise from the armoured warriors he knew to be nearby. In choosing a squad of assassins to slaughter the sorceress, Malus had selected warriors not from his own army but from that of Tullaris. Disciples of Khaine, the executioners considered murder a sacred act and they harboured no love for either Malekith or the sorceresses of Ghrond. Killing Drusala, for them, would be more than vanquishing an enemy. It was an act that would bestow upon them the blessing of their god.

Twenty Bloodseekers led by the infamous Sarkol Narza. More than a match for one exhausted sorceress and her freakish bodyguard, Silar thought.

Drusala had been cautious enough to light no fires. There would be asur scouts in the area and stragglers from the vanquished Ellyrian armies. It was prudent for her to exhibit a modicum of wariness. She'd have been better served, however, to draw less heavily upon the energies streaming down from the mountains. With the aethyric emanations visible even to Silar's sight, seeing the energies converging at a single point, spiralling down to a rocky outcropping was like the blast of a trumpet or the burn of a beacon. It announced Drusala's presence for any who cared to look.

'The witch dies by my blade,' Sarkol hissed in Silar's ear. 'Do you understand that, Hag-rat? She dies in the name of Khaine, not for your master!'

Silar could see the fanatic gleam in the executioner's eyes above the face-wrapping he'd adopted. Given the slightest excuse, he knew Sarkol would leave him dead among the rocks. Cautiously, the noble nodded his understanding. 'I am here only to ensure she dies. How she dies, why she dies, is your business.'

The executioner drew back. 'See that you remember your place, then,' he warned. Sarkol pointed an armoured finger at the outcropping. 'She is there. Half of my followers are working around to the other side. We will strike from here. Between us, there will be no escape for the witch.'

Again, Silar nodded. His fingers tightened around the bronze charm the Blood Coven had bestowed upon each elf in the murder squad. In the event that Drusala wasn't as weak as they expected, the charm would offer some protection against spells. Not immunity, but a degree of resistance. Sarkol and his Bloodseekers had taken the charms with a good degree more confidence than Silar felt. Then, the killers probably thought themselves protected by Khaine and with little need for talismans and charms in the first place.

Beside him, Silar watched Sarkol's fingers rubbing a braided strangler's cord, his thumb working at the rope with careful, measured rotations. It was an old assassin's trick, a way of measuring time and synchronising an attack. At least one of the executioners circling the outcropping would be keeping time the same way. When they were in position, they would wait for the agreed upon moment to strike.

The superstitious dread of a lifetime raced down Silar's spine. It was no easy thing, killing a sorceress. If the witch was able to identify her killers before she died, her curse would haunt their bloodline to the eighth generation. It was why Sarkol and the others wore wraps across the lower half of their faces, a precaution against the death-curse. Silar swore at himself for not exhibiting similar caution, but when he'd left camp he'd been more worried about his murderous companions than Drusala's spells.

'Be ready, Hag-rat,' Sarkol whispered. 'Be vigilant and report to your blasphemous master how the children of Khaine ply their trade.'

Silar could feel more than see the Bloodseekers rise from the rocks and rush towards the outcropping. He rushed after them, determined to carry out the duty Malus had charged him with. When Sarkol struck, he intended to see every sweep of the executioner's blade.

Behind the outcropping, they found Drusala sitting on the ground, her legs folded beneath her. What seemed a column of dancing fireflies was spiralling down around her, but the glowing flickers weren't insects. They were motes of aethyric power drawn down from the mountains, seeping into Drusala as she replenished her magic. The sorceress's skin pulsed with a purple light, her clenched teeth and rolling eyes crackling with energy.

Beside her stood Absaloth, as grim and sinister as ever. The voiceless warrior had drawn his sword and turned to receive Sarkol's attack. The bodyguard appeared oblivious to the dark shapes hurrying out of the darkness behind him. As arranged, the other executioners were striking at the same moment Sarkol had chosen.

Only they weren't Sarkol's elves. Silar hissed a warning when it was obvious to him that there were too many shapes rushing out of the dark. Even as he realised the peril, crossbows were sending bolts into the charging executioners. Five of the killers, half of Sarkol's force, collapsed under the barrage. The survivors rushed onwards, determined to strike down their quarry before they too were slain.

The foe was quicker than the Bloodseekers, intercepting them before they could get close to Drusala. They were wiry, lean elves, their bodies cloaked in black, their skins pale where they hadn't been stained with tribal markings and tattoos. Autarii! The savage tribesmen of Naggaroth's wastelands, descendents of those renegades who'd been exiled from the cities and condemned to fend for themselves in the unforgiving wilds. Silar recognised the nature of the shades at once and an awful suspicion rose into his mind.

The same spiral of magic that had allowed them to find Drusala had also guided these shades to her.

The sorceress had foreseen treachery and countered it with a trap of her own.

With cruel knives and crooked swords, the shades flung themselves upon the executioners. Three of the autarii were cut down by the massive blades, hacked to ribbons by the angry steel of Har Ganeth. In return, however, the cloaked savages brought down all of their foes. In the space of only a few heartbeats, only Silar and Sarkol remained.

Sarkol brought his draich crunching through the skull of one autarii and opened the belly of a second. Kicking the wretch from his path, the incensed executioner tried to reach Drusala. Absaloth fended away the butchering sweep, his sword ringing as it crashed against Sarkol's. The executioner backhanded the bodyguard, laying his cheek open to the bone. Absaloth gave no reaction to the wound, but instead slashed at Sarkol, forcing the warrior back.

The duel that ensued was as brief as it was amazing. Thrust and parry, feint and riposte, Sarkol and Absaloth circled one another. Whenever the executioner seemed about to butcher his foe, the bodyguard's sword would dance against the draich's cruel edge. When it appeared that the Voiceless One would prevail, some killer's instinct would preserve Sarkol at the last second, causing him to weave aside or intercept the blade with the weighted hilt of his draich.

Silar was too busy trying to fend off the attentions of the autarii who came rushing at him to see the end of the fight. The shades came at him from every side, pushing him back to the edge of the outcropping. With nothing behind him except a hundred-foot fall, he had no choice but to fight. The first shade to come at him was sent rolling to the dirt, clawing at the stump of his arm. The second went hurtling to his death when Silar caught hold of his cloak as the shade lunged at him and spun the elf over the edge.

The autarii circled around him now, wary as old wolves. A snarled command from a shade with a face dominated by black tattoos caused them to back away. Falling back, they unlimbered the crossbows hidden beneath their cloaks.

'Merikaar! Leave him be!' The commanding voice boomed like a clap of thunder. The shades flinched at the sound and slipped their crossbows back beneath their cloaks. The tattooed leader scowled, but his eyes were wide with fear.

Silar looked past his attackers. He could see Sarkol staggering on his feet, a gold-hilted dagger piercing the back of his neck. While he watched, the executioner fell. Absaloth, bleeding from a deep gash in his left arm, thrust his sword into the ground and bent down to remove the dagger. Almost gingerly, he restored it to the one who had put it there.

Drusala didn't even glance at her mute bodyguard when she took the dagger from him. Her eyes were fixed entirely upon Silar. 'You will excuse Merikaar. His tribe, the Knives of Khaine, are quite devoted to me. Sometimes that devotion can be carried too far.'

The sorceress walked towards the embattled highborn, paying no notice at all to the corpses strewn about her feet. She smiled as she noted the bronze charm Silar wore. Her fingers hovered before it for an instant. She closed her eyes and sighed. 'Each spell bears a signature, and I know this one from long ago.' She opened her eyes and her smile took on a mocking quality. 'Aren't you going to attack? Aren't you going to fulfil your master's purpose?'

Silar managed to smile back at her. 'All I was supposed to do was watch and report,' he said, nodding at the dead Sarkol. 'I was warned against taking any hand in the attack.'

'You killed two of my kindred,' Merikaar accused, gesturing at Silar with the knife in his hand.

'Do be fair, Merikaar,' Drusala told the shade. 'After all, they were trying to kill him.' Her face lightened, almost wistful. 'This is Silar Thornblood, one of the highest of the highborn of Hag Graef. We mustn't be too capricious about allowing him to die.

'After all, if something were to happen to Malus Darkblade, Lord Silar would be the logical choice to succeed him as drachau.'

SEVENTEEN

Twenty asur captives had been the price set by the Blood Coven to work their magic and conceal the Bloodseekers of Sarkol Narza during the battle. In their time as refugees under the protection of Hellebron in Har Ganeth, the three sorceresses had many centuries to hone their craft, to merge the ritualistic powers of the cult of Khaine to their own dark sorcery. The end result had been a debased and abominable kind of magic, a magic that drew its strength from blood and suffering.

The witches gazed cruelly, hungrily, upon their prisoners. The great Tullaris himself had brought them here, bound to stakes that were driven into the ground in such a way that from the sky, from whence the gods observed the mortal realm, the stakes would form the mark of Khaine. Blood and slaughter delighted the Lord of Murder, and the witches intended to give their violent deity quite a spectacle in exchange for their own revitalisation.

Flinging aside their crimson cloaks, the witches drew long, fang-like knives from their girdles. Sacrificial blades long in the service of Har Ganeth's witch elves, the weapons exuded an aura of atrocity, the stink of blood and death soaked into the ancient bronze, perverting the very metal with the stain of murder. Gleefully, the Blood Coven kissed the hoary blades and ran their tongues along the sides. Blood welled up from the tiny scratches the knives cut into their tongues. The witches laughed in delight, rolling the blood around in their mouths until their teeth took on a crimson hue.

From the stakes, the captive asur looked on with horror and repugnance as the sorceresses worked themselves up into a frenzy, playing the knives across their nubile bodies, unheeding of the cuts and slashes they inflicted on their bare flesh. They threw themselves into a wanton dance of madness and bloodshed, cutting at one another as their bodies writhed and gyrated as though in the thrall of some phantom musician. Wilder, faster, crazier the dance became. The Blood Coven raised their voices in animalistic screeches, howls that mimicked the slavering growls of hounds and the shrieks of hawks on the hunt. The bestial chorus increased in malignance and savagery, dipping into the hisses of jungle saurians and the hellish abominations of the Wastes.

With a final wail, the Blood Coven broke away from their dance of self-mutilation. The witches rushed at the bound captives, slashing at them with their grisly knives. One after another, the asur wilted in their bonds, throats slashed and hearts stabbed as the sorceresses ran amok. Blood fountained from each of the butchered elves, the sanguine fluid taking on a lustrous black sheen as it slopped from the wounds. Ecstatic squeals leapt from the witches as they raced amongst their victims, sacrificing each in turn. The earth within the symbol of Khaine formed by the stakes soon became a bog of dark, shimmering blood.

As their last victim died, the Blood Coven returned their knives to their girdles and hurled themselves to the ground. In a spasm of obscenity, the witches squirmed and writhed through the gory mire, letting the blood soak into their pale skin. As they slithered through the muck, each of them could feel the dark magic they had trapped in the blood passing into themselves in turn. Their bodies tingled, their souls sickened, their stomachs turned as the aethyric powers were drawn into their flesh.

Abruptly, the blood-caked witches looked up, their heads snapping around to stare past the ring of stakes that surrounded them. Beyond the perimeter, they could see a lone druchii, a she-elf dressed in black, her dark hair layered in tiers upon a silver headdress. She leaned against a ghoulish-looking staff, its head aglow with the sorceries bound inside it. An expression of derisive contempt was written across her face and her eyes gleamed with the malice of an old hate long deferred.

'Wallowing in the mud like hogs,' Drusala sneered. 'Is this why you betrayed your mistress?'

One of the Blood Coven, the eldest of the trio, climbed to her feet and pointed a clawed finger at the handmaiden. 'You are a fine one to speak of betrayals. Is your place not in Ghrond, with your mistress Morathi? Do not lecture us about loyalty, Drusala!'

'And who commands your loyalty now that you have fled Hellebron?' Drusala asked. Before the witches could answer, she opened her hand, displaying the protective charm she had stripped from the body of Sarkol Narza. 'An interesting curio to find in the possession of an assassin,' she said. 'And even more curious to find each member of his entourage carrying the same.'

The Blood Coven glanced at one another uneasily. They had imagined Sarkol and his killers had simply missed Drusala in the dead of night. The foothills were, after all, quite a vast wilderness.

'You needn't worry,' Drusala told the Blood Coven. 'They are all dead... well, most of them.' She smiled at the bloody sorceresses. 'There are none left to bear witness against you.'

One of the witches uttered a dry, scoffing laugh. 'There is still you, Drusala. You are alive to bear witness against us.'

Drusala smiled coldly. 'Indeed, and what will three refugees of the convents do about that?'

Again, the witches exchanged a look, but this time there was a sly quality about it. 'We have called upon the old magic. We have drawn the blessing of Khaine into ourselves, transformed our bodies into reservoirs of dark magic. You bring your scorn and mockery at a poor time, harlot of Morathi. The Blood Coven has bathed in the favours of Khaine. Our powers are at their peak!'

'Yes,' Drusala conceded, strangely calm before the threats and boasts of the Blood Coven. 'You are indeed at the height of your ability and power. I have waited many hours to see you at your strongest. It will make beating you still more satisfying.'

A feral snarl rose from one of the witches. Throwing out her hand, the druchii sent a wave of rolling, smouldering darkness at Drusala. As the tide of darkness sped forwards, its essence pitted the wooden stakes and decayed the asur bodies bound to them.

The sorceress gestured with her staff, causing the noxious darkness to fold in upon itself. The cloud quickly disintegrated, dripping into the earth like some malefic dew. 'That was... unimpressive,' Drusala sneered.

Snarling their rage, the three witches made cabalistic symbols with their fingers, the eerie glyphs blazing for an instant in the air. As each symbol flashed into life, the blood-soaked flesh of the conjurers likewise took on a spectral glow. When the Blood Coven unleashed their fury against Drusala, the spell drew nourishment from all three witches rather than one alone. The enchantment took shape as streamers of gore flew upwards from the ground. In a few breaths, a long spear of pulsating blood hovered above the earth. Throwing their hands forwards in unison, the Blood Coven sent the gruesome lance straight at the sorceress.

Drusala drew back as the lance sped towards her. Quickly she threw the folds of her robe about her face, her staff held crosswise against her breast. The bloody spear hurtled straight at her. Like the ball of darkness, it broke against the defensive counter-spell she'd evoked. Unlike the black cloud, however, the spear didn't dissipate. Instead, it exploded into a great morass of blood, a writhing mass of gore that wrapped itself around the sorceress.

The Blood Coven laughed as the blood coiled around Drusala. Each of the witches made pulling motions with her left hand. In response the shattered spear threw more tendrils of itself about their foe. Soon, Drusala's very shape was lost beneath a blanket of pulsating liquid. Grimly, the witches stopped the pulling motions with their left hands. Now, they extended their right hands, slowly closing their fingers. In response, the shell that had formed around Drusala began to collapse in upon itself, shrinking more and more as the Blood Coven closed their hands into fists.

'Broken bones and mangled meat,' one of the witches chortled. 'A fitting end for any of Morathi's trash.' Her eyes took on a light of sadistic glee as she watched the shell contract still further, reducing itself to something on the order of a large pumpkin.

'There won't be enough of her left to fill a thimble,' a second witch observed, cackling with obscene mirth.

'Are you impressed now?' the third witch taunted the shell as it reduced itself to the size of a melon.

'Not particularly.'

The Blood Coven spun about as they heard Drusala call to them. The voice came not from within the shrinking shell, but from the centre of the sacrificial ground. The sorceress stood amongst the stakes, the unnaturally decayed husks of the asur crumbling around her. She held her staff before her, as she had at the start of the attack.

Now she thrust it towards the witches, a purplish light erupting from the head of the staff.

'Let's see how you like my magic,' Drusala hissed.

The Blood Coven railed as lashes of purple light whipped around them. One of the elves was struck on the shoulder, a livid scar appearing as the arcane light seared her skin. Before another lash could strike true, however, a slobbering chant erupted from the lips of all three of the witches. The tonalities weren't entirely of elven speech, but derived from the susurrations of ancient amphibian mage-priests and the cachinnations of daemons.

The sounds themselves seemed to take on a phantasmal substance, speeding away from the witches like a storm of fireflies. Each of the knife-edged motes slashed through the whipping tendrils, sending streamers of purplish light to dissipate in the night air.

Before the lashes could be completely vanquished, Drusala magnified their power, drawing them together into a single great cord of pulsating light. Swirling her staff skywards, she caused the purple cord to shift along with it. When she brought the staff striking earthwards, the phantom luminance did likewise. The ground shook as Drusala's spell slammed against it, quivering with violent tremors that toppled many of the stakes. The purple light exploded in a burst of sound and energy, casting slivers of itself in every direction. The robes of the sorceress were slashed by the burning slivers, her pale skin cut in a dozen places. She dabbed a finger in the blood flowing from her cut cheek, for an instant her body flickering, assuming a different visage. Quickly, she reasserted her will and repaired the momentary dissipation of her protective wards.

The Blood Coven had been sent flying by the aethyric explosion. When the witches picked themselves up from the mire of blood, their bodies were scraped and bruised, the patina of sacrificial blood upon them crumbling into black ash with their every breath. The loathsome coating had preserved them against the worst of the attack, but it had drawn heavily upon their powers. They glared at Drusala as they wiped long locks of blood-matted hair from their faces.

'Enough!' Drusala shouted, slamming the butt of her staff against the earth. A sympathetic tremor rolled through the ground, causing the Blood Coven to stumble. 'You have seen that my magic is greater than yours. Must I destroy you to prove it?' She laughed, a tone of withering scorn. 'I can afford to spare you because your sorcery is no threat to me. And now you know it!'

The witches continued to glare at the sorceress. 'We know you too, Drusala. We know your devotion to Morathi. Whatever lies you've told Malekith, we know who you serve,' the eldest of the witches snarled.

Drusala nodded. 'You know much,' she said. 'But do you know enough? Do you know that Morathi is prepared to forgive your betrayal? Do you know she is prepared to welcome back her sisters? Think of it. You can slip away from the pious madness of Hellebron. You can return to the true sisterhood of sorcery.'

'What if we prefer freedom?' one of the witches demanded.

'What if we have come to favour the Lord of Murder as He favours us?' another asked.

The sorceress laughed. 'Then you are fools,' she declared. 'Think! For all of your magic, even united, you could not oppose me. And I am but Morathi's servant! How should you fare if the Queen herself were here? Do not be so foolish as to think she will be content to be exiled to Ghrond. She will stir herself when the time is right. When she does, she will know her loyal servants... and her enemies. The walls of Har Ganeth will not protect you when she does.'

A murmur swept through the Blood Coven. The three witches turned to one another, conversing without speaking, debating the things Drusala had said.

Drusala watched them with no small amount of misgiving. Their magic had been almost enough to destroy her. But for the hasty translocation spell she'd employed, their gruesome blood spear might have overwhelmed her. Certainly escaping such a fiendish evocation would have been arduous. Then there had been the ghastly survival of the witches against the malign ferocity of her own assault. Any sorceress in Naggaroth should have been obliterated, yet these renegades were merely bruised.

An offer of truce and a promise of rehabilitation hadn't been in Drusala's mind when she'd come here to confront the Blood Coven. Yet, as any druchii general knew, no plan remained intact after contact with the enemy. She felt she knew how they would decide. They had existed for too long in fear of Morathi. The chance to escape that fear was too great to let slip through their fingers now. They'd agree to Drusala's proposal.

Malus and Tullaris would find it exceedingly difficult to act against Drusala now that their pet witches were under her control. She decided not to disillusion them, however. Let them think the Blood Coven was a resource they could draw upon. Their mistake would provide her with early warning of any plan they concocted.

That was if Malus Darkblade was even around to hatch any new plots after this night. Drusala rather hoped he would be. She had a bit too much invested in Malus to see him go to waste.

Darkness had settled over the compound in which the surviving Naggorites were held. Kunor Kunoll's Son had shown unusual restraint following the vicious battle against the Ellyrian army. He'd only executed every third slave-soldier who tried to desert and escape into the hills. Barely a score of Naggorites had been impaled and set as a warning at the perimeters of the enclosure. As atrocities went, it was scarcely worth noting.

Of course, much of that restraint had to do with the attrition the Naggorites had suffered. From thousands of war-slaves, they had been bled into a force of only hundreds. Less than a twentieth of those who'd surrendered when Hag Graef defeated the black ark remained. Even Kunor recognised that the time would soon come when his slaves could no longer field a viable fighting force.

The sons of Naggor had sought noble death in battle, an end that might draw the attention of Khaine and Ereth Khial, a finish that might be worthy of the gods. To such an end they had suffered the indignities and cruelties heaped upon them by Kunor and his minions. They had forgotten their pride and sworn their service to their conqueror. At every turn, Malus had betrayed them, dispatching them not into battle, but into massacres. They weren't deployed as warriors; they were used as fodder for the arrows and blades of the enemy. Even the illusion of a glorious death in combat was stripped away from them, left to rot alongside the butchered dead.

This last callous deployment against the Ellyrians had seen the slave-soldiers decimated by their fellow druchii, shot down without remorse alongside the asur. It was the final affront for those who survived.

Through the darkened camp, three shadows moved. Silently they stole past the rows of tents in which the surviving Naggorites slept. Only a few of the survivors knew the plot that was unfolding this night. They were the only ones in the enclosure who slept the sleep of the just and whose dreams were happy ones.

The time for action had come. Now, while they yet had the strength to strike, to avenge themselves upon the tyrant who had abused them so capriciously. One last act for the glory of Naggor! One last moment when the sons of the black ark could hold their heads high and remember the pride that had once been theirs.

Bragath Blyte ran his thumb along the back of the knife he carried.

The blade itself had been anointed with hydra venom during the battle for the Eagle Gate, dipped into the poison gushing from the torn remains of Griselfang. Using secrets taught to him by the Witchguard, Brek Burok's Son had preserved the envenomed blades, maintaining their potency throughout the long march across Ellyrion.

Bragath could feel the lethal power of the weapon he held. He could feel its strength flowing into him. Should he but reverse his grip, brush his finger along the edge itself, there would be an end to it all. No more doubt and fear, no more suffering. An instant of pain and it would all be over. To hold such power in his hand made his heart beat faster, made his chest swell and his stomach tighten. Death was in his hand and before the night was over, that death would sheathe itself in the breast of Malus Darkblade.

To kill the tyrant. The last act of defiance that was left to the Naggorites.

Three avengers, Brek Burok's Son, Lorfal the Sly and Bragath himself. There'd been only enough venom to anoint three blades. The other members of their conspiracy had been compelled to remain behind. It would be up to these three to bring all their plans to fruition.

The complexity of the intrigue had been complex in itself. Bribes of treasure looted from fallen asur on the battlefield had bought the service of a wine steward of Hag Graef, an elf with his own grudge against Malus having found his entire household left behind in the exodus from Naggaroth. After their victory over the Ellyrian host, the druchii had celebrated far into the night. The bribed steward had ensured drugged skins of wine reached the people Bragath needed them to reach. He was only sorry the resources weren't available to put something stronger in the wine.

Creeping through the darkness, the trio of killers soon passed the perimeter of the Naggorite compound. The sentry who should have spread a warning turned away when he saw Bragath and his companions. Suddenly he found the eerie mage-light in the sky above of far more interest than the killers slinking over the enclosure wall. It had taken a good deal of gold to buy the cooperation of guards like this, but many harboured their own resentments where the drachau was concerned and they could be depended upon to look the other way if it boded ill for Malus.

'I still think it would be wiser to wait for Lord Silar to return,' Lorfal whispered as they stole down the narrow alley between the rows of tents. Inside each bivouac, ten warriors of the Hag slumbered. There was no knowing how many of them had celebrated with a skin of drugged wine and how many would need but the slightest noise to spring from their sleep. This was the most dangerous leg of their excursion, and the murderers knew it well.

Bragath scowled at Lorfal's trepidation. 'Silar could help us,' Bragath agreed. 'But would he? It is better to strike now while he is away with Sarkol Narza. Once the deed is done, he will be unable to deny the role thrust upon him as the new drachau.'

'But would he thank us for his succession?' Brek shook his head.

'He could be no worse to our people than Malus,' Bragath answered. 'Even a quick death would be preferable to this slow hell of denigration and humiliation.'

The killers had moved through one lane and were stealing towards another when Lorfal suddenly stopped. He shook a trembling finger at one of the tents. An armoured druchii was slumped on a bench outside, her head cradled against her shoulder and a skin of wine lying at her feet. It wasn't the sight of a drugged guard that provoked Lorfal, however. Jubilantly, he wagged his finger at the banner leaning against the sleeping warrior, and at the glyph emblazoned across it. It was a symbol known and reviled by all the Naggorites.

'Kunor Kunoll's Son,' Lorfal spat. 'The swine must be inside that tent.' The murderer started towards the structure, but Bragath caught him by the shoulder.

'There isn't time,' Bragath hissed. 'We must strike down Malus before sunrise. Think of the greater goal.'

Lorfal pulled away from Bragath's grip. Scowling, he turned his head and displayed the scar on his neck, a scar left by Kunor's whip. 'I can think of no greater goal than this. Malus will wait. If there isn't time for Kunor, then we *make* the time.'

Bragath would have protested further, but Brek was already rushing past him, stealing like a hungry wolf towards the slavemaster's tent. Conceding defeat, he followed after Lorfal. While Brek stabbed his poisoned blade into the sleeping guard, Lorfal tore open the flap covering the door of the tent.

Kunor lay sprawled upon a bed of furs, moaning slightly in his drugged sleep. A skin of wine lay dangling from one hand, spilling its last dregs onto the ground.

The three Naggorites glared balefully at the sleeping slavemaster. Kunor had been their persecutor long before the invasion fleet landed in Ulthuan, but it was those recent indignities that were the most fresh in their minds. To an elf, not one of them had failed to dream of a scene like this: their enemy lain out helpless before them.

Lorfal charged at the sleeping druchii. Knife raised high, he drove it full into Kunor's chest. Dark blood was just bubbling up from the wound when Lorfal struck again. In rapid fashion, the vengeful slave-soldier stabbed his victim over and over, spattering the walls of the tent with Kunor's blood. The killer's hands became foul with gore, his face splashed crimson, yet still he stabbed and struck.

'Enough,' Bragath finally declared, pulling Lorfal away from his mutilated prey. 'He is dead.'

'I wanted a scream,' Lorfal growled, still glaring at Kunor's body. 'The drug has cheated me of my scream.'

'Then we had best find the drachau's tent,' Brek stated. 'Malus fears poisoners so he keeps his own stock of wine. He won't be drugged insensible like this dog. Stab Malus and you'll have your scream.'

Leaving the butchered Kunor behind them, the Naggorites slipped back into the night.

Silar Thornblood's heart felt as though it would burst. For hours he had been racing back to the druchii war-camp, scrambling through the underbrush and rocks as he hurried down from the foothills. His elven stamina had been taxed to the utmost by his ordeal and the haste with which it was made. Every time his boot slapped against the ground he could feel the impact throbbing in the small veins behind his eyes. The sound of his pounding blood was like a dull roar in his ears. His breath came in thin, burning gasps now, scorching his lungs and sending little slivers of suffering throughout his body.

The need for haste had never been greater. Silar was the lone survivor of the attack on Drusala. Why the sorceress had spared him and commanded the Knives of Khaine to let him go wasn't a mystery, however. Drusala had been obliging enough to explain that Silar was necessary for continuance, that the host of Hag Graef might soon demand a new leader. If Silar wasn't there to step into such a role, she was concerned that Tullaris Dreadbringer would appoint himself general. She was quite frank about her doubts that she could enjoy the same influence over the executioner that she did over the drachau. Whoever the drachau might be.

Silar clenched his teeth tight against the sensation of self-reproach that flared through him. Why had he allowed himself to be involved in the schemes of Bragath Blyte? Had it been pity for the Naggorites that kept him silent about the plot, or had he been looking for some opportunity to exploit the scheme towards his own ends? Whichever way, he knew Drusala was aware of his involvement. If anything happened to Malus, the sorceress would have a powerful piece of blackmail to wield against him. As drachau, Silar would be little more than her puppet. He knew he didn't have the strength of will to resist Drusala. It needed a resolve as mighty as that of Malus to oppose Morathi's handmaiden.

The highborn pushed himself still faster, moaning as he saw the stars of early dawn begin to creep up over the horizon behind the sheen of swirling magic crackling down from the Annulii. By the hints and suggestions Drusala had made, Bragath and his conspirators would be making their move before sunrise, while the camp was asleep. If Silar was going to warn Malus, he had to reach the camp before dawn.

The faintest hint of a rustle among the underbrush had Silar whipping around, sword in hand. The Knives of Khaine. He was certain that at least a few of the autarii were following him. Their master, Merikaar, had taken Drusala's decision to let Silar go with ill grace. He wondered if Merikaar had given the shades special orders to attend to him once he was away from the sorceress.

Silar forced his sword back into its scabbard. Even if the shades were following him, he couldn't let their presence distract him from his purpose. He had to take it on faith that Merikaar and his tribesmen understood the scope of Drusala's powers and the impossibility of concealing any treachery from her. Silar could testify to that last part from his own experiences.

After what seemed a lifetime, Silar saw the watch fires burning around the perimeter of the camp. Carefully, he forced his racing steps into a trot, smothered the panic he was feeling inside. He'd be within sight of the sentries soon. Warriors of the Hag might allow a calm, commanding highborn into the camp without too much question, but they would be certain to detain one who looked as though he'd just slipped past Nethu's gate. Adopting an imperious aloofness he didn't feel, Silar unclasped the brooch pinning his cloak in place. It was the representation of a Naggorite murderhound, a favourite emblem of Malus's inner circle and one that would be known to any soldier of the Dark Crag.

Ahead of him, two guards materialised out of the darkness. One held a crossbow at the ready, while the other gripped the lethal length of a barbed spear. Before the soldiers could issue a challenge, Silar was holding the brooch towards them.

'Lord Silar Thornblood,' he announced in his haughtiest tone. 'Returning from an errand for the drachau.' His lip curled in a withering sneer. 'If you value your heads, let me pass.'

The spearman gave a brief inspection of the brooch and an even briefer glance at Silar. The guard turned pale as he found himself recognising both. 'Forgiveness, Lord Silar,' he said, bowing before the highborn.

Silar ignored the soldiers, marching past them with long, stately strides. The sky overhead was growing darker now, the false night before the first dawn. It was a monumental effort for Silar to maintain a measured pace until he was within the camp itself. Once out of sight of the guards, however, he broke into a frantic run. Bragath and the others had had months if not years to make their plans. Even Malus might not be able to slip through their scheme.

Hurrying towards the grand tent where the Scion of Hag Graef had ensconced himself, Silar saw the first intimations of disaster. The guards outside the tent were laying face-down in the dirt, their hauberks slashed in such a way that the mail looked as though it were partly melted. As he rushed towards the tent, Silar saw a pair of shadowy figures dart inside. A third assassin charged towards him, streams of smoke rising from the poisoned weapon in his hand.

The killer froze in mid-strike, Bragath gazing in shock at the elf he had been about to attack. 'Lord Silar?' the Naggorite gasped.

'It is I, Bragath,' Silar answered. 'Stay your hand.'

Bragath smiled at the highborn. 'With the dawn, you will be drachau. Stand with us, Lord Silar. Keep your promise to my people.'

Silar looked past Bragath, at the tent where Malus slept. There was no time for debate. He had to act now. Before the Naggorite knew what was happening, the noble's sword was flashing from its scabbard and slicing a deep furrow in his chest. 'I must do what is best for the Hag,' Silar hissed. 'I must keep the oath I made to Malus!' He blocked the vengeful sweep of Bragath's blade and knocked the killer back with a kick of his boot. 'Alarm!' Silar shouted. 'Lord Malus, awaken! The daggers of Naggor are upon you!'

Snarling like a beast, Bragath hurled himself at Silar. A downward slash of the highborn's blade took the ear from the killer's head. The anointed knife raked across Silar's shin, the acidic hydra venom sizzling against his steel armour. The noble buffeted Bragath aside with the pommel of his sword, smashing the killer's jaw and spilling teeth into the dirt. With the Naggorite at bay, Silar hastily cut free the plate the dagger had scratched, knocking it loose before the caustic venom could burn its way down to his flesh.

Bragath glared at Silar, but instead of lunging at the highborn who had betrayed them, he spun about and charged towards the tent. Divested of his compromised armour, Silar hurried after the killer. He was just a few steps behind Bragath when the Naggorite threw open the flap.

Bragath froze in the doorway, stunned by the scene unfolding before him. That moment of surprise was all that Silar needed. Rushing up behind the Naggorite, he slammed his sword into the elf's back, driving it up under the steel backplate Bragath wore. Shuddering, the killer slid downwards, blood bubbling from his mouth as he collapsed onto the woven mats lining the floor of Malus's tent.

Silar stepped over Bragath's body. It was his turn to share the sense of shock and surprise experienced by the Naggorite. Far from finding Malus asleep and defenceless, Lorfal and Brek were engaged with a furious, armoured drachau!

'Your warning is appreciated, Lord Silar, if a bit tardy.' Malus whipped a heavy dragon-skin cloak at Lorfal, snagging the poisoned knife the Naggorite held. While Lorfal struggled to free his blade, Malus spun around, slashing the warpsword across Brek's neck. The killer's head rolled from his shoulders, bouncing across the tent. Before the decapitated body could collapse, Malus was lunging at Lorfal.

The Naggorite had just ripped his envenomed knife free of the cloak when he found the drachau charging him. Lorfal slashed at his foe, but the enraged Malus ducked beneath the sweeping blade and drove the warpsword full into the druchii's chest. Snarling at the thwarted assassin, Malus plunged his sword still deeper into Lorfal's body, impaling him upon the hungry steel. When a foot of blade stood out from the Naggorite's back, Malus gave a sidewise twist, ripping the warpsword free in a move that cut Lorfal in two.

Silar gazed in awe at the havoc his master had wrought in but a few heartbeats. Malus sneered at the dead slaves. 'When you kick a dog, sometimes it shows its teeth.' He spat into the cold eyes of Brek's head. 'When that happens you have to kick it harder.'

Silar bowed, nodding his head. 'The Naggorites sought your life, my lord.'

'And they will suffer for it,' Malus vowed. 'The cold ones will be wanting lively fare before they are fit to march and we took too few asur captive to suit that purpose.' His eyes narrowed and he studied his vassal for a moment. 'How is it that you have had the good fortune to arrive just when you did? Shouldn't you be with Sarkol Narza?'

Silar winced at the accusation, but kept all emotion from his face. Drusala had told him what to say, the explanation that would satisfy his tyrannical lord. She'd promised to fabricate whatever evidence Silar needed to back up his story. 'Sarkol Narza was a traitor, dreadlord. He plotted with Tullaris to dispose of you and me so that they could assume control of your forces. That is why he urged you to kill Drusala and abduct the Blood Coven. He knew that sorcery was the one thing that could upset his plans.'

Malus paced across his tent, blood still dripping off the warpsword's blade. 'If Sarkol wanted your life, how is it you are here to tell the tale?'

'Drusala foresaw my peril and sent her vassals, the Knives of Khaine, to intercede. They killed Sarkol and his retinue,' Silar said. 'I knew if they'd been bold enough to murder me, they wouldn't fail to send someone against you.'

The drachau paused above the body of Bragath. The Naggorite stirred feebly. Blood streaming from his mouth, the dying elf glared at Silar and reached a trembling hand towards him. 'This one seems to know you, Silar,' Malus said. He punctuated the statement by stabbing the warpsword into the druchii's back. Bragath shuddered once and fell still.

'He doubtless hoped I might display mercy towards him,' Silar suggested. 'He wouldn't be foolish enough to expect such weakness from the drachau.'

Malus nodded, satisfied with the explanation. 'You have fought beside me a long time, Silar. You would do well to remember your oath.'

'I remember my duty to the Hag,' Silar answered. He frowned, considering the implications of Drusala's lie about Sarkol and Tullaris. 'What will you do about the executioners?'

'Nothing. For the moment,' Malus said, wiping the warpsword clean on Bragath's vestment. 'They have made their play and failed. It will be a time before they work up the courage to try again. Until they do, it will be best to feign ignorance. Tullaris will fight harder if he thinks I'm unaware of this plot of his. Once his usefulness on the battlefield is at an end, so is he.'

'And... Drusala?' Silar wondered.

'A reprieve,' Malus decided, the word sour on his tongue. 'She will be needed now to counter the Blood Coven. The irony of that isn't lost on me, Silar. I don't appreciate being made a fool of.'

An ugly light shone in the drachau's eyes. 'I think a hundred Naggorites fed alive to the cold ones will remind everyone what comes of trifling with me.'

EIGHTEEN

There was a chill in Malus Darkblade's heart as he received the dignitaries Drusala conducted into his tent. Not so long ago, these elves would have been his most dire enemies. Now, by the edict of the Witch King himself, all who wore the World Dragon were allies to the druchii.

It wasn't the presence of the three Caledorians that discomfited the drachau. It was the knowledge that beyond the perimeter of his camp the beasts these princes had ridden awaited their return. Dragons. The strength of Caledor and by extension the might of all Ulthuan. On its own, one of the reptiles could slaughter hundreds of soldiers. In concert with its fellows and with the strategic guidance of the elven princes, the havoc these wyrms could wreak was incalculable. The threat of having such power unleashed against his troops was exceeded only by the intoxicating vision of what Malus might do with three such monsters under his command.

'Prince Iktheon of Caledor and his brothers,' Drusala announced as she presented the Caledorians. The bows they sketched might hardly have qualified as a nod. Malus wasn't certain if that was more due to arrogance or contempt for the alliance Prince Imrik had forged between their peoples.

'Well met, Iktheon,' Malus greeted the Caledorian. He glanced around at the generals and nobles who'd come to attend this audience between the dreadlord and their new allies. He noted with some pleasure the hint of uneasiness exhibited by Tullaris. First Sarkol Narza was slain in the failed plot against Drusala and now the sorceress was bringing to the army a power far in excess of the Ossian Guard and all of Tullaris's executioners. Even if Malus didn't need the dragons for the battles ahead, they would be useful to remind Tullaris who was in charge. While the wyrms were around, Malus would be able to depend on the sincerity of the Chosen of Khaine.

The more troubling issue was determining how much control Drusala had over the Caledorians that she could draw them away from the armies ransacking Tor Elyr. The sorceress was taking pains to make herself indispensable to Malus. He didn't care for that, because he knew there would be a price for her services. And when it came to a sorceress as powerful as Drusala, he was certain the price would be too dear to pay.

'It is an ill wind that brings eagles among ravens,' Iktheon replied. He cast a scornful gaze across the assembled druchii, his air as disdainful as that of a huntmaster inspecting a pack of curs in his kennel. 'My duty to Prince Imrik has never been as onerous as it is today.'

Malus leaned forwards on his wooden throne, raising one of his mailed hands and motioning for his courtiers to be silent. 'If you provoke an incident here, do not think it will shatter the alliance between your prince and my king. The dream of conquest doesn't die so easily.' The drachau smiled as he saw a little of Iktheon's haughtiness crack, the slightest sag in the proud, out-thrust chest.

'Caledor fights beside Naggaroth now. There is nothing either of us can do to change that. We are friends and as friends, we must seek out our mutual enemies.'

Drusala stepped closer to the seated drachau. In the presence of Tullaris and so many of his officers, Malus noticed that the sorceress kept close to him. He wondered if she would be quite so cosy if she knew it was he who had dispatched Sarkol to kill her.

'You have scouted the terrain between here and Avelorn,' Drusala said. 'Tell the drachau what you have seen.'

Iktheon hesitated a moment, the Caledorian choking on a revelation that only weeks before would have been the basest, most vile treachery. 'A great force marches into Ellyrion. By their deployment, it can only be that they mean to hunt down the host of Hag Graef and cut it down.' The dragon prince paused again, fighting to find the strength to disclose the rest. 'The force marching from Avelorn is much smaller than your army, Lord Malus. Perhaps as little as a fifth the size.'

Malus tapped one finger against his chin. 'But there is more, is there not? Something you feel uneasy sharing with friends?'

The Caledorian glared at Malus. For a breath, it seemed he would draw his sword and leap upon the drachau. The moment passed, and instead, Iktheon spoke. 'The Phoenix Guard march in the vanguard of the army, led by Caradryan himself.'

Silar Thornblood stepped out from among the druchii nobles. 'If the Phoenix Guard is there, then they will have phoenix riders as well.' That statement brought a few uneasy mutters from Malus's generals.

The drachau clapped his armoured hands together. 'Be at ease,' he said, the commanding note in his voice brooking no dissension. 'We have friends with us now who will do their utmost to defend us from the phoenix riders.' He nodded to Iktheon. 'Surely your wyrms are the equal of any firebird?' Malus laughed at the impotent hate he saw in Iktheon's eyes. The prince's sense of duty would carry him through.

'And we have the unmatched sorcery of Lady Drusala to help us prepare for battle,' Malus declared, letting his hand fall on the sorceress's shoulder. She'd made a mistake in underestimating how fully the drachau might lean on her powers. Before the battle was through, Malus intended to drain her to the dregs. The Blood Coven could wait; Drusala was the more immediate concern. His only hesitancy came from the worry that it was Tz'arkan making that determination and not his own assessment of the threat she posed.

'If we give battle to the Phoenix Guard, it must be on ground of our choosing, not theirs,' Tullaris declared. Malus was impressed that the executioner didn't colour his words with talk about the will of Khaine and other such zealot doggerel.

Drusala opened her hand, a soft purple fire rising from her palm. In a matter of heartbeats, the fire expanded into a representation of the Ellyrian countryside. Standing stark from the rolling hills and meadows was a jagged landscape of volcanic outcroppings. 'Reaver's Mark,' Drusala explained. 'Here the aethyr hangs close to the earth and my powers will be at their strongest. It is here that I should be able to cast the glamour you wish of me. The Phoenix Guard won't see a single druchii until it is much too late for them.'

Malus nodded, appreciating the ploy. He would discuss the details with Iktheon, Tullaris and his generals later. For now, there was only the need to remind Drusala of her place. 'It isn't what I wish that concerns you, enchantress, but what I command of you. Beware you do not disappoint me.'

Reaver's Mark was a blight of ugliness marring the tranquillity of Ellyrion's eternal summer. Great heaps of volcanic rock lay strewn about the plain, breaking the landscape into eerie expanses of wind-swept cliffs and jagged gullies. Through this haunted terrain, the asur force marched, nearly a thousand strong. No scouts ranged ahead of the army, an oversight that would have bespoke perfect arrogance in any other warriors. The Phoenix Guard were different, however. To an elf, they had walked within the Shrine of Asuryan. They had formed a compact with the Creator God, binding their lives to Asuryan in exchange for the honour of serving him and the glory of his divine blessing. To them was bestowed a sense of purpose denied to other elves; in their souls each of them had been shown the place and hour of his death. In order to preserve such dire portents, to defend the sanctity of prophecy, the Phoenix Guard took an oath of silence that no foreknowledge might slip from their tongues and send ripples of discord through the skein of things yet to come.

More than any of the others, it was their leader, Caradryan of the Flame, who had been afflicted with the curse of foreknowledge. The proud lordling had violated the holiest of holies within the Shrine of Asuryan, penetrating into the sacred Chamber of Days. What secrets had been revealed to him there were known to none but himself, yet from that hour onwards, Caradryan had borne a terrible sense of destiny and upon his brow the rune of Asuryan marked his flesh in a glowing tattoo of arcane flame.

The foresight granted to Caradryan had guarded him well through the centuries. Warriors under his command knew the tide of battle before the first blow had been struck. The disposition of enemy forces, the strength of their leaders and their regiments, these were no secrets to the captain of the Phoenix Guard. To him, the outcome of any fight was already known, the lay of any battlefield already mapped in his mind. For Caradryan, even more than the warriors of his Phoenix Guard, the future was already fact, not simply a fog of possibility and potential.

Malus could have chosen no more dangerous an enemy to face. The greatest strength the druchii had lay in deceit and treachery – strengths that would count for little against a foe who already knew the future. The only counter to the divine magic of Caradryan, of course, lay in more magic. Magic of his own. Magic ruthless enough to tear apart the veil of time and space, to mock the very essence of the future. He'd heard from Lady Eldire how dangerous such magic was – only the toad-priests of the jungles could perform such violations with impunity. A lesser mage risked not simply life but soul as well attempting such a terrible ritual.

Fortunately, Malus had a sorceress on hand who would accept such risk. By playing up to her pride, Malus was able to manipulate Drusala into becoming the vital element in his battle plan. Exterminating the Phoenix Guard would be a terrible blow not simply to the defenders of Avelorn but to the asur as a whole. The key was getting around their insufferable prescience.

Much depended upon the sorceress now. Malus looked over at where Drusala stood, the blood of a dozen slaughtered Naggorites bubbling in the cauldron before her. Arrayed about the cauldron, in a twist of irony that wasn't lost on him in the slightest, were the Blood Coven. Handmaiden of Morathi and witches of Hellebron united in common purpose, determined to bring victory to the host of Hag Graef.

Spite snarled uneasily as the taint of dark magic seeped into the air around them. A spiral of darkness was growing around the cauldron, streamers of sorcery wrapping themselves about the sorceresses. Malus watched as the pale skins of Drusala and the Blood Coven blackened, becoming as dark as malachite. From their splayed fingers, sparkling flares of magic shot upwards, zipping off across the plain until they wrapped themselves about each of the assorted regiments in his army.

'Dreadlord,' Dolthaic hissed in a subdued tone. Malus turned his head slightly, trying to keep his gaze on both the knight and the witches. 'The Phoenix Guard are almost clear of Reaver's Mark. If they reach the open plain, our ambush will have no chance of stopping them, whatever magic the sorceress has promised us.'

The back of Malus's mailed fist caught Dolthaic in the side of his mouth. The knight's cold one snarled hungrily at the scent of the fresh blood dripping from its rider's face. 'I have eyes to see the same as you,' the drachau said. 'And I have a mind capable of forming my own appraisal of the situation. I suggest you hold your opinions in silence. If I want to hear anything from you, I'll tell you what to say.'

Malus left Dolthaic to nurse his wounded pride. He had bigger worries than the esteem of a chastened minion to concern him. The dire assessment Dolthaic had given echoed the thoughts running through his own mind. If Drusala's promised spell didn't exert itself quickly, the entire plan would come apart. Malus needed to cage the Phoenix Guard in Reaver's Mark, prevent them from slipping through to the plains. If a single asur survived to make his way back to Avelorn, there would be small chance of penetrating deep within its borders before Malekith's own forces were on the move again. The Witch King had already claimed victory at the Eagle Gate and would doubtless take credit for the conquest of Ellyrion. Malus was determined that the crushing of Avelorn would belong to him alone. With the Phoenix King dead, the greatest victory the druchii could have would be the capture of the Everqueen. With one blow, the battle for Ulthuan would be decided. Without their king, the asur were a shell of themselves. Without their queen, they would be nothing.

The tendrils of coruscating energy bound themselves in spectral rings around the Knights of the Burning Dark and the drachau who was their master. Malus felt the hairs on his neck prickle as the weird energies swirled faster and faster around him. He could see similar rings taking shape around the Har Ganeth regiments, Silar and the Hag Graef dreadspears, the Iceblades of Ghrond, even Drusala's sinister autarii devotees, the Knives of Khaine. Iktheon's dragons snarled as the dark magic circled them, the great wyrms voicing their distaste for this sorcery to their riders. He watched as Tullaris and his Ossian Guard closed ranks and chanted to Khaine for guidance as the spell wrapped its coils around them as well.

Malus didn't bother to hide his amusement at the sight of Tullaris's devotions. The executioners were praying to be guided into the thick of battle. Well, their prayers were going to be answered, more completely than they hoped. They would play an important role in the battle, but probably not the one Tullaris expected. He could pray to Khaine, but it wouldn't be the Bloody-handed God's doing. It would be the plan conceived by Malus and executed by Drusala.

The arcane ring circling the Knights of the Burning Dark flared, sending a pulse of energy wafting across the plain. The gyrations of the magical power grew faster, becoming more intense with each rotation. Again a pulse of power sped away from the ring. Malus could smell a copper tang in the air and felt a clammy taste in his mouth. His mind shuddered as weird sensations forced themselves into his thoughts. He could touch the colour purple, smell the sound of his heartbeat, hear the flavour of the slime oozing from Spite's scales. The drachau clamped his hands to the side of his head, trying to blot out the obscene impressions.

Then, in a blaze of light, the bizarre sensations were gone. Malus blinked in astonishment as he found himself down in one of the gullies that scratched their way across Reaver's Mark. Around him, Dolthaic and the knights muttered in confusion. They could be thankful their reptilian steeds lacked the wits to be similarly discomfited by the disorienting experience. Prepared as they were for Drusala's spell, the druchii couldn't help the awe that such mighty magic provoked in them.

What Malus and his warriors didn't expect was the sight of the Phoenix Guard just starting to march into Reaver's Mark. When he had last seen them, the asur were leaving the battleground Malus had chosen. The explanation was a simple one, though chilling for that very simplicity. Drusala's spell had moved the army not merely in place but in time as well. They'd been projected forwards to Reaver's Mark, but backwards to that moment when the sorceress had started her ritual. The realisation made Malus's stomach clench. He could hear several of the knights being sick as the same impression struck them.

Dolthaic drew his sword, ready to lead his knights to the attack. A look from Malus made him lower his sword. 'Wait,' the drachau said. 'Wait and watch. I will let you know when to sound the attack.' Dolthaic looked doubtful as he sheathed his sword. The charge of the knights was the signal that would send the rest of the Hag Graef forces into battle. Until the knights attacked, the rest of the regiments would remain where they were, in the gullies and behind the rocks Drusala's spell had sent them to.

Malus could understand Dolthaic's concern. He thought the asur would escape unless the druchii attacked right away. What the knight failed to appreciate was the bloodthirsty impetuousness of Tullaris Dreadbringer and his Ossian Guard.

As the Phoenix Guard entered Reaver's Mark, the executioners came charging out from the gully they'd been transported into. The heavily armoured druchii shrieked a murderous war cry as they flung themselves at the asur. Black draichs slashed down into shining armour and golden surcoats, rending flesh and bone with each strike. The asur were taken utterly by surprise, their shock doubled by the fact that for once Caradryan's foresight had failed to predict the ambush. Drusala's great conjuration had cheated the divine blessing of Asuryan's anointed.

Lesser warriors would have broken under the ferocity of Tullaris's attack. The Phoenix Guard, however, were the staunchest of Ulthuan's soldiers. Under the ghastly punishment of the Ossian Guard, the warriors reformed their ranks, drawing back in orderly fashion. Golden halberds crunched down into the blackened mail of the executioners. Now it was the druchii who paid a butcher's bill. The spearmen and swordsmen with Caradryan's force entered the fray from the side, assaulting the flank of the Ossian Guard. Caught between the two forces, Tullaris was swiftly outnumbered. Malus had no fear that the Chosen of Khaine would try to escape, however. The executioners would fight so long as they had the opportunity to take some of their foes with them. Final offerings for the Lord of Murder.

'Tullaris will be overwhelmed,' Dolthaic pointed out.

Malus turned a contemptuous look on the knight. 'The Ossian Guard will keep the asur pinned down while our forces recover from Drusala's spell,' he declared. 'Tullaris will simply have to hold until we are ready to ride to his relief.'

A seething roar from the rocks to his left had Malus spinning around in Spite's saddle. He turned his eyes skywards as three immense creatures took flight. Crimson wings flashed overhead as the Caledorians guided their dragons across the battlefield. Malus slammed his fist against Spite's side in a pique of frustration. Iktheon, for all his distaste for the role, was behaving like a good ally. Despite the change in allegiance, the dragon prince was still thinking like an asur and no asur would sit back and watch comrades in arms being massacred.

As the dragons flew towards the fray, twelve fiery shapes arose from the asur ranks. Phoenix riders, and leading them, mounted upon the back of the ice-winged Ashtari, was Caradryan the Flame. The captain of the Phoenix Guard was himself taking the fight to the dragons. If the sorcerous ambush had taken Caradryan by surprise, it seemed the treachery of Caledor hadn't. Without hesitation, the phoenixes hurtled towards the dragons like arrows loosed from a bow.

'Sound the charge,' Malus growled at Dolthaic. He'd wanted to wait until the problem of Tullaris was settled, but the honour of Iktheon had made that impossible. The druchii had to attack now and in full force. If the dragons were overcome by the phoenixes, the devastating toll on the morale of Malus's troops would render them almost useless. If the wyrms made short work of the phoenixes, then the asur would break and any chance of striking Avelorn with any element of surprise would be lost.

As the cold ones charged out from the gully, hundreds of darkshards and dreadspears marched out from their own positions. The Iceblades, the grisly swordsmen from Ghrond, filed out from behind an outcropping of black volcanic rock. The Har Ganeth warriors came rushing out from one of the gullies, eager to aid their embattled Chosen of Khaine. Stealing along the periphery of the battle, the autarii, Merikaar and his shades worked their way towards the rear of the Phoenix Guard.

Cries of alarm rose from the soldiers supporting the Phoenix Guard. But for the stolid presence of the warriors of Asuryan, the rest of the asur would have broken and fled. The size of Malus's army was incomparably vast compared to their own. It was the presence of the Phoenix Guard that made them stand their ground, the reminder that they fought beside elves whose devotion to their god was stronger than fear. Unlike the Voiceless Ones from Ghrond, the Phoenix Guard held their silence not from physical mutilation but from their own oaths and determination. When one of them was cut down by an executioner, even at the moment of death he refused to let a sound pass his lips. No screams, no cries, only the silent acceptance of his doom. As the vast druchii horde came thundering down upon them, the Phoenix Guard displayed the same iron resolve, prepared to meet the foe with the same fatalism that guided all their deeds.

Malus spurred Spite onwards, reaching the asur battle line at the forefront of his knights. The warpsword flashed down, splitting the helm of a warrior of the Phoenix Guard while the flashing fangs of his horned one ripped open a second elf's pelvis. A twist of Spite's head and the asur was dragged from his regiment and tossed under the driving claws of the cold ones charging into the fight.

'Send them to sleep with their king!' Dolthaic roared, laughing as he skewered the throat of an asur spearman.

The laugh ended in a wet gurgle as the warpsword raked across Dolthaic's neck. The knight slumped in his saddle, his sword falling to the ground as he clapped his hands to his mangled throat. His eyes stared in horrified confusion at his murderous lord.

'Poor choice of words, old comrade,' Darkblade snarled as the last flicker of life left Dolthaic. The knight really had brought his execution upon himself. He should have remembered the details of his lord's parentage.

Spite shifted beneath Malus, the reptile's jaws snapping off the arm of an asur spearman as the warrior tried to attack the drachau. Malus turned away from the murdered Dolthaic and brought the warpsword shearing through the spearman's shoulder, leaving the elf's other arm lying in the dirt. The mangled body staggered back, collapsing against the warriors in the rear ranks. Spite lunged into the gap, shaking its horned head and snapping its fangs at the enemies around it. Malus played his blade about him, shattering shields and breaking spears at every turn.

Cries of dismay rose from the embattled asur. Malus saw several of the warriors in the rear ranks pointing up at the sky. Overhead, he could hear the shrieks of the phoenixes and the roars of the dragons. A hasty glance showed him Caradryan attacking Iktheon. A pivotal duel, one that might shatter the enemy's resistance if it favoured the Caledorians.

Careful to keep the asur at bay with his sword, Malus watched as Ashtari dived down upon the red-scaled dragon. Iktheon's sword crashed against Caradryan's halberd as the two elves struck at one another. Then the claws of the icy phoenix were ripping at the dragon's hide, clumps of frost forming with each buffet of the great bird's wings. The dragon gnashed its jaws, trying to snatch Ashtari from the air. The reptile's reward was the bite of Caradryan's halberd, the Phoenix Blade. Wreathed in flame, the enchanted weapon shattered several of the wyrm's fangs and drove a shard of tooth up through the top of its mouth.

Snarling in pain, the dragon started to roll in mid-air, trying to knock Ashtari loose. The roll, however, brought unintended disaster. While the wyrm seemed largely impervious to the cold generated by the phoenix, the chains holding Iktheon's saddle were far less robust. As the dragon rolled, chains already turned brittle by Ashtari's frost snapped. Iktheon managed a single wail of terror as the saddle tore loose and he plummeted to the ground far below.

Even as the dragon prince died, his monstrous steed sought to avenge him. Flipping back, turning its roll into a climb, the dragon soared upwards. Craning its head around, the brute breathed a gout of flame full into Ashtari. The cold phoenix shrieked, some of its icy feathers melting in the dragon's malignance. The pain was enough that the bird pulled its talons from the scaly hide. As it tried to glide away, the wyrm's jaws snapped at Ashtari, tearing into its left wing.

Before the dragon could work further havoc, Caradryan struck at it. Forged in the almost legendary time of Kor-Baelon, the first captain of the Phoenix Guard, the Phoenix Blade pierced the dragon's eye. Fiery ichor and molten jelly spurted from the wound, bathing Caradryan in burning slime. The stricken dragon released Ashtari, vengeance and the fallen Iktheon forgotten as it bellowed in anguish. Beating its mighty wings, the reptile soared away, driving back towards the south and the volcanic mountains of Caledor.

The asur warriors began to cheer the destruction of Iktheon and the routing of his dragon, but the celebration quickly fell silent. Ashtari, its wing maimed by the dragon's bite, came hurtling down from the sky. The bird crashed to the earth with the ferocity of a comet, scattering druchii and asur alike. Slivers of ice slashed at the elves while those closest to the impact were crushed by the phoenix.

A ragged shout did sound from the asur as the wounded phoenix stirred. Even in its fall, Ashtari had tried to protect its elven friend. Loyal to the end, the bird had shielded Caradryan from much of the impact. Now the hero emerged from the devastation, the dragon slime still steaming on his golden armour. Caradryan the Flame, bathed in smoke and wielding the fiery Phoenix Blade, stood beside the crippled Ashtari and prepared to receive his foes.

Malus sneered. It was a futile act of defiance. The asur were still vastly outnumbered. All Caradryan could do was try to sell his life as dearly as he could. The drachau was determined the elf would find no heroic end. Urging Spite away from the melee, he drove the horned one towards the regiments under Silar's command. He'd have the darkshards deploy against the arrogant lordling. There wasn't too much honour in being pierced by a hundred bolts and dying like a sick dog in the dirt.

Riding towards Silar, Malus heard a disconcerting sound ring out across the battlefield. Turning about in his saddle, he felt ice crawl down his spine. The sound was that of horns, the sharp keening blasts of war and the promise of combat. He could hear the thundering hooves of hundreds of horses, see the bright gleam of armour in the sunlight. Then Malus saw the standard of the Phoenix King, rising above a vast company of asur knights. Finubar was dead, that much Malus knew for certain. He also knew who it was who had been appointed Regent of Ulthuan.

An army was riding to rescue Caradryan and the Phoenix Guard, an army commanded by the most famed of all Ulthuan's heroes.

Prince Tyrion, the Dragon of Cothique!

NINETEEN

Malus could see the magic burn of Tyrion's sword, Sunfang, as the hero led his knights across the plain. Malus had imagined the Regent of Ulthuan would be far from the battlefields of Ellyrion, that he would be ensconced in some stronghold somewhere orchestrating the defence of the ten kingdoms against the elven and daemon enemies who threatened the realm. He hadn't considered that the blood of Aenarion truly coursed through Tyrion's veins, or that the regent would be as loathe to keep himself from combat as his famed ancestor.

The first victims of the asur knights were a group of Ghrondian spearmen acting as bodyguard for one of the *Eternal Malediction*'s sorceresses. As the knights thundered towards them, the dreadspears tried to brace for the assault. The sorceress drew upon her magic, hurling arcane fire into the charging Ellyrians. A clutch of knights were blasted into oblivion, their flesh melting into the backs of their panicked steeds. The malefic spell wasn't enough to break the attack. Voices raised in a cry of vengeance, demanding justice for the slaughtered elves of Tor Emyrath, the cavalry slammed into the dreadspears. The force of their impact buckled the formation, spilling druchii warriors in every direction. Tyrion himself, upon his noble stallion, Malhandhir, charged towards the sorceress.

The druchii witch hurled a blast of black lightning full into the elven prince's face. The great blood-red ruby Tyrion wore upon the brow of his winged helm pulsed and flashed with a crimson glow. The black lightning parted before him as though swept away by a spectral wind. Before the stunned sorceress could unleash another spell, Sunfang came slashing down and sent her head tumbling from her shoulders.

A flash of ghostly light, and suddenly the charge of the Ellyrian knights was blocked by a regiment of warriors from Clar Karond. The druchii soldiers locked their shields and received the brunt of the assault, resisting the driving hooves and stabbing lances of the asur.

More of the weird luminance played about the battlefield now. A company of darkshards were transplanted from where they had been menacing Caradryan and moved to the flank of the elven knights instead. Drusala and the Blood Coven, working once again their uncanny violation of space and time. Now it was only their place in the material plane that the sorceresses adjusted, allowing the temporal positioning to remain unaffected. They didn't confine their effort to the druchii, however, and soon the spiralling rings of arcane energy were swirling about the blocks of advancing infantry moving to support Tyrion's knights. A company of Lothern archers found themselves flung to the far side of Reaver's Mark, spun around so that the arrows they loosed fell upon a cove of sun-bleached trees instead of druchii flesh. A complement of sea guard was cast full into the blades of Malus's soul-bonded dreadspears. The careful formations of the asur general were thrown into utter disarray as Drusala's sorcery scattered them about the plain.

Malus laughed. He'd thought to end Caradryan quickly, to content himself with sacrificing Tullaris and the Ossian Guard in exchange for a speedy victory. Now he found himself with a prize even greater than anything he had imagined. The Regent of Ulthuan, the mighty hero the asur had rallied to in their moment of crisis and calamity. If he could take Tyrion's head he wouldn't need to lay waste to Avelorn and capture the Everqueen. He could break the asur here and now. He could claim a victory that Malekith wouldn't be able to take from him. With the head of Tyrion hanging from his belt, the Witch King would have no choice but to make Malus his seneschal, to elevate him to a rank second only to the king himself.

Roaring commands at Silar to bring his troops, shouting threats at the Knights of the Burning Dark to follow him, Malus whipped Spite away from the Phoenix Guard and towards the new prey he had chosen for himself. The warpsword would hew the head from Tyrion's shoulders. It had been a long time since he'd faced the hero, but Malus was confident that this time their meeting would be different. He could feel the strength of Tz'arkan within him, filling his veins and muscles with power. The daemon had retreated into the hinterlands of his soul after Drusala had pacified it, but Malus found he could still call upon the fiend's strength. Even better, since the daemon wasn't trying to exert its control over him at the same time. Perhaps it understood the danger of confronting Tyrion – the Sunfang was a weapon forged to slay its kind after all. Perhaps Tz'arkan understood that if it were to endure it had to invest Malus with its strength without the usual distraction of its plots and schemes.

For Malus to endure, he had to be the one to strike down the elven prince. Yet even as he spurred Spite away from the Phoenix Guard, he could see that he wasn't alone in his ambition. Tullaris

Dreadbringer had seen the Dragon of Cothique as well. A blood-curdling howl rose from the Chosen of Khaine. Driving the First Draich clean through the body of the asur he was fighting, ripping the dying elf from his blade as though he were nothing more substantial than a leaf, Tullaris turned and forced his way back through the ranks of the Ossian Guard. Those executioners too slow to part ranks for their maddened master were cut down with the same ruthlessness he had shown the asur.

There was a bitter hatred between Tullaris and Tyrion, but Malus knew on the part of Tullaris that hate was wrapped up within the divine visions and whispers the executioner believed himself to receive from Khaine. The fire that burned in Tullaris was more than simple madness: it was a religious mania that could sate itself only with the blood of the asur hero. Malus wanted the prince's head to secure his power; Tullaris wanted it merely as an offering to the Lord of Murder.

The Scion of Hag Graef was certain his claim was better, and he would make sure it was the warpsword that ended the legend of Tyrion this day. Leaning from his saddle, Malus glared back at Silar. He gestured at Tullaris and crooked two of his fingers against one another. It was an old signal between them, one that had been developed when Malus still dwelled in his father's tower and Silar was but a simple retainer. It was a sign that had brought death to a great many Malus had found inconvenient over the years. Now it would initiate still another murder.

Leaving Silar to attend the details, Malus spurred Spite onwards. Around him, the Knights of the Burning Dark urged their blood-maddened cold ones onwards, the reptiles' roars thundering across the battlefield.

The asur infantry, seeing the threat posed by the cold one knights, moved to intercept the charge, to thwart the druchii rush towards

Tyrion and his cavalry. A phalanx of Sapherian spears interposed themselves in Malus's path. The spearmen were too few to overcome the knights, but they were enough to act as an obstacle to their advance. A sickening groan rattled across the field as the ponderous cold ones slammed into the hastily assembled fence of asur spears and shields. Druchii lances pierced the silverwood shields, gouging hideous wounds in the warriors behind them. A few of the cold ones were brought down, impaling themselves upon the waiting spears in their savage rush. Most of the knights on their backs were able to kick themselves free of the dying reptiles, but a couple of the elves weren't so fortunate, crushed beneath the bulk of their beasts as the brutes writhed in their death throes.

Malus brought the warpsword slashing out. Powered by the infernal strength of Tz'arkan, he sent a spearman hurtling overhead, flung like a bullet from a sling by the impact of the drachau's blade. The mangled asur crashed violently among the ranks of her comrades, breaking arms and backs as her armoured weight slammed into them. Malus urged Spite forwards, lunging into the gap he'd created; then he began to slash his enchanted blade to right and left, reaping a ghastly toll from the Sapherian soldiers. A silver-helmed champion chopped at him with a gem-encrusted axe but the elf's first blow merely glanced from the drachau's spiny sabaton. Malus answered the assault with a cleaving strike of his blade that sliced the face from the champion's head and left a screaming skull behind.

The slaughter among the Sapherians was woefully one-sided. Scores of the spearmen were cut down by the Knights of the Burning Dark or mangled by the fangs and claws of their cold ones. The stubborn defence the asur offered soon crumbled as the determination of the survivors faltered. The spearmen broke and fled, ironically causing Malus more problems in retreat than they had in battle. Bellowing threats and curses, he commanded his knights to restrain their reptilian steeds and keep them from pursuing the fleeing asur. Subduing the bestial instincts of the cold ones was a task easier said than achieved. Several of the knights broke ranks as the hungry reptiles defied their riders and loped after the Sapherians. One of the cold ones was so opposed to the idea of lingering behind that it flung its head back and caught its rider's arm, pulling the limb from its socket before any of the other druchii could come to the knight's aid.

In the confusion of restoring order among the knights, Malus looked away to the south. He could see that Tullaris had taken control of another contingent from Har Ganeth, the Bloodseekers, executioners who had once served Sarkol Narza. The Chosen of Khaine led his warriors at a loping trot across the plain, still intent on reaching Tyrion and his knights. Like Malus, however, the executioners found their path blocked, this time by a regiment of Chracian warriors. Draped in the pelts of white lions, the spearmen of Chrace met the glaives of the Bloodseekers in a display of primitive savagery that recalled to Malus the feuds of skin-clad barbarians in the Wastes. It was a forbidding reminder to him of the brute hiding beneath the veneer of civilisation, that thousands of years of culture and refinement were but a mask the elves wore to restrain the savage underneath. For the Fangs of Chrace and the Bloodseekers, such restraint had been cast into the winds.

Malus smiled when he saw Silar leading his darkshards towards the rear of the Bloodseekers. The crossbows would quickly turn the tide and settle the problem of Tullaris Dreadbringer.

Standing in his stirrups, Malus cried out to his knights. 'I want the regent's head,' he shouted. 'The knight who kills Tyrion will be given the weight of his cold one in gold! The knight who lets the regent escape will be fed to his cold one!' He brought his sword swinging down, thrusting its point to where Tyrion battled the warriors of Clar Karond. The asur were winning, but if the druchii fighters could hold out just a few minutes more, Malus could bring his cavalry smashing into the Ellyrian flank. They'd have half the asur knights lying in the dirt before the Regent could react.

Then it would just be a small matter of killing the greatest asur hero of the age. Malus was going to enjoy that. Despite his promise of reward, he would kill any druchii who tried to steal that glory from him.

Tullaris Dreadbringer hurled himself into the fray with the wanton abandon of a blood daemon. The First Draich slashed and gouged, hacked and stabbed its way through the Chracian warriors. The executioners around him gave a wide berth to the Chosen of Khaine, all too aware how easily it could be them rather than the asur who were claimed by their lord's murderous fury. Their hesitancy caused more of the asur spearmen to rush Tullaris, thinking to bring down the infamous villain before meeting the glaives of the Bloodseekers.

The song of Khaine thundered through Tullaris's veins as he met the Fangs of Chrace. Ten, then twenty of the elves lay butchered at his feet. The gore of his victims dripped from his armour and plastered his face, lending him a fiendish aspect. The slaughter thrilled Tullaris, made his heart swell inside his breast. Death! Blood! Skulls for Khaine! He would glut the Lord of Murder with the souls of his victims this day. The First Draich would reap a harvest of carnage undreamed of.

Through the blood frenzy, Tullaris could yet hear the voice of his god. Khaine's words pulsed through his very soul. The executioner snarled in rage, his entire being revelling in the havoc around him. Yet the commandments of a god couldn't be ignored.

While Tullaris wrestled to pull himself free from his own frenzy of slaughter, the commander of the Chracians fell upon him. The elf's gleaming axe came chopping down, striking for the villain's head. In a blur of motion, Tullaris spun his draich around, the ancient blade cleaving through the haft of the Chracian captain's axe. As the ancestral axe was cut in half, the draich continued its vicious sweep, slicing through the heavy lion pelt the asur wore, crumpling the steel helmet beneath and crunching through the skull inside. Before the horrified spearmen knew what was happening, their captain fell at the feet of Tullaris.

The killer's face split in an ophidian smile of diabolic satisfaction. Tullaris would heed the words of Khaine, he would march to the destiny that awaited him. But there would be blood every step of the way. Tullaris would find Tyrion even if he had to turn the whole of Reaver's Mark into a charnel house to do it.

Away from the roar of battle, Drusala watched as the asur poured more forces into the fight. With the arrival of the Ellyrian host, Caradryan had been saved. She had detected the presence of Korhil among the relieving force, Charandis-bane as the elves of Chrace had named him. An almost legendary warrior, renowned as the captain of the fearsome White Lions, Korhil would prove a formidable adversary for Malus. Perhaps too much for Darkblade to overcome.

From atop one of the volcanic spurs that rose above the field, Drusala observed the well-ordered ranks of infantry being brought into the battle. Already engaged with the Phoenix Guard and their supporting troops, the army of Hag Graef was too dispersed to react quickly enough to Korhil's advance. She could see the tall, powerful elf lord, his body draped in the hide of Charandis as he led his White Lions towards the fray. Regiments from Ellyrion and Lothern and Avelorn followed, their banners snapping in the fading light. The druchii had lost the advantage of numbers, and likewise the advantage of cohesion. There was little Drusala could do about the former, but she had tried to influence the latter, shifting regiments around the battlefield with her dark magic.

The violation of time and space had sapped her powers, however. To work the feat she now had in mind, she would need to draw upon the powers of the Blood Coven.

'Sisters, I must call upon your strength,' Drusala called to the three witches. It was a formality, really. When she'd defeated them before, she placed upon each of them a binding that laid their souls bare to her. They were as much her slaves as Absaloth and the Voiceless Ones, even if they weren't aware of it.

The Blood Coven clawed handfuls of gore from their cauldron, bathing themselves in the lifeblood of murdered druchii, drawing into themselves the terrible potentialities of the aethyr. To Drusala's attuned eyes, the three witches began to blaze with flames of dark power, each becoming a crackling pillar of arcane energy. Stretching forth her hand, she began to draw that energy into herself, to use it to shift and manipulate the fabric of reality. She ignored the cries of pain her leeching drew from the Blood Coven. It was their honour to be used by the sorceress, to fuel such a vast magical working. What matter if it would shred their souls and shatter their minds? They should be thankful for the opportunity to serve Queen Morathi.

Scattering the strands of reality, Drusala wove them into new patterns and shapes on a far greater scale that she had before. The last of the Clar Karond beastmasters in the host of Hag Graef found themselves transplanted from the flank of Caradryan's encircled forces to the fore of Korhil's White Lions. The remaining hydras in the druchii force snapped and tore at the stunned asur, decimating their front ranks as they suddenly appeared right in the path of their march.

All about the battlefield, the theme was repeated. Dreadspears manifested upon the rear of Avelorn archers, bleakswords were transferred into the path of marching Ellyrian warriors. Malignantly, Drusala stretched her will to seize the well-ordered asur regiments. One by one she scattered them about Reaver's Mark in chaotic disarray. Warriors who thought themselves protected on either side by friends now found themselves surrounded by foes. Archers ready to loose their arrows reappeared far across the field with no enemy within range. The Lothern Sea Guard were dropped in the midst of the Iceblades and the corsairs, the bewildered asur hurriedly locking their shields together in a circle of protective steel.

Drusala laughed in vicious triumph, channelling more and more power through herself. She could feel the Blood Coven being sucked dry by her magic, but it was of no concern to her. To feel this kind of power, to exert this kind of force, she would drain the lives of a dozen sorceresses! A hundred!

Lost in her hubris, Drusala failed to notice the tiny strands of magical energy that were being diverted away from her. The Blood Coven were bound to her now, and compelled to obey her, but still they had found a way to defy the sorceress. Each little coil of power that they diverted away from Drusala they sent pouring into Malus Darkblade. The process had started with the first great ritual that had sprung the drachau's ambush against Caradryan. Now, as Drusala drew more heavily upon her living fuel, so did the witches send more aethyric power into the drachau himself.

Through their arcane connection to Drusala, the Blood Coven had learned of Tz'arkan. Now they were feeding the daemon, using it to empower Malus. With enough power, the drachau would be free of Drusala's control. When he was, he would come seeking his revenge.

It was only when one of the witches was finally drained dry and her withered body wilted to the ground that Drusala noticed the energies that were being redirected. With a shriek of fury, she cut off the flow of power, leaving the two surviving witches collapsed upon the ground.

Drusala didn't spare the prostrate witches another thought, but immediately focused on what they had done. She could see the dark energies blazing within Malus. The witches had stirred up Tz'arkan's power while leaving the daemon's consciousness in retreat. Malus Darkblade with the full might of a daemon king flowing through his flesh! The prospect was one that made even her shudder.

To stop Malus now would mean horrendous risk, risk that Drusala didn't dare. Casting her awareness about the battlefield, she hesitated, wondering if there weren't perhaps another way. She saw Tullaris and the Bloodseekers cutting their way through the Fangs of Chrace. Just as they had their foe on the run, a company of darkshards under the command of Silar began to shoot down the executioners. More deceit and treachery from Malus. First the drachau had connived to have Drusala transplant Tullaris and the Ossian Guard nearest the enemy, now the drachau set his soldiers the task of outright assassination.

The Chosen of Khaine harboured a long grudge against the Scion of Hag Graef. This treachery on the battlefield would only enflame that hate. Tullaris would be her weapon against Malus.

Unable to tap into the Blood Coven's magic, Drusala exerted her own energies to once again pervert the rules of time and space. A ring of coruscating light formed around the Bloodseekers, whirring about them in a blinding spiral. When it seemed the light could spin no faster, both it and the Bloodseekers vanished. Right from under the bolts of Silar's troops, Tullaris was snatched to another part of the field, dropped down some little distance from Malus and his Knights of the Burning Dark.

Exhausted by her exertion, Drusala sank against the side of the volcanic spur. She had seen the executioners safely across the field, placed Tullaris where he could exact revenge upon Malus. What she didn't see as she tried to regain her strength was Tullaris order his troops away from the Knights of the Burning Dark. She didn't see him lead his elves towards the Ellyrian knights.

Revenge was a powerful force in the heart of Tullaris Dreadbringer, but the voice of Khaine was more powerful still.

Malus felt as though the strength of a god were in his limbs. The asur he struck down were cut asunder as if their armoured bodies were no more than pieces of bread. By his strength alone, the knights ruptured the asur regiment, decimating the warriors in an orgy of bloodshed. Cold ones ripped gory giblets from the slaughtered foe while knights stabbed their lances into the wounded elves writhing on the ground. Malus held the banner of the vanquished regiment overhead. He waved it back and forth, mocking the rest of the enemy army. Then, with no more than a snap of his fingers, he broke the stout silverwood pole and tossed the broken banner into the bloody morass of shattered warriors and feeding reptiles.

The whole of Ulthuan would tremble at his name. The asur would cower in their palaces and temples, praying to Asuryan and all the indifferent Cadai for deliverance from Malus Darkblade. He would raise a mountain of skulls such that even Malekith would beg him for mercy!

A low hiss from Spite drew Malus's attention. He followed the horned one's gaze. Red fury boiled up inside him. He'd been aware that Drusala and the Blood Coven were continuing to bend space and time to shift forces about the battlefield so that the fighting would favour the druchii. What he hadn't been aware of was the translocation of Tullaris and the Bloodseekers. The executioners had appeared a few hundred yards from the Knights of the Burning Dark. Malus could see Hag Graef crossbow bolts sticking in the armour of the Har Ganeth killers, some of them dropping to the ground from their wounds even as he watched. The sorceress had used her magic to save Tullaris just as Silar was about to destroy the Chosen of Khaine.

Drawing back on Spite's reins, Malus expected the executioners to come rushing at his knights. Instead, Tullaris goaded them forwards. It took only a second for Malus to understand his rival's intentions. Tullaris was still focused on his original purpose – determined to strike down Tyrion. Even balanced against the recent treachery of the drachau, Tullaris was intent on the asur prince. Malus felt a cold chill rush through him, wondering if the fanatic thought the voice of Khaine were guiding him to such an encounter. More disturbingly, he wondered if that voice might in fact be real.

Real or not, he was determined to reap the glory from this battle. 'The Regent!' Malus shouted at his knights, jabbing the warpsword in the direction of the Ellyrian reavers. The cavalry had won their battle, scattering the Clar Karond contingent, but it had been a costly fight. They started to turn back towards the asur positions, but thanks to the shifting magic of Drusala, there was no battle line to return to, only a hundred small skirmishes unfolding all around Reaver's Mark.

Malus saw Tyrion raise Sunfang over his head, a gesture of challenge as ancient as Aenarion. The drachau hefted the warpsword in reply, accepting the call to battle. But when the Ellyrians came galloping across the field, they wheeled to the right, away from the cold ones and their lord! Malus roared in outrage when he saw that they were charging the Bloodseekers. Tullaris, too, had raised his weapon in challenge and it was to Tullaris that the asur now drove their frothing steeds.

'I want the Regent,' Malus snarled at his knights. 'I want his blood. I want his flesh. I want his soul!' Spite growled hungrily as the drachau urged the reptile to greater effort. 'The Regent,' Malus snapped at the knights riding around him. 'Kill anyone who stands between us and the Regent!'

He knew his Knights of the Burning Dark. They wouldn't hesitate to obey his command, however murderous. The execution of Dolthaic would be a reminder to them of what it meant to offend their master.

Panic gripped Silar Thornblood when he saw the Bloodseekers vanish right from under the assault of his darkshards. From his vantage, he could see the executioners reappear across Reaver's Mark. They had rematerialised only a small distance from Malus and the Knights of the Burning Dark. At once he recognised the treachery at work here. Drusala had employed her sorcery to bring Tullaris against Malus. After the murderous fire from Silar's troops, the Chosen of Khaine would be even more enraged and maniacal than usual. He'd avenge himself on Malus, given the opportunity.

The drachau was the only one who could hold together the dwindling might of Hag Graef. Malus was the only lord with the strength and determination to rekindle the blood of the Dark Crag. Silar felt this in his heart. If his people were to have any legacy at all, Darkblade must live!

Spotting one of the mounted messengers who relayed commands between the drachau's generals, Silar broke away from the darkshards and waved the horseman towards him. As soon as the messenger was near, the noble seized him and dragged the elf from the saddle. A slash from his sword ended the messenger's protest at Silar's thievery. The smell of its former master's blood excited the black charger, the horse rearing and snorting as it tried to throw Silar from its back.

The noble jerked the reins savagely, forcing his new mount to turn. Once he had the horse pointed towards the Bloodseekers, Silar swatted its flank with the flat of his sword. The steed galloped off, its hooves pounding across the corpse-littered terrain. Dead and dying elves were smashed by the racing animal. Asur stragglers stabbed at Silar with spears and swords, druchii survivors cried to him for aid. Silar ignored them all, intent upon the desperate purpose that now ruled him. He had to save Malus. He had to honour his old oaths. The future of the Hag depended upon it.

Ahead, Silar could see the Ellyrians rushing to engage the Bloodseekers. For a moment, he debated drawing back, leaving the asur to settle with Tullaris. With Tyrion commanding them, there was every chance the Chosen of Khaine would meet his end.

Silar shook his head and urged his horse onwards. He couldn't take the chance. If Tullaris survived, it was certain that he would prosecute his vengeance against Malus. Silar was realistic about his chances against the executioner – at least in a fair fight. But he didn't intend to fight Tullaris at all. He intended to ride him down while the killer was focused on the Ellyrians.

Away to his flank, Silar could see Malus and his knights charging towards the melee. The proximity of his lord made him hurry his mount to still greater effort, lashing its flank until blood streamed down its legs. He couldn't let Darkblade fall! Not when it had been his duty to kill Tullaris in the first place. Not when so much depended on the drachau's survival.

Murderous and vicious as they were, the Bloodseekers still had a certain degree of discipline. Those at the rear of their formation parted ranks to allow Silar to pass through them, mistaking him for a mounted messenger. The noble drove his horse between the executioners. From his vantage, he soon spotted Tullaris.

Lashing the horse once more, Silar drove for the infamous fanatic. This time he didn't wait for the Bloodseekers to step aside, but used the mass of his horse to batter them aside. He saw the Ellyrians being cut down by the vicious Tullaris. He could hear the grisly Khainite chant that rose from the executioner's lips.

Raising his sword high, Silar charged his horse straight for the embattled Tullaris. Something, some uncanny sense, warned the executioner at the last instant. In a blindingly fast motion, Tullaris shifted away and brought the First Draich sweeping upwards. The murderous blade struck the horse in the neck, shearing through muscle and bone to send the animal's head flying away. The decapitated brute ploughed onwards for several yards, crashing into the Ellyrians.

Silar tried to leap clear of the saddle, but his boot caught in the stirrup. When the momentum of the beast was spent and its carcass crashed to the earth, he was pinned beneath its weight. Desperately, he tried to free himself, tried to drag his now broken leg clear of the dead animal.

A dark shadow suddenly fell across the trapped Silar. He grabbed for his sword, but even as he did, the gory blade of the First Draich came scything down, shearing through his shoulder and leaving his arm lying in the dirt.

'Loyalty to that cretin was ever your weakness, Silar,' Tullaris snarled at the maimed noble. A cruel smile twisted the executioner's face. 'Khaine warned me you would try to save your master. Fear not, he will be joining you soon enough.'

Tullaris hefted the First Draich, swinging it high above his head and bringing the murderous blade crunching into the trapped Silar's skull.

The Ellyrians crashed into the ranks of the Bloodseekers, lances piercing mail and stabbing flesh, bones crushed beneath the pounding hooves of elven steeds. Tyrion was there at the centre of the fight, his burning sword strewing the corpses of executioners all around him, his great stallion, Malhandhir, cracking skulls and shattering ribs with every kick of its powerful hooves.

Amidst the carnage, Tullaris butchered his way towards the Regent, his draich impaling foes on its blade with every thrust. Elves and horses died wherever the Chosen of Khaine stepped, their blood added to the gore already coating the butcher's armour. A low, sadistic chant rasped across Tullaris's lips as he stalked through the melee, an appeal to the Lord of Murder that the massacre should never end. A world of endless blood and slaughter, such was the only prayer Tullaris thought fit to offer up to Khaine.

When the Knights of the Burning Dark crashed into the fray they attacked with wanton abandon. Executioners were crushed beneath the claws of cold ones even as Ellyrian cavalry were lifted from their saddles by druchii lances. The warpsword sang its deathly song as Malus carved a path through enemy and ally alike. The strength of the daemon made his muscles feel as though they were corded iron; every slash reduced his victim to a mangled heap, every cut ripped through armour and pulverised bone. The drachau shouted at the magnitude of his havoc, exuberant in the glory of his might.

Ahead of him, Malus could see the banner of the Phoenix King, the standard that had been entrusted to Tyrion as Regent of Ulthuan. Redoubling his assault, the drachau cleared a way ahead. As the last Ellyrians were hacked to pieces by the warpsword, Malus drove Spite forwards in a ferocious charge that demanded every last mote of the reptile's strength.

Malhandhir smelt the horned one before it charged. Whinnying in warning, the elven steed turned towards Malus as the drachau came rushing at Tyrion. By the narrowest margin, the Regent raised Sunfang and blocked the descending strike of the warpsword. Sparks of antithetical magic flew from the crashing blades. Despite the daemonic strength flowing through the drachau's arms, Malus was unable to shatter the enchanted sword as he had the lesser blades of lesser foes. But he could see that Tyrion trembled from the strain of trying to drive back Malus's strike.

Malus reared back in his saddle, driving the warpsword again and again at Tyrion. Sunfang parried each blow, the two swords shrieking as they scraped against one another. With each strike, Malus could see Tyrion's endurance put to the test. Each assault made him drop a little lower in the saddle, each parry was just that little bit slower than the last to intercept his blade. The Regent was weakening while with every breath Malus felt his own strength growing.

Spite snapped at Malhandhir with its fangs, forcing the horse to shift and dodge the flashing jaws, further taxing the skill of its master to block Malus's attacks. Breath by breath, heartbeat by heartbeat, the drachau was winning.

Emboldened by the weakening of his foe and the daemonic might burning within his own body, Malus wasn't prepared when Tyrion changed his tactics. When the warpsword came flashing down at the Regent's head, instead of blocking the blow as he had before, Tyrion urged Malhandhir into a sidewise twist. Malus's sword cleft nothing but empty air. Without the expected impact of blade against blade, the drachau was overbalanced, falling forwards across his saddle.

Instantly, Tyrion slashed at Malus with Sunfang, but he didn't reckon upon the speed and agility of the drachau. Malus's reflexes and instincts had been honed in the horrors of Naggaroth and the perils of the Wastes. As Tyrion's blade came for him, he threw himself backwards, lying flat across Spite's back. Instead of skewering him, Sunfang merely slashed his cheek. Even so, the glancing wound brought a cry of sheer agony from Malus. The filth that bubbled up from his wound wasn't blood alone, but had within it dark purple strands of obscene ichor.

Infused with the might of a daemon, Malus's flesh had taken on some of the properties of the daemonic. Sunfang had been forged to destroy such entities in the days of Aenarion, the first Phoenix King. The agony that wracked Malus's body from even so slight a scratch was crippling. He sagged weakly against Spite's side, the warpsword dangling from his hand. His other hand clawed desperately at his scarred cheek, as though he could rip out the pain.

'Now you answer for your outrages, Tyrant of Hag Graef,' Tyrion snarled. He raised Sunfang for the killing blow. Malus saw death in the Regent's eyes.

Before the blow could land, however, Tyrion cried out in shock. Blood erupted from the hero's side, spilling across the ancient dragon armour he wore. It took Malus a few breaths to understand what had happened. When he did, a bitter laugh fell from his lips.

While drachau and Regent duelled, another foe had intruded into the fight. Tullaris drove the First Draich into Tyrion's back, the ensorcelled weapon tearing through the hero's enchanted mail, its murderous energies too great even for the armour of Aenarion to defy. Tyrion writhed in agony, his body spitted upon the unholy glaive. The executioner howled the name of Khaine as he lifted Tyrion from Malhandhir's saddle and threw the Regent to the ground.

Malus clenched his teeth as he watched Tullaris stalk towards his fallen enemy. It seemed the glory of killing the Regent would belong to Tullaris.

The satisfaction of killing Tullaris once the deed was done, however, would belong to Malus Darkblade.

TWENTY

Tyrion's cry echoed across Reaver's Mark as Tullaris drove his blade into the hero's back. Up on the volcanic spur, the scream stabbed into Drusala's mind, rousing her from her stupor. The sorceress turned her witchsight across the field and cursed herself for the mistake she had made.

Until that moment, she had believed Korhil was leading the asur reinforcements. She had been unaware of Tyrion's presence. The jewel the Regent wore, the Heart of Avelorn, rendered him resistant to magic. It would have taken a more direct focus for her sorcery to detect him upon the field. Even so, Drusala berated herself for allowing such an oversight. She should have considered the possibility the moment the reinforcements had arrived.

She had hoped to employ Malus Darkblade as a counter against Malekith, a pawn to send against the Witch King. Far more vital to Morathi's plans, however, was Tyrion. If the Dragon of Cothique fell, the consequences would be dire. Because of her mistake, her complacency, Drusala knew there was now a very real chance that the Regent would be killed. Alone, either Malus or Tullaris was enemy enough to test Tyrion's mettle. Against both of them, the sorceress feared Tyrion would fall. He might slay one, but then the other would pounce on the weakened hero and cut him down.

Drusala had no choice. She had to cast aside her pawn to save Tyrion. She couldn't act directly against either of the druchii warlords. The risk of her actions being made known to Malekith, the chance that the Witch King would discover her treachery, was too great. She had to act more subtly. She had to take a terrible risk, one that would allow the Regent a better chance than the odds he faced now.

Weakened by her onerous castings, Drusala turned back towards the Blood Coven. The surviving witches were only now beginning to stir. It was partly their duplicity that had brought things to such an impasse. It was only fitting that they should help set things right. Boldly, Drusala walked over to the witches. Before they could react, she clapped one of her hands against each of their foreheads.

'Your queen needs your power,' she said, a malignant glaze falling across her eyes. A sinister scarlet glow spread from Drusala's hands, slithering down into the bodies of the Blood Coven, worming through the essence of their souls for every speck of energy that yet lingered within them.

At the Eagle Gate, Drusala had re-caged the daemon Tz'arkan. A link yet existed between them. The peril was enormous and it would take more magic than she could safely harness on her own in her weakened state, but she intended to exploit that connection.

By Hekarti, she only prayed she was able to act before it was too late to salvage her carefully laid plans.

Even as Drusala began her spell, she felt the aethyric vibration sweep through her. Far away some tremendous and profane ritual had been performed, a feat of magic so colossal that its echo was roaring through the winds of magic with the fury of a tempest. The sorceress exerted her will, trying to draw down the energies

blown ahead of that storm, trying to harness the magic she needed
before the aethyric tidal wave struck.

Tyrion lay in the dirt, blood streaming from the wound in his back.
He glared up at Tullaris as the executioner raised his bloodied draich. It was an unsettling thing, to watch as his blood dripped from
the ghoulish weapon.

'Khaine told me I should find you here,' Tullaris declared. Slowly,
the executioner raised the First Draich.

As Tyrion saw the murderous weapon poised to take his head,
a ghastly sensation turned his insides cold. A profound sense of
loss, a loneliness that gnawed at his vitals and made his heart feel
as cold as iron, a numb misery that washed through him with an
agony unspeakable. His daughter, Aliathra, was dead. He didn't
know where or how, he only knew that she was. For an instant, he
seemed to feel her soul reaching into his own. Then she was gone.
Even her spirit was no more – it had been consumed by the same
atrocity that had taken her life.

Fury blacker and more terrible than anything he had ever felt
before filled Tyrion's mind. Long had he feared the curse of Aenarion, the murderous madness that plagued all those of the first king's
bloodline. Now, he didn't care. He didn't care if this was the curse,
if this was madness. All he cared about was the pain inside him. All
he cared about was making it stop. All he cared about was making
something suffer as he suffered.

He no longer felt the wound in his back or the weariness in his
limbs. Strength poured through him – the power of rage and unbridled hate. Snarling like a rabid beast, Tyrion lunged at Tullaris
as the executioner brought his draich slashing down. The Regent
slid beneath the cutting blade and slammed into the druchii killer,
bearing him to the ground. Roaring an inarticulate cry of unfettered

savagery, Tyrion brought Sunfang stabbing into the executioner's side. Tullaris struggled against the blade as it punched its way deeper into his body, puncturing armour, crushing bone and rupturing organs. Blood gushed over Tyrion's hands as he ripped the sword free, severing the executioner's spine.

Tullaris flailed his arms on the ground for a moment and then fell still. His eyes struggled to focus on the asur prince who stood over him. 'Khaine told me I would find you here,' he repeated. 'I hear His voice even now, thundering through my brain. When this shell of flesh is finished, I will join Him.' The executioner reached his hand out, fumbling blindly at the air. 'Finish me. Set me free. Set yourself free.'

Tyrion glared down at Tullaris Dreadbringer, recounting in his mind the many atrocities, the countless sorrows this villain had inflicted upon Ulthuan. There was no mercy in him for this monster, no pity for this fiend. Let him die like a dog in the dust. It was a kinder doom than he deserved.

'You are weak,' Tullaris spat when Tyrion failed to deliver the killing blow. A cruel smile formed on the druchii's bloodied face. Attuned to the Lord of Murder, long in the service of death and slaughter, Tullaris had felt that fleeting instant when Aliathra's spirit had reached to her father. The executioner forced his paralysed body upright. His blind eyes struggled to find his enemy. A blue and gold blur was all he saw, yet towards this he turned a mocking smile.

'You are weak,' the executioner snarled again. 'That is what killed your daught–'

Tyrion drove Sunfang into the executioner's head before he could finish, cleaving it in half and spilling the fanatic's brains. 'This is what killed you,' he spat. Tyrion pressed his boot against Tullaris's chest and tried to wrench his burning blade free.

It was then that he heard Malhandhir's warning snort and he remembered that his fight wasn't with one infamous fiend but with two.

Like a jackal after the wolf is gone, Malus Darkblade came rushing in to finish the wounded Tyrion.

Tyrion's horse tried to intercept Malus as the drachau charged towards the Regent. Spite barged past Malhandhir, sending the horse stumbling back with its side torn by the reptile's claws.

Malus had eyes only for his intended prey. He had bided his time, waiting to see which of the combatants would prevail. He had to admit he was surprised to see Tyrion triumphant. He was grateful, in his murderous way, that the Regent had eliminated Tullaris for him. Now he wouldn't have to bother about that small detail. He could devote his attention fully to the asur prince. The glory of killing the Dragon of Cothique would be his and his alone.

As Tyrion struggled to free Sunfang from Tullaris's body, Malus charged. Not for an instant did he question the honour of striking his enemy from behind or taking advantage of a wounded foe. Such compunctions were for those too weak to endure, too soft to rule. He had made himself drachau by his own hand only by divesting himself of such foolish ideas as these. There was nothing, absolutely nothing, that he wouldn't do to expand and maintain his power. The head of Tyrion would help him accomplish both, and no druchii would ever question how he had claimed his trophy.

Malus raised the warpsword, ready to cut down the Regent. The strength of iron was in his arm as he hefted the blade high. Then he felt that strength expand still further, felt waves of power rushing through him. His sword fell from his hand, clattering to the ground as a spasm of searing agony coursed through him.

The drachau cried out as the familiar, hideous sensation pulsed through his body. After so long thinking the daemon subdued, he could feel Tz'arkan rising once more. The daemon brushed aside the barriers presented by Malus's mind and soul. Like wine pouring into a glass, the fiend was expanding to fill every corner of the elf's essence.

It was the change, not brought on by any act of will on the part of Malus but by Tz'arkan itself!

Spite hissed in fright and tried to unseat its master as it sensed the change that was consuming Malus. This time the transformation was too swift for the horned one. Howling in pain, the reptile collapsed beneath the expanding mass of Tz'arkan as the daemon distorted flesh and bone, twisting the form of its mortal host into a shape more to its liking. Spite flopped against the earth, its back broken by the daemon's weight. Tz'arkan grinned down at the crippled beast and brought one of its cloven hooves smashing down into Spite's skull.

'Does that make you sad, flesh-worm?' Tz'arkan taunted the retreating soul of Malus. The daemon's face twisted in a grisly leer. More of its essence came boiling up, driving the spirit of its host still further and further back into the darkness.

'The witch, I warned you about her,' Tz'arkan hissed. 'Her magic caged me, now her magic frees me.' Tz'arkan's head rotated back on its neck, staring across Reaver's Mark, glaring at the volcanic spur where Drusala stood. 'Of course, she meant only a half-measure, to leave us a quivering heap of flesh, neither Malus Darkblade or Tz'arkan. We couldn't have that, though. We're much too strong for that now.' The daemon paused, its leer turning into a snarl. 'Still, your soul acted as a bridge, a chain she used to bind me again.'

Inside it, Tz'arkan could hear Malus pleading with it, begging it for mercy.

'Shut up, mortal,' Tz'arkan growled as it sent its essence flooding into that last tiny corner where the soul of Malus Darkblade lingered. The drachau's spirit shrieked as the daemon smothered it into nothingness.

Tz'arkan's eyes glowed with vindictiveness as it stared at the spur and Drusala. 'What will you do, witch? How will you cage me now?' The daemon laughed as it plucked the sorceress's thoughts from the aethyr. 'I think I'll punish you by finishing what Malus started.'

The hulking daemon swung around. Asur and druchii alike had fled from the monster, drawing away and forgetting their own battle in the presence of this monstrous fiend. Only Tyrion remained, his blade finally torn free from the skull of Tullaris.

'An elven princeling as an appetiser and then two armies to devour,' Tz'arkan hissed at Tyrion. 'Or should I save you as a dessert and let you watch all the others die before you? Would that...' The daemon hesitated, its burning eyes shifting colours as it became aware that something wasn't right with the elf who stood before it. There was a shadow, an aura hanging over the Regent of Ulthuan, something of such ghastly power that it caused even a daemon king like Tz'arkan to feel the icy touch of fear.

Tyrion stared up at the fiend. 'What's wrong, daemon? Have you lost your appetite?'

Bellowing its fury, Tz'arkan lunged at the asur prince. Its great claws tore at the ground as Tyrion nimbly darted away. 'I shall give your soul to the furies as a plaything,' Tz'arkan vowed, venom dripping from its fangs. Again the beast charged at its foe, but this time Tyrion darted beneath the sweep of its claws. The enchantments woven into Sunfang blazed into brilliance as he raked the blade across the daemon's hide. Flesh bubbled like wax, ichor steaming from the hideous wound as writhing worms of dark magic slopped from the daemon's marrow.

The daemon shrieked, its painful screech causing hundreds of elves across the battlefield to clap their hands to their ears in a futile effort to blot out the sound. Those closest to the fray collapsed to the ground, their bodies quivering in agony as Tz'arkan's scream ripped at their souls.

Tyrion alone stood immune to the daemon's howl. Rushing in, he slashed at the injured monster, raking its flesh again and again with the burning Sunfang. Step by monstrous step, he drove the fiend back. Tz'arkan plucked elves from where they lay in the dirt, flinging both the living and the dead at its foe. The asur prince deftly avoided each flailing body. Only when he was beside the carcass of Spite did he hesitate in his pursuit of the monster. Reaching down, Tyrion retrieved something from the bloodied earth. When he stood again, he held two blades in his hands. In his right, the holy energies of Sunfang blazed. In his left, the malefic power of the warpsword.

Tz'arkan growled at its enemy, a final snarl of hate and defiance. It had felt the bite of Sunfang and it knew the power of the warpsword. Against these weapons, in the hands of a mortal who had such an ominous presence lingering around him...

The daemon turned to flee, but as it did so it found its path blocked by a force of elves who, like Tyrion, didn't cower before it. Caradryan and his Phoenix Guard had fought their way clear of the druchii and now hurried to support the Regent of Ulthuan. Their halberds stabbed at Tz'arkan, driving the beast back towards Tyrion.

Tz'arkan rounded on his pursuer. The daemon's eyes blazed with infernal fires, scorching the waxy flesh of its face. Leathery lips pulled away from monstrous fangs in a grotesque leer. 'Are you the best your people have to send against me?' Tz'arkan hissed, its voice searing across the field like some morbid echo of the ancient volcanoes beneath Reaver's Mark. The daemon cackled derisively. 'You wear the trappings of a dead maniac and you think yourself a hero? The blood of madness pulses through your veins and you think yourself virtuous? You bear the blades of both righteousness and depravity in your hands and you do not see the hypocrisy?'

The elf stalked towards Tz'arkan, Sunfang and warpsword held at his sides. 'I am Tyrion of Cothique, heir of the line of Aenarion, son of Morelion! By the faith of my people am I Regent of Ulthuan–'

A cruel laugh rumbled from the massive daemon. 'Regent? Then they would not have you as their king?' Tz'arkan's fiery eyes diminished into little slivers of malice. 'Tell me, mock-king, why do you think that is? Could it be they know you for the mad dog you are? Could it be your gods have turned their faces from you?' Tz'arkan laughed again as he saw the doubt that made Tyrion halt in his advance. The shadow of power still clung to the asur prince, but Tz'arkan thought of its own imprisonment within Malus Darkblade. However magnificent the power, the vessel was still but a mortal, and with that came mortal weakness.

'Shall I tell you of the petty scavengers you call gods?' Tz'arkan sneered. 'I have seen them, little mock-king. I have seen them cast about themselves a veil of deceit and trickery that they might drain the strength of your foolish people and fatten on them like so many leeches! You place your faith in weak parasites who will not dare stir themselves in your hour of need.'

Tz'arkan saw the doubt spread, the hissing corruption of its voice clawing into Tyrion's soul, drawing out all the doubts and fears that lurked within the hero. Still, the aura of power was there, wrapped all around the elf's essence, almost blinding the daemon in its awful potency.

'I may be benevolent,' Tz'arkan declared. 'If you like, I shall allow you to fly back to your court, mock-king. You can hide behind your fortress walls and the spears of your armies. You can find the safety of wizards and mages. Go, little mock-king! I allow you to run back to your castle. After all, if you die here, who will lead the asur in the futile fight to save their land?'

The seeds of doubt and fear provoked by the daemon's voice dropped away from Tyrion as he raised his face and stared into Tz'arkan's eyes. 'It isn't I who will die here this day, daemon.' Grimly, he hefted Sunfang and warpsword, bringing the two crashing together above his head. The clash of their antithetical enchantments was like a clap of thunder, an explosion of arcane energy that went rippling away from the Regent.

Tz'arkan felt the force of those crashing swords. It could feel the mongrel vibrations caused by their collision, vibrations magnified far beyond the magic of either sword on its own.

Brazenly, the daemon tried again to cripple its foe with doubt. 'You think to kill what is eternal, mock-king? Do you know what it is you stand before? I am Tz'arkan the Render. Tz'arkan the Woe. Tz'arkan the Blight. I was there when the star-gods fell. I was there to watch the first apes climb up from the slime and call themselves elves. I have seen the rise of continents and the collapse of empires. I have been there from before the beginning, when all was raw, primal and untainted by the unnatural harmonies of what you call order. I will be there when all of this is cast down, ravaged until it is less than dust. I will be there when Great Khorne calls the Last Slaughter and all is drowned under a tide of blood. You think to kill me, mortal? I am destiny! I am eternity! I am–'

Only two words passed Tyrion's lips as he glared at the daemon. It was the elf who now wore the mocking smile, the haughty arrogance of disdain. 'Prove it,' he challenged the daemon.

Ancient beyond even the reckoning of elves, versed in all the evils and horrors of a million nightmares, Tz'arkan was nevertheless oblivious to its own weakness. Something it had absorbed from its mortal host after so many years. Of all the things to spur the rage of Malus, the jeers of an enemy were the most certain. Now, it was the daemon who had consumed the druchii lord who felt the primitive, unthinking fury of its vanquished host boil within it. Roaring, Tz'arkan lowered its horned head and charged at Tyrion. The aura of power clinging to the elf was forgotten in the blind urge to rend and maim. The enchanted swords were dismissed as brutish blood-lust filled Tz'arkan's mind.

With the huge daemon rushing at him, Tyrion threw himself forwards in a diving roll. As he came up under the driving daemon, he stabbed his swords into Tz'arkan's body. The monster howled in pain, aethyric blood steaming from its wounds. Tyrion clenched his jaw tight, straining his muscles to their utmost, forcing the warpsword and Sunfang to shift and turn inside the daemon's body. Inch by gory inch, he forced the weapons together.

A withering blast of power exploded from Tz'arkan as the warpsword and Sunfang touched. Magnified still further by the aethyric essence of the daemon, the magical discharge ripped Tz'arkan apart. The beast's torso was flung high into the air, collapsing hundreds of yards away in a heap of bubbling corruption. The lower part of the fiend's form was blasted into dripping giblets that spattered the armour of the asur and druchii, who had forgotten their own fights to observe the Regent's duel with the daemon king.

Despite the fury of Tz'arkan's destruction, Tyrion himself was unfazed. Standing right at the centre of the arcane explosion, he was unmarred by either the violence or the gore of his enemy's annihilation. He held the warpsword before his face, watching as the fragments of Tz'arkan's essence were sucked down into the depths of the unholy blade. A fitting death for a monster that had brought such misery into the world.

* * *

As Tz'arkan's corpse corroded into puddles of stagnant filth, clouds soared into the sky, seemingly sucked into the void left by the daemon's passing. Thick, syrupy drops of black rain began to shower down upon Reaver's Mark, drawing shouts of confusion and alarm from the elves below. It seemed the very heavens were mourning the daemon king's destruction.

Only a few knew better, those who had sensed the far-distant ritual that had unleashed an unprecedented surge of magical energy across the world. The storm that swept across Reaver's Mark was much more than cloud and rain. It was the fury of the aethyr unchained.

Drusala could feel the obscene taint of Death Magic that coloured the storm. She knew that far across the sea a great evil had been revived. The clouds to the east blazed with violet fire, lightning boiling and flashing from within their smouldering depths. A deathly chill swept across Reaver's Mark, silencing the sounds of battle that yet lingered. The druchii and their asur foes drew back, gazing uneasily at the comrades around them, feeling at the very core of their beings the occult force that rippled all around them.

Then the arcane taint seeped down into the bodies lying strewn about the battlefield. The corpse of Tullaris rose to its feet, brains drooling from its split skull. The carcass of Spite slithered across the earth with its broken back. The dead of both druchii and asur rose again, granted a ghastly semblance of life by the forces surging through them. Bony hands clawed their way upwards as still more ancient dead were awakened, pulling themselves from the ground on skeletal arms and withered talons. Barbarian marauders who had been slain millennia before rose alongside skeletal elves and the rotten husks of goblins that had been slain during the rampage of Grom the Paunch.

Living warriors cowered before the graveborn, drawing away with the instinctive repugnance of all things living for all things undead. The animated corpses made no effort to close the gap between themselves and those who had been their comrades in arms. The graveborn simply stood where they were or stumbled about in directionless idiocy. It was only when the surviving witches of the Blood Coven appeared upon the volcanic spur that the undead found motivation and purpose.

The red-clad Blood Coven sent their magic wafting across the battlefield, binding those undead closest to them to their power. Following their example, the other sorceresses yet remaining to the host of Hag Graef began to exert their own power. Coldly, they stirred the desiccated hearts and tattered mentalities of the graveborn, turning them towards the asur, driving them into battle once more. Fallen asur now crossed swords with their living kinsmen while once-slain druchii were given the chance to avenge themselves against their slayers.

'Aid us,' one of the Blood Coven snarled at Drusala. 'Lend your magic to our purpose and we may yet win the day!'

Drusala knew she didn't have the power to fight the witches. Not now. She had expended too much energy releasing Tz'arkan. What little she still possessed was sustaining the glamour that cloaked her. There was nothing she could do to defy the Blood Coven. Nothing she could do to keep the graveborn from slaughtering the asur and killing Tyrion. She had risked so much to preserve the hero that now all she could do was watch impotently as all her plans were unravelled.

As she turned her eyes towards Tyrion, Drusala saw him step boldly towards the nearest of the undead. The asur hero raised the warpsword high, brandishing it before the oncoming horde of graveborn horrors. 'This is the Warpsword of Khaine!' Tyrion shouted, his voice booming across the battlefield. 'Dead of Ulthuan, attend me!

This is the blade of the Destroyer, the Murderer of Nations, he who cut the life from you and cast you into the dominion of corpses!'

The undead froze as they heard Tyrion's cry. Sightless skulls and rotting eyes turned towards him wherever the graveborn fought, staring in sepulchral fixedness at the black blade he held overhead. The Blood Coven raged and shrieked, trying to coerce the undead back into the fight, but the carcasses refused their commands. All across Reaver's Mark, the druchii sorceresses were finding themselves unable to break the uncanny fascination Tyrion exerted over the graveborn.

'I speak for the Destroyer,' Tyrion declared, slashing the warpsword through the air before him. 'You belong to Khaine. By right of conquest and death, you are the slaves of the Bloody-handed God. My enemies are the enemies of Khaine. The enemies of Khaine are your enemies.' The Regent's face became a mask of unbridled hate as he gazed across the horde of graveborn and turned towards the druchii. He thrust the warpsword towards the black-armoured warriors. 'Slay them all!' he commanded.

By the hundreds, by the thousands, the undead set themselves against the druchii, stabbing at them with splintered spears and broken swords, clawing at them with rotten fingers and bony claws. The warriors of Har Ganeth, of Clar Karond and Hag Graef met the attack with the iron resolve of their own hate, striving to push the undead back that they might again close with the living asur and sell their own lives in the killing of their ancient foes.

Upon the volcanic spur, the witches of the Blood Coven loosed their magic against the tide of skeletons climbing up towards them. Dozens of corpses were blasted into splinters by their spells, but for each corpse they vanquished three more graveborn seemed to take their place. Again, the witches called for Drusala to help them, but this time their cry was one of abject terror. Frantically they looked about them for the sorceress, but of Morathi's handmaiden there was no sign. In the confusion of shifting battle, with the Blood Coven fixated upon their undead warriors, she had vanished.

At last the undead reached the top of the spur. The first few were sent falling to earth by the sorcerous wind the Blood Coven summoned, but there were too many for the witches to resist. Their magic faltered and they were dragged beneath the oncoming swarm. Shrieking, they were torn asunder by the rotten hands of the graveborn.

Across Reaver's Mark, the sinister undead crashed against the shields and blades of the druchii. Fighting like fiends, the sons of Naggaroth tried to drive them back. Hundreds of the graveborn were cut down, but the dead cared not. Relentlessly they continued to throw themselves at their enemy. Finally, even the hate-ridden resolve of the druchii could take no more. First one regiment, then another, turned and fled, retreating back across the fields of Ellyrion they had ravaged only days before.

Tyrion raised his sword once more, but this time it was Sunfang he held and it was living warriors he addressed. 'Defenders of Ulthuan,' he shouted. 'Khaine demands blood! The blood of Naggaroth and Malekith's slaves!' A terrible cry of ancient hate and savage violence sounded from every asur on the field as they heard the song of Khaine in Tyrion's words. Viciously they followed their Regent as he led them across the field in pursuit of the broken druchii. Like wild animals, the asur fell upon their foes, hacking them to pieces when they caught them, rending their foes to ribbons even as they lay dead upon the ground. Only the Phoenix Guard, exalted and marked by Asuryan, maintained the discipline of warriors. Over them, Khaine's Bloodsong held no power.

While Tyrion led his maddened army in the massacre of their

routed foe, a lone figure prowled amidst the carnage they left behind. Drusala picked her way carefully among the corpses as she emerged from the fissure at the base of the volcanic spur that had become the grave of the Blood Coven. As she drew some of the fading energies rising from the twice-slain graveborn, she found enough power to adjust the glamour she had cast about herself.

For the merest instant, the image of Drusala, handmaiden of Morathi faded. It had been a wondrous mirage, crafted from the murdered handmaiden's own soul, a semblance that had deceived even other spellcasters. Morathi was almost reluctant to cast it aside, but she knew the role of Drusala had served its purpose. The situation had changed and she had to change with it. Using the magical energies she'd gathered from the undead, she transformed herself into the likeness of a Sapherian mage.

Teasing one of her now blonde tresses behind her ear, the sorceress turned to join Tyrion in his hunt. There was a delicious flavour to the idea of hunting down the shattered druchii host. If the massacre were complete enough, it might even cause some delay in her son Malekith's schemes.

As she started towards the asur army, Morathi noted a broken corpse dragging itself along the ground. She recognised the animated remains of Spite, Malus Darkblade's steed. The thing was crawling towards the puddle of corruption that had been Tz'arkan. Even in its undead state, despite the horrific transformation of Malus's body, the reptile was trying to reach its master.

Morathi shook her head at the pathetic display and smiled. 'You were a useful pawn, for a time, Malus Darkblade. But you were, after all, only a pawn in a much greater game.'

Her eyes already envisioning the new steps she must take to ensure her plans came to fruition, the sorceress hurried to join Tyrion's triumphant asur.

ABOUT THE AUTHOR

C L Werner's Black Library credits include the Space
Marine Battles novel *The Siege of Castellax, Mathias
Thulmann: Witch Hunter, Runefang*, the Brunner the
Bounty Hunter trilogy, the Thanquol and Boneripper
series and Time of Legends: The Black Plague.
Currently living in the American south-west,
he continues to write stories of mayhem and
madness set in the worlds of Warhammer
and Warhammer 40,000.

WARHAMMER®
THE END TIMES

THE CURSE OF
KHAINE

GAV THORPE

An extract from

The Curse of Khaine

by Gav Thorpe

Despite the forlorn situation, Malekith admired the knights and warriors bearing down upon the defenders. It was rare for him to contemplate such lowly subjects but he took a moment to acknowledge the unswerving dedication and bravery demonstrated by their sacrifice below. Many of them would die, of course, without knowing such regard existed, but the fortunate few that survived to see the dusk Malekith would reward for their endeavour, further undermining Malus's power. He was, after all, a magnanimous ruler when required. That which could not be coerced with dread was easily bought with gold and favour, and in the new world they would carve on these shores the druchii knew only a few would rise to the top of society and would happily betray each other for such position.

There was a great commotion at the front of the assault, but Malekith could not see clearly what passed. He saw an explosion of daemonic energy and the asur army was in disarray for a while. No doubt Malus had unleashed whatever power it was Malekith had sensed at the council. It mattered little, the assault was grinding to its inevitable stop.

The mountains rang then with deafening roars, followed by a tumult of cheering from the ramparts of the Gate. A palpable aura of despair engulfed the druchii host pressing into the valley, from spearmen to knights, sorceresses to the beastmasters that drove Malus's two monstrous hydras into battle. Malekith turned to the south, knowing what it was that had caused such consternation so quickly, broken lips twisted into a smile.

Dragons.

There were dozens of the immense creatures, each ridden by one of the proud knights of Caledor. A rainbow of colours against the summer sky, a glittering chromatic display of raw strength. The surprise and delight of the defenders was all the greater for recent events. Imrik of Caledor had declined to help Tyrion against the daemon assault and had withdrawn his forces to the borders of his kingdom.

His aid had been unlooked for, but now it seemed the tide would be turned by Imrik's intervention.

Such relief and joy was untimely.

Malekith pulled himself up into Seraphon's saddle-throne and picked up the iron chains of her reins.

'Go,' he whispered. 'Go to your cousins.'

Shouts of encouragement from the druchii followed Malekith into the sky as those below thought he sought to take on the squadrons of Caledor single-handed. Jeers rang out from the defenders, mocking his arrogance.

The jeers faded and the praise of the druchii fell to silence as Malekith and Imrik guided their monstrous mounts towards each other, weapons bared. As he closed with the Caledorian prince, Malekith was surprised by just how alike he was to his ancestor whose name he had taken.

He fixed this new Imrik with his dread gaze and lifted *Urithain*.

Cries of surprise and dismay sounded from the mountainsides as Imrik saluted with his lance and the two dragonriders turned towards Eagle Gate, the lord of Caledor following behind the Witch King of Naggaroth. In their wake came the gold and silver and red and blue scales of Caledorian mounts, but amongst them more ebon-hued beasts raised by the masters of Clar Karond and Karond Kar.

There was already fighting on the walls as Caledorian knights that had been part of the garrison revealed their true loyalty. Even as the dragons descended with claws and deadly breath the great portal of Eagle Gate's seventh wall was opening.

The druchii roar of glee was almost as thunderous as the cries of the dragons as Malekith's followers surged into the pass, intent on the doomed fortification.